"The breezy, well-plotted book moves at a fast clip, fueled by Viets's perfect comic timing. But she also knows when to keep the plot serious, as *Pumped for Murder* explores extreme fitness fanatics, steroid use, alcoholism, and corrupt businesspeople." — *Miami Herald*

"Viets offers a smooth blend of humor and homicide in her tenth mystery. . . . The antics of fitness fanatics and some supercharged libidos in one case and a trip back to the drug-fueled wildness of the 1980s in the other keep Helen and Phil hopping in another satisfying outing."
— *Publishers Weekly*

"With each hilarious novel, [Viets] takes ordinary jobs and creates extraordinary mysteries. Her main character, Helen Hawthorne, is the lady-next-door who finds herself knee-deep in mischief no matter what she's doing. . . . *Pumped for Murder* is this summer's quintessential workout companion."
— *Fresh Fiction*

"Elaine Viets provides another great mystery worth reading as, even with her name cleared, the heroine ends up working a dead-end job, albeit undercover."
— *Genre Go Round Reviews*

continued . . .

Also by Elaine Viets

The Dead-End Job Series

Josie Marcus, Mystery Shopper Series

Pumped for Murder

A DEAD-END JOB MYSTERY

• • • • • • • • • • • • • • • •

Elaine Viets

AN OBSIDIAN MYSTERY

OBSIDIAN
Published by New American Library, a division of
Penguin Group (USA) Inc., 375 Hudson Street,
New York, New York 10014, USA
Penguin Group (Canada), 90 Eglinton Avenue East, Suite 700, Toronto,
Ontario M4P 2Y3, Canada (a division of Pearson Penguin Canada Inc.)
Penguin Books Ltd., 80 Strand, London WC2R 0RL, England
Penguin Ireland, 25 St. Stephen's Green, Dublin 2,
Ireland (a division of Penguin Books Ltd.)
Penguin Group (Australia), 250 Camberwell Road, Camberwell, Victoria 3124,
Australia (a division of Pearson Australia Group Pty. Ltd.)
Penguin Books India Pvt. Ltd., 11 Community Centre, Panchsheel Park,
New Delhi - 110 017, India
Penguin Group (NZ), 67 Apollo Drive, Rosedale, Auckland 0632,
New Zealand (a division of Pearson New Zealand Ltd.)
Penguin Books (South Africa) (Pty.) Ltd., 24 Sturdee Avenue,
Rosebank, Johannesburg 2196, South Africa

Penguin Books Ltd., Registered Offices:
80 Strand, London WC2R 0RL, England

Published by Obsidian, an imprint of New American Library, a division of Penguin Group (USA) Inc. Previously published in an Obsidian hardcover edition.

First Obsidian Mass Market Printing, May 2012
10 9 8 7 6 5 4 3 2 1

Copyright © Elaine Viets, 2011
All rights reserved

OBSIDIAN and logo are trademarks of Penguin Group (USA) Inc.

Printed in the United States of America

For Paulita Zimmerman, who showed me

the killer world of the fantastically fit

ACKNOWLEDGMENTS

Helen Hawthorne still works those dead-end jobs, but for a different reason. She and her husband, Phil, started Coronado Investigations, their private-eye agency. They needed help for their new venture, and they got it.

The Florida Association of Licensed Investigators' 16th Annual Professional Development Conference was a terrific resource. Lynette Revill of Revill Associates in Sarasota, Florida, was especially helpful, as were Tim O'Rourke and K. C. Poulin of Critical Intervention Services, Inc.

Special thanks to senior editor Sandra Harding at NAL, who gave this novel a detailed and much-appreciated critique. Her assistant, Elizabeth Bistrow, is always helpful.

Copy editor Eileen G. Chetti did a superb job.

My husband, Don Crinklaw, shares Phil's fascination with orange junk food, but he's always there when I need him—even when I have panic questions at three a.m. Thanks to my agent, David Hendin, whose advice is always good.

Jan Kurtz is not an adulterous gym trainer. She gave a generous donation to charity to be libeled in this novel. Nancie Hays let me turn her into a lawyer. Opera lover Valerie Cannata became a hard-hitting investigative reporter for this book. Did she have a fling with Phil before his marriage? Both maintain a discreet silence.

Many other people helped me with this book. Thanks to Molly Portman and Alan Portman for their St. Louis and family expertise. Librarian Doris Ann Norris told me about Fostoria, Ohio. Thanks to Kay Gordy, Karen Grace, Jack Klobnak, Robert Levine, William Simon and Janet Smith. I can't forget supersaleswoman Carole Wantz, who could sell sand on a beach.

Thank you, Detective R. C. White, Fort Lauderdale Police Department (retired), Synae White and Rick McMahan, ATF special agent. To the sources who can't be named, I appreciate your legal, medical and tax information.

Boynton Beach librarian Anne Watts lent me her six-toed cat, Thumbs, for this series. Once again, I am grateful to the librarians at the St. Louis Public Library and Broward County Library. Yes, the information is on the Internet, but librarians helped me sort out what was accurate.

Thank you, blog sisters. I rely on the advice and encouragement of the women in the Lipstick Chronicles (www.thelipstickchronicles.typepad.com) and the Femmes Fatales (www.femmesfatales.typepad.com).

I'm grateful to the booksellers who recommend my novels to their customers and encourage me.

Finally, any errors are my own. You can tell me about them, or better yet, tell me you enjoyed this novel, at eviets@aol.com.

CHAPTER 1

H elen Hawthorne wished Eric Clapton would shut up. She didn't want to listen to him croon about cocaine.

"She don't lie, she don't lie . . . ," Eric sang.

Enough, Helen thought. She sat up in bed and pulled the black satin sheet up to prepare for the first fight of her marriage. She didn't want to be totally naked.

Phil, her husband of thirty-three days, looked lean and white against the dark sheets. She admired his young face, a startling contrast to his silver-white hair. His eyes were closed as he listened to the music.

Here goes, Helen thought. As soon as I open my mouth, our honeymoon is over. But she couldn't stop herself.

"I hate that song," she said. "Clapton sounds bored."

Helen waited for Phil to defend his guitar hero. He gave a lazy stretch, sat up and said, "You're right."

"I am?" Helen raised one eyebrow in surprise. Her husband worshiped Clapton. He even had a "Clapton Is God" T-shirt. Helen expected Phil to be struck by lightning every time he wore it.

They'd spent the sizzling September afternoon in his

bedroom, listening to Clapton sing about hopeful love, hopeless love, and shameful, sinful love while they indulged in legal, married love. The cool music and green palm fronds shading the window turned Phil's bedroom into an oasis at the Coronado Tropic Apartments.

Phil reached for the CD clicker and switched to an old favorite, "White Room," with the howling guitar sound. "There. Is that better?"

"Much," Helen said.

"You have to admit the guitar riffs in 'Cocaine' are elegant," he said. "In his defense, Clapton thought he was singing an antidrug song."

"Not to me," Helen said. "Sounds like he's in love with the white lady."

"A lot of people think that," Phil said. "You heard the audience cheering in that live recording. That's why he quit singing it for a while. Coke was the evil lady of the eighties, and 'Cocaine' was her anthem. When Clapton brought the song back for his North American tour, he added the line 'that dirty cocaine' for his backup singers. It's my least favorite Clapton song. He sounds depressed."

"Did you ever use coke?" Helen asked.

"Did I *what*? I. Hate. Coke." Each word was a separate sentence. Phil threw back the sheet, slipped into his white robe and paced up and down. With his silver hair, he looked like an agitated ghost.

"I hate the whole cocaine culture: the destruction, the corruption, the killings. I worked a case here in South Florida in the mid-eighties, in the days of the cocaine cowboys."

"Sounds very *Miami Vice*," Helen said. "I loved that TV show."

"*Miami Vice* was a Disney movie compared to Miami in the eighties," Phil said. "Coke isn't romantic pink sunsets, throbbing sound tracks and drug dealers' yachts."

"I wouldn't know," Helen said. "I was in high school then. Our wild St. Louis drug scene was kids smoking pot under the bleachers."

"I'm only five years older," Phil said. "I was a PI trainee on my first major case. I was only twenty-one and my hair was blond. They thought I'd be good at finding a sixteen-year-old runaway because I looked young. Her name was Marcie. I was supposed to bring her back to Little Rock."

"Did you?"

Phil was still pacing the terrazzo floor in his bedroom, avoiding their scattered clothes.

"I tracked Marcie to some clone of Studio 54, then bribed the doorman with a hundred bucks. Put the bribe on my expense account. Thought I was quite the stud."

"You are," Helen said. She tried to put her arms around him as he paced past her, but Phil shook her away. He seemed eager to tell this story, maybe for the first time.

"I followed Marcie into a club packed with half-naked people. It looked like every club then: tropical neon and a shiny black bar with mirrors. Behind the bar, Tom Cruise wannabes mixed flashy cocktails."

"Sounds interesting," Helen said.

"It wasn't," Phil said. "The crowd was mostly fat, balding men or Don Johnson look-alikes with designer stubble, and very young women. Couples were having sex everywhere: behind the curtains, in bathroom stalls, even right on the tables."

"Ew," Helen said. "I want to wash my mind out after that image."

"Well, I can't. I also can't forget the black bowls of coke. They sat around like party favors."

"What happened to Marcie?" Helen said.

"I don't want to talk about it."

"Did you find her?"

"Yeah," Phil said. "I found her. I sent her home—in a box. I'd like to forget her. I'd like to forget the whole ugly decade."

Phil seemed to shut down. He stopped pacing and sat down on the bed next to her.

"It must have been horrible for you," she said.

"It was no fun for Marcie, either. She didn't deserve what happened to her."

Helen traced the outline of his thin, slightly crooked nose with her finger and kissed the bump where it had been broken years ago. "Let's talk about something pleasant: our new detective agency. Do you still like the name Coronado Investigations?"

"It's perfect," Phil said. "Classy with a retro feel, like the Coronado Tropic Apartments. Our office could be the set for an old private-eye movie: the rattling window air conditioner, the monster gunmetal gray desks, the battered file cabinets. I can see Bogart sitting behind my desk in a wifebeater undershirt, drinking cheap whiskey."

"I'd rather see clients," Helen said. "Our savings will run out soon. We have to find some. How do we start looking for work?"

"That's what I asked Ed, my PI friend. I had breakfast with him this morning. I was working while you slept in. He's a retired cop who's with a big agency now."

"You were supposed to tell me what he said when you came back," Helen said.

"It's not my fault. I was distracted by this tall brunette with great legs."

Helen tucked her legs under her. "There. The distraction is gone. Why should he help us? Aren't we competition?"

"Not really. He works for a huge agency that specializes in private security. It started as a small shop run by two friends and grew. Ed says we need a PI license and a computer. I already have both. We need insurance, and we have the money for that."

"What about me?" Helen said.

"The state laws on private eyes are changing. We can get you in under the wire as my trainee, but you'll have to take classes. So will I, if we want the business to succeed.

"Ed says we have another important asset—our reputation. I'm glad we went back to St. Louis and cleared up your troubles with the court. That's out of the way."

Troubles with the court. Helen felt like a boulder had been lobbed at her gut. She'd divorced her lying, cheating ex more than two years ago. That's how she wound up in South Florida. She was on the run, avoiding an outrageous divorce settlement. A St. Louis judge had given her greedy ex-husband Rob half of Helen's future income.

Helen had hidden in Fort Lauderdale, working jobs for cash under the table. Rob had tracked her down, demanding thirty thousand dollars. With the help of a St. Louis lawyer, Helen had just recently cleared her name with the court.

"Has Rob shown up in court to contest the new divorce settlement?" Phil asked.

Helen felt her mouth go dry as Death Valley. Alkaline dust seemed to coat her tongue. "Uh, no. The process server can't find him. My lawyer published all the legal notices. Rob never appeared."

"He disappeared at the wrong time," Phil said. "Your legal troubles are over."

"Almost over," Helen said. "I didn't file any taxes while I was on the run. My St. Louis tax attorney is working on that problem."

"We'll soon be free," Phil said.

Helen felt a second boulder land on her back. She'd have to carry that crushing burden the rest of her life. She hated keeping a secret from her husband, but if she told Phil what had really happened to Rob, she'd ruin an innocent young life.

"What's the matter, sweetheart?" Phil asked. "You look pale."

"Nothing," Helen said, adding yet another lie to the layers of deceit. "What else did your PI friend tell you?"

"Lots. Maybe too much. I'll tell you more as I remember it. Ed suggested I hang around the courthouse and watch for new case filings. He says I should find a small, hungry law firm and do its investigative work. Our business will grow with the firm's."

"What do we do in the meantime? Live on love?"

"Find our local niche," Phil said. "Florida has more private eyes than any other state except California."

"Because this is such a rootless society?" Helen asked.

"Partly. Also, a lot of old cops retire down here. They live on their pensions while they start up their own agencies."

"Makes it tough for us," Helen said. "We don't have their investigative skills."

"We have our own advantages," Phil said. "Old cops can be set in their ways. They're used to getting what they want through the power of the badge and don't learn how to coax information out of people. And you're a genius at getting dead-end jobs."

"Thanks, I think," Helen said.

"Low-paying jobs are good ways to observe subjects. The people who do the work see things the bigwigs never do. They're more likely to talk. You've worked as everything from a hotel maid to a bookseller. You're a good listener."

"You're good at disguises," Helen said. "I've seen you look like an outlaw biker, a homeless man and a businessman. A cop looks like a cop no matter what he puts on."

"Ed says we could try to specialize in background checks or insurance-agency work."

"So we follow some guy suing someone because he hurt his back and catch him mowing the lawn?"

"Something like that," Phil said.

"Sounds boring," Helen said.

"Could be," Phil said. "Is it any duller than standing at a shop counter?"

"I guess not," Helen said. "Maybe Margery has some ideas to make a more lively living. Our landlady has a stake in our future, too. Our office is in her apartment complex. Is it time for the nightly poolside gathering?"

"It's seven ten," Phil said, checking the bedside clock. He pulled on his jeans. "Should be just starting."

"Wait. We haven't fed the cat yet," Helen said, buttoning her blouse. "Thumbs is at my place."

"Are you sure it's a good idea to keep two apartments?" Phil asked.

"My tax attorney said no major lifestyle changes until I settle my IRS problem," Helen said.

"Getting married isn't a lifestyle change?"

"He meant we shouldn't throw money around buying luxury cars and mansions. Besides, keeping my own apartment and sneaking into yours makes marriage seem illicit."

A furious cat greeted Helen at her apartment door with loud yowls of protest. Thumbs was mostly white with gray-brown patches. His giant six-toed front paws gave him his name. Thumbs followed Helen into the kitchen. He flipped over his food bowl with one huge paw.

"Hey! That's not nice," Helen said.

Thumbs stared at her with angry green eyes.

"I should know better than to lecture a cat," she said, flipping his bowl back over and pouring his dinner. Thumbs edged her hand out of the way and buried his face in his food.

Helen found a box of white wine in her fridge, rummaged for a can of cashews and headed outside.

The Coronado Tropic Apartments, built in 1949, looked like a white ocean liner. A hot breeze stirred the palm trees in the courtyard, and small waves rippled the pool's tepid water. Margery Flax and their neighbor Peggy were stretched out on the poolside chaise longues like Victorian maidens.

The real maidens would have fainted if they'd seen Margery. Helen's seventy-six-year-old landlady was wearing a purple romper. Her long, tanned legs ended in eggplant espadrilles. Marlboro smoke veiled her face. Her sunset orange fingernails glowed through the cigarette smoke.

Margery's face was wrinkled, but she wore her age like an exotic accessory. Her steel gray hair ended at a necklace of charms—Helen saw martini glasses, wine bottles, olives, lemons, wineglasses, drink stirrers and a small corkscrew, each about the size of a beer cap.

"Cool necklace," Phil said.

"It's called a statement necklace," Margery said.

"Looks like yours says it's time for a drink," Phil said.

"Drink!" came a raucous voice. "Drink!"

"Pete's learned a new word," Peggy said. Her Quaker parrot was perched on her shoulder like a corsage. Pete was the same bright green as Peggy's long gauzy dress.

"And a useful word it is," Margery said. She raised her wineglass in a salute to the gray-headed parrot. "Let's drink."

"Good boy," Peggy said. "Here's your reward." She gave the bird a bit of broccoli. The parrot dropped it on the pool deck.

"Poor Pete," Helen said. "That's some celebration when all you get is broccoli. Can he have a cashew?"

"Sorry. That's on his no-fly list," Peggy said. "He's still two ounces overweight."

Helen closed the lid on the can of nuts and stuck them under her chair.

"Bye," Pete said sadly.

"We came here for help," Phil said, dragging a chair over to the group. "Coronado Investigations needs to specialize to succeed. Any suggestions?"

Peggy said, "Based on my past experience with men, you should investigate potential spouses and lovers. Right now, I'm dating a good guy, but my friend Shelby at work is looking for a detective. She's having problems with her husband, Bryan. About a year ago, she bought him a gym membership. Bryan has lost twenty-five pounds. He works out seven days a week. He's got a killer body."

"What's wrong with that?" Helen asked.

"Shelby hasn't had sex with him since he started looking good. She's convinced he has buffed himself up for another woman."

"Or man," Phil said. "Fort Lauderdale may have more gays than San Francisco."

"Whoever it is, Shelby needs an answer," Peggy said.

"Sounds promising," Phil said.

"I think you should help families," Margery said. "The average person can afford you better than they can a big agency. You can investigate situations when the family can't—or won't—go to the police."

"Like finding runaways and deadbeat dads?" Phil said.

"Partly," Margery said. "My mechanic has a problem. Gus thinks his brother's suicide was a murder. He wants to hire an investigator to prove his brother was killed. He died in the eighties."

"Opening a cold case can cost a lot of money," Phil said.

"He's got it," Margery said. "Gus charges me eighty bucks an hour to work on my car. He specializes in vintage restorations."

"I thought your Lincoln Town Car was fairly new."

"Then I'm the vintage restoration," Margery said. "You want the job or not?"

"What's his number?" Phil asked.

"I have him on speed dial." Margery opened her cell phone and hit a number.

"Gus?" she asked. "You still want that detective? I've found a good agency—Coronado Investigations." She listened a moment, then asked, "Can you meet him at his repair shop?"

She looked at Phil. He nodded. So did Helen.

"It's *they*, Gus," Margery said. "You're hiring the best team of shamuses in South Florida. They don't come cheap, but you can afford it after my car bills. What did you do last time on my Lincoln—a heart transplant? Coronado Investigations will see you at seven tomorrow night."

Peggy had her own cell phone out. She snapped it shut and said, "My friend Shelby really wants you to start, too. She'll stop by at seven tomorrow morning before she goes to work."

"Amazing," Helen said. "We got two jobs sitting by the pool."

"Enjoy the honeymoon," Margery said. "It won't ever be this easy again."

CHAPTER 2

Shelby Minars was blond, desperate and drop-dead gorgeous—the proper client for a couple of PIs drunk on the romance of their profession.

"Welcome, Shelby." Phil smiled at Coronado Investigations' first client. "You're here at seven a.m. on the dot."

Shelby teetered in on red heels and flashed an uneasy smile. Helen thought Shelby looked young enough to be a schoolgirl in her red polka-dot sundress. She clutched her little white purse as if it were a life preserver.

Helen and Phil sat in their matching black-and-chrome club chairs. Shelby arranged herself in the yellow client chair, crossing her pale legs. The painted toenails peeping through the open toes looked like Red Hots.

Phil stared at Shelby's toes with that silly smile still plastered on his face. He pulled himself out of his toe trance and raised his eyes to Shelby's face.

"How can we help?" Phil asked.

"I'm going to kill my husband," Shelby announced.

"Be careful with statements like that," Phil said. "We're required to report threats to the police."

"I think my husband, Bryan, is cheating on me," she said. "I think it's true, but I don't want it to be. I hope it's not true. That's why I need your agency."

We need you to pay the electric bill, Helen thought. "We can't help you without facts," she said. "Why do you believe your husband is unfaithful?"

"I met Bryan in high school. We've been married seven years," Shelby said. "We've always been happy. At least, I thought we were. We have a four-bedroom house in Rio Vista."

She paused, waiting for the congratulations.

"Nice neighborhood," Helen said. It was, too. Rio Vista's biggest crime problem was golf-cart rustling.

"Yes," Shelby said. "Bryan got us a good deal on our home."

"Is he a doctor?" Phil asked.

"A lot of doctors live in Rio Vista, but Bryan is a successful real estate salesman. At least, he was until the Florida real estate market tanked. My husband has been restless and worried since the housing market fell apart. He's not getting commissions like he used to. Real estate isn't expected to spring back anytime soon. We have plenty of money to live on, but Bryan had too much free time. He started drinking too much and taking long lunches. He put on twenty-five pounds. I couldn't have my honey slipping into a depression, so I bought him a membership at Fantastic Fitness of Fort Lauderdale."

"That's the big gym on Federal Highway?" Phil asked.

Shelby nodded.

"When did you buy the membership?" Helen asked.

"Last June," Shelby said. "Bryan didn't seem enthusiastic about my gift at first. He'd work out maybe once a week and come back in forty-five minutes—and that included his drive time. About a month into his membership, Bryan changed. Now he goes to the gym seven days a week. He can spend five or six hours there."

"Is he really working out," Phil asked, "or watching babes?"

"He's definitely working out. He looks so hot. Bryan is a mass of rippling muscle. Put him in a pirate shirt, and he could model for romance-novel covers."

"What's wrong with that?" Helen asked.

Shelby studied her red-painted nails. "There's no romance," she said. "Not for me. My husband has lost interest in me."

"Maybe he's tired from working out," Helen said. "How old is Bryan?"

"Forty," Shelby said. "I'm two years younger. Forty is a dangerous age for men. They get restless. There's someone else. I'm sure. Almost sure. I need you to make sure."

"Have you seen any signs of infidelity?" Phil said.

"I never caught him with another woman," Shelby said.

"There are other, less obvious clues," Phil said. "One giveaway is when a spouse uses a different soap than you have at home."

"We use Irish Spring. But Bryan showers at the gym, so that won't help."

"Have you found matchbooks from strange restaurants? An earring or feminine item of clothing in his car or gym bag? Numbers on his cell phone he calls often that you don't recognize? Odd charges on your credit card statements?"

"Bryan has lots of callers I don't know on his cell phone," Shelby said. "It's part of his real estate job. There are no unusual charges on our credit cards. I haven't found any lipstick on his shirts.

"But I did catch him lying. A month ago, Bryan told me he was showing a house in Victoria Park. He left at noon Sunday, saying he was going to meet the Jacksons. At twelve thirty I got a call from Bryan's office. Renee said the Jacksons were waiting at the office to see the house. She asked if I knew where Bryan was. His cell phone went straight into voice mail. I called, too, and he didn't answer. Renee said not to bother; she'd take the Jacksons herself.

"Bryan came back about five that afternoon and said the Jacksons had looked at the house, but he didn't think they were interested. I didn't mention Renee's call, but I was suspicious. We hadn't had . . ."

Shelby stopped and looked at Helen and Phil with sad hazel eyes. "We haven't had marital relations in more than six months. I'd asked him again and again if anything was wrong. He insisted he was fine. I offered to go to a marriage counselor. He said nothing was wrong. I didn't believe him.

"Bryan did something strange the next morning. He said he had to go to work—at six a.m. Nobody shows houses that early, and I said so. Bryan said he had a lot of paperwork. After the day before, I was suspicious. I waited fifteen minutes, then drove to his real estate office. No one was there. The lights were off. Fantastic Fitness is on my way home. I saw his car parked in the lot. I peeked in the gym window. Bryan was sweating on a treadmill."

"Anyone working out with him?" Phil asked.

"Lots of people," Shelby said. "But they were all men. I thought maybe Bryan wasn't interested in me because I'm not as fit as the women at his gym."

Shelby gave a long pause, as if she expected Helen or Phil to protest that she looked fine. Both kept silent on that subject.

"So what happened?" Helen said.

"I bought a membership, too. I thought we could work out together. But Bryan wouldn't go with me. If I went in the morning, he went in the afternoon. If I worked out in the afternoon, he went at night. I started dropping in at different times, hoping I'd catch him. As soon as he saw me, he'd make some excuse and leave. Then he'd sneak back to the gym later when I wasn't around."

"How do you know that?" Phil asked.

"I paid Carla, the girl at the reception desk, twenty dollars to let me see the check-ins on the computer," Shelby said. "Bryan is shaping up for someone, and it isn't me. I want you to find out who he's seeing."

"I could work out at the gym and follow him," Phil said.

"That could be difficult," Shelby said. "Bryan is

sneaky and observant. It would be too easy for him to figure out he's being followed and change his hours like he did with me."

Shelby slipped off her red high heel. It dangled from her painted toes as she slowly swung her leg back and forth. Phil's eyes were drawn to those Red Hots toes as if they were little magnets.

"I have a better idea," Shelby said. "The gym is looking for a receptionist. Maybe Helen could work there as a receptionist. If you wouldn't mind, I mean."

"Why would I mind?" Helen said.

"Well, being a detective is highly skilled. Receptionists just answer the phone and check in members. The job may be too low for you."

"No job is too low," Helen said, and then looked at Shelby's startled face. "I mean, I wouldn't mind working as a receptionist."

"There are mirrors everywhere, and you could watch Bryan without him knowing he's being watched," she said. "You could keep the money you'll make as a receptionist and I'll pay, too. That way you get paid double, Helen."

"Nice," Phil said. "I can answer phones. I'd make a terrific receptionist."

"I'm sure you would," Shelby said. "But the club doesn't hire guys for the reception desk. That job is for women only. The men are trainers and salesmen. They make more money."

"That sounds like a lawsuit," Helen said. "I used to be a director of human relations at a big company. They were careful about gender bias."

Shelby nervously swung her leg. Her red heel dangled from a single toe. Phil's eyes were glued to the painted pinkie.

"The club promotes the women to trainers, too, as soon as they buff up," Shelby said. "The women are so happy to make more money and get away from the desk, they never complain. The club lets the receptionists work out for free, so you could get in shape, too. I mean, if you wanted. You look just fine."

"I hate working out," Helen said.

"Me, too," Shelby said. "At the gym the trainers said an early-morning workout gives you energy for the rest of the day, but it just left me exhausted. Phil, you're ripped enough to be a trainer, but Bryan already has one. Her name is Jan Kurtz."

Phil tore his eyes away from Shelby's tootsies to ask, "Could Bryan be having an affair with this Jan?"

"I don't think so," Shelby said. "Carla at the front desk says Jan is having an affair with Nick. He's another client. Nick is married, but that doesn't seem to stop anyone there."

"Sounds like an interesting place," Phil said. "Helen, you could get paid to be in this soap opera."

"We'll need a recent picture of Bryan," Helen said.

"I have one with me," Shelby said, pulling a snapshot from her purse. Helen raised one eyebrow. Bryan wore a Speedo that barely covered his private parts. The man had to shave down there, too.

"Isn't he amazing?" Shelby asked.

"Let me get you a contract, Shelby," Helen said. "If you come over to my desk, I'll explain the terms and rates."

Shelby slipped her red heel back on and trotted over to Helen's desk. She nodded as Helen talked about the payment schedule, barely glanced at the contract before she signed it, and wrote a check for one thousand dollars.

"These desks are amazing," she said, running her small, painted paw over the beat-up gray surface.

Phil looked like a pooch that had been patted on the head. He was proud of the battered gunmetal desks. To him, they were vintage. As a final romantic private-eye touch, he'd added a framed poster of Humphrey Bogart as Sam Spade.

"They're so old," Shelby said. "Did you get them at a museum or something? And who's the funny-looking guy with the bird statue in the poster?"

"Sam Spade," Phil said. "From *The Maltese Falcon*. It's a classic detective movie."

"I don't like old movies," Shelby said, wrinkling her nose, "but my grandfather watches them. He's got lots of time now that he's in assisted living."

Phil looked like he'd been walloped with a walker. Shelby waved good-bye as she tripped across the terrazzo.

"Thank you, Shelby," Helen said.

"Bye," Phil said.

Helen kissed Phil on his ear and said, "See you, Gramps. I'm off to get a job at the gym."

CHAPTER 3

Fantastic Fitness of Fort Lauderdale looked like a gym on steroids. Walls stuck out at gravity-defying angles. Windows appeared in improbable places. The gym was bigger than many corporate headquarters.

The automatic doors opened with the *whoosh!* of a spacecraft's air lock. Helen was hit with a blast of refrigerated air and pounding techno-pop. A wall of muscle blocked her way inside.

"I'm Logan," he said.

Logan was built like an anatomy chart. All the muscle groups were visible under his skin. Helen could even see his chest muscles through his tight tank top. She caught the outline of more muscle under his tiny white shorts. Veins were popped out on his neck, thighs and biceps. Even his chin had muscles. The center dimple looked like it had been installed with a drill bit.

"I'm here to apply for the receptionist's job," Helen said.

"Oh," Logan said, not bothering to hide his disappointment. "We're offering some fantastic deals."

"I'm sure you are," Helen said. "But I want to work here, just like you."

"I'm the head salesman," Logan said, as if he were a god frowning down from Olympus. "I have two Testarossas and a ten-bedroom house. I doubt if you could sell half as well as I do."

"Probably not," Helen said. "But I'm good at dealing with customers."

"You need to talk to Derek, the day manager. I'll have the girl at the desk call him."

Logan gave orders to the "girl." Helen wondered if a phone receiver was too heavy for the musclehead to lift. Everything about him was too much, from his muscles to his mansion. Why did he need to tell her he had two Ferraris?

A bouncy brunette in a short skirt strutted through the door. Logan's muscle mass headed her way, cutting off a pack of other overdeveloped salesmen. Helen saw Logan steer his prey toward a cubicle by the window.

She turned back to the jutting steel reception desk.

"I'm Carla," the receptionist said, flashing a warm smile. "The manager is on his way down. I hope you get the job. I need help at this desk."

The light darkened behind Helen as though an approaching storm front had moved in.

"I'm Derek." His voice was surprisingly light and his Caribbean lilt was pretty.

Derek's muscles stood out in hard lumps, like monster roast coffee beans. His shaved dark head looked obscenely naked. A road map of veins snaked across his abdomen.

"You're here for the receptionist's job?" Derek asked. "I need you to fill out an application. Sit down at the desk in that cubicle and start writing."

Helen did. The gym's treadmills and stationary bikes hummed like beehives. The music pounded and the weight machines clanged.

Ten minutes later, Derek's bulk nearly filled the glass cubicle. The chair groaned as he sat down. The gym manager frowned at Helen's application and said, "You're a smart lady with a college degree. Why do you want to work here? We can only afford to pay minimum wage."

"I like the atmosphere," Helen said. "Lots of energy. I want to work at something more exciting than retail."

"Some days, you'll get more excitement than you want," Derek said. "I can promise that our customers are never dull. The pay isn't much at first, but there are opportunities for advancement and your workouts are free. It wouldn't hurt you to buff up. I see the beginnings of a belly and some biceps sag."

Derek's assessment of her figure stung, but Helen reminded herself that Shelby Minars was paying her to work here and investigate Bryan. Those free workouts would give Helen more time to study their client's husband.

"Anyone can benefit from exercise," Helen said and smiled at Derek.

I've started exercising already, she thought. I read somewhere it takes fifteen muscles to smile and only seven to flip someone off.

"That's the right attitude," Derek said. "Can you start work today? Carla's going to be here all day, and I want her to train you."

Carla was on the phone when the manager took Helen back to the reception desk. "Yes, ma'am," she said. "I'm sure it was the bank's mistake. If you could get the money to us before your next training session . . . Thank you."

Carla hung up the phone, pushed her dark curls off her face and sighed. "I wish you didn't have to hear that, but it's part of the job. We have to make clear-up calls when members get behind in their payments."

"I used to be a telemarketer," Helen said. "People can be pretty rude on the phone."

"This woman wasn't bad," Carla said. "She didn't hang up or cuss me out. She used the old 'bank mistake' routine. You'll hear more inventive excuses now that you're working here. Welcome aboard. Let's start with a tour of the place. I'll ask Derek to watch the desk for me. He's a sweetheart."

She waved Derek over to the reception desk. "No problem," he said with the lovely island accent and smiled. Even his teeth looked strong.

Helen could smell the women's locker room at the end

of the hall, a pleasant scent of steam and coconut soap. Three women lounged on flowered couches, sipping ice water. A fourth dried her hair in the dressing area.

"It's nicer than the country club where I used to work," Helen said.

"This is a club for our regulars," Carla said. "Heck, it's home. That's the lounge with the couches. The showers and toilets are in here. The stall doors go down to the floor for privacy—in some cases, a little too much privacy. We get same-sex couples in the stalls. The day managers have to break up fights in the men's locker room when a gay guy hits on a straight one."

"What about the gay women?"

"Straight women usually don't get upset if gay females make a pass at them. Guess they don't feel their womanhood is in question. Some gay women use the sauna or hot tub as a trysting place. If you get a complaint at the desk, you'll have to tell the ladies to find a more private location."

They walked down a white-tiled corridor where the air reeked of warm chlorine. "That's our pool. Over on that side is our Kiddy Kare room. Some women get a membership just for the free babysitting. They're allowed to drop the kids off for five hours at a time. You'll get used to the cries of abandoned babies."

Helen shuddered.

"Treadmills are on the first floor. Stationary bikes are next to them. Weight and exercise rooms are upstairs, along with the basketball and racquetball courts. That's the short tour. Now we'd better get back to the reception desk because Derek has work to do in his office.

"Thank you, Derek," Carla said as they rejoined Derek at the front desk. "I'll take over here again."

"No problem," Derek said. His accent was an island vacation.

Carla and Helen slid behind the reception desk, and Carla swung the computer screen so Helen could see it.

"The check-in routine is simple," she said. "Members show their cards. You run the cards through the computer.

A red box comes up on your screen if the members are three months behind on their payments. If that happens, you have to tell them their membership is frozen until they pay up. Some get embarrassed. A few turn nasty. If they get abusive, press that red button under the counter here and Derek will come running. The sales boys are right over there, but they're usually trapping anyone who comes in wearing civilian clothes."

"I know," Helen said. "I ran into Logan."

"That scumbag," Carla said. "Stay away from him."

Before she could explain why, a perky brunette interrupted them. "Hey there," Carla said. "It's Beth." She cocked her brown head to one side, like a sparrow.

Beth had a cheerleader's compact, muscular body and a soccer mom haircut. Her red workout suit seemed to be a series of holes. The interconnected fabric barely covered the vital spots.

"Could you check the computer and see if Jon is here yet?" She put a twenty on the counter.

"Sorry," Carla said. "We're not allowed to do that."

"Oh." Beth looked sweetly confused. "I thought—"

"Helen here is a *trainee*," Carla said.

Beth fumbled in her purse, found another twenty and put it in front of Helen.

"We're both risking our jobs," Carla said.

Two more twenties appeared. Carla clicked the computer keys and said, "Jon arrived ten minutes ago. He's probably in the weight room now."

"There he is!" Beth said, running upstairs to the weight room.

"If she sneezes in that workout suit, she'll be arrested for indecent exposure," Helen said. "How does she exercise in that thing?"

"She'll get quite a workout—in the towel closet with Jon," Carla said. "Those holes are artistically arranged to make a quickie quicker."

"Why don't Beth and Jon get a motel room?" Helen asked.

"Most couples do," Carla said. "But not those two. Jon's

splitting with his wife. He's afraid she has detectives sneaking around watching him."

Helen hoped she wasn't blushing.

"Is Beth going to marry him once he's divorced?" Helen asked.

"No way," Carla said. "Jon doesn't make enough money as a car salesman. Beth's husband is an anesthesiologist, and she doesn't want to lose her meal ticket.

"What I told Beth was true. We are not supposed to give out that information. When a couple is having an affair, they'll ask if their lover is at the gym now or was in earlier for a workout. You can see the full day's check-ins and check-outs by hitting this key."

"May I?" Helen said. She checked the names. Their client's husband—Bryan Minars—had come in at seven ten, about the same time his wife hired Helen to watch her possibly wayward husband. He'd left ten minutes before Helen arrived at the gym.

"Hitting that key is the best way I know to boost your income," Carla said. "The going rate for adultery information is twenty bucks, but if they're desperate you can milk them for forty. That's your split. Don't let Derek see you. Taking bribes is a firing offense."

"You keep it." Helen slid the cash toward Carla.

The receptionist flushed with surprise and pocketed the eighty dollars. "Thanks. Just keep it quiet."

"I won't tell," Helen said. "I need this job."

"Me, too," Carla said. "I can't afford Fantastic Fitness's high ethics."

A scream split the air, a sound louder than the pounding music. "Listen! I want to watch Fox News. Give me the clicker." A woman's voice, low and rumbling.

"Oh, no, you don't, Debbi. It's my week. I get to watch *my* station." This voice was higher and lighter, like a yappy Yorkie.

"You're full of it, Heather. And you're fat." Debbi said the F word as the ultimate insult.

"You could use some fat," Heather said. "You might look like a human instead of a freak."

Two women were scuffling over a TV clicker. Debbi, the taller one, had a body like a strip of beef jerky—long, thin and dried out. Her hair was short yellow tufts, like a dandelion plopped on her head. Heather, the short redhead, was a wet dream of creamy skin, curves and curls. She made a jump for the black clicker and missed.

"Oh, lordy," Carla whispered to Helen. "Debbi is in another 'roid rage. She's in training for a bodybuilding competition. These last days are making her crazy. Watch how I break up this fight. It may be your turn tomorrow."

Carla marched out onto the floor. Stick-thin Debbi towered over the curvaceous Heather.

"Debbi, put down that clicker," Carla commanded. "You know this is CNN week. Switch the station."

Debbi glared at Carla. Her chest heaved. Muscles rippled up and down her abdomen.

"We agreed in November that we would alternate weeks on the television in the stationary bike room," Carla said. "Switch it back now or I'll revoke your membership."

Debbi raised her arm and slammed the clicker on the floor. The black case popped open, and the batteries rolled under a bike.

"Change it yourself," Debbi said, storming off toward the locker room.

CHAPTER 4

．．．．．．．．．．．．．．．．．．．．．．

Helen didn't bother trimming calories after seeing Debbi's stylized starvation. She ate her chicken sandwich with relish—plus mayonnaise, a fat bun and a pile of potato chips.

Thumbs, Helen's six-toed cat, sat at her feet, staring hopefully at her dinner.

Phil had already put his plate in the dishwasher. "The meeting with our second client, Gus Behr, is at seven tonight," he said. "We have to leave in ten minutes."

Thumbs sprang up on the table and streaked toward the last bite of Helen's sandwich. She caught the cat and dropped him on the floor. "You know better, Thumbs."

The cat slunk off to his food bowl and crunched resentfully on his dry dinner. Helen finished her sandwich and dashed into the bedroom to freshen up.

"Don't do anything fancy," Phil said. "We're going to a car repair shop."

At six fifty-five, Phil's Jeep bumped across the railroad tracks that ran along Dixie Highway. Boy Toys Restoration and Car Repair was straight ahead, a showy hot pink and turquoise building surrounded by a gleaming metal fence.

"Look at that," Phil said, and gave a whistle. "That is purely beautiful."

Helen saw a stocky man with grease up to his elbows bent under the hood of a needle-nosed car.

"He is?" Helen said.

"Not the guy, the car," Phil said. "That looks like a 1965 Jaguar XKE, the most beautiful sports car ever made. I'm in love."

"Should I be jealous?" Helen asked.

"No," Phil said. "I can't afford her. She costs more than a hundred grand."

"Thanks a lot," Helen said. "Glad I'm cheap."

Phil swung his beat-up black Jeep next to the sleek red Jaguar, jumped out and said, "Hi. Gorgeous Jag."

Gus Behr wiped his hands on an oily rag. "Isn't she? You're looking at two years of restoration. Too bad she's going to sit in some doctor's garage."

Phil peeked in the driver's window. He looked at the black leather interior and wood steering wheel like a starving man in a bakery shop.

"My husband, Phil, was struck speechless by that car," Helen said. "I'm Helen Hawthorne. We're the co-owners of Coronado Investigations."

"I figured," Gus said. "Let's go in my office and cool off." Sweat cascaded down his forehead.

Helen and Phil followed Gus through an open garage that smelled pleasantly of engine oil. The gray painted floor was clean and shiny. Tools were neatly hung on a pegboard or stowed in metal cabinets. Inside Gus's office, it was thirty degrees cooler—and frozen in the 1980s. Gus sighed with relief as he sat behind a black lacquer desk piled with papers and parts catalogues. A framed autographed photo of Don Johnson as Sonny Crockett took up one corner. The actor stood next to the black Ferrari from *Miami Vice*.

Gus opened a water bottle for himself and drank thirstily. Helen and Phil said no thanks and opened their notebooks.

"We can talk prices and stuff when I finish," Gus said. "If I don't tell my story now, I'll lose my nerve. This goes way back to the eighties, when my brother Mark died. I'm fifty-seven now. Mark was two years younger. In 'eighty-six, Mark had just turned thirty. He died of a gunshot wound to the head. The police said it was suicide, but I know he was murdered."

He paused for another drink. Helen said nothing. Phil nodded at him to continue.

"My family is from Fostoria, Ohio," Gus said.

"Where they made the glassware?" Phil asked.

"Right. Fostoria is about ninety miles from Columbus," Gus said. "Lot of Germans, Irish, Italians and Belgians did the grunt work at the glass plants. The powers that be looked down on us because we were blue-collar Catholic. My dad, Frederick, saved up enough to start a gas station. He pumped gas and fixed cars. My mom, Roseanna, took care of us three kids. The Three Behrs, they called us. We were all redheads. You see what's left of mine." He ran a grease-stained hand through his rusty fringe.

"Mom named my sister Bernadette for the humble French saint who saw Jesus's mother. Bernie hated the name. She was no saint and she sure wasn't humble. She and Mom had some complicated mother-daughter thing and fought a lot. Bernie didn't like leaving her friends in high school. My brother, Mark, and I got along fine with Dad. We loved cars.

"Back in Ohio, we were the perfect Catholic family, right down to the concrete Virgin in the yard. When Dad got older, he got sick of working in the Midwest winters. He said the cold would kill him. He moved the family to Fort Lauderdale in 1980 and opened Fred's Garage. Mark and I worked at the garage, lived in a bachelor dive and had a great time.

"Mom acted like she never left Ohio. She had her Fort Lauderdale volunteer groups and went to church every Sunday. Even had the same damn concrete Virgin in the yard. Mom insisted we kids show up for Sunday dinner. Bernie gave her a hard time, but Mark and I never missed a meal."

Gus patted his gut as if it were a prize pumpkin.

"Dad was a good mechanic, but he struggled to stay in

business. Winter didn't kill him. The Florida heat got him. He died of a heart attack in July 'eighty-five.

"Dad's death was a shock. Mom wanted to sell the garage, but Mark and I talked her into letting us run it. It was Mark's idea to change the name and redo this building. He made the business upscale. We were no longer a neighborhood garage.

"When Dad died, our family lost its anchor. Mom quit cooking Sunday dinners. Bernie started coming home late, then staying out all night. Mom didn't say anything. I think she was tired of fighting. Bernie was seventeen, a real looker, with long red hair. Guys would stop and stare, she was that beautiful.

"I should have kept an eye on my little sister, but I was working ten-hour days at the garage. I'd also met my wife, Jeannie, and was wrapped up in her. I was doing the work of two men. Mark showed up when he felt like it, which wasn't often.

"Mark and Bernie started running with a wild crowd. Bernie was dating a rich Turk named Ahmet Yavuz. Ahmet was Hollywood handsome. Mom didn't like my sister hanging around with him. The more she objected, the more Bernie said she loved him."

"What did you think of this Ahmet?" Phil asked.

"He was bad news. Ahmet had an import-export business, but I thought it was a cover for drug dealing.

"Mom wanted Bernie to date a nice Catholic boy. She insisted I lay down the law. I told Bernie if she kept going out with Ahmet, she couldn't live at home with Mom. Bernie said fine and moved in with the drug dealer."

Phil and Helen said nothing, but Gus read their disapproval. "I know, I know. That's not a smart way to treat a headstrong young woman. I was head of the family and I had a lot of worries. Mark was throwing money around. He tried to help, even if he didn't work much. He sent customers with flashy cars—Lamborghinis, Ferraris, Bentleys. The customers paid cash and never questioned the bills. I suspected they had drug money, but I didn't look too close. Cash was rolling in.

"Worse, Mark's mental problems surfaced again. In his early twenties, he'd been diagnosed as manic-depressive. I guess they use 'bipolar' now. Mark was fine if he took his medication. When he ran with the party crowd, he stopped. Six months after Dad died, I found Mark walking naked down Dixie Highway, babbling that he could save the world. I hauled him off to a mental hospital. Later, I learned Mark used coke to make the voices in his head go away."

"What happened after you committed Mark?" Phil asked.

"Mom wasn't happy with me. I tried to explain my brother needed professional help—a naked man wandering the streets could get shot.

"After Mark got out of the hospital, he worked even less, but he sent me new business. He and Bernie partied harder than ever. One night I came home from work and found Bernie had moved in with us. She said she'd left Ahmet, but she wasn't going home to Mom. She didn't want to hear Mom say, 'I told you so.'"

Gus took another gulp of water. "I— He— This next part is hard to say." He took a deep breath. "That was a Monday. A week later, Mark was shot. My sister said the accident happened in Plantation."

"The Lauderdale suburb?" Phil asked.

"Yeah," Gus said. "I was here at the shop when Bernie called. She said Mark was in Broward Hospital in bad shape. I ran over there. He was in a coma.

"I got the rest of the story in bits and pieces. Ahmet told the police that Mark came to his import-export business talking crazy and waving a gun. He said my brother shot himself in the head before Ahmet could take the gun away.

"I know Ahmet lied. He hated my brother. Ahmet wouldn't lift a finger to help Mark. My brother never came out of the coma. He died in the hospital two days later. The police said Mark committed suicide."

"I'm sorry," Helen said.

Mark's death was twenty-five years ago, but his brother's grief still seemed raw.

"I know Mark didn't kill himself," Gus said. "Our family is Catholic. Suicide is a mortal sin."

"But Mark quit going to church," Phil said. "He used coke. Your sister lived with a drug dealer."

"Everyone was wild back then," Gus said. "Most of Mark's friends straightened out. Mark and Bernie had good values. They lost their way for a while.

"I know what really happened, but I can't prove it: The police hushed up Mark's murder. I need you to get the evidence."

Gus's heavy shoulders seemed bowed by the weight of his story.

"I don't know if we can help, Gus," Phil said. "The mid-eighties were the heyday of the cocaine cowboys. There were definitely corrupt cops. But it will be hard to prove Mark was murdered. Why investigate your brother's death now?"

"I make a good living restoring classic cars," Gus said. "I got my start thanks to Mark. My son, Gus Junior, is in business with me. I'm a grandfather."

Gus pointed proudly to photos of a red-haired boy ranging from newborn to about age four. In the latest, his curls were covered by a fire hat. "That's Gustav Behr the Third. He likes cars as much as his dad."

"What a cutie," Helen said. "He inherited your red hair."

"I'm worried he inherited something worse," Gus said. "My wife's grandfather killed himself. Jeannie's mom hanged herself after her fourth kid. I don't want my grandson thinking we're a family of suicides. I want you to prove Mark's death was murder."

"How does Bernie feel about this investigation?" Phil asked.

"My sister turned into Mrs. Solid Citizen. She's completely changed. Bernie was real depressed after Mark died. She kept saying it was 'all her fault.' I guess she felt guilty she'd taken up with a drug dealer. She had her own drug problem. Bernie went into rehab and spent six months in a mental institution.

"Once she recovered, Bernie went to med tech school and became a phlebotomist—she draws blood at a hospital. She married Kevin Bennett, some big executive. They live in Weston and have a kid in college. To look at her, you'd never guess my sister had a wild past. My poor mom died of cancer about a year after Mark's death."

"Is Ahmet still alive?" Phil asked.

"He's even more respectable than Bernie. Ahmet is a big-time real estate dealer. Belongs to the chamber of commerce, serves on a bunch of charity boards. Makes me sick to see him grinning in the society pages."

Gus seemed to run out of steam. A heavy silence fell over the room.

"Do you have any paperwork?" Phil asked. "Your brother's death certificate, the police reports, his autopsy?"

"Mom and Bernie had those," Gus said. "I couldn't face Mark's death for a long time. I couldn't even think about it. I never believed he killed himself. I know I'm right. It's only since little Gus came along that I knew I had to find out what really happened. I need you to find the facts."

"This case is cold," Phil said. "The records—if there are any—could be lost or missing."

Gus pulled out a checkbook. "Your landlady said you were the best. Margery is one smart lady. Here's two thousand dollars. There's more where that came from."

Gus signed a contract and the paperwork giving Coronado Investigations permission to act as his agent.

"We'll need the names of your brother's friends," Phil said.

"I've already made a list and included Mark's Social Security number, the hospital and the funeral home. Here's an old video of Mark's thirtieth birthday party at a Lauderdale bar called Granddaddy's. You can see my sister, Mark, me, Mark's friends and Ahmet. All the major characters."

"Digging into family history is dangerous," Phil said. "Are you sure you want this investigation?"

"I need to know," Gus said.

On the drive back home, Helen was the first to break the silence. "Are you worried we won't find Mark's killer?"

"The job is impossible," Phil said. "And if we succeed, Gus may be sorry. Remember Marcie, my first case?"

"The girl who died," Helen said.

"Her parents wanted to know the truth. I had to tell them their baby had become a coke whore. I watched them die in front of me."

"Maybe Mark's story won't end like that," Helen said. "Let's get the facts first."

Helen and Phil watched the old VCR tape that night. Helen snuggled next to her husband on the black leather couch in Phil's living room. She had Gus's list of names on a clipboard.

The homemade tape started with a burst of sound and static. Then the video camera righted itself and panned the room.

The walls were painted dark blue and hung with glowing beer signs. Granddaddy's Bar, Helen thought. A neighborhood bar with chrome stools and a long, polished lane of dark wood. The bottles on the lighted back bar were a skyline of liquor, a promise of good times. A neon palm tree proclaimed it was a Florida bar.

"We are definitely in the mid-eighties," Helen said. "I see the styles I coveted as a teenager: headbands, frizzy hair, purple-red lipstick, blush like racing stripes. I wore blush like that, and my mother made me wash it off."

"For once, I agree with your mother," Phil said. "You don't need makeup. Your skin is naturally beautiful." He kissed her cheek, then her ear. His kisses traced the long line of her neck down to her open shirt collar.

"We should be working," Helen said and sighed.

"We're newlyweds." Phil put the tape on pause. "I like making love to married women. This will help me forget my troubles." He took her in his arms, and Helen's clipboard slid to the floor.

A half hour later Helen and Phil went back to the tape of Mark's birthday party. They were still captivated by the outrageous eighties fashions.

"Look at the brass earrings on that woman," Phil said. "They're like something in *National Geographic*."

"How about the rhinestone chandeliers on the brunette?" Helen asked.

Most of the women were twentysomething. They showed off their lean bodies with crop tops, ripped jeans, leggings and tiny flared "ra-ra" skirts.

"What does that blonde have on her legs?" he asked. "They look like leg sweaters."

"Those are leg warmers," Helen said. "After *Flashdance* we all dressed like we'd just come from a dance studio. Check out the guys' hair—more mullets than a fish shop. Half the men are wearing Members Only jackets."

"I had one. I liked it," Phil said with a touch of defiance.

"You were young," she said. "You didn't know better."

The camera panned the glowing jukebox. Kool & The Gang sang "Celebration" at full volume. Phil turned the sound down a notch. Men waved beer bottles and danced with women drinking wine coolers or pale peach drinks.

"What's in the highball glasses?" Helen asked.

"I think the women may be drinking Sex on the Beach," Phil said.

"I snuck one at a graduation party," Helen said. "Sex on the Beach was peach schnapps, vodka and some things I can't remember. I never forgot the hangover, though. I spent the next morning worshiping the porcelain goddess."

The music switched to "Every Breath You Take." The Police promised "I'll be watching you" when a woman with red-gold hair cruised past the beer-swilling mullets.

She was arresting, even in the grainy video. Her hair glowed like a bonfire. She had snow-maiden skin, a black leather jacket with shoulder pads, wicked leather pants and a bra the same fiery color as her hair.

Every man in the room swiveled to stare at her.

"Damn. Gus wasn't kidding," Phil said. "That has to be Bernie. She is breathtaking."

"The guy with her isn't bad, either," Helen said. "I bet that's Ahmet, the drug dealer. He looks like a young Omar Sharif. Lovely olive skin, eyes like twin pools of chocolate."

"Corn as high as an elephant's eye," Phil teased.

"I'm just saying the man is eye candy," Helen said. "No wonder Bernie fell for him. They make a striking couple.

Both know how to dress. She looks like a rock star. He's wearing Armani with a black T-shirt."

"How do you know the designer when you can't see the label?" Phil asked.

"Years of working retail," Helen said.

A doll-like dark-haired woman walked carefully through a back door, carrying a birthday cake with candles. She held the cake out to keep the icing away from her sparkling cobalt blue top.

"Sequins and shoulder pads," Helen said. "Wouldn't be the eighties without them."

The shoulder-padded woman set the cake down and lit the candles.

The camera panned to Bernie. She was wrapped around Ahmet, kissing him. The partygoers chanted, "Go! Go! Go!"

Someone turned down the music, and another mullet-head yelled, "Hey, Danny, put that videocam on a stand and come here. We've gotta sing 'Happy Birthday' to old Mark. Where are the birthday boy and his brother? Mark? Gus? We need you."

A broad-chested young man crowned with red-gold hair entered, his arm around a thin, fashionably frizzy-haired blonde. He had the dazed smile of a man in love.

"Is that Gus?" Helen couldn't hide her shock.

"Hi!" The red-gold prince waved to the partygoers. "You all know my Jeannie. Mark will be in, soon as he parks his car."

"You're looking at Gus with fifty fewer pounds and a lot more hair," Phil said.

"You don't have to sound so happy." Helen felt sad that Gus's good looks were gone.

The cheers grew louder.

Helen and Phil stared at the man striding on-screen. "That has to be Mark," Helen said. "He looks like a young god."

The crowd parted for Mark. He towered over everyone. Helen couldn't tear her eyes away. Mark's face was sculpted perfection. The man was a Viking warrior in a pink Italian sport coat and artfully wrinkled white linen pants.

He should be holding a sword, Helen thought.

"Mark is wearing Ray-Ban sunglasses at night," Phil said. "The man was a player."

"That's all you can say?" Helen asked. "He's the most beautiful man I've ever seen."

"Hey!" Phil said.

"You don't even notice Gus next to him," Helen said, "and Gus was no slouch. It's hard to believe someone as vibrant as Mark is dead. No wonder Gus still grieves for him."

Someone handed Mark a frosted mug of beer. He shouted at the camera: "Hey, Danny Boy, get your ass over here, so I can blow out these candles." Mark's grin took the sting out of his command.

"You can't talk to me like that in my own bar," a reedy voice called back. Danny Boy's speech was slightly slurred. A small rodent with slicked-down black hair appeared next to Mark. Danny Boy barely came to Mark's shoulder, even in his red cowboy boots.

"I'd wear sunglasses, too, if I had to stand next to Danny Boy's Hawaiian shirt," Phil said.

Helen studied Gus's list on her clipboard. "He's the bar owner. Gus says he was Mark's best friend."

Danny Boy swayed in his cowboy boots and poked a finger at Mark's massive chest. "Hurry up and blow out your candles, before the fire inspector shuts me down. Damn. Thirty candles. You're old, man."

Danny led the crowd in an off-key version of "Happy Birthday."

Mark, smiling, golden, glowing, blew out his candles and bowed. His friends shouted, "Speech! Speech!"

Mark held the beer mug aloft in a toast. "May you live forever, and may I never die."

Then Mark blew out the candles on his last birthday cake. The screen went dark.

CHAPTER 5

"Jack the Dripper, I'm gonna break your face. I want you out of this gym! Out!"

Debbi's shriek made Helen drop the notebook she'd been studying behind the desk at Fantastic Fitness.

Yesterday, the young bodybuilder had battled for the TV remote. This morning Debbi was boiling over with fresh rage. Her eyes bulged with fury. Her face was as hard as her muscles. "Carla, damn it, do something!"

"What did he do this time?" Carla asked. Helen was grateful the receptionist stepped up to handle this complaint.

"What he always does," Debbi said. "Jack won't wipe down the weight bench. It's disgusting, the way he sweats. Look at my hand. It's wet with his sweat." The furious bodybuilder flicked the drops at Carla.

"Hey!" Carla said. She ducked, but not fast enough.

Jack the Dripper ambled over to the desk. He was pale as a cooked noodle and about as muscular.

"What's she complaining about now?" he asked. "You're supposed to sweat at a gym. Real men sweat."

"Real men wipe down the bench when they finish,"

Carla said. "That's why we have sanitary wipes here. Unless you're too weak to lift one." She stared pointedly at his concave chest.

"Hey, I'm a member here," Jack said.

"We can change that," Carla said. "You have ten seconds to wipe down that bench, or I'll revoke your membership."

Jack reluctantly returned to the weight bench and gave it a halfhearted swipe.

"Thank you," Debbi said. "It's about time." She forced a smile, but it looked like it hurt. That set of muscles was underused. Then she adjusted the weight bench and began a ferocious set of power sled chest flies.

"Good thing those weights are made of metal and rubber," Helen said. "Debbi is slamming them hard."

"I just hope the weights are the only things she hurts," Carla said. "That woman scares me."

"She does have a temper," Helen said.

"She's out of control," Carla said. "Debbi is going to kill someone. I wish Derek would talk to her about her anger. As the manager, he might be able to get her to listen."

"She seems to be taking it out on the free weights now," Helen said. "It's only six thirty-five in the morning and we've already had our first crisis."

"You ain't seen nothing yet," Carla said.

Fantastic Fitness quickly settled back into its regular routine. Men ran nowhere fast on treadmills. Women pumped iron. Helen heard the *tock!* of racquetballs hitting the walls. The workout music pounded. She hoped this distracting medley would shake her sadness. Watching Mark's final birthday video last night had left her feeling depressed.

So far, Helen had checked in three guests under Carla's watchful eye. One of them was her client's husband. Her face didn't even twitch when Bryan Minars said his name. No wonder Shelby was upset that she wasn't having sex with her man, Helen thought. Bryan looked rock hard, but his physique hadn't crossed the line from Gibraltar to grotesque.

He had other endearing qualities: His dark wavy hair formed a question-mark curl over his eyebrow. His trainer,

Jan, was putting Bryan through his paces with the barbells. Jan was a fortysomething brunette. She had muscles but still looked softly pretty.

"Come on," Jan said to Bryan. "You can do it. One more dead lift and then you can do thirty minutes on the treadmill." The trainer made it sound like that half-hour run would be relaxing.

Carla caught Helen staring at Bryan. "He's easy on the eyes, isn't he?"

"Definitely," Helen said. "Does Bryan have a girlfriend?"

"He doesn't act like it. No woman's dropped twenties on me to find out if he's at the gym. His wife works out here, too."

Rats, Helen thought. I knew it wouldn't be that easy.

Suddenly, the *tocking, clanking* and humming seemed to stop. The gym doors whooshed open to reveal a goddess wearing two well-placed scraps of spandex. The goddess wafted through the front door. Her hair was blond silk. Her breasts were twin cantaloupe halves. Her bottom was two honeydew globes.

"That's Paula," Carla said. "Watch Paula's suckers."

Paula paraded down the aisle of treadmills, each whirring machine topped by a sweating man. As Paula passed the men, they automatically sucked in their guts and kept running. Even Shelby's husband pulled in his six-pack of muscle. Helen wondered if Paula was the reason Bryan was killing himself at the gym.

"See how the dudes sucked in their guts when she walked by?" Carla said. "Watch what happens next."

Paula ignored the men. She made a left at the end of the treadmill aisle and turned into the hall to the women's locker room. Once she was out of sight, the guts flopped back into place. Fat, red-faced men gave small, relieved sighs. The well-built ones like Bryan relaxed a bit.

"I hope she has the same hypnotic effect on the judges at the upcoming East Coast Physique Championships," Carla said. "Paula is training for the bikini competition."

"She doesn't have muscles like Debbi," Helen said.

"She doesn't need them," Carla said. "Not with that body. The bikini contestants look like regular people."

Who stepped out of a centerfold, Helen thought.

A trim fiftysomething woman with pretty gray hair waved to Carla and Helen as she headed out the door with a full gym bag.

"Did you check in Evie this morning?" Carla asked.

"Nope, just three guys."

"Hm," Carla said. "I didn't check her in, either. Must be something wrong with her card. Remind me to check it when she comes back. She usually works out in the morning and again before closing. Are you okay?"

"Sure. Why wouldn't I be?"

"Usually after a new receptionist encounters Debbi in one of her rages, she quits."

"I've seen worse," Helen said. "I like it here. Might even work out on my break."

"That's coming up," Carla said. "You'll get fifteen minutes. If you're new to exercising, try riding the bike on a low setting. And don't be late. When you return, you have to fill in at the Xtreme Shop."

Helen pedaled the stationary bike for four minutes and felt good, even invigorated. She decided to step up her workout and punched the buttons to the highest setting. Pedaling at that level was harder, but not that hard.

I'm in better shape than I thought, she congratulated herself. She was surprised when the timer dinged and she had to return to the reception desk.

Carla was waiting for her. "Hurry! Kristi is going on break. You have to watch the Xtreme Shop for her."

"What do I do?" Helen said.

"Ring up the members' purchases on the cash register. Everyone puts them on their gym account, so you just run their membership cards through the machine. Be careful around Kristi. She's in training for a bodybuilding competition. She and Tansi are Debbi's mentors."

"Do you have to have a name like a Playboy centerfold to be a female bodybuilder?" Helen asked.

Carla pushed Helen into the Xtreme Shop, a cubicle

stocked with protein powders and bodybuilding supplements. "Promotes skin-tearing muscle pumps!" screamed a drum of "muscle amplifier." A fat bottle declared it was a "pre-contest physique repartitioning compound."

Sexual metaphors abounded: "explosive strength," "increases powerhouse pumps," "extreme stimulation."

I've spent too much time on my honeymoon, Helen decided. I need to get my mind out of bed.

"Extreme" was definitely the word for Kristi. She showed off her muscles in yellow spandex. The grotesque development looked like a set of clothes. Kristi had a shelf of muscle on her shoulders. The sides of her chest were like an insect's carapace. She was so deformed by her shoulder and upper-arm development, she walked slightly hunched.

A grumpy Kristi glowered at Helen. "You're late," she said. "I'll be back in sixteen minutes."

"Nothing wrong with that girl a good meal wouldn't fix," Carla said as Kristi scuttled to the free weights.

"Wow," Helen said. "Kristi has some serious muscle."

"Serious is right," Carla said. "She and Tansi are going out for the Women's Muscle title in the upcoming East Coast Physique Championships. They're training Debbi for the Women's Novice Muscle title. They think she's a shoo-in."

"Do they get paid for mentoring her?"

"No. They get the glory if their protégé wins," Carla said. "If they rack up enough winners, they can call themselves 'trainers to the pros' and make big money. I wish Debbi's two mentors didn't start her on steroids."

"Aren't those illegal?" Helen said.

"We don't allow steroids at our gym," Carla said. "But some of our bodybuilders inject. You can tell who uses them. Take a look at Kristi's back and you'll see the telltale acne.

"And talk about 'roid rage. Kristi saw me eating a burger and nearly bit my head off. She said I was deliberately trying to make her lose the competition. I was just eating lunch."

"Can't she eat, too? I thought workouts made you hungry."

"They do," Carla said. "But right before a competition,

some serious builders go into starvation mode to show every muscle fiber. They live on two ounces of chicken."

"That's all they eat for one meal?" Helen said.

"For one day," Carla said. "They eat protein only—no fruit or bread. They avoid carbs the way you'd run from heroin."

Debbi approached the reception desk. This time, she seemed shy and tentative. "Excuse me," she said with a small voice. She pushed what looked like a candy bar toward Carla. "That's for you. It's an energy bar. Double Dutch chocolate. When I can eat, it's my favorite. It has no carbs and three grams of protein. I'm sorry I yelled. I tell myself I won't get mad and next thing I know, I'm screaming. I'm just so angry since my dad died."

Carla's face softened. "I'm sorry. That was awful."

"Nobody's sorry he's dead," Debbi said.

Helen noticed a brief flare of anger, like a lit match in the dark.

"He killed a harmless old lady when he held up that convenience store," Debbi said. "I'm glad the manager shot him. Except everyone knows I'm the Granny Killer's daughter."

"Nobody blames you for what your father did," Carla said.

"They do," Debbi said. "I hear them talking about me wherever I go."

"They are talking about you," Carla said. "You're a strong woman. Your trainers say you'll be a star. You'll get that trophy."

"I want it bad," Debbi said. "I want everyone to know that I'm a champion. I'm not worthless like my father."

"You're not, sweetie," Carla said.

"Are you still mad at me?"

"I'm concerned," Carla said. "We all want you to succeed. If you yell at a judge, you could be disqualified. Maybe a doctor could give you something so you wouldn't be so angry."

"Can't afford a doctor," Debbi said.

There it was again, Helen thought. That flash of anger.

"Mom and I don't have health insurance. But once I win the novice title and the endorsement money rolls in, I can see a doctor. I'd better leave now."

Debbi bobbed her head good-bye and walked awkwardly toward the door.

"That poor thing," Helen said. "Starving herself for a trophy. Why do the women do that to themselves?"

"For the glory, the awards and the prizes," Carla said. "Same as the male athletes. Too bad women don't win as much money. Guys can win ten times more. There's a lot of discrimination against strong women, but not at Fantastic Fitness. If any of our members—Paula, Kristi, Tansi or Debbi—wins a title, we'll display their photos and trophies in our Hall of Fame, along with our other winners' prizes."

The hall trophy case was just outside the Xtreme Shop. It could have been in any high school hall—if the students were built like comic-book superheroes.

CHAPTER 6

"**H**oney, I'm home!" Helen called out the old sitcom line as she breezed into Phil's apartment. "It's only two o'clock and I've finished work. I even got some exercise, and then I walked home. I—"

Helen saw Phil's face and stopped her runaway report. "Something's wrong," she said. The apartment smelled of burnt coffee. Half-empty mugs were scattered on the table and the kitchen counter. Three cups were on his desk next to the computer, mute testimony to Phil's frustrated efforts.

"Way wrong," Phil said. "Our case is dead before I even started. I can't find any official paper on Mark's accident. I spent the morning searching for the records in Plantation. There's no police report, no incident or accident report, no autopsy."

"Gus was right," Helen said. "There is a conspiracy."

"Not necessarily," Phil said. "Mark has been dead a quarter of a century. Paper trails are easy to lose. Could be the police report was destroyed after all this time. I talked with Barry, an old-timer who retired from the force. Barry doesn't remember any suicide shooting from 1986."

"It's been a while," Helen said.

"It has," Phil said. "But Mark's accident was dramatic, and Barry has a good memory. He was new to the force twenty-five years ago. I checked with Gus again. He insisted his brother's shooting happened in Plantation. Gus says his sister told him it was there. I need official paper."

"What about the murder investigation files?" Helen asked. "The murder book, I think it's called. Don't the police keep that?"

"Could be the cops never started one," Phil said. "Barry said they could have closed this case before it became a murder investigation. I spent the morning checking records and drew a blank.

"I called Gus once again and went over the timeline with him. The first day, Mark went to the hospital with a gunshot wound to the head. He was in a coma. The surgeons operated. Mark died two days later. A week or so after, someone told the cops that Mark was bipolar and suicidal, and the case was closed."

"Wouldn't Ahmet tell the cops that the day of the accident?" Helen asked. "If the shooting took place at Ahmet's import-export business like Gus said, I assume the cops questioned the drug dealer after the shooting."

"The cops wouldn't take Ahmet's word alone," Phil said. "They got confirmation from someone. Gus said Mark died the third day and the police closed the case as a suicide. That's all he knows."

"Gus doesn't want to believe his brother killed himself," Helen said.

"It's a typical reaction when a family member commits suicide," Phil said, "especially if they are Catholic or some religion that has strong prohibitions against it. Gus hung on to his grief for twenty-five years. We're supposed to exorcise it."

"I can understand why he'd have trouble with his brother's death," Helen said. "I have a hard time believing that gorgeous man is gone, and I only saw him in a scratchy old video. He was so alive."

"I feel like a fraud taking a grief-stricken man's money," Phil said.

"We've just started," Helen said, rubbing his back. "You've worked cases before. You know they take time. Why are you reacting like this?"

"At my old job, I mostly did work for rich people or corporations who used me like a servant. Gus isn't rich like they are. He can get hurt. He's hurting now."

"But that was true of that drug case you did so many years ago. That family wanted their daughter found."

"That was different," Phil said. "I'm in charge now. I can't blame my bosses anymore when things go wrong. I make the screwups."

"We do," Helen said. "Together. Gus needs us. He needs to know what happened to his brother."

"Please don't say he needs closure," Phil said.

"No," Helen said, "but he needs to know the facts, and we need to find them. It's too soon to give up. Maybe you're looking for the records in the wrong place. Lots of Florida communities are brand-new. Did Plantation exist when Mark died in 'eighty-six?"

"The city has been around since the fifties," Phil said. "It has an important place in film history. The *Caddyshack* pool scene was shot at the Plantation Golf Course. It's also a rich city. Mark died July seventh. Plantation has no record of any similar incident for four months either side of his death date. If we can show Gus the official records, maybe he will accept his brother's death."

"If we need paper, why don't we start with Mark's funeral records?" Helen asked. "When my mom died, the funeral parlor had stacks of paperwork about her life and death."

Phil kissed her. "Did I say you were brilliant?"

"Not often enough," Helen said. "Do you know where Mark was laid out?"

"It's on Gus's list. His brother's visitation was at the Becca Funeral Home in Fort Lauderdale," Phil said. "It's a family-owned business. Been around since the 1920s. It's only three o'clock. We have time to go there."

The funeral home was pink stucco with a red tile roof flanked by the inevitable palm trees. Inside, the satiny gold wallpaper made Helen feel like she was trapped in a giant jewelry box. Dark red flowers and pale torch lamps added to the gloom. Helen shivered. The funeral home was cold, even by summer-in-Florida standards.

"May I help you?" The woman had a severe gray suit, short gray hair and a face so immobile it seemed frozen by the funereal cold.

Phil's smile should have melted the woman. "We're with Coronado Investigations. We are looking for records of a visitation you had here some time ago."

The glacier face shifted slightly. Now the woman seemed worried.

"It's okay," Helen added. "We're helping a family look into the cause of the man's death. There's no problem with the funeral home."

Phil showed her the paperwork Gus had signed.

"I'm Jessica," she said, her face thawing slightly. "Let me present this to our director. Mr. Harold is the fourth generation to run the Becca Funeral Home. Please take a seat."

Helen sat on a couch upholstered in mournful brown velvet and felt it swallow her. She'd have to punch her way out of its pillowy depths. The air was thick with the lifeless perfume of hothouse flowers.

"Looks like a horror movie set," Phil whispered.

"Shush," Helen said. "If I start giggling, we'll be kicked out."

Jessica returned. She was smiling, but her face looked— Helen's mind skittered away from the word—stiff.

"We'll be happy to help," Jessica said. "Follow me."

They trailed behind Jessica like lost ducklings down the drab gold hall with the dark visitation rooms. Helen was relieved they were all empty.

The ordinary office with its oak veneer desk, fax, phone and computers seemed almost cheerful. Jessica pulled a leather-bound ledger off a shelf. "We did our records by hand back then," she said. "I think they have more dignity than the computer entries."

She opened the pages to Mark Behr's "Record of Funeral." It had cost $6,518.61. Mark had been buried in a Regal Steel Blue casket. Helen read the details with horrified fascination. Each seemed to add more weight to this sorrowful story. The funeral home had charged extra for dressing the body, for underwear, for hose (were those socks?) and slippers.

Mark's family had paid for candles and candelabra, for an organist and a singer. They'd paid $150 for a second limousine. Flowers had cost $410. They'd ordered five hundred prayer cards for $50. The family had rented a tent to shade the mourners from the hot summer sun.

The last detail was the saddest: Mark's mother had paid for the funeral in installments. It was stamped PAID a year after her son's death.

Helen fought back her tears. That poor woman. Every month, she got a fresh reminder of her son's death. You never knew Mark, she told herself. Quit being so dramatic. You have a job to do.

She heard Phil ask, "Is there a death certificate?"

"Let me check the files." Jessica opened another door, and Helen got a glimpse of gray ranks of file cabinets.

Jessica was back in five minutes. "Here's a copy."

Phil's eyebrows shot up when he read the certificate. Helen knew he'd found something. Phil put on his poker face. "I appreciate your time," he said. "What do we owe you for the copy?"

"Nothing," Jessica said. "We're happy to be of service. We hope you'll remember the Becca Funeral Home in your time of need."

"We will," Phil said. "We hope we won't need you anytime soon."

Helen couldn't wait until they got to Phil's Jeep.

"What is it?" she said. "Tell me."

"The death certificate says Mark died of a self-inflicted gunshot wound."

"That doesn't explain your smug look," Helen said. "We already knew that."

"Look." His finger pointed to a box that read PLACE OF INJURY. Typed in it was "a motor vehicle" at "3868 Palmwood Blvd., Sunset Palms, FL."

"Sunset Palms is nowhere near Plantation," Phil said. "Why did Gus tell us the wrong town?"

CHAPTER 7

"**L**ook at that knockout!" Phil said. "She's amazing."

Helen studied the boxy turquoise-and-white beast with vestigial fins. Its grill had a smug grin, as if it knew it was a classic. Gus had the hood open, a blanket protecting the front fender.

"Is that an old Chevy?" Helen asked.

"That's like asking if the Mona Lisa is an oil painting," Phil said. "Gus is working on a 1956 Chevy Bel Air. A two-tone convertible with fabulous chrome." His voice was soft with reverence for the old beauty.

"Evening," Gus said, and wiped his hands on a rag. He looked beat. A red-haired boy sat in a toy car next to Gus. His pedal car was a miniature version of the gleaming '56 turquoise Chevy.

"Cool car," Phil said. "Are you Gus the Third?"

"Yeah!" The boy held up a yellow plastic wrench. "I help Paw-Paw!" he said.

"He loves cars just like you do," Helen said.

Gus straightened his shoulders and patted his grandson's fiery curls. "I'm hoping he'll take over the shop when he grows up."

Gus smiled hopefully at Phil and Helen. "You find out something already?"

"We did," Phil said. "Mark's shooting didn't happen in Plantation. It was in Sunset Palms. Why did you send us to the other end of Broward County?"

Gus looked confused. "What do you mean Sunset Palms? Mark was shot in Plantation. My mom and my sister said so. They can't both be wrong."

"They were," Phil said. "Look, Gus, it's your money. If you want to pay for a wild goose chase, that's fine with me."

"I don't know how things got so tangled up," Gus said. "Mark died a long time ago. They were in shock. We all were."

"So shocked *both* women got the scene of the shooting wrong?" Phil asked.

"You weren't there," Gus said. "You don't know what our family went through. You never knew Mark. That's why I showed you the video, to give you some idea what he was like. When my brother was shot, it was total confusion at the hospital. First the doctors said he was going to make it; then they did a one-eighty and said he wouldn't pull through.

"Mom was so upset I thought she was gonna die before Mark. My sister was half crazy. Mom and Bernie wandered around the hospital like lost souls. I had to sit them down and force them to eat. I don't think Mom ever got over Mark's death, and Bernie changed completely. I can ask her myself why she got the location wrong."

"No!" Helen said.

Gus frowned. "You're telling me I can't talk to my own sister?"

"Of course you can," Helen said. "But it would be better if we asked Bernie the details about Mark's death."

"When it's an emotional issue, it's helpful to have a third party ask the tough questions," Phil said. "It's our job. We can ask the hard questions you can't. That's why you're paying us. Remember, when this case is over, we'll never see you or your sister again. You'll have to sit across the table from her at Thanksgiving dinner."

"Can I at least call Bernie and tell her you're coming?" Gus asked.

"We'd rather you didn't," Phil said. "Helen will ask the questions. She's good with people. We want you to be by your phone, in case Bernie calls you to confirm that you've hired us to look into Mark's death. We need you for backup, Gus."

"Okay," he said, but Gus wasn't happy. "When are you going?"

"I thought I'd drive out about nine tomorrow morning," Helen said.

"If you need to reach me, have Bernie call my cell," Gus said. "I'll be here at the shop."

He carefully eased his head back under the Chevy's hood, like a lion tamer sticking his head in the mouth of a beautiful killer. Little Gus waved good-bye.

On the ride home, Helen said, "Little Gus's pedal car was amazing. I can see why Gus worries that his grandson may have the family tendency for suicide. He has everything else—their looks, their hair, their fascination with classic cars."

"You don't have to turn into your family," Phil said. "You aren't anything like your mother."

"I try not to be," Helen said. "But sometimes I look in the mirror and think I see her."

Phil laughed, leaned over and kissed her. "Not a trace," he said. "I'd know."

The car behind them honked, and the Jeep inched through Fort Lauderdale's rush-hour traffic. Heat shimmered on the road, and the air was thick with car exhaust and the stink of melting asphalt.

The Jeep was not air-conditioned. Phil didn't seem to notice the heat. Helen felt like she was on a griddle instead of Federal Highway. The cool Coronado seemed light-years away.

"You sure I can't go with you tomorrow morning to talk to Bernie?" Phil asked.

"Nope," she said. "Bernie's interrogation requires my special skills. I'll do the talking."

"I might be better at talking to women," Phil said and waggled his eyebrows.

Sweat dripped down Helen's forehead. "This could turn into girl talk," she said. "A man would be a liability when we really dish. I'll handle it."

"You aren't worried, are you?" Phil asked. He grinned at her.

"Of course not," Helen said.

She hadn't forgotten how Bernie had undulated into Granddaddy's Bar during Mark's birthday video, wearing skintight leather and a flame red bra. Helen knew Phil was nothing like her unfaithful ex-husband, Rob, but the man was human. Helen had been a trusting fool during her first marriage. She wouldn't make that mistake again. She wouldn't push her new husband into the path of a fiery-haired temptress.

"Bernie and her husband, Kevin, must have some bucks if they live in Weston," Helen said. "Didn't some magazine say Weston had some of the richest residents in the country? I wonder what Bernie's husband does."

Phil turned off Federal toward tree-shaded Las Olas. Helen felt cooler already. Almost home.

"I can answer that," Phil said. "I checked him out. Kevin Maynard Bennett is a health insurance executive. Their son, Kevin Maynard Junior, goes to Nova University. Your husband, Phil, could use a drink."

"You're about to get it," Helen said as the Jeep rumbled into its parking spot. "We're back at the Coronado in time for the sunset salute."

Every evening, the Coronado residents gathered around the pool to toast the day. Peggy and Margery were sitting on chaise longues, sipping box wine. Helen's landlady looked mysterious in her perpetual haze of Marlboro smoke. Her purple caftan gave her a languid air.

Red-haired Peggy seemed tired and drained after a day's work. Pete was perched on her shoulder.

"Hello!" the parrot said, nibbling a strip of green pepper.

"Hi, Pete. Still on a diet?" Helen asked.

"Poor Pete!" the parrot said.

"How about a cold glass of wine?" Margery asked.

"Count me in," Helen said.

"I'll get myself a beer and be right back," Phil said. He returned shortly with a chilled bottle, a bag of tortilla chips and a jar of salsa.

"Don't take the lid off that salsa until you open your present," Margery said.

She handed Helen and Phil two long, thin boxes wrapped in silver paper and white ribbons. Helen ripped off the shiny paper and opened a white box.

"Business cards!" she said. The cards read:

CORONADO INVESTIGATIONS
HELEN HAWTHORNE

They had the agency's address, phone number and license number.

"Love the typeface," Helen said. "Straight out of a noir movie. How did you know our agency license number?"

"That took some real detecting," Margery said. "You have it framed in your office. I love that Florida private investigators are licensed by the Department of Agriculture. They regulate vegetables, fruit, milk, pawnbrokers, dance studios, shellfish and pest control."

"I assume we come under pest control," Phil said.

"Should be food service, as often as your wife is in the soup," Margery said.

"Seriously, Margery, these cards are lovely," Helen said. "I don't know how to thank you."

"Be successful," Margery said. "I need your agency to overcome what happened in Apartment 2C."

A young woman had been murdered there. Margery blamed herself, though she had nothing to do with the untimely death. Their landlady's guilt had eased some with time, but all the paint and disinfectant in Florida couldn't make that tragedy go away.

Margery had pulled the apartment off the market and given it to Helen and Phil as an office for one dollar a month, until their agency turned a profit.

"I can't make a profit until you two succeed," she said.

CHAPTER 8

W eston had cornered the market on beige paint. Helen drove through what seemed like miles of monotonous minimansions on carefully curved streets. Each had its own pool. Most were covered with black mosquito cages. Weston was the gateway to the Everglades, and the mosquitoes never let anyone forget that.

Weston was born a decade after Mark Behr was buried, the brainchild of real estate developers. Bernie's flirtation with exotic men was long gone: Weston looked rich and regimented.

Bernie and Kevin Bennett lived well off the misery of others. Their home was a brownish stucco mansion on a perfectly landscaped cul-de-sac with palm trees as skinny as flag poles. A four-car garage stuck out of the front like a tumor. Helen heard the distant thrum of a lawn crew manicuring grass and trimming hedges.

Helen parked the Jeep and hoped it wouldn't leak on the beige pavers in the circular drive. She stood on a narrow, arched porch and pressed the doorbell. Through the door glass, she glimpsed beige marble and mirrors. Helen heard footsteps. Someone was coming.

The woman who opened the door was big breasted and wide hipped. Her hair was cropped short and dyed the same brownish beige as the house. She wore no makeup, green surgical scrubs and white nurse's shoes. Helen thought that was an odd outfit for a maid.

"May I help you?" she asked with an impersonal smile.

"I'd like to speak to Bernie Bennett," Helen said.

"That's me."

Helen stared at the woman. Hidden in that heft was the former temptress Bernie Behr. The barroom stunner was now a hundred pounds heavier. She looked as drab as her new neighborhood. The shock froze Helen.

"If you're collecting for the Sagemont School benefit, I'll be at the meeting Wednesday," Bernie said and smiled again.

Helen didn't know whether to be flattered or insulted that she'd been mistaken for a prep school mom. Maybe marriage made her look more respectable.

"Uh, no." Helen recovered her scattered wits. "I'm here for a different reason. It's about your brother."

"Gus?" Bernie asked. A frown creased her smooth skin. "Is he okay?"

"Gus is fine," Helen said. "He asked us to look into the circumstances surrounding your brother Mark's death."

"Who *are* you?" Bernie asked. The smile was gone, replaced by angry suspicion.

Helen produced one of her new business cards.

"Coronado Investigations?" Bernie said. "My brother Gus hired you to look into Mark's death? Why?"

"He doesn't believe Mark committed suicide," Helen said. "You can call him and talk to him if you want."

"Oh, I'll call him—don't you worry," Bernie said. "But not while you're here. I don't believe in airing our family business, but Gus sent you here, so the gloves are off.

"My brother, a *car mechanic*"—Bernie said his profession as if it were somehow shameful—"doubts the decision of the police and medical professionals? He's going to get an earful from me. Look, Miss Hayward—"

"Hawthorne," Helen corrected.

"Whatever," Bernie said. "My brother Mark's suicide was a terrible shock to our family. But even before Mark died, Gus was strange. The rest of us knew how to have fun, how to relax. Gus always had his head under a car hood.

"Mark gave Gus's business a jump start. He sent Gus a lot of luxury-car business. Gus has plenty of bucks. He could have sent his son to a good prep school like Sagemont or Pine Crest. But he and Jeannie let Gus Junior go to public school, and the kid turned out exactly the way you'd expect: He's nothing but a mechanic, like his father."

Helen did not like Bernie, not at all. "Gus is a good, honest mechanic," Helen said. "My landlady uses him, and she's no fool."

"I never said Gus was dishonest, did I?" Bernie asked. Her eyes were narrow, flat and yellow. The fine beauty was gone from her face. "But I made something out of myself. I married an executive."

Helen didn't think a health insurance executive was anything to brag about, but she kept quiet.

"Gus has never accepted Mark's death. If you knew my brother Mark, you'd understand why his death was so hard on our family. After Mark died, I tried to get Gus in treatment, but he refused to talk to a counselor. That was Gus's problem. Now he's made it mine.

"Mark shot himself. The police investigated his death and said it was suicide. The case is closed. My poor mother is dead. I've moved on with my life. Only Gus stays stuck in the past."

Bernie stopped her tirade long enough for Helen to squeeze in a question: "Why did you tell Gus that Mark shot himself in Plantation, when he really died in Sunset Palms?"

"Is that what Gus told you?" Bernie said. "He has a bunch of weird theories about Mark's death. My therapist said it's guilt that makes him talk crazy."

"If I could just come in for a minute," Helen said.

Bernie blocked the door. "There's nothing to talk about. There's nothing to investigate. My brother Mark killed himself. The past is dead. Only Gus tries to keep it alive."

Her face turned as hard as the driveway pavers. "Goodbye," she said. "I have to go to work now. If I catch you near my home again, I'll sue you up one side and down the other."

She slammed the door in Helen's face. Helen heard her turn the dead bolt.

CHAPTER 9

T hat was some skilled interrogation, Helen told herself as she drove home from Bernie's house. If you'd
worked for the Allies during World War II, the Nazis
would be goose-stepping down Federal Highway.

Every time Helen thought about her talk with Bernie,
she burned with shame. She'd bragged to Phil that she
would be better at getting information from the woman.
Deep inside, Helen knew she'd steered her husband away
from Bernie because she'd seen the opulent redhead strut-
ting on that video. Bernie had been shockingly sexy—a
quarter century ago. Bernie had grown up since then.

Helen tormented herself all the way back to the Coronado. When she wasn't giving herself a blistering lecture, the
heat scorched her. Sweat soaked her blouse and plastered
her damp hair to her neck. Even when the Jeep got rolling
on the road, the air was like a burning breeze through a
blast furnace.

I need a car with air-conditioning, she told herself. A few
more successes like this morning and we won't be able to
afford gas for this one. I have no business being a private

detective. I couldn't find the cap on the toothpaste. I'm lucky I found my way home.

Helen parked the Jeep in its slot at the Coronado. Her sandal sank into the soft, melted asphalt. She pulled it out, then slogged up the stairs to the Coronado Investigations office.

Phil greeted her with a smile. "How did the interrogation go?"

"Bernie threw me off her property." Helen opened a bottle of cold water from the office fridge and flopped into her desk chair. It squeaked in protest.

"Good." Phil looked pleased. "That means you've hit a nerve."

"I didn't come close," Helen said. "I couldn't even get in her house. Bernie ordered me off the front porch. She doesn't want us looking into Mark's death. She implied that her brother Gus was nuts and said she'd sue us sideways if we bothered her again."

"Even better," Phil said. "When a subject overreacts, it means something."

"It means I did a lousy job," Helen said.

"No, it doesn't," Phil said. "I see two signs of success: Bernie ordered you off her property. She said her brother Gus was crazy. We're getting somewhere."

"It would help if we knew where we were going," Helen said.

"My turn to use the wheels," Phil said. "I'm interviewing one of Mark's friends, a guy named Joel who lives in Boca. Can I give you a ride into work?"

"After I change my shirt," Helen said. "I've been sweating like a stevedore in your Jeep."

She showered, changed into a cool blouse and combed the wind tangles out of her hair. On the short ride to the gym, Helen said, "Any way we could afford a car with air-conditioning? Showing up for interviews sweaty and wind-blown isn't professional."

"The heat doesn't bother me. I'm naturally cool." He grinned.

Helen kissed him. "I know," she said. "I love you any-way."

"I hate to give up my Jeep," Phil said. "It blends in so many places. I think we could find you a good used car. Want me to start looking?"

"Yes," Helen said. "You can save me from the clutches of the car dealers. I don't care what I drive as long as it has air-conditioning. I'm guessing we don't want a flashy ride for our business. We're at the gym already. Thanks for the ride."

The doors to Fantastic Fitness opened with that weird air-lock whoosh, and Helen was gratefully enveloped in its chilled atmosphere. Carla was at the reception desk. Bryan was leaning across it, talking to her.

As she approached, Helen heard him say, "I have a session this afternoon with my trainer, Jan. Is she in yet?"

Carla checked the schedule. "Jan's due here in about ten minutes."

"Okay." Bryan shrugged and his shoulders rippled. "I'll warm up on the stationary bike until she comes in."

Bryan mounted the first bike in the front row when a scream split the gym air: *What the hell are you doing on my bike?*

Helen recognized the roar: Debbi the bodybuilder was in another rage. Her chest heaved. Her yellow hair stood up in outraged spikes. Helen feared she would black out from fury. Helen had never seen a young bodybuilder who looked so lean. There wasn't enough fat on her to fry an egg. The corded muscles twisting on her arms, legs and shoulders made her look like a science-fiction creature.

Carla pushed Helen toward the stationary bike. "Go break up that fight!" she said. "I got her last two tantrums. I can't deal with Debbi today."

Bryan didn't want a confrontation with Debbi. He dismounted from the bike and tried to soothe her. "Sorry," he said. "I didn't know you were using this."

"Everyone knows I always use the first bike. Even you should know."

Debbi's anger sizzled and crackled around her like an electric field. Helen approached the bodybuilder warily, like a zookeeper approaching a wild animal.

Bryan stayed sweetly apologetic. "I didn't see anyone on the bike. I didn't think anyone was using it."

"It's bad enough I have to watch that crap CNN instead of seeing the truth on Fox News," Debbi said. "Then I go hydrate and you steal my bike."

"Here," Bryan said. "Take it."

Helen saw that Debbi's face was stroke red and her eyes were jaundice yellow. Even her skin had a yellow tinge. She looked trapped and hurt.

I should have a tranquilizer gun for this assignment, Helen thought. She tried to tell herself that Debbi was young and damaged by her father's misdeeds, but it didn't help.

"Debbi," Helen said softly, working to keep the fear out of her voice. "Bryan didn't mean to take your bike. He's rooting for you just like everyone else here. We all want you to succeed. Remember your talk with Carla? Anger is bad for your career."

Debbi whirled on Helen as if she was going to attack her. Then her face grew softer. Her eyes looked wounded. "You're right," she said. "It's not worth it. He's not worth it."

Bryan had climbed on another bike farther down the row and was pedaling hard. He didn't look their way.

Debbi took a seat on the bike she'd claimed as her own. "I'll try to do better," she said.

"Good work," Carla whispered when Helen was back at the reception desk. "She still scares me."

"She's better after you talked to her," Helen said. "This time Debbi made an effort to calm down. Look at her. She's fine now."

Debbi was pedaling so furiously, Helen thought the bike might burst into flames.

"*After* she lost her temper," Carla said. "Mark my words. That woman will kill someone. When she goes postal and the reporters are here interviewing the survivors, I'm going to tell them I warned everyone she was dangerous."

"At least there are plenty of people here with muscles if she goes ballistic," Helen said. "They'll protect us."

"Hard bodies are no protection if someone comes at you with a gun," Carla said.

"Gun?" Helen said.

"Debbi's father killed a woman in that botched holdup," Carla said.

"That's unfair," Helen said. "You told Debbi you didn't blame her for her father's mistakes."

"I don't," Carla said. "But I'm not going to forget what he did, either. Emotions get stirred up in gyms. People get murdered. Nearly everyone comes in here with a gym bag. You can hide a handgun or a rifle in one. Nobody checks gym bags. We don't have metal detectors here. And it's happened before.

"At a competitor's gym, a lesbian flirted with another woman. Her partner shot her. At another gym, a man thought his girlfriend was cheating on him. He hid a gun in his duffel bag and opened fire on her aerobics class. His girlfriend was shot in the leg. Four innocent gym members died.

"Sweat, sex, ambition and half-naked people are a dangerous combination. We have cheating couples here. We have 'roid-raging bodybuilders who want to win medals. We have people working out practically naked. See that woman over there on the treadmill? She's wearing more makeup than clothes."

"Is she wearing lace underwear?" Helen asked.

"That's lingerie; that's no workout suit," Carla said. "Her panties don't cover her butt cheeks."

"She certainly can't conceal any deadly weapons in that outfit," Helen said. "Unless you count her implants."

"Helen, be serious." Carla nodded toward a massive bald bodybuilder doing pull-ups with giant chains slung around his neck. The chains could have anchored a cruise ship, but he wore them like necklaces. The links were thicker than his blush-worthy thong.

"Look at that hulk in the banana sack," Carla said.

"Cashew sack is more like it," Helen said. "Doesn't look like the guy has much down there."

"Steroids, probably," Carla said. "Do you think that mastodon could move fast enough to help me?" Helen heard the fear in Carla's voice. "He may be built like Superman, but he can't stop bullets. When it comes down to it, we're alone at this desk."

Treadmills and bicycles whirred. Basketballs thumped and barbells clanged. Workout music pounded and the television blared.

Helen realized if she or Carla was in danger, no one would hear them. The gym was too noisy. They were marooned on a stark black-and-steel island.

She hoped Debbi's workout would leave her too tired to follow in her father's footsteps.

That thought made Helen feel guilty. Poor Debbi was right to worry. No wonder her eyes seemed stricken. She was tarred by her father's lethal legacy.

Helen thought of a little red-haired boy pedaling his retro car. Would Gus the Third escape his family's sad past?

CHAPTER 10

Helen sat up on the weight bench, gasping for breath. Her midsection felt like it had been gouged out, then wrapped with iron bands. Fantastic Fitness indeed. This place was an air-conditioned torture chamber.

Derek kept smiling. The massive manager was a sadist in spandex.

"Come on, Helen, you can do it," Derek said. "One more set of crunches. No pain, no gain."

"What the heck does that mean?" Helen said.

Derek ignored her surly words. "Pain means you're achieving your goal. You have to work through your pain to get to a better body." He flashed those blinding white teeth.

"What idiot believes that?" Helen said.

"Jane Fonda," Derek said. "My mom had her exercise tapes. I grew up listening to Jane say, 'No pain, no gain' and 'Feel the burn.'"

"Derek, I'd punch you, except I'd break my hand on your rock-hard abs."

Derek remained relentlessly upbeat. "Come on, Helen. You're a good-looking woman. You could be hot if you got rid of that flab. You're a bad example to our members."

"Flab?" Helen said. "That's not flab. I have curves."

"You've got Dunlap disease," Derek said. "Your gut Dunlapped over your jeans."

"You're exaggerating. It's not that bad," Helen said.

"How old are you?" Derek asked.

"Forty-one," Helen said.

"You're too young to think like that. One more set; that's all I'm asking."

"I don't want a better body," Helen said. "I like this one. So does my husband."

"But you do want to keep your job, don't you?" Helen heard the threat. Derek's smile didn't look quite so friendly. "You could have finished the next set in the time you've been arguing with me."

"I'm making minimum wage for maximum pain," Helen said. She could feel the burn, all right. Her abs and biceps felt like they were on fire. She needed this job to watch their client's husband, the heroically chiseled Bryan. Helen put her aching arms behind her neck and positioned herself on the bench for ten more agonizing crunches.

"One!" Derek said.

Derek had volunteered to train her for free after work. Helen hoped she would discover Bryan Minars's partner in adultery so she could quit her job at the gym.

"Two!"

She could see Bryan now. Helen had watched Shelby's husband every time he came to work out, and the man never did anything remotely compromising.

"Three!"

After Bryan had finished his training session this afternoon with Jan, he had stopped briefly to flirt with Carla at the reception desk.

"Four!"

Now Bryan was deep in conversation with "What a Waste" Will, the sweet-natured gay guy who made the men and women gym members sigh. Will disappointed everyone. He was faithful to his partner, despite constant temptation. Helen had seen at least four gym members hit on him, including a smoking-hot firefighter. The man had a will of iron, as well as buns of steel.

"Five!" Derek counted. "Halfway there."

Bryan isn't having an affair, Helen decided. He liked hanging out at Fantastic Fitness and he had lots of friends. Too bad Shelby wasn't one of them. Shelby wouldn't like hearing that.

"Six!"

If your marriage was over, Helen thought, it was better to know than to delude yourself.

She'd made that mistake herself, and the results were more painful than anything this gym could inflict.

"Seven! Eight! Nine! One more. One more!" Derek called.

Helen finished her ten crunches and collapsed on the bench in a puddle of sweat.

"Good," Derek said.

"There's nothing good about this." Helen dragged her tortured body to the showers. Soaking under the steaming water, her sore muscles slowly unknotted. Helen dried herself with a scratchy gym towel, dressed, then poured herself a glass of ice water in the women's lounge. She'd earned her rest on the flower-patterned couch and hoped it would give her the strength for the hot walk home.

She watched gray, mouselike Evie scurry toward the lockers. The tiny woman was back for her second workout of the day. Evie was pretty, but her slender white body never developed muscles—or curves. Helen wondered why Evie spent so much time at the gym. She was glad Evie was a member. The quiet creature never caused a moment's trouble.

Wish we had more people like you, Helen thought, and fewer overdeveloped divas. She swallowed the last of her water.

The walk to the Coronado was a trek through a steam bath. All the way home, Helen cursed their client and this pointless job.

She should have spoken up when Shelby saddled Helen

with the receptionist gig. Hell, Phil should have said something. Instead he sat there, transfixed by Shelby's Red Hots toes, and Helen got stuck with mandatory musclehead workouts.

By the time she dragged herself upstairs to Coronado Investigations, she'd worked up a full-blown case against her husband and declared him guilty. It didn't help when he greeted her with a big smile.

"Helen!" Phil wrapped his arms around her.

"Ouch! Don't touch me," she said. "I'm sore."

"How about a massage?" he asked.

"How about hands off?" she said.

He kissed her lightly on the cheek and started to unbutton her blouse. "We could do it on the desk," he whispered in her ear. "We haven't christened our office yet. I've been thinking all afternoon about that."

"I've been thinking all afternoon about how I got stuck with this lousy job at the gym," Helen said. "You don't have to exercise to keep it—I do."

"I'm sorry," he said. "I feel your pain."

"You couldn't begin to," Helen said.

Phil wisely changed the subject from sex to work. "Any progress on the case of the wandering husband?"

"None. A lot of women look at Bryan, but I've never seen him step out of line."

"Cheaters can be accomplished sneaks," Phil said. "His wife goes to that gym. She called me and asked if she should continue working out there. I advised her to quit going there. It may take him a while to drop his guard. Just watch him a little longer."

Helen didn't want to hear that. "I'm working *two* cases. You're working one."

"I'm sorry," Phil said.

Was he trying to look sincere? Or was a smirk hovering around his lips?

"How can I make it up to you? Helen, I haven't been sitting on my hands. I've been working on Gus's investigation. I drove up to Boca this afternoon and talked with Joel, Mark's friend from the old days. Have I got news."

She sat down gingerly in her office chair, careful of her sore glutes and thighs. "Spill," she said.

"Joel says Mark and Bernie were running with a party crowd—and he was one of the hell-raisers. He bragged about his wild past. Gus didn't hang around with them. Joel liked Gus well enough—they all did—but Gus only cared about cars and Jeannie. He'd just met her and he knew she was the one. Jeannie didn't do drugs and didn't like wild parties.

"Bernie was living with the drug dealer, and Joel thought she had her nose in the snow. Joel says Gus didn't see much of his brother or his sister, except at Mark's thirtieth birthday. Right after that party, Joel says Bernie called her brother."

"Which one?" Helen asked.

"Mark," Phil said. "She couldn't go to Gus with this problem. Bernie was in a panic. She told Mark that Ahmet wouldn't let her leave his house. The drug dealer hid her clothes and locked her in his house."

"That's kidnapping," Helen said.

"Taking a woman's clothes is a common trick to keep her in her place."

"She could have run out the door," Helen said.

"Naked? With no money?" Phil said. "Not the way she looked then. If Bernie attracted the attention of the law, she'd have to listen to an 'I told you so' lecture from her mother and the cops might get interested in her party crowd. Instead, Bernie searched Ahmet's house when the dealer was out and found where he hid the phone. Then she called Mark and begged him to get her before the dealer got home.

"Joel says Mark drove to Ahmet's house, broke down the side door, wrapped Bernie in a bedspread and carried her to his car."

"Dramatic," Helen said.

"It was," Phil said. "And everyone in their crowd knew the story. Joel says Bernie couldn't go home to her mom. She told Gus she'd broken up with Ahmet and stayed in her brothers' apartment."

"With no clothes?" Helen said.

"She put on Mark's old T-shirt and jeans, and he took her shopping for clothes. Joel said she hid out there at her brothers' place, too afraid of Ahmet to leave. About a week later, Mark was shot.

"Joel has no doubt that Mark committed suicide. He described Mark as 'messed up' and said he 'wanted to die' and talked about killing himself."

"You don't believe that, do you?" Helen asked.

"No," Phil said. "We've found too many red flags. This gave Ahmet a good motive to kill Mark. You don't diss a drug dealer the way Mark did and live long. But there's an even stronger reason why Mark had to die: He owed Bernie's boyfriend three thousand dollars. He was running up a coke bill and couldn't pay it."

"Wouldn't it make more sense to keep Mark alive and get the money from him?" Helen said.

"Not according to Joel. He said Mark was growing unstable, between the coke and his bipolar disorder. Joel wasn't sure Mark could concentrate enough to work anymore. Joel said with Mark's death, the permanent party was over. His friends sobered up and settled down."

"What's Joel do these days?" Helen asked.

"Not sure," Phil said. "He's definitely lost the mullet and Members Only jacket. Joel has a big office with a corner window and enough plants to stock a rain forest. His card says he's a 'financial consultant,' but he's not affiliated with a bank or a brokerage firm."

"Sounds vague," Helen said.

"It is," Phil said. "Maybe deliberately. Joel's schedule was wide open when I stopped by. He was friendly, took the time to talk to me, had his secretary bring in coffee. Joel remembers Mark as 'a party animal.' Called him a 'good-looking dude.'"

"That's an understatement," Helen said.

"Joel said he lost touch with the Behrs after Mark's funeral. He asked after Gus and Bernie. He wanted to know if Gus was still crazy about cars. Joel said Mark's sister is the most beautiful woman in South Florida."

"Do you believe him?" Helen asked.

"From the way he described Bernie, I'd say yes," Phil said. "In his mind, she's still a knockout."

"Any way we can verify this story?" Helen asked.

"There's no police report. It's all hearsay, gossip. But after the way Bernie overreacted when you talked to her, I'm sure there's something there."

"Gus isn't going to like hearing this," Helen said.

"I know," Phil said. "I won't enjoy telling him, either. I warned him what happens when you dig around in your family's past."

CHAPTER 11

K risti looked like she'd escaped from Area 51 in Ros-
well, New Mexico. The bodybuilder had huge round
eyes, a wrinkled face and a furtive manner. With her
misshapen muscles, Helen thought Debbi's mentor could
pass as an extraterrestrial.

Tansi, the other mentor, looked like a creature from this
planet—a reptile with yellow eyes and smooth scales for
skin. The Lizard and Space Alien, Helen thought. What a
pair.

"You look perfect, Debbi," Kristi said. There was a cos-
mic emptiness in her smile.

Debbi preened, if a strip of leather could preen. She
stood before the mirror in the middle of Fantastic Fitness.
Helen and Carla were at the reception desk some thirty feet
away. Debbi was obviously proud of her stringy body in her
posing suit, a black bikini with yellow sparkles.

"I can see you onstage, picking up that trophy," said
Tansi.

"Nice suit," the Space Alien said. "Looks expensive."

"Four hundred bucks," Debbi said. She couldn't hide her

pride—or her need for their praise. She craved it like an addict needed heroin.

Helen gasped. "Did I hear right?" she asked Carla. "There's barely room for a dozen gold sparkles on that teeny bikini."

"Four hundred dollars is what a good competition suit costs," Carla whispered. "I know competition bodybuilders who spend a thousand bucks or more on their posing suits. They cover them in emeralds, Swarovski crystals, or real gems. One competition builder couldn't pay her rent. All her money went into—or rather on—her suit."

"You've done a good job maintaining your base tan," the Lizard told her protégé.

"The day before the competition, I'll go in for a spray tan," Debbi said. "Then I'll get another coat before the prejudging and another coat before the evening show."

"Make sure you get a dark tan," the Lizard said. "East Coast Physique judges like a natural bronze—nothing sparkly. You're using the competition spray tanner I gave you?"

"*We* gave you," said Kristi, Debbi's other mentor. The Space Alien smiled and distant suns darkened.

"Tanning is too important to get wrong," their protégé said, as if the universe would implode should she miscalculate the color.

"We've done good," the Alien said. "If the competition was today, you'd have the Novice Women's Muscle title."

"I hope that 'we' includes me," the reptilian Tansi said. "I've been working with her, too." She smiled, and Helen thought of dinosaurs and extinct volcanoes.

"Debbi reminds me of myself when I started bodybuilding," Tansi said.

"That's been a while," Kristi said.

The Lizard frowned. Planes of muscle shifted in her forehead like tectonic plates. No wonder Tansi looked unhappy. Racing Father Time was one competition that bodybuilders couldn't win. They could only stave off the effects.

"Another year and Debbi will be serious competition for both of us," the Alien said.

Debbi's jaundiced eyes glowed yellow with pleasure. In her black posing suit with the amber beads, she looked like a feral cat. A starving cat, lapping up that praise.

"Let's put you through your poses," the Lizard said. Kristi nodded agreement.

These were not runway-model poses, but highly structured ways to show off muscle development.

"Front double biceps pose," the Lizard said.

Debbi pressed her heels to the floor, flexed her calves and hamstrings and raised her arms.

"Push your glutes back slightly," the Lizard said.

Now the Alien jumped in. "Raise your elbows until they are slightly above your shoulders. Now squeeze your biceps hard. Harder! No, you're shaking. Keep your legs flexed and try it again."

"It's not enough to have a good body," the Lizard said. "You have to know how to show it. Do it again. Keep your chin up and smile."

Every muscle was gruesomely defined. When Debbi moved, she was an animated anatomy chart. Helen could make out the lean muscles in her jaw and forehead even from a distance. Mountain ranges of muscle jutted along the young bodybuilder's shoulders and down her arms. Helen was tempted to pound out a xylophone tune on her corrugated abs.

The two trainers put Debbi through the six major stage poses for more than an hour.

"I'm exhausted watching her," Helen said.

"It's intense," Carla said. "Like tai chi for the chiseled."

"Poor Debbi," Helen said. "It's sad she needs those two to tell her she's good."

"Somebody has to," Carla said. "Her mom works two jobs, and her father was worthless. He couldn't even die right. He killed an innocent grandmother and ruined Debbi with that same shot. She feels like she has to atone for his crimes."

"I wish she'd do it at college instead of in a gym," Helen said.

Carla shrugged. "We can't all be college students. Debbi has made herself special. She'll win that championship."

Debbi's two mentors finally stopped the exhausting round of poses.

"Good, good," Kristi said. "Now, smile and keep your chin up, Debbi."

"But don't get a big head," Tansi told her. "You've got a long way to go before you're in our league. Relax, concentrate, look the way you do today and you'll be in the Fantastic Fitness Hall of Fame."

The mentors started double-teaming their protégé with advice.

"No food this close to the competition," Kristi said. "And no more water to drink."

"Can I at least suck on ice cubes?" Debbi asked.

"Sure, if you want to lose the trophy," the Alien said. "Too much water can bloat you."

"I'm so thirsty," Debbi said.

"Think how good you'll feel when you have that trophy," Tansi said. "We'll take you out for a big dinner afterward to celebrate."

"No guts, no glory," Kristi said.

Helen wondered why bodybuilders were so fond of slogans.

"You don't want to eat your way out of a trophy," Tansi said. "We have too much at stake. We don't want to lose our investment. We'll build our pro training business on your success while you pump up your career and grab the prize money and product endorsements."

"What about my special medicine?" Debbi asked. "Do I need another dose?"

"I may have some in my car," Tansi said.

"I'll go out with you to get it," Debbi said.

"Me, too," Kristi said. "I could use some fresh air."

Helen and Carla watched the three women head out of the gym, a solid wall of muscle. Acne spotted their backs like malign polka dots.

"Squeezing those overbuilt bodies into Tansi's Neon will

be a real feat," Carla said. She checked the gym clock. "Three o'clock. Right on schedule. They're going outside to shoot up steroids. Stay away from them until the competition is over. They're as unstable as old dynamite.

"I hope you understand that ninety percent of women won't develop the kind of muscles you see on those three," she said. "It takes more testosterone than women normally have. They've been chemically altered. I love these women who come in here and are afraid to lift two-pound weights because they think they'll get huge. Heck, their purses probably weigh more."

The gym doors whooshed open, and Paula entered in shining perfection. White light surrounded her. Bits of over-stretched spandex barely covered her body. Her white silk hair shimmered. If she was suffering jitters over the upcoming competition, Helen saw no sign of them.

Once again, Paula was oblivious to the line of admiring males sweating on the treadmills. She swept triumphantly down the aisle as if she were at the bikini competition, accepting her trophy.

CHAPTER 12

E ven the makeup couldn't hide Debbi's mustache. It was thick as cake icing. The layers seemed to emphasize the dark hair on her upper lip. The acne lurked underneath, making her look like she was being eaten by a deadly disease.

Helen shifted her eyes away from Debbi's damaged face down to her black suit and saw something worse. Round craters appeared at the tops of the bodybuilder's thighs where they joined her stringy torso. They looked as if someone had peeled back the skin and scooped out the tissue underneath with a melon baller.

Helen wasn't sure how to react, so she pretended nothing was wrong. "Hi, Debbi. Eight days until the East Coast Physique competition. Bet you can't wait."

"What are you, stupid?" Debbi asked. "You think I can compete looking like this? Where is that pair of dildos?"

"Which ones?" Helen asked, and then regretted she'd answered.

"Tansi and Kristi, my so-called mentors. Their 'advice' " — Debbi sliced the air with angry finger quotes — "helped me right out of the competition."

"Uh." Helen was afraid to say they were upstairs in the free-weight room.

"Never mind," Debbi said. "I can see them myself."

Helen was relieved when Debbi charged up the steps. Carla, the curly-haired receptionist, said, "Hunker down, girl. Somebody miscalculated her steroid dose. That caused the facial hair and acne outburst. Debbi also depleted her carb and water intake, which made the—well, I can't say fat because I don't think she has any—whatever that is under her skin collapse. She won't be able to compete after all that work and it can't be fixed in time. Expect an explosion any moment."

Debbi's rage started on cue: *"You dipwads,"* she shrieked. *"I was perfect! Perfect! Look at me now. I can't compete like this."*

All activity in the gym stopped. Treadmills no longer ran to nowhere. Bicycles didn't whirr. No one grunted in the weight room or sweated on the benches. Even the televisions seemed silent. Logan and the other salesmen tiptoed out of their area to see Debbi's epic fury.

Debbi had cornered her two trainers upstairs in the weight room. From where Helen stood, she could watch them behind the room's glass partition, like a giant television. Debbi was standing by the weight rack, rows of weights arrayed like ammunition.

Her muscle-bound mentors made sure they had a massive weight machine between themselves and Debbi before they started talking. "Calm down," Tansi said. She looked like a lizard coming out from under a rock. "Getting angry will just make it worse."

"Worse! How could I possibly look worse?" Debbi shook with rage.

Good question. Angry acne mountains pushed their way through the layers of makeup. Rivers of sweat ran between them.

Debbi lumbered toward the pair, an uncontrollable force deformed by her rocklike outcroppings of muscle. Her screams ripped through the weight room: "Can you make this go away in time for the competition?"

The trainers stayed silent.

"I'll get you! I'll get you both. Everyone will know what you did. When I finish, you won't be allowed to train a poodle."

Debbi hurled a fifteen-pound metal weight at Tansi as if she were flicking a Q-tip. The reptilian trainer deftly dodged the weight, and it slammed on the floor beside Evie. The small, gray-haired woman had been quietly pumping two-pound weights.

The mouselike Evie stood up and roared, "Hey! Watch it! I wasn't bothering you."

Helen was stunned by Evie's sudden display of anger. It was as if a butterfly had grown fangs and attacked.

Evie drew herself up to her full height, which wasn't much. In her sagging sweats, she looked like an animated ragbag. Debbi pushed her aside, and Evie fell against a black bench.

The two mentors could have easily subdued Debbi and protected Evie. The overbuilt cowards stayed barricaded behind the weight machines while Debbi focused her rage on Evie. Helen could see the little woman was shaking with outrage and adrenaline, but her burst of courage was spent. Evie was too frightened to run. She was frozen by the bench.

Debbi looked crazed and ready for another attack.

"Carla, get Derek, quick!" Helen said. "I have to rescue Evie before Debbi kills her."

Helen ran upstairs to the weight room, dragged the cowering Evie away from the bench and pushed her toward the door. "Have a soothing glass of water in the lounge," she said.

Debbi grabbed another weight, ready to lob it at Helen.

"Put that weight down," Helen said. "Evie, go!" She shoved Evie through the door. The escapee scuttled downstairs toward the women's locker room.

Helen turned to Debbi. "Don't take out your anger on Evie. She never hurt you."

"Shut up!" Debbi's voice rose to a siren wail as she repeated, "Shut up! Shut up! Shut up!" She couldn't stop shouting those words. They turned into a chant.

Debbi tossed the twenty-five-pound weight back and forth in her hands, enjoying its heft. Then she hurled it at Helen's head. Helen ducked, and the weight hit the glass wall. The wall broke into pieces, falling outward in one giant section until it shattered on the hard gym floor.

"Look what you made me do!" Debbi howled.

"I didn't make you do anything," Helen said. "Calm down, Debbi. Please, get your temper under control, for the sake of your career."

"What career?" She pointed at her trainers, still huddled behind their metal barricade. "I could have been in the Hall of Fame here. Now I'm ruined. And I'm going to ruin you."

She grabbed a monster thirty-pound weight off the rack as if it were made of foam rubber, and charged like a maddened rhino. Helen stepped backward and ran into something solid, warm—and human.

The darkly handsome Derek pushed Helen out of his way and stepped in front of Debbi.

"You're out!" he said. "You've attacked gym members. You've destroyed property, which you will pay for. Your membership is canceled. Clean out your locker and leave."

"But—," Debbi said.

"Go!" Derek pointed a finger the way God must have when She banished Adam and Eve from Paradise.

Debbi couldn't slump her shoulders. The muscle plates wouldn't permit that. But she slunk toward the women's locker room. Helen watched her retreat from the top of the stairs.

Helen thought the trouble was over. Then she saw Heather, the contender in the recent TV-channel battle, bar Debbi's way. Was Heather going to fight her rival again?

The red-haired beauty planted herself boldly in the bodybuilder's path and held out a twenty-ounce go-cup. "I have a present for you," she said.

Debbi looked stunned. "Me? Why?"

"Because I don't want to exercise at a gym when someone is angry at me," she said. "The bad vibes disturb my workout. I've brought you a protein shake I made myself.

All natural, with real strawberries, blueberries, a banana for potassium and organic soy milk."

"I can't drink it," Debbi said. "I'm not — " Then she realized her circumstances had changed. "No, I can. I'm not competing in this contest. Not this time. I've had a setback, but that's all it is, a setback. Next time I'll find real trainers, not those two losers."

Debbi forgot she was banished from the gym, Helen thought. Or maybe she thought Derek would forgive her. Maybe he would. Everyone said she was a surefire winner.

Debbi stabbed the plastic cup lid with a straw and drank the shake in three long gulps, not bothering to hide her thirst. The straw made empty sucking sounds.

"That was so good," Debbi said.

"Shake?" Heather asked.

"Definitely. I have to get the recipe," Debbi said. "It's the best protein shake I ever had. What kind of protein did you use: whey or soy?"

Heather hesitated. "Vanilla soy," she said. Her pale skin flushed slightly. "I meant could we shake hands—like friends?"

"Sure," Debbi said. "I'm sorry I flew off the handle. I'm trying to control my temper, but I don't always succeed."

Flew off the handle? Helen wondered. Debbi had destroyed the upstairs weight room less than two minutes ago.

Debbi tossed the empty cup in the trash and shook Heather's pale hand. "I'm glad we're on better terms," she said. "I'm going to change."

Helen didn't know if Debbi meant her attitude or her clothes, but the tension seemed to lighten. Heather waved and walked lightly out the doors, as if a burden had been lifted from her.

Helen, still shaken by the encounter with Debbi, held on to the stair rail.

"Are you hurt?" Derek asked.

Helen was trembling now that the danger was over. "No." Her wobbling voice betrayed her.

"You did a good thing when you stepped in and saved

Evie," he said. "You look shaken. Go home. Take the day off. Watch that broken glass."

As she stepped carefully across the crunchy glass, she heard Derek chastising the two would-be trainers. "You were using steroids, weren't you? I turned a blind eye to that. Now I'm giving you fair warning. Any hint—and I mean *any*—that you two freaks are shooting up on this property and you're permanently barred. And that includes those little trips to Tansi's Neon. If you get anyone here hooked on steroids, I'll call the cops."

"We just did what any trainers would," Kristi said.

"No, you didn't," Derek said. "You took a promising bodybuilder and ruined her. Debbi is so out of control, she could have murdered someone. Do you want a list of everyone at this gym she's started a fight with?"

More silence.

"Good," Derek said. "Because I don't have time to name them all. Debbi even picked a fight with little Evie, the most harmless person here.

"Get out of my sight. Both of you. You disgust me."

Helen left before the two trainers, eager to be away from the gym. She dreaded coming back tomorrow morning.

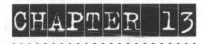

At five forty-five, the morning air felt like warm soup. Helen kissed Phil good-bye in the parking lot at Fantastic Fitness and slid out of his Jeep, gym keys in her hand. Even the sun isn't up yet, she thought as she made her way to the front door.

But the gym members were. The door was blocked by bodies. Some were thick with muscle, others larded with fat. The fat ones wanted to punish themselves for their excesses. The fit ones were anxious to keep their glow of sweaty grace.

"Excuse me," Helen said, pushing her way through the spandexed throng. "The gym will open in fifteen minutes. Give me fifteen minutes, please."

She tapped in the security code on the pad and turned the key in the lock, then opened the doors just wide enough to slide in. Disappointed gym members pounded on the doors, their paradise denied.

Helen flipped on the lights and savored the cool, still air, then turned on the pounding workout music. That made her move faster. To the relentless techno-beat, she booted up the reception desk computers and took the phones off the automatic answering system.

She opened the men's locker room. All the showers were clean, their white curtains uniformly pushed back. Not so much as a damp towel marred the dressing room benches. She refilled the water dispensers and sliced lemons for the garnish and crossed toward the women's locker room.

Helen checked the clock. Two minutes to go. She refilled the water pitchers in the women's lounge and set out a new stack of plastic cups and another plate of sliced lemons. Then she checked the women's locker room.

All of the shower curtains were pushed back, except the curtain on the shower in the far corner. It hung oddly. Derek must have been in a hurry last night and missed it when he checked the gym. Helen went into the locker room to push it back. There was a black gym shoe on the floor near the showers. Someone must have forgotten her shoe. Helen moved closer and saw the shoe was still on a foot. Which was attached to a leg. A muscular leg that ended in cratered skin where it joined a ripped body. A body where every muscle was stripped of fat. Debbi, now gray-green under the acne bumps, lay faceup inside the shower.

"Oh, no! Oh, please, no. Don't be dead," Helen begged.

But she knew this prayer would not be answered.

The gym's most promising bodybuilder would not be competing anymore.

CHAPTER 14

H elen fumbled with the gym phone for almost a full minute before she could dial 911.

"Help!" she cried when the 911 operator answered. Her shrill, scared voice seemed to belong to someone else. "There's a dead woman here. At Fantastic Fitness. In West Hills. In the locker room. No, I don't think the paramedics can help her. But you can send them. I'm not a doctor."

She knew she was babbling. As she talked, Helen began to absorb the 911 operator's calm strength and speak more slowly.

She sat down at the registration desk, took a deep breath and said, "Yes, ma'am, I'm here alone. There's no one else in the building with me. I don't think so, anyway. I don't know if the woman was killed. There's no blood or bruises. I can't step outside to wait for the police. There's a crowd by the door, and they want to kill me."

Helen could see an angry mob of gym members, shouting and smacking the locked doors.

"Get off the phone and open up!" screamed a bullet-headed man. Bullet Head slammed a meaty fist against the metal doorframe. Helen hoped he'd bruise his hand.

"It's six twelve," his beefy sidekick yelled. He kicked the door so hard the glass rattled, but it didn't break. The gym building was stronger than the members—so far.

"No, I'm not in that kind of danger," Helen tried to explain over the cries of the furious rabble. "The members are angry because I didn't open the gym on time. Wait! The police are here. I see their car in the parking lot. I'm going to hang up and unlock the doors for them. No, I won't open until the officers are at the doors."

Helen was relieved when two muscular West Hills cops in their mid-twenties climbed out of a patrol car in front of the building. The woman officer looked strong enough to rescue an entire orphanage. She was so close that Helen could read her name tag—M. DORSEY.

"Get the yellow tape," Officer Dorsey told the other cop. His name tag said N. PICKARD. He jogged back to the patrol car, elbowing protestors out of his way.

"I got a right!" shrieked a well-toned woman in navy shorts.

"This is *my* gym," a man in baggy orange shorts yelled.

"This is *my* crime scene," Officer Dorsey said. The sturdy woman cop grabbed Baggy Shorts by his stretched-out shirt and said, "Get out of here, you idiot."

"Get your hands off me," he shouted. "I'm a lawyer. I'll sue."

"I love lawyers," Officer Dorsey said. "How much do you make an hour?"

"Five hundred dollars." He puffed out his narrow chest, proud of his earning prowess.

"How about if I slap the cuffs on you and arrest you for failure to obey the lawful order of a police officer? That could take several thousand dollars of your valuable time."

The lawyer slunk off, trailed by Ms. Toned. The rest of the throng refused to move.

"Crime scene?" a man in green Nike shorts asked. "Was there a murder?"

The word "murder" bounced through the crowd like a loose balloon on a windy day. A man in a faded black T-shirt shouted, "Who died?" The crowd was growing larger.

"Is Carla safe?" a man called out. That was Bryan Minars, hunky husband of Coronado Investigations' client Shelby. When did he join the party? Helen wondered. And why was he asking about the curly-haired receptionist?

"Is Carla safe? She's such a sweetie." "What a Waste" Will stood next to Bryan, a frown creasing his smooth brow.

Logan pushed his way to the front. "It's not Heather? Is Heather dead?" Since when was the salesman worried about the cute, creamy redhead?

"Please tell me it wasn't pretty Paula," one of her suckers begged. Helen recognized him as one of the treadmill runners fixated on her fabulous body. Helen wondered if the chubby older man would bother holding in his gut for anyone else.

She saw several women gym members in the crowd. Why weren't they asking about Derek? Didn't they care about the men? What about the less spectacular women? Did only the beautiful deserve to live?

"We aren't telling you anything until we know something," the fearless Officer Dorsey said.

"Even if somebody was killed, you wouldn't have to close the whole gym," Logan said. "They didn't die in the sales area, did they? I can still sell memberships. Look at this crowd." The gym's number one salesman was prowling for prospects. Even death didn't stop him.

"Out!" the woman cop commanded. "Leave. All of you."

Camera phones flashed and photographed the police officer shooing away the crowd. This time, they scattered like spandexed chickens. Helen heard engines start as the stragglers trickled across the parking lot.

Officer Pickard, the male cop with the burred blond head, ran back with a roll of yellow tape.

"What took you so long?" Officer Dorsey asked.

"You can open that door now," she told Helen.

Helen flipped the door lock open for the two West Hills cops and discovered that at least two gym members had stayed behind. Bullet Head and his beefy friend tried to shove Helen aside and enter the gym.

"You should have opened at six," Bullet Head said as he

pushed Helen against the doorframe. His faded red shirt stank of old sweat. Helen couldn't breathe.

"Move!" she gasped.

He didn't budge.

Helen kneed Bullet Head in the groin, and he doubled over, yowling in pain.

"Hey," Mr. Beefy said. "You didn't have to do that."

"Sorry," Helen said, though she wasn't. "There's been an emergency. The gym is closed."

"When can we come back?" Mr. Beefy wasn't quite so belligerent now that his bullet-headed friend couldn't stand up straight.

Officer Dorsey stood behind him, looking like a rescuing angel—to Helen, anyway. "When we say so. I already told you: Get outta *my* crime scene."

Suddenly, the doorway was deserted.

"I liked that hurricane-safety procedure you performed on the idiot who tried to push his way in. I'm Officer McNamara Dorsey," she told Helen. "I go by Mac."

"What hurricane procedure?" Helen asked.

"You clipped his coconuts," she said. "That's the first thing you do when a big wind is on the way."

"My manager won't be happy that I kneed a client," Helen said.

"I didn't see anything," Officer Mac Dorsey said. "I wasn't officially in the building. You see anything, Pickard?"

Her partner shook his head. "I was getting the yellow tape." He held up the roll.

"Thank you," Helen said. "The dead woman is in the locker room. This way."

The two officers followed her through the ranks of bikes and treadmills to the women's locker room.

"Nice setup here," Officer Dorsey said.

"Don't let Logan hear you," Helen said. "He'll sell you a membership."

"I already have a gym," she said. "Let's see the victim."

"She's in there," Helen said. She stopped at the entrance to the locker room and pointed toward Debbi's shoe.

The room's silence seemed to suck out the air. Helen

didn't want to get near Debbi. Officers Pickard and Dorsey walked closer to examine the body.

"Look at those pecs," Dorsey said. "She was ripped. EMS can't help her. She's DRT."

"That means dead right there," Officer Pickard told Helen. "Officer Dorsey will call Ever Ready. That's Evarts Redding, West Hills homicide detective. He's always ready for a case—and to nail a suspect. Don't ever mention his nickname to his face."

His partner glared at him. "Are you a cop or a color commentator?"

"Can I call our manager?" Helen asked. "Derek needs to know we have a problem."

"We'll do the contacting," Dorsey said.

The two police officers studied the body without touching it. Poor Debbi, Helen thought. She'd sweated, starved, sacrificed and ended up like this.

Finally, she broke the deadly silence. "Debbi had high hopes of getting her picture and trophies in the Fantastic Fitness Hall of Fame," Helen said. "She was training for the Women's Novice Muscle title in the upcoming East Coast Physique Championships. Some here thought she was taking steroids."

"Looks like it. Major acne on her face," Dorsey said. "And a better mustache than you have, Pickard. And what's this on the floor?" Officer Dorsey bent down to examine a white pill.

"An aspirin?" Helen guessed.

"Nope. Looks like oxycodone. Hillbilly heroin. Same thing that got Rush Limbaugh busted, except he was no bodybuilder. Better get CSI to bag that. Where I work out, I see some older bodybuilders who push themselves so hard they take pain meds."

"Do you think she OD'd on steroids?" Helen asked.

"It's harder to overdose on steroids than you'd suspect," Dorsey said. "We won't know how she died until we hear from the ME—and he needs a tox screen. But it looks like she was taking oxy. Add that to fat burners—gonadotropins—and 'roids, and you got sort of a steroid-laced speedball. Was her death suicide or murder? That's a question for the medical examiner. Glad I don't have to answer it."

"She was definitely upset yesterday," Helen said. "Debbi planned to walk off with a trophy. Practically had the spot picked out for it in our trophy case. She was all set to win. Then she showed up here with acne so bad it looked like smallpox, a mustache like a seventies disco dude and these odd craters under her skin."

"Overdid it," Dorsey said. "Wrong dose of steroids, not enough carbs or water."

"She was crazed when she first realized she couldn't compete," Helen said. "Started screaming, threatening, throwing weights at people."

"Homicide will want the names and numbers for everyone who was here yesterday when she went ballistic."

"Those are in the computer at the reception desk," Helen said.

"We'll wait till CSI prints that area," Dorsey said. "Then you can get the contact information. Someone's rattling the door now. Looks like the party is about to start."

The two cops followed Helen toward the front door. Yesterday, Derek the manager had brought in a crew to clean up the shattered glass after Debbi's 'roid-rage tantrum. Now the window overlooking the inside of the gym was boarded up. The free weights had been moved to an empty workout studio. The weight machines were off limits until the glass was replaced. The former weight-room door was strung with yellow CAUTION tape.

"Whoa!" Officer Dorsey said. "What happened upstairs?"

"Someone threw a twenty-five-pound weight at the glass, and it shattered."

"Someone with anger issues," the cop said. "Who?"

"Debbi, the dead woman."

"Who was she aiming for?"

"Me," Helen said.

CHAPTER 15

H elen hated Homicide Detective Evarts Redding
from his first comment about Debbi Dhosset.

"Did she want to look like that? On purpose?"
he asked.

What? Helen thought. Dead? Of course she didn't want
to be dead. Then she realized the detective was talking
about Debbi's sinewy carcass, all muscle and gristle.

Detective Ever Ready's funereal gray suit was perfect
for viewing a dead woman. Helen wondered how he could
stand a suit and tie in the swampy South Florida summer.

He looked down on Debbi. The sneer on his face seemed
permanent. His white flyaway hair and age-spotted hands
marked him ready for retirement, but Helen suspected that
was one conclusion he wasn't going to jump to anytime
soon.

"Debbi was a bodybuilder," Helen said. "She devoted
her life to stripping every last ounce of fat off her muscles."

"Mother Nature will do that now," Ever Ready said. "No
one's thinner than a skeleton."

Helen felt a weird urge to defend Debbi. "Competition

bodybuilding is not my world. But she supposedly had a real chance to be a champion."

Poor Debbi did look grotesque. Her washboard abs were hard knobs under her black suit. Her biceps were croquet balls. A dragon ridge of muscle ran along her shoulders. The bodybuilder looked inhuman in death. Even her mustache seemed thicker. Was the old wives' tale true? Did hair grow after death?

"That girl needs a shave," the detective said, and rubbed his own smooth chin. "You sure this Debbi wasn't one of those he-shes? Looks kinda tiny on top for a girl. Guess you can't develop *those* chest muscles or surgeons wouldn't be selling implants. She sure overworked everything else."

Detective Ever Ready gave his own gut a self-satisfied pat and said, "Granted, I could lose a few pounds myself."

You could lose more than a few, Helen thought. You're on the express train to Fat City.

She made a superhuman effort to keep her mouth shut. The last thing Helen needed was to attract the fury—and curiosity—of a homicide detective. There's a body buried in a St. Louis basement, she reminded herself. It has to stay that way for the sake of your sister and your innocent nephew, Tommy Junior. Be cooperative. Don't confront Ever Ready.

She forced herself to smile. "None of the women in the locker room complained that Debbi wasn't a woman," Helen said, "and they would know when she undressed. Looks like she didn't change out of her clothes from yesterday. She's still wearing the same workout suit."

"What was her race? Was she black, white, Mexican, or mutt? Her skin color doesn't look right. It's got a shine like a rotten fish," Ever Ready said.

"That's a spray-on tan," Helen said. "Many bodybuilders prefer to spray on several coats of color rather than risk a sunburn. It looked better when she was alive."

"Anyone here at this gym have a reason to kill Miss Dhosset? I'm assuming she's not married. Not the way she looks."

"I don't know her marital status," Helen said. "I've only

worked here a short time. She wasn't popular. Debbi got in fights with gym members, but I don't think someone would kill her over a TV clicker."

"You'd be amazed what people kill each other over," Ever Ready said. "Athletic shoes, pocket change, video games. Just tell me what you know. It's my job to think. I need to sit down. Let's use one of those empty desks over there."

Crime scene techs were at work, crawling on the floor, measuring, videotaping, dusting for prints. They'd finished the reception desk, then moved to the women's locker room.

A uniformed officer stood at the Fantastic Fitness door, keeping out gym members and delivery people. So far as she could figure, Helen was the only non–law enforcement person in the gym. She followed Ever Ready on his march to the sales area.

The detective flopped down at Logan's desk, his belly vibrating a bit. Helen was secretly gleeful that he'd commandeered the salesman's desk. She wondered if Logan could sell the fathead a fitness package. Would Ever Ready slap the cuffs on Logan for daring to suggest it? The thought made her smile.

"Something funny, Miss Hawthorne?" Ever Ready asked.

"No, no," she said. "Must be hysteria." She figured he'd like that excuse. This man believed women were the weaker sex, no matter how many muscles they had.

"Nothing to be worried about now." Ever Ready gave her a condescending smile. "I know you girls get scared when you see a body, but I'm used to it." He straightened his tie and tried to smooth down his flyaway hair.

Was he preening for her? Helen twisted her gold wedding band, hoping he'd notice she was married.

"Now, tell me what happened with Miss Dhosset," he said.

Helen told him about the bodybuilder's fight with the cream-skinned Heather over the TV channel and yesterday's battle with her would-be trainers, Tansi and Kristi.

"Our manager, Derek, barred Debbi from the gym for her abusive behavior," Helen said. "That practically made her an orphan, she spent so much time here. I don't know where Debbi lived, but this was her real home."

"Doesn't sound like a happy family," Ever Ready said.

"It had good and bad moments," Helen said, "like any family."

"But these family members liked to feud," Ever Ready said.

"She got in fights," Helen said. "But she felt bad about it later. She and Heather made up yesterday."

"Who started the fence-mending?" Ever Ready asked.

"Heather. She brought Debbi a fruit smoothie and they shook hands."

"And Miss Dhosset didn't have any more fights after the one with Heather?"

"Well, no," Helen said. She really didn't want to say this, but he'd find out anyway. "Debbi ticked off Evie."

Ever Ready sat up, a glint of interest in his eye. "Think Evie killed her?"

"Evie isn't strong enough to swat a fly," Helen said. "She works out with weights the size of toothpicks."

"Size doesn't make any difference," Ever Ready said. "I had a wife kill her husband because he said, 'What, meat-loaf again?' when she served him dinner. She was a little bitty thing, weighed seventy pounds soaking wet. She put antifreeze in his beer while he watched TV that night and murdered him.

"I've been a homicide detective for going on thirty years, up north in Wisconsin and now down here in Florida. I know more about murder than you ever will, Miss Haw-thorne. Here's the most important fact: Watch the quiet ones. They take it and take it, and then one day that rage busts loose and they start killing. Sometimes the little ones are deadlier than the big guys. Sneakier, too.

"You don't need muscles to poison someone," Ever Ready said. "When I see funny-looking pills at a murder scene, I naturally start wondering if the death was suicide or murder."

"Suicide," Helen said. "I think it was suicide."

"There you go thinking again," he said. "That's my job. I'm the murder expert." Another condescending smile.

"I know that," Helen said. "But I saw Debbi yesterday. She was so disappointed when she couldn't compete. She carried on like her life was over."

Maybe she was laying it on a little thick, but Helen was frightened. She couldn't have Ever Ready go after poor little Evie. Was he ready to jump to one of his conclusions?

"But if you're right"—the detective said that as if he was sure Helen was wrong—"Miss Dhosset would consider herself a work of art. She wouldn't destroy the body she was so proud of building. She was still young. She had lots of chances to win competitions."

"She did say something like that," Helen said. "Debbi seemed in a better mood after the reconciliation with Heather. Heather gave her a drink. Maybe there was poison in it. The cup is still in the trash."

"I know how to do my job, Miss. Hawthorne," he said. "It will be bagged and tagged, along with all the other evidence. Sounds like Miss Dhosset had a real gift for stirring up people. She was asking for it."

"You think she caused her own death?" Helen didn't try to hide her disbelief.

"In a way, yes. She chose her killer, too. Vics like Debbi have a sixth sense for choosing their killer. I want to talk to this Evie. What's her full name? How old is she?"

"Evie Roddick," Helen said. "I don't know her exact age. She's fiftysomething."

"Women that age are unstable," Ever Ready said. "They get jealous of younger women when they go through the change of life."

Helen had her mouth clamped so tightly she could feel her jaw muscles cramp. She was afraid to say a word while Ever Ready leaped from one crazy conclusion to another, like a madman skipping across the rocks on a creek.

"You got a contact number?" he asked.

Finally, a question she could answer safely. "I can look it up on the computer at the reception desk," she said.

"CSI is finished over there. Get me Evie's contact information and everyone else the vic had a fight with. I want all the major players at this gym."

"Major how?" Helen asked.

"Managers, salespeople, trainers, all the gym personnel. And the gym members she had fights with."

It was a long list. Helen delivered the first page with Evie's name at the top, then returned with another batch of printouts.

An angry Ever Ready thumbed his cell phone shut as she handed him the second pile. "I thought you gave me the phone number for Evie Roddick."

"I did," Helen said.

"Some guy answered and said she doesn't live there. Moved out weeks ago. You got a cell phone for her?"

"Sorry," Helen said. "That's the only number we have. Guess she didn't update her contact information."

"She's hiding something," Ever Ready said.

"Could be she's going through a bad divorce and doesn't want her husband to know where she's living now," Helen said. She'd been in that situation herself, but she wasn't about to tell the detective.

Too late. Ever Ready had already made his leap.

"Mark my words," Ever Ready said. "She's guilty."

CHAPTER 16

After her day with Detective Ever Ready, Helen felt like she'd been run over by a trash truck. She trudged home from the gym, limp hair straggling down her sweat-damp neck. Her clothes were wrinkled and her makeup was gone, except for the raccoon eyes created by her smudged liner.

At the Coronado apartments, she ran into Margery hosing the pool deck. Actually, her landlady was hosing down her feet in their purple flip-flops. She reminded Helen of a kid playing in a lawn sprinkler. A cynical kid with gray hair who smoked Marlboros.

Helen waved and called her name.

Margery turned off the hose and said, "You look like hell. Get in my apartment and cool off. Get yourself a drink."

Helen obeyed. She fixed herself a tall ice water and collapsed at Margery's kitchen table.

Her landlady nuked a brownie the size of a potholder. Margery kept an endless supply in the freezer for emotional emergencies. When Phil joined them, their landlady nuked another, then fixed herself a screwdriver that was short on orange juice and long on liquor.

Margery sat at her kitchen table, smoking, sipping and watching Helen and Phil demolish their brownies. Helen turned down the offer of the screwdriver, then tore into her warm brownie and wished she could make Detective Ever Ready disappear as fast.

As she revived, she told Margery and Phil about Debbi's death, the angry mob of gym members and the West Hills detective who jumped to conclusions.

"Ever Ready has decided—on no evidence at all—that Evie poisoned Debbi," Helen said. "When I told him that Heather had given Debbi a fruit smoothie, he wasn't interested. It seems to me, Heather had the easiest way to poison Debbi—if she even died that way."

"And you think this Heather woman would poison Debbi over a fight about a television channel?" Margery said.

"People kill for stupider reasons than that," Phil said.

"That's exactly what Ever Ready said," Helen told him. Her tone made it clear she didn't appreciate Phil's conclusion.

"Sounds like you need a drink after the day you had," Phil said.

"I'd rather work on Gus's case," Helen said.

"If you're sure," Phil said. "You look like you've spent the day in a cement mixer."

"I've spent the day with an idiot," Helen said. "I want to spend time with a smart man."

"Glad you put me in that category," Phil said. "The paperwork is at my place. I'll make us coffee."

Ten minutes later, Helen settled on Phil's couch with a stapled pile of paper and a cup of strong coffee.

"This is a copy of Mark's 1986 accident report from Sunset Palms."

"How did you get that?"

"It's public record," Phil said. "Easy to find once I had the right city. I've made copies for both of us."

Helen was surprised the report was so thick—twenty

pages. The report reduced Mark's fatal beauty to gray language, neat numbers and check-mark choices. Each small detail added to its chilling weight.

The report, numbered 86-3866, was signed by Officer Dolan Hayward. His clear writing was back-slanted, as if pointing backward in time.

"Florida Uniform Accident Report," it began. "Agency Name: S.P.P.D." That must be Sunset Palms Police Department, Helen decided. The location was Broward County, the street address 3868 Palmwood Boulevard. Hayward had recorded the accident time as 1:43 p.m. "Time notified" was the same.

"One injured," Hayward had written. "Number of vehicles involved—three." Not just cars were damaged— Mark also had crashed into a building, Ahmet's Elegant Imports Co.

Mark had been driving a black '85 Chevy Monte Carlo, sporty wheels for a single man. Helen could see the car in her mind—shiny, chromed, fast.

Officer Hayward had used a diagram on the form to show the accident damage to Mark's Monte Carlo. The front end and fenders had been crushed. He must have hit the building hard.

Before Mark crashed into the building, he'd also smashed into Ahmet's car—a parked red '83 Mercedes registered to Ahmet's Elegant Imports. After Mark damaged the front end of the Mercedes, he drove into the building. Ahmet's wounded red Mercedes spun around and collided with a parked white Ford belonging to Lorraine Yavuz.

Black, white, red—cars the colors of death.

"Who is Lorraine Yavuz?" Helen asked. "A relative?"

"Ahmet's mother," Phil said. "His father is dead. I found that out myself."

Helen went back to reading. Officer Hayward had found Mark in his black car, covered with red blood. His account was less colorful: "Upon arrival I observed Driver No. 1 sitting in the driver's seat," Hayward had written. "He was bleeding very heavily from the left side of his head and he appeared unconscious."

The dazzling Mark was now dreary Driver No. 1.

"The Sunset Palms paramedics then arrived at the scene," the officer reported. "The paramedics began first-aid treatment. As the paramedics were lifting Driver No. 1 from the auto, I observed an automatic pistol on the driver's side floorboard, a .32 Mauser. The pistol was taken by this officer and given to P.O. Stone, who was assisting at the scene, who later tagged it into evidence."

While the paramedics fought to save Mark, Officer Hayward charged him with two felonies: "destruction of private property and unlawful use of a weapon."

"How did the officer know the weapon was used?" Helen asked.

"He could tell the weapon had been discharged," Phil said. "He'd smell the cordite. It's an overpowering smell. Even on a rifle range the smell is pervasive. You don't get rid of it."

"How did he know that Mark fired it?"

"He couldn't know that," Phil said. "He made an assumption."

"And passed it off as fact," Helen said. She thought the passionless prose provided cover for the police officer's wild speculation.

Officer Hayward dutifully recorded that the unconscious Mark was not given a Miranda warning. "At this time, P.O. Stone located several witnesses. Their statements are included in report 86-3867."

Hayward's report was written in soothing, stilted official-ese. Helen could almost hear him reciting it to a jury. Mark wasn't "taken by ambulance"; he was "conveyed." Officer Hayward did not go with him to the hospital; he "responded" there.

While at Broward County Hospital, "this officer was advised by Dr. Wiley that Driver No. 1 was being treated for the head injury and would be admitted to the hospital. I then responded to the station, where I contacted Sgt. Clark, who advised me of the following:

"Sgt. Clark spoke with Ahmet Yavuz (owner of Ahmet's Elegant Imports), who stated that he had known Mark B.

(Driver No. 1) for about five years. The last time that he saw Mark B. was in September 1985, and at that time Mark B. had suffered a nervous breakdown. Ahmet Yavuz further advised that in speaking with Mark B., he began talking 'very crazy,' telling him he could save the world.

"This officer was advised by the Broward County Hospital staff that Mark B. was being treated for a possible gunshot wound to the head. Dr. Wiley confirmed that the bullet entered the left side and exited the right side. I was further advised that Mark B. was in stable condition; however, he was unable to talk at this time.

"Sgt. Clark then responded to the tow yard and conducted a search of Vehicle No. 1. Sgt. Clark seized a slug found on the right front seat. Also seized was an empty casing found on the floorboard under the right front seat and a blue cotton blanket found on the floorboard, right front side. NOTE: The blanket appears to have a bullet hole in same."

Helen stopped reading. "Why would someone shoot a blanket?"

"Blankets, couch cushions and pillows can be homemade silencers," Phil said.

"But the police said Mark committed suicide," Helen said. "He wouldn't need a silencer." She stopped. "This is more evidence that he was murdered, isn't it?"

"I think so," Phil said. "But the cops won't. They'll tell you that suicides do strange things. It's how they dismiss any loose end—and there are always loose ends."

Helen read a "property disposition report" for Mark's "auto accident/suicide attempt." It said that the ".32-caliber W-W auto casing, copper slug and .32-caliber W-W auto unfired round" were held for evidence in a property cabinet. So was the blanket. A wallet, ID and thirty dollars were in "safekeeping; pending claim."

"What's a W-W auto casing?" Helen asked.

"That stands for Winchester-Western," Phil said.

Officer Hayward's report continued, stately, sad and strangely hypnotic: "As the paramedics responded to the scene, P.O. Stone observed and seized a .32 Mauser pistol that was lying on the floorboard of the driver's side of the vehicle. See attached for a description of the pistol. The same was loaded with one round in the chamber and two rounds in the clip. Above scene was photographed by the undersigned officer. Vehicle No. 1 was then towed from the scene to 104400 Commercial."

The weapon was a ".32 automatic Mauser Brand 3-inch pistol #765 steel blue," also held for evidence.

"I'm confused," Helen said. "In the earlier report, Officer Hayward saw the gun, picked it up and gave it to Officer Stone. Now we have Stone seizing the same gun from the floorboards. What's going on?"

"Looks like ass covering to me," Phil said. "I'm guessing Hayward saw the gun during the confusion and kept it, but something interfered with the chain of custody. So he rewrote history here to make it official."

"Huh," Helen said. "Another reason to suspect this report—and the police conclusions."

The two witness reports were next, dutifully documented by Officer Hayward:

"Sgt. Clark also spoke with Witness No. 1, Cleveland Berlin, who stated just prior to the accident he heard a car that sounded like it was traveling south on the driveway at a high rate of speed. Berlin heard the tires squealing and it sounded like the car was coming north and then south again. He then heard the crash.

"Witness No. 2, Lorraine Yavuz, stated she was inside the building that was struck, and that she was the nearest person to the point of impact. Witness No. 2 stated that she was not injured and that no one else was near nor was anyone else injured."

Helen stopped reading. "The police don't say that Witness No. 2 was Ahmet's mother," she said.

"There's a lot the police don't say," Phil said.

"Both witnesses heard the crash," Helen said. "But nobody heard the gunshot."

"The blanket was a silencer," Phil said. He handed Helen one more page. "Here's the final report." It was dated three days after the accident.

"On today's date at about 1400 hours, Sgt. Clark received a phone call from Mr. Harcourt Revill, an investigator with the Sunset Palms Medical Examiner's Office. He advised that Mark Behr had died at 1230 hours at Broward County Hospital and had been pronounced dead by Dr. Wiley of the staff of the hospital. The medical examiner's office is investigating the incident and requested a complete copy of the reports be sent to their office. At this time the medical examiner has not released his findings as to cause of death."

Helen stared at the single gray typed paragraph. "That's it?"

"That's all I found," Phil said. "We know the cause of death. We saw the death certificate. The medical examiner said Mark committed suicide."

"Did the police test Mark's hands for gunpowder residue to find out if he actually fired the gun?" Helen asked.

"No," Phil said. "They couldn't. The doctors and paramedics were trying to save his life. That evidence would have been destroyed while they were treating him."

"Why didn't the police check out Ahmet Yavuz?" Helen asked. "Did they know he was a drug dealer?"

"The patrol officer might not have known Ahmet was a dealer," Phil said. "He was never convicted or arrested. Once Mark died, there was no reason to investigate the accident further. It was closed as a suicide."

"So there was a conspiracy," Helen said.

"I don't think so," Phil said. "Sunset Palms is a small force. A couple of overworked cops were offered an easy answer, and they took it."

"Mark was murdered," Helen said. "This report says he shot himself and he used a silencer."

"Not quite," Phil said. "It says a blanket with a bullet hole was found in his car. I said it could have been a silencer."

"And he brought a silencer to commit suicide? I don't think so," Helen said. "Where did Mark get the gun? Did he own a Mauser? What happened to it?"

"More questions we'll have to answer," Phil said.

"Is there paperwork that says what happened to Mark's gun?" Helen asked.

"There should be," Phil said. "I'll keep searching in the Sunset Palms files. I hope the rest of the paperwork hasn't been lost after twenty-five years."

"Maybe it's missing for a reason," Helen said.

CHAPTER 17

Peaceful Rest Cemetery was flat, hot and treeless—more like a doormat for hell than a place of remembrance.

Helen didn't like South Florida graveyards, especially this one. In her hometown of St. Louis, cemeteries celebrated the drama of death with weeping willows, mournful monuments and mausoleums with stained glass their occupants never saw. St. Louis death was personal. The loss was commemorated with permanent reminders.

South Florida did not indulge in funereal flights of fancy. Many of its cemeteries didn't even have tombstones, just flat plaques set flush with the ground so the grass could be easily trimmed. Eternal rest had to be convenient for the endless lawn mowing.

Helen found Mark's grave shockingly spare: a flat metal plaque with his name and death dates next to a stingy bunch of artificial flowers.

"This is depressing," Helen said as she surveyed the grim plot.

"It's supposed to be depressing," Phil said. "It's a cemetery."

"Some cemeteries have real tombstones that say something," Helen said. "'Beloved Husband' or 'Resting with Our Savior.' People put flowers, toys or balloons on the graves. Look at this. I've seen more personal markers for water mains. At least Mark could have a granite tombstone."

"Helen, we live in a hurricane zone," Phil said. "Windstorms topple tombstones."

"But this flat"—Helen struggled for the right word—"nothing is like Mark never lived."

"His brother remembers him," Phil said. "The memories are still alive. That's why we're investigating his death. I'm glad the gym is closed for a few days so we can work on Mark's case. I wanted to see Mark's grave to check the death dates. So much information about his case has been wrong or missing. These dates match his death certificate. We're making progress."

"It doesn't seem like progress," Helen said. "But I'm in this for better or worse. What's the next stop on the Behr death tour?"

"The scene of Mark's accident," Phil said. "He was shot in an industrial park in Sunset Palms. That may be more depressing than this cemetery."

Federal Highway was a four-lane griddle, and Phil's Jeep scooted along like it had been scalded.

"Any leads on finding a car with air-conditioning?" she asked.

"Yeah, Gus has one he wants to sell—a PT Cruiser."

"Those are cute, but they're not collectibles," Helen said. "I thought Gus handled luxury cars."

"He got it in a trade along with a Jaguar," Phil said. He turned on Broward Boulevard, then waited to make a left onto Third Avenue. They were in the heart of Fort Lauderdale's downtown, surrounded by expensive cars. Helen watched wistfully as they drove by, remembering the days when she was a high-paid executive with a sleek silver Lexus. That car was long gone, along with her life as a corporate wonk.

"Could we afford a Jag?" Helen asked. She could almost

feel herself sinking into its luxurious leather seats, icy air blasting in her face. The Jeep hit a pothole, and she clutched the door to keep from bouncing out of her seat.

"We can't afford a car that's too noticeable," Phil said. "We're private eyes, remember? We have to follow people into all sorts of neighborhoods. A Jaguar would stand out too much."

"I could handle the luxury end of our trade," Helen said, "and try to blend in."

"Nice try," Phil said. "But that's not our niche. Coronado Investigations does affordable family investigations. Maybe I could get you a nice minivan."

"No!" Helen said. "If I drive a minivan I'll wind up with two preschoolers and Happy Meals on the seats."

Phil grinned at her. "We can take a look at the PT Cruiser the next time we see Gus."

"Soon, I hope," Helen said. She fanned herself with Mark's accident report and succeeded only in stirring up the hot air. "Is the drug dealer—Ahmet what's-his-name— still working in Sunset Palms?"

"No," Phil said. "I checked the street directories while you were dealing with the 'roid rager at the gym. Ahmet closed his import-export business six months after Mark died. He opened a real estate office in Pompano Beach in north Broward County. He outgrew that building ten years ago. Now his office is in downtown Lauderdale. We'll pass it on our way to Sunset Palms."

Helen groaned. "Not more time in this rolling furnace. This summer is so hot, it doesn't even cool down after sunset."

Helen's dark hair was plastered to her neck. Sweat ran down her face, and her shirt looked like someone had thrown a bucket of water on it. Phil stayed annoyingly cool, from his silver-white hair to his blue T-shirt.

"Think how cool that minivan will feel," Phil said, keeping his face straight. "A peek at Ahmet's office won't eat up more time—I promise. It's the other side of the Third Avenue drawbridge."

They heard a distant horn, the signal that the drawbridge

was going up. The Jeep idled in a long line of traffic waiting for the sailboats and yachts to pass under the bridge. Helen swallowed exhaust fumes and more complaints about the un-air-conditioned Jeep. She could see a gold minivan two cars ahead. The innocuous van looked like a warning.

"See the dark gray skyscraper?" Phil pointed to a building like an upended marble shoebox. "That two-story pink stucco building next to it is Yavuz Elegant Homes. Ahmet owns it."

"Huge parking lot," Helen said. "He's doing well if he can afford a block of downtown real estate. Either that, or he's still dealing drugs."

"Careful," Phil said. "Save those comments for me. Ahmet and his old girlfriend Bernie Behr are now solid citizens. Neither one was convicted or even charged with any wrongdoing. They won't like it if they hear a couple of upstart PIs are spreading rumors about their pasts. Rumors we can't prove are true."

"Who am I going to tell?" Helen said. "The muscleheads at the gym? They can't see past their barbells."

Helen felt like she was marinating in oil for the rest of the drive to Sunset Palms but decided silence was the wisest choice for marital harmony.

Phil noticed her discomfort, kissed her and said, "I'll see about getting your air-conditioned car by tomorrow night."

Phil drove into a run-down industrial park the color of a mustard-stained tie. A rusty fence protected the potholed parking lot. Plastic grocery bags clung to the chain-link.

"Mark's accident happened by this building here," Phil said, parking in front of the fence. A broken plastic sign proclaimed FLORIDA'S BEST MINIBLINDS: MADE TO YOUR SATIS-FACTION.

Phil and Helen walked to the padlocked gate and peered inside. "I don't see any trace of Mark's accident," Helen said. "Not even a scrape on the walls where he crashed his car."

"Let's see if we can get a better picture by going through the accident report." Phil unfolded his copy and started reading.

"Mark's black Monte Carlo came in through this gate," Phil said. He rattled it.

"Then he crashed into Ahmet's red Mercedes, parked over there by the building entrance." He waved his hand to the left.

"Ahmet's Mercedes spun and hit the Ford belonging to his mother, damaging it." Phil twirled his hand. "Sometime during this chaos, Mark shot himself—or was shot—and crashed into the side of the building."

"Ahmet and his mother weren't on the lot at the time of the shooting," Helen said. "I think that was in the police report."

Phil checked the report. "It was. Lorraine Yavuz told the police she was inside the building. She said she heard the car hit the wall. I'm guessing Mark's Monte Carlo plowed into that flat stretch of cinderblock next to the blue Dumpster."

"Where was Ahmet?" Helen said.

"The report doesn't say," Phil said. "And the police didn't ask. When did the drug dealer come running out? Before the shooting—or after it?"

"Or did he fire the fatal shot?" Helen asked.

CHAPTER 18

. . . .

"Coffee?" Phil handed Helen a warm mug. She sat up in bed and inhaled its dark, strong fragrance.

"You think of everything." Helen gave her new husband a love-drunk smile. "I'm glad I have you instead of one of those hardbodies at the gym."

"Thanks," Phil said. "I think." He looked down at his bare chest and said, "I'm not that flabby, am I?"

"I meant those men are too muscular."

Silence.

"Unnaturally so," Helen added.

"Bet that foot tastes delicious," Phil said. "If you'd like to take it out of your mouth, I can fix you toast and eggs for breakfast."

"I meant it as a compliment," Helen said. "I should know better than to make conversation before I've had my coffee." She took a long drink and settled back on the pillows. "That's better. I'm fortified with caffeine. And I don't have to go to the gym today. I wonder how long the police will keep it closed."

"It's a big homicide scene," Phil said.

"I'm hoping three or four days," Helen said.

"You may get your wish," he said. "Maybe they'll keep it closed long enough that those hardbodies you admire will get soft." He kissed her, a long, slow kiss.

"I never said I admired them," Helen said as she pulled him back on the bed. "And what's this about hard?"

After another session of love, they were awakened by Thumbs, howling indignantly and demanding breakfast.

"All right, all right, I hear you," Helen said. "What time is it?" She checked the bedside clock. "It's noon. No wonder Thumbs is angry."

"Let's skip breakfast and go out to lunch," Phil said. "Then we can see Gus. I want to ask him a question about Mark. Your PT Cruiser should be ready this afternoon. We can pick it up after we eat."

"Air-conditioning at last," Helen said. "I'll shower and be ready in no time."

Helen thought she looked good in her black dress and sandals. So did Phil, judging by his appreciative appraisal. He was wearing her favorite blue shirt. Thumbs twined around his legs while Phil poured the cat his food.

Out by the pool, they were blasted by the noonday heat. Margery was skimming bougainvillea blossoms off the pool surface and flipping them onto the lawn with swift, expert movements. Helen thought the pile of damp purple flowers was too pretty for yard trash.

"Good morning," Helen called.

"Good afternoon," Margery said. "Off to work?"

"Out to lunch," Phil said. "Want to go with us?"

"No thanks, I have a date with a rake."

"Sounds racy," Helen said.

"There's nothing romantic about yard work," Margery said, "though it is forever. Where are you going?"

"Thought we might try the Fifteenth Street Fisheries," Phil said.

"The last time I was there, the place was overrun with tourists," Helen said.

"You make it sound like it has roaches," Margery said. "They're not an infestation. If we're lucky, we get tourists. We live in a tourist destination. We all make our living off tourists, one way or another. We spend millions luring them down here. Then we don't want to be around them. I don't know why. People from the Midwest are more polite than Floridians."

"The New Yorkers aren't," Helen said.

"*Some* New Yorkers," Phil said. "I like the Big Apple variety."

"I said midwesterners," Margery said. "We can debate the other states later. Midwestern tourists are polite. They're less likely to cut you off in traffic. They're quieter than Floridians. They don't drink as much as we do or run around naked, except during spring break. So why do Floridians think there's something wrong with a restaurant when the tourists go there?"

"It's not the tourists," Helen said. "Restaurants cut back on the quality of the food and service if they get too many tourists. They figure the tourists won't be back again, so they can treat them badly. A restaurant that caters to locals has to keep higher standards, all year long."

"The Fifteenth Street Fisheries is under new management," Phil said. "We'll look at the boats in the marina, have a drink and lunch."

"I'm finally getting my car," Helen said.

"That's right, use me and cast me aside," Margery said, grinning at them. "Get out of here, you two. I hope you fed that beast. I don't want to listen to Thumbs yowl while you're gone."

The Fifteenth Street Fisheries Restaurant was some thirty years old, a survivor by South Florida standards. The two-story Caribbean-style building with the cool verandas sprawled along the Lauderdale Marina. Tarpon swam near the docks, waiting for their daily feeding.

Helen and Phil took a table with a water view and watched the sleek greenish blue game fish dart and circle in the water. A little girl tossed a french fry in the murky water, and the fish—some nearly six feet long—fought over it. The girl squealed in delight as her cautious mother held her hand.

Helen virtuously ordered a tomato and buffalo mozzarella salad, then swiped Phil's french fries. At first she ate them one at a time. Now she reached for six.

"Hey!" he said after she helped herself. "Get your own."

"Can't," she said. "They're fattening. I have to stay in shape to keep my job." She picked up Phil's last fry, examined it, then put it back on the plate.

"What's wrong with that one?" he asked.

"Overcooked," she said.

"So it's good enough for me? Thanks a lot."

"Look at how I've saved you. There are about fourteen hundred calories on that plate," Helen said.

"Were," Phil said.

"I was only thinking of you," Helen said. "I'm worried about your health." She smiled at her husband. "Why do you want to talk to Gus?"

"I want to clear up a couple of questions about his brother's gun. The police report said Mark was right-handed. Gus confirmed that. The police said the gunshot wound was on the left side of Mark's head."

"That doesn't make sense," Helen said. "Mark would have to reach around his head to shoot himself."

"I think the wound on the left side supports Gus's theory that his brother was shot by someone," Phil said. "The killer could fire into the car from the driver's side and drop the weapon on the floorboard. Except the police recovered a shell casing from the front passenger seat."

"So if someone shot Mark, they'd have to run around the car and throw the shell casing on the passenger side," Helen said.

"Not necessarily," Phil said. "The shell casing could have bounced or fallen onto the passenger-side seat. It could have been moved when his body was taken out of the car. Paramedics aren't careful about preserving crime scenes. They only wanted to save Mark."

"That's a reasonable explanation," Helen said. "But if the killer shot Mark, there's no mention in the police report of a bullet hole in the driver's window."

"No. Mark must have rolled down the window," Phil said. "That tells me Mark either knew and trusted his killer or wanted to talk to him, so he rolled down his window. Even in 1986 most cars had air-conditioning, and Mark's Monte Carlo was only a year old."

"Ahmet," Helen said. "Mark went to talk to Ahmet at his import business."

"I want to ask Gus if his brother had a gun," Phil said. "Maybe Mark wasn't there to talk to Ahmet. What if Joel's story was true? The dealer kept Bernie a prisoner in his house and Mark had to rescue his sister. She was still hiding at the brothers' apartment, afraid to leave. Maybe Mark went there to kill Ahmet."

"Then how did Ahmet shoot Mark in the head?" Helen said.

"That's one more question we can't answer," Phil said. "It will get worse when I ask Gus about Joel's story: Did he know his sister, Bernie, was rescued by Mark? I also suspect Mark was dealing drugs."

Helen winced. "You really think Mark was a drug dealer?"

Phil nodded.

"Those questions will shatter Gus's last illusions about his family," Helen said.

"Gus will have to face a lot of painful things before this investigation is over," Phil said as he signaled the waitress for the check. "Brace yourself. Our client may fire us."

Helen ate the last overcooked fry.

CHAPTER 19

H elen was wilting in the soupy heat as Phil's Jeep
idled in the beach-bound traffic. The salt air smelled
like exhaust and warm asphalt. She hoped this was
the last time she'd have to inhale that particular perfume.
She couldn't wait to drive her cool PT Cruiser.

"What color is my new Cruiser?" Helen asked.

"That's a surprise," Phil said.

"You won't give me a hint?" she asked.

"We're almost at Gus's. You'll find out soon enough. Besides, you said you didn't care as long as it had air-
conditioning."

Helen hoped it was bright red or a vibrant blue. A wicked
black Cruiser would be fun. It would look like a bootlegger's
getaway car. Maybe she could put a fake bullet-hole decal
on the back window. Then she remembered Mark and his
real bullet wound. Bullet holes were not funny. Not now. Not
with this client.

"How much is the car costing us?" she asked.

"It's two years old," Phil said, "has about fifteen thousand miles, one owner and not a scratch on it. Gus is giving
it to us for eight thousand."

"Giving?" Helen said. "Eight grand is a lot of money for a used car."

"I checked the prices," Phil said. "We're getting a deal. He's charging us about four thousand below what it's worth."

"We're working for Gus and we'll wind up owing him money," Helen said.

"You wanted a car," Phil said. "I got you the best deal I could."

"Eight thousand is not too bad," Helen said.

"With taxes, tags and insurance, you'd better add another two or three thousand."

"That wipes out our startup money," Helen said. She was getting an old familiar feeling. "Can we afford that much?"

"We have to," Phil said. "If you're going to be an equal partner, you need a car. I know it's a scary chunk out of our stash, and neither of us has a regular paycheck."

"I have my job at the gym," Helen said.

"Which will be over as soon as our case is finished," Phil said. "New clients aren't lining up at our door. So we have to be careful for a while. But this is a justifiable expense. We have to spend money to make money."

"I have a little money tucked away in a St. Louis account that we can use now that the terms of my divorce have changed."

"A little?" Phil said. "You have three hundred thousand dollars stashed there."

"But no money coming in," Helen said. "And I still have to work out my problems with the IRS and pay the lawyers."

"You don't owe that much," Phil said.

That old feeling was growing darker, blacker and more threatening, like an approaching storm system. Soon it would become a constant, full-blown worry. Helen had lived with many kinds of worries: the vague unhappiness when she had a dull, well-paid corporate job that ate up her life and gave her nothing but money. The ferocious anger when she'd discovered her husband, Rob, was unfaithful. Heck, she didn't discover it. She stumbled over her buck-naked husband doing the wild thing with their next-door neighbor Sandy. Helen had picked up a nearby crowbar and hurt the one Rob loved most—his SUV. Rob had wept real tears over that loss, and Helen hadn't felt one bit better.

Her dull anger morphed into blind rage when the divorce judge gave her ex-husband, Rob, half of her future income—a rage so ferocious that she fled St. Louis. Helen had driven around the country in hate-crazed lunges—over to Kansas, then south until she finally landed in Fort Lauderdale, nearly broke and jobless.

There she'd learned to live with a different worry: fear ate away at her while she struggled to avoid her ex. She swore Rob would never see a nickel of her money, and she'd kept that vow—at a terrible cost. She'd give every cent she had, plus all her future earnings, if her worthless, bloodsucking ex were alive again.

Now Helen lived with the fear that Rob's body would be discovered, but that was a worry she could bury deep—just like Rob. She hadn't killed her ex. He'd died accidentally. Her innocent nephew, Tommy Junior, swung his bat and hit Uncle Rob when he attacked Helen. Helen and her sister, Kathy, had begged Rob to go to the emergency room, but the man had refused. He wasn't going to the ER because a ten-year-old smacked him in the head with a bat. Rob died. Helen's innocent nephew would have to live with a burden he didn't deserve, all because of Rob's selfish, careless decision.

Helen had wanted to call the police and say that she killed Rob, but her sister, Kathy, refused. She was afraid her son would confess that he'd hit Uncle Rob, and Tommy Junior would be branded for life as a killer, teased by thoughtless classmates, mocked and shunned until he became an outcast. Helen and Kathy had both seen an innocent classmate ruined that way.

So Helen swore she'd never tell anyone what really happened, not even Phil.

Now she lived with that decision daily. It had become part of her marriage, an unwelcome third party. Helen had pledged herself to Phil for better or for worse, and this was bad. She felt like she'd broken her vows before she'd even married Phil. She'd dragged her dead ex into their life.

Still, she couldn't sacrifice her nephew. Helen had had to choose between blood and love, and blood won. She'd buried that fear so deeply, even she couldn't bear to acknowledge it, but it was always there, a dark shadow beside her. Sometimes she wondered why Phil couldn't see it.

Now she was facing a familiar fear, the one she'd learned to live with after she'd quit her high-paying job and gone on the run—the fear of not having enough money. The fear of living with no comforting paycheck. At least this fear was well-known. It moved in again, like a houseguest who didn't know when to leave. Worrying about money added another shade of gray to her world, but Helen could live with this dreary problem. She'd endured it for more than two years before she married Phil. Heck, most of America lived with it.

Phil brought her back to the present and the traffic jam on Federal Highway. "Helen, we'll be okay. Margery hasn't raised our rent in years," he said. "She's giving us the Coronado Investigations office for a dollar a month. We're not going to be thrown out on the street tomorrow. You worry too much."

And Phil refused to worry. Helen thought that was another fault.

"I have to worry for two," she said.

He put his arm around her, drew her near and kissed her forehead. "Then find a real worry. We don't have any credit card debt, just the utility bills. We only have to feed ourselves and the cat."

"He's a fat cat," Helen said, but she couldn't help smiling.

"Forty percent of the homes in Broward County have underwater mortgages," he said. "How many of the people stuck in this traffic jam are worse off than we are?"

Helen studied the parade of painted snails stranded on the highway.

"How about that woman in the red Mercedes?" Phil said. "She looks prosperous, but she could be in debt up to her designer sunglasses. And that poor guy in the rusty dark blue Datsun. Wonder if he's seen a process server on his doorstep."

Those cars inched forward and the Datsun driver honked at them. Helen sat up and straightened her black dress. Phil waved at the Datsun and moved forward.

Now the Jeep was next to a silver convertible packed with shirtless, sunburned students. Loud bass blasted from its speakers. Three guys clutched beer cans, and two blondes in bikinis sat on their laps. The wind blew the telltale odor of burning leaves Helen's way. Party time. If this traffic jam went on much longer, she and Phil would have a contact high.

What about you, kids? she wondered. Are you in debt already for school? Or will your troubles begin later, when you're further down the road? The party car moved past them, and Phil said, "Get ready, Helen. As soon as we cross these railroad tracks, we'll be at Boy Toys Restoration. There's Gus, working on an old black Imperial. Look at that amazing beast."

The Imperial was as big and square as Kansas. The fenders were draped with protective cloth, like a patient undergoing surgery. Gus had his hands in the Imperial's guts. He looked up, saw the Jeep bouncing over the tracks, wiped his oily hands on a rag and waved.

Helen caught the first glimpse of her new car, parked in front. It wasn't red, black, silver or even a cool blue. To Helen, it seemed older people drove cars this color. Even Margery, a woman who never showed her true years, had that one telltale sign of age.

"It's so . . . white," Helen said, hoping she kept the disappointment out of her voice.

"The official color is stone white," Gus said proudly. He opened the door and started the engine. "The interior is slate gray. It's loaded with extras—bucket seats, air bags and tinted glass to make it even cooler in summer."

I said I didn't care how it looked, Helen told herself. I only wanted a car with air-conditioning. I didn't want to trudge around the used-car lots. I got what I wanted.

Gus and Phil grinned, proud as new parents.

"Wait till you feel that cooling system," Gus said. "Sit down."

Phil virtually pushed her into the seat.

"It's as cold as—," Helen began as the arctic air blasted her face.

"It's a rolling igloo," Gus said.

Helen knew her car had been named.

"I have the only igloo in South Florida," she said.

Phil gave Helen a warning look, then said, "Before we hit the road, Gus, I have to ask you a question about your brother's gun."

"The .22?" Gus said.

"No, the Mauser the cops found in his car."

"Mark never had a Mauser," Gus said. "He had a little Walther P22 pistol he kept for protection."

"Maybe your dad brought a Mauser home after World War Two," Phil said.

"My dad served in Korea," Gus said. "He never had guns. My brother bought a little .22 pistol for protection."

"When?" Phil said.

"When he started hanging out with that wild crowd," Gus said. "The grip was so small I could hold it and shoot it using two fingers and a thumb. Only had a five-inch barrel. I asked him what he was doing with a lady's gun. He said the .22 was accurate and easy to conceal."

"Are you sure?" Phil asked.

Gus was clearly steamed. "Of course I'm sure. I know the difference between a Mauser and a .22. Just because I fix cars doesn't mean I'm stupid."

"Whoa!" Phil said. "I didn't mean to upset you. But the police didn't find a .22 in Mark's car. They found a blue steel Mauser .32 automatic."

"It was not Mark's gun," Gus said. "We lived together in an apartment so small there wasn't room for the roaches to hide. He never owned a Mauser."

"Gus, did you ever wonder if your brother might have been a drug dealer?" Phil said.

"No!" Sweat poured down Gus's face.

"I didn't mean to upset you," Phil said.

"I'm not upset," Gus said. His clipped words and stiff body said otherwise.

"Where did Mark get all that money?" Phil asked. "It had to be drugs. Mark probably peddled a little coke at parties."

"That couldn't be," Gus said.

Helen thought he was really saying *That's not what I want it to be*.

"Where did you get the money to keep this garage going?" Phil asked. "You said Mark steered exotic-car owners your way. You spent major money restoring Boy Toys in the eighties. How did you keep going until your income picked up?"

"Mark found an anonymous investor to lend me two hundred grand," Gus said.

"Did you pay back this investor?" Phil asked.

"No. Only Mark knew the name. I waited for the guy to come forward after my brother died, but he never did."

"There was no investor," Phil said. "Mark gave you that money. He was dealing."

"No! I built this shop through hard work." Gus wiped more sweat off his forehead, leaving a dark oil smear.

"I know you did," Phil said. "I didn't say you were a dealer. But I think your brother was. I'm guessing Mark was a small-timer. He gave you the money and called it a loan. When his bipolar problem kicked in, he started sampling his product and wound up behind in his payments to Ahmet."

"Maybe," Gus said, his face sullen.

"Your brother owed Ahmet three thousand dollars when he died," Phil said gently, as if his softer voice would make those words easier to swallow.

"I might have heard something like that," Gus said. "Maybe. I don't know for sure. I don't know anything."

Helen wished Phil would stop talking so they could leave. Gus was getting upset.

"You asked me to talk to his friends," Phil said. "One of them said Mark rescued your sister from Ahmet's house. Ahmet kept Bernie prisoner there. Mark had to kick down the door to get her out. She hid at your apartment, too afraid to leave."

"Bernie never said anything like that to me," Gus said. "Mark didn't, either. Why are you telling me this?"

Because you insisted you wanted to know, Helen thought. But she didn't say it.

"Because it means you were right: Mark was murdered," Phil said. "I think Mark went to Ahmet's business to kill him. Instead, the drug dealer shot him."

Rivers of sweat cascaded down Gus's forehead and drenched his shirt. His shoulders were bowed.

"I didn't know any of this," he said. "All I know is I love Mark and Bernie."

CHAPTER 20

H elen fell in love with the Igloo on the ride back to
the Coronado. The white PT Cruiser rolled coolly
down the highway, encasing her in a lovely chilled
bubble. The car had lots of legroom and a cargo cover, so
she didn't have to worry if she left something valuable inside. Her neighborhood had suffered a rash of car break-ins.
The thugs smashed windows with a spark plug and went
after laptops, iPods, purses, even pocket change.

Helen admired the Igloo's retro dashboard clock. The
temperature gauge told her it was a sizzling ninety-six degrees outside. She waved at Phil, following in his open Jeep,
his long silver hair tied back in a ponytail. The man wasn't
even breaking a sweat.

Helen was still shaken after their scene with Gus. He was
clearly hurt by their new information, even if it did bolster
his belief that Mark was murdered.

At the Coronado, she parked in the spot where the Toad
used to squat. The Toad was an ugly green monster she'd
driven when she'd worked at the Superior Club, a not-so-
superior country club. The Toad had been junked long ago,
but the miserable creature had leaked nasty bodily fluids in

the lot, a permanent memorial to a moody, bad-tempered car.

A purple cloud drifted to the gate. Margery, in a gauzy eggplant caftan and lavender sandals, lifted a chilled glass of white wine in a salute. "Like the new ride," she said. "Gives my white car some company. How is the Cruiser?"

"Cool, in all senses of the word," Helen said.

Phil kissed their landlady on the cheek and said, "You look like a glamorous hostess in a magazine."

She kissed him back lightly and said, "You're sweet."

Margery flirted outrageously with Phil. Helen wondered if her husband would have married Margery if she'd been thirty years younger. Their landlady was glamorous at seventy-six. She must have been devastating in her forties.

"You two want to join me in a drink?" Margery asked.

"We'll take a rain check," Phil said. "Helen's gym is closed tomorrow while the crime scene unit goes over it. We want to make some progress on Gus's case."

They retreated upstairs to the Coronado Investigations office. In the kitchenette, Phil poured Helen a glass of wine, opened himself a beer, and pulled a bright orange bag out of the cabinet.

"What's that?"

"Spicy snack mix," he said. "Jalapeño cheese crackers, hot pretzels, salsa-flavored corn chips and more."

"More what—heartburn?" Helen asked. She thought Phil had a touching faith in the promises on junk food labels.

"More ingredients," he said. "It also has spicy SunChips. Those are multigrain, so they're good for you. So are the peanuts. The spicy snack mix has no trans fat and sixty percent less regular fat."

"Than a can of Crisco?"

"Than other potato chips," Phil said. "You're always after me to eat healthier. Then when I try, you make fun of me."

He tilted his head like a puzzled pup. Helen laughed and kissed him. "I love you," she said. "I'm glad 'for better or worse' doesn't mean eating your snack mix."

Phil kissed her back and Gus's case was forgotten for more than a half hour. That old-fashioned desk was surprisingly roomy.

"We have to get serious now," Helen said, straightening her black dress. "No more newlywed breaks."

"We had to christen that desk," Phil said. "That's why shamuses hang around leggy brunettes. Now we have to figure out who shot Mark."

"With a gun his brother says he didn't own," Helen said. "Is part of that police report missing? Do we need to go back and check for more of it?"

"By we, I assume you mean me," Phil said. "Sure. It won't be the first wild goose I've chased. I need to poke through those old records anyway. I have a hunch there's more in those files. Those cops loved filling out forms."

"They were better paper pushers than investigators," Helen said. "I didn't realize how hard it would be to tell Gus what we found out."

"We haven't confirmed it yet," Phil said. "We're just repeating old stories."

"I think on some level, Gus believes them," Helen said. "Can we conclude that Ahmet shot Mark?"

"For now," Phil said. "Unless someone else in the drug business killed him. Mark was hanging around with a dealer. He bought a gun for personal protection. He was scared and doing something dangerous. Ahmet had the most likely motive for Mark's murder: Mark was acting crazy. He'd insulted the drug dealer and broken into Ahmet's house to rescue his sister. Ahmet couldn't tolerate a challenge to his authority like that. He had to send a message. Mark was shot. Shortly after that, Ahmet quit dealing and became a solid citizen."

"He became a real estate dealer," Helen said. "Not sure how solid that is."

"He became a rich real estate dealer," Phil said. "I know that for sure. He's living on four acres of waterfront property on Hendin Isle. That's several million for the land alone. And he's not sleeping in a double-wide. His house has eight bedrooms, a tennis court, pool and private dock."

"Now, that sounds like a *Miami Vice* drug dealer," Helen said.

"I think Ahmet got scared out of the drug business."

"Can he just leave like that?" Helen asked.

"On his level, yes," Phil said. "It's not the mob. You've seen too many movies. You're still thinking about those two Colombians meeting in a parking lot with a suitcase full of cash. Drug dealing is a business. There are six or seven levels before the drugs reach the actual consumer. Nice white kids buy drugs from their nice white friends. Middle-class people do not go into the ghetto. They get the drugs from other middle-class people.

"Ahmet was probably at level four or five. Mark and his friends were at level six or seven. Mark made a lot less money because he was so far away from the source.

"Drug dealing is a business, like Kmart, Home Depot or McDonald's. The dealers set up a surprisingly corporate structure with a regular chain of command. There's a CEO at the top, far removed from the street sales. The lower levels have lots of employees. Ahmet was like the manager of a McDonald's, and Mark was a lowly burger flipper. He'd be wearing a hairnet at Mickey D's.

"Dealers usually let the low-level players walk away. They can't kill them without a good reason. A death invites too much attention. Drug dealing breeds in the dark, like vermin."

"Gus insists his brother didn't sell drugs, even as a low-level player," Helen said.

"Gus doesn't know what he's talking about," Phil said. "Dealers do not hang around with users. Ahmet wouldn't have let Mark near him if he'd only been a user. Mark was selling drugs first, then fell nose-first into the snow and became a user. Most of those guys eventually wind up dead."

"Like Mark," Helen said.

Phil took a long sip of his beer. "I hate drug cases. Hate them." His blue eyes flashed with anger, and Helen wondered if he was thinking of Marcie, the lost girl from Little Rock. His first case and his first failure. Marcie had been buried as long as Mark.

Helen tried to bring Phil back to their case. "So we've got low-level Mark selling drugs, asking people if they want fries with their coke. Why did he need a gun? Was he afraid someone would shoot him when he hung out in the projects?"

"Mark? Selling in the projects? Not a chance," Phil said. "People like Mark would not go into that neighborhood. He doesn't belong there. He probably peddled coke at parties."

"I've never been to any parties like that," Helen said.

"Yes, you have; you just didn't know it," Phil said. "You were probably drinking or dancing in the main rooms. The drug users congregate in a basement, a rec room or a bedroom. They use coded language like *I'm really stressed. I need to relax and mellow out.* Or *I need some energy.* That's the cue to bring out the drugs."

"That's just middle-class drug use," Helen said and shrugged.

"Drug dealers are businessmen, Helen, and the middle class has lots of those. The good dealers are smart businessmen. They have to be.

"In the eighties, it seemed like everyone was either using coke, selling it or both. Ordinary blue-collar guys were stashing drug money in their closets. The handy ones built secret compartments in the bedroom closet. The cops always knew where to look. They'd lift up the carpet on the closet floor, and the secret was revealed. Or the cops would see some cheesy door cut into the sheetrock closet wall with boxes of Christmas decorations piled in front of it. Obvious as hell. Once the small-timers were caught, they usually folded."

Phil paced up and down on the terrazzo floor, trying to work off his anger.

"Rob and I were offered a chance to bankroll a couple of drug dealers in St. Louis," Helen said. "They promised we could make fifty thousand dollars. It was presented as an investment opportunity."

"And you turned them down?" Phil said.

"Of course. Rob wanted to go for it. He thought we could make one big score and quit. I was too scared."

"You were too moral," Phil said.

"No, I knew I'd get caught."

"You might have," Phil said. "But you'd be surprised who got away with dealing. A lot of respectable businesspeople got their nest egg selling drugs. They got in, made some money and got out. When I was on that drug case, I kept hearing, 'I'm just in this until I can buy a house.' Sometimes it was a restaurant. Or a boat. Or a flashy vacation. They had a goal. They wanted to make a hundred thousand or two hundred thousand. Enough to open the restaurant, take the luxury cruise, or start their dream business.

"The 'buy the restaurant' guy was more likely to quit when he reached his goal. Some small-timers did that in the eighties. They scored and got out of the business. Or something happened and the middle-class ones got frightened back into being so-called good citizens. The ones who didn't either died or got busted."

"Behind every great fortune is a great crime," Helen said. "And behind many small fortunes are small crimes."

"You'd be surprised how many comfortably off people are living off a small, tainted fortune," Phil said.

"Or their brother's dream business," Helen said. "Poor Gus. Do you really think it's better that he knows everything?"

"Maybe if he quits idealizing his brother," Phil said, "he can live with the memory of the real Mark."

CHAPTER 21

"Helen!" The telephone could not hide Kathy's cry of primal fear. Helen could hear her sister's anguish a thousand miles away in St. Louis.

"Kathy, honey, is that you?"

"Of course it's me," Kathy said, but Helen could hardly understand her sister, her voice was so distorted by tears. "Tom's taken the kids out for ice cream. Are you alone so you can talk?"

Helen heard Phil whistling in the shower. "For a little while."

More tears. "He called, Helen. He promised he'd go away, but he called."

"Who?"

Anger spiked in Kathy's voice. "The blackmailer, that's who. That dirtbag—" Kathy stopped to calm herself. "The one you paid five thousand dollars a month ago. Now he wants twice as much—ten thousand dollars—or he'll ruin Tommy's life. He knows Tommy killed Rob. He saw it. He must have. He asked me how it would feel to be the mother of the Killer Bat Boy."

More tears. Helen's gut squirmed like a basket of snakes.

She could see the sensational headlines now: KILLER BAT BOY WHACKS UNCLE. Tommy had swung at Helen's worthless ex-husband with his aluminum bat, and Rob had died soon after. Rob had refused to go to the hospital. He'd laughed when Kathy had suggested it. Right before he died.

"Tommy didn't kill Rob," Helen said. "I did. Rob woke up again, and I bopped him with the bat."

"I told the blackmailer that. He laughed. He said he'd tell the police he saw Tommy swing at Rob and his mother and Aunt Helen bury Uncle Rob in the church basement. He said it would make a touching story about families working together—mother, aunt and the Killer Bat Boy. The blackmailer said you could say what you wanted, but that title would stick to Tommy like Velcro. For the rest of his life, my boy will be known as the Killer Bat Boy."

"No, he won't," Helen said. "I'll FedEx you the money."

"You can't. There isn't time. He wants the cash tomorrow night or else. It's eight thirty in Fort Lauderdale right now. The FedEx pickups are over."

"I can wire transfer the money to your bank account," Helen said.

"No!" Kathy sounded crazed with terror. "Tom will find out. My Tom. He'll go to the police. You know he's a straight arrow."

So is Phil, Helen thought. Her new husband was whistling his Clapton favorites. He'd switched to a slightly out-of-tune version of "Layla," the Clapton song about hopeless love.

"Then I'll hop on a plane and bring the money myself," Helen told her sister. "I still have that St. Louis bank account. I have to tell Phil about the blackmailer, Sis. He can help us. He's a detective. I don't like lying to my husband."

"You don't like lying?" Kathy said. "What about me? What if Tom finds out his boring suburban wife buried a body in the church basement? Bringing Phil into this mess will make it worse. You promised, Helen. You promised not to tell." Her sister's voice rose to a panicked shriek.

"Take it easy, Kathy," Helen said. "What if Tom and the

kids walk in and hear you? Take some deep breaths. Fix yourself a soothing cup of tea."

"Tea, hell," Kathy said. "I want a glass of wine."

Helen spoke slowly, as if she were talking her sister off a ledge. "Good. You do that. Do you have a bottle open?"

"Yes," Kathy said in a small voice.

"Pour yourself a big glass and take a drink. I'm going to put the phone down and check the flights to St. Louis on the Internet. I'll be right here, Kathy. I won't hang up. Give me just a minute."

Helen booted up Phil's computer and checked the flights, then got her credit card. She had one, now that she was no longer on the run from the law. It was one benefit of being a solid citizen. She couldn't have bought a last-minute flight with cash before she'd settled her problems with the court.

Helen picked up the phone. "Kathy, are you still there?"

"Of course I am," Kathy snapped. "Where do you think I'd go?"

Crazy, Helen wanted to answer. My little sister is going crazy. She could see her in her kitchen. Kathy was two years younger and four inches shorter. She had a generous figure, a touch of gray at her temples and a nice smile, though Helen was sure Kathy wasn't smiling now.

"I need you to be strong for Tommy," Helen said. "There's a flight that leaves Fort Lauderdale at six thirty tomorrow morning and gets into St. Louis at nine twenty-five. I'll stay overnight with you, then catch the afternoon nonstop back to Lauderdale. I can be home again by five o'clock the next day. I'm booking the flight while we talk."

"How will you explain this trip to Phil?" Kathy asked.

Helen could hear her husband whistling Clapton's "The Way You Look Tonight" as he shut off the water. Whatever she told Phil, it would have to be soon.

"I'll tell him my lawyer, Drake Upton, wants to talk to me about a possible settlement with the IRS. I'll call Drake when I get to St. Louis. He might be able to see me on short notice."

Helen could hear her sister sniffling, then taking a gulp

of wine. Kathy's tear storm was nearly over. "Do you think you could? Do you mind?" she asked.

"Of course I don't mind, you little twit," Helen said. "I want to help my nephew. Tommy doesn't deserve to have his life ruined because I married the wrong man."

"There's the sister I know and love," Kathy said. Now Helen could hear her sunshine smile. "Allison and I will pick you up at the airport tomorrow."

Helen hung up the phone as Phil stepped out of the bathroom in a cloud of steam. Wrapped in a thick terry robe, he flopped down on the bed beside Helen. "Did I hear the phone ring?"

"That was our lawyer, Drake Upton," Helen said. "He wants me to make a quick run to St. Louis tomorrow to talk about a possible settlement with the IRS."

"Short notice," Phil said. "It's late for Drake to make a business call."

"It's only seven thirty in St. Louis," Helen said. "This is a real shot in the dark, but I think it's worth the risk. I can stay with Kathy. She'll be happy to see me. So will Allison and Tommy Junior."

"Well, okay," Phil said. "If that's what you want."

There. She'd said it. She'd lied to Phil. She'd tried to tell him the truth about Rob before they married, but he thought she was having bridal jitters and kissed her fears away. And it had been so easy to forget her lies during their honeymoon. She almost convinced herself it had never happened. But this St. Louis trip was a deliberate choice. She felt numb. Is this the first sign of marital death? she wondered. Helen tried to bury her unease under more talk.

"I've already booked my ticket, Phil. My flight is at six thirty tomorrow. We'll have to leave here at five in the morning. Do you mind taking me to the airport, or should I drive the Igloo and park it there overnight?"

"I'll take you," he said.

"I'm sorry I won't be able to help you with Gus's case tomorrow."

"It's okay," he said. "I'll look for more pages to Mark's

accident report. While you're in St. Louis having fun, I'll be going through Sunset Palms police records."

"You're still convinced there's more paper?"

"Let's just say I have a strong hunch," he said. "And I'm usually right. That search will probably take up most of tomorrow. Maybe part of the next day, too. Sounds like you're getting back early enough that we could do some research at Granddaddy's Bar. Have drinks and dinner. You might have to eat some french fries."

Helen buried her face in Phil's bathrobe, ashamed to look him in the eye. She licked a drop of water off his ear. "French fries. That's my kind of research," she said.

Phil pulled her closer, and she kissed him. "Glad the gym is still closed," she said. "Derek says it won't open for at least another two days. I'd risk losing my job if I asked for time off so soon after getting hired."

"Any news for our client Shelby?" Phil asked.

"Nothing. I think my first case is a bust. Bryan never looks at another woman except Paula—and everyone looks at her."

"Which one is Paula?"

"She's a gorgeous woman who makes dramatic, actressy entrances into the gym. She's competing in the bikini competition at the upcoming East Coast Physique Championships. When Paula floats down the aisle, all the guys on the treadmills suck in their guts. For some of the older ones, that's the heaviest lifting they do at Fantastic Fitness."

"It doesn't mean Bryan is unfaithful because he stares at Paula," Helen said. "Any man with a pulse would. I even look at her. The only other woman I've seen Bryan spend time with is his trainer, Jan Kurtz. She puts him through his paces five or six hours at a time. He's only interested in her professionally."

"Are you sure?"

"Positive," Helen said. "I watch them in the mirrors when they think no one is looking. It's strictly business."

"Maybe Bryan knows you're a plant," Phil said.

"I don't think so," Helen said. "When the gym reopens,

I'll spend one more day, then tell Shelby what's going on: Her husband is faithful, but he's lost interest in her."

"She'll hate to hear that," Phil said.

"The truth hurts," Helen said. "I get the feeling Shelby might prefer a husband who's cheating on her to one who's faithful but uninterested."

Phil kissed Helen good night and was soon snoring softly. Helen stared at the ceiling, thinking about faithful husbands and painful truths.

CHAPTER 22

....

Helen's alarm went off at four the next morning. She swatted the clock like a fly, and it tumbled off her bedside table.

The clatter woke up Phil. "Huh?" he said, sitting up in bed. "What's wrong?"

"I have to fly to St. Louis," Helen said. "You go back to sleep. I'll leave the Igloo in the airport parking lot."

Phil rubbed his hands through his thick silver hair and said, "No, there's not enough time for you to catch the parking shuttle. I'll drive. I just need some coffee."

"Me, too," Helen said, staggering into the bathroom. She flipped on the light, looked in the mirror and winced. Was that red-eyed creature really her? No need to get her suitcase out of the closet. She already had the bags under her eyes.

When she emerged damp from the shower, Phil handed her a mug of hot coffee.

"You've saved my life," she said, gulping coffee while she threw a pantsuit into her rolling bag in case she really did see the lawyer. She packed a black long-sleeved shirt and scarf so the blackmailer wouldn't see her. She planned to stake out the money drop. That creep was getting fifteen thousand dollars of her cash, but it would be his last payday. This time, Helen would catch him.

Five o'clock was too early for the sun to be up. The air was so thick, Helen thought she might drown if she inhaled. The Coronado's window air conditioners rattled and insects hummed, a comforting summer symphony. She heard the low rumble of thunder in the darkness and hoped this trip wouldn't be canceled by bad weather. She had to get to St. Louis.

She rolled her suitcase down the narrow sidewalk to the parking lot. As they passed Margery's apartment, Helen saw the yellow glow of their landlady's kitchen light and caught the faint whiff of cigarette smoke seeping through the glass slats on the jalousie door. The rest of the Coronado was ghostly white.

"My car or yours?" Phil whispered.

"Mine's air-conditioned," Helen said. "You want to drive the Igloo? You're more awake." She handed him the keys.

"I like this car," Phil said as he eased the PT Cruiser through the small, tight traffic jam in front of the terminal.

"You can't have it," Helen said. She kissed him good-bye and rolled her suitcase toward the airport security line. She'd packed light, but Helen felt the heavy burden of her lie to Phil.

Her fellow travelers seemed abnormally chipper for six a.m. Helen's head ached and her eyes felt like someone had tossed sand in them. She'd spent the night beating herself up.

I can sleep on the plane, she told herself as the jet pushed back from the gate.

She didn't. The plane bounced through the thunderheads for more than a thousand miles. Even seasoned travelers grabbed their seat arms as the plane dipped and pitched. The captain ordered the flight attendants to stay seated.

Helen blessed Phil for that morning coffee. No beverages were served on the three-hour roller-coaster ride.

The clouds cleared a hundred miles before their destination. When the flight finally touched down in sunny St.

Louis, the passengers applauded. Helen felt like she'd walked there from Lauderdale.

The graceful steel and glass curves of Lambert International Airport made a sunlit cage. Kathy was waiting at the terminal entrance, looking even more frazzled than Helen. She noticed her sister's hair was a trace grayer at the temples and her smile was tentative.

Her niece, Allison, looked so much like Kathy, back when Helen's sister had been carefree. Before my ex and I ruined my sister's life, Helen thought.

"Aunt Helen!" Allison cried. A flurry of pink ruffles ran toward her.

Helen hugged her niece. "You're so big," she said.

Allison twirled to show off her outfit, her round face lit with a smile. "See my Disney princess backpack? I'm wearing princess ruffles, too."

"Pretty," Helen said. "I like the pink sparkles on your shoes."

"The other mothers say this princess phase will pass," Kathy said and rolled her eyes.

"I got to come to the airport," Allison said. "Tommy had to go to school."

"Tommy was not happy," Kathy said. "You look exhausted, Sis. Bad flight?"

"Like being in a cocktail shaker going six hundred miles an hour," Helen said. "It's over. I'm here."

"I'm so glad," Kathy said, hugging her. "Thanks for coming here."

The searing heat hit them when they left the terminal. "Fall definitely hasn't arrived yet," Helen said. "St. Louis seems hotter than Florida."

"The only sign of fall is the dogwood in my backyard," Kathy said. "My poor little tree is doornail dead. This was the fifth-hottest summer in city history."

"Do dogs like dogwood?" Allison asked.

"No, but cats like cattails," Helen said.

"You're silly," Allison said, giggling.

They climbed into Kathy's blue minivan, the same one Kathy had used to haul Rob's body to his clandestine burial.

Despite the brutal heat, Helen couldn't help shivering at that memory.

"Hungry? Want to stop for breakfast?" Kathy asked.

"Food later," Helen said. "Let's get the money now, in case there's a problem at the bank. I'll call Drake Upton while you drive there. Maybe he can see me while I'm in town."

The lawyer answered his own phone and gave Helen a mild chiding. "I wish you'd given me more notice."

"I am sorry," Helen said. "I had to see my sister in a hurry. Unfinished business after Mother's death."

"I can fit you in at nine thirty tomorrow for twenty minutes," Upton said.

"I'll be there," Helen said.

She hit END on her phone and said to Kathy, "I can leave straight for the airport after the lawyer's appointment. If you can't take me, I'll catch a cab. I have to find some way to tell him about that money we're giving our friend."

"Why?" Kathy asked.

"Deposits and withdrawals of ten thousand dollars or more are reported to the IRS."

"We could take out six thousand now," Kathy said, "and four thousand this afternoon."

"It still adds up to ten thousand, and that has to be reported," Helen said. "I'll ask my lawyer how I should handle it."

Kathy's van swerved slightly, and a red Nissan honked at her. "Does that include deposits, too?" she asked. "Does that mean the bank reported the twenty-one thousand dollars I found in Mom's cookie jar when I put it in the kids' college fund?"

"Sure does."

Helen watched the color drain from her sister's face.

"It's okay," Helen said. "Make sure you tell your accountant and pay taxes on it. You can say it was a gift from Mom before she left on her trip."

"What about Mom's not-so-grieving widower, Lawn Boy Larry?" Kathy asked. "Will he find out?"

"The IRS won't report the transaction to Larry. He never

bothered knowing his wife well enough to find out about that cookie jar. Have you heard anything from old greedy guts?"

"He held the estate sale the day after Mom's funeral and put her house up for sale a week later. I drive by it nearly every day. It sold three weeks ago, and a family moved in before school started. I'm sure Larry kept all the house sale money."

"I'm sure he did, too," Helen said. "He only married poor Mom for her money. She wouldn't be buried next to Dad if she didn't have a prepaid plot. At least she can spend eternity with the man she loved. Mom and I have some track record when it comes to men."

"You've got a gem now," Kathy said. "Phil was worth the wait."

Helen checked her niece before she asked her next question. Allison was asleep in her car seat. "What time do you leave the package?"

"Nine o'clock," Kathy said. "It should be dark by then."

She stopped the minivan in front of a beige cube and said, "Here's the bank. Take this bag for the money." She handed Helen a reusable Schnucks supermarket bag.

"Go green for blackmail," Helen said.

CHAPTER 23

· · · · · · · · · · · · · · · · · · · ·

E leven thirty-two.
Nine hours and twenty-eight minutes before
Kathy had to deliver the blackmail money, Helen
loped out of the bank with the ten thousand dollars. She
dropped the cash-crammed Schnucks bag in the minivan's
cargo compartment and climbed into the front seat.

"What now?"

"Home to Webster Groves," Kathy said, "and an early
lunch."

Allison woke up at the word "lunch." "Mommy made us
special Ooh and Aah's Wrap 'Em Ups." She could barely
contain her excitement. "I'm having them for my birthday
party."

"Who are Ooh and Aah?" Helen asked. "And why are
they rapping?"

"You've been neglecting your Disney Channel," Kathy
said. "Ooh and Aah are two monkeys. The Wrap 'Em Ups
are chicken-lettuce wraps—sandwiches, not singers."

Allison collapsed into giggles at this news. "Singers!" she
said. "They're not singers. We're having Monkey Face salads, too."

Helen raised an eyebrow.

"That's fruit salad," Kathy translated. "Allison will drink milk and we'll have grownup jungle juice."

"Made from fermented grapes, I hope," Helen said.

"White grapes," Kathy said.

"Good. Jungle juice contains lots of antioxidants for Aunt Helen."

Helen admired the scenery on her way to Kathy's house. The summer sun had wilted the gardens and burned lawns brown, but St. Louis still looked lush. The last time Helen had been home was for her mother's funeral almost two months ago. It was Phil's first visit to the city, and he'd praised St. Louis's beauty extravagantly. Helen had felt a childish compulsion to defend her adopted state of Florida, as if every boost for St. Louis knocked Fort Lauderdale.

Today, without her husband beside her, Helen could admit to herself that the tree-shaded suburban streets looked cool and inviting. She wondered if she'd disagreed with Phil to convince herself that she didn't want to come back home.

Florida was built yesterday, except for its prehistoric swamps and eternal ocean.

St. Louis was older than the United States. It started as a French trading post in 1767 and grew into a nineteenth-century river and railway hub. Some say the city reached its peak with the 1904 World's Fair. There was even talk of moving the U.S. capital to St. Louis. That went nowhere, as so many of the city's grand plans would, but mansions and generous homes from its glory period survive. They wear their age well. St. Louis's older homes promise stability, though like all white elephants, they can be a burden as well as an honor for their owners.

Kathy and Tom's two-story home had stained-glass windows and a gingerbread porch. "That's our house!" Allison shouted. "Daddy burned the paint off the porch. He's going to make it white and pretty."

"Daddy better hurry," Kathy told Helen. "Winter is on the way. Tom will freeze his tail off soon, even working with a blowtorch."

My sister had a nearly perfect life, right down to the

white picket fence covered with rambler roses, Helen thought. Until Rob and I ruined it. Another guilt boulder was piled on top of her lies to Phil.

Kathy helped her daughter out of her car seat, and they gathered in the comfortable kitchen with the rooster wall clock. "Is it lunchtime? I get lunch with Aunt Helen," Allison shrieked. "You said so. Ooh and Aah Wrap 'Em Ups!"

Helen winced. The little girl had a loud, shrill voice.

"Allison, what did I tell you about using your indoor voice?" Kathy said. "Go wash your hands while I heat up our lunch."

The lettuce wraps were made with ground chicken, mushrooms, soy sauce, onions, garlic and mint on tender butter lettuce. They tasted deliciously grown-up. Allison was proud of her Monkey Face salads.

"I made them myself," she said. "Mommy cut up the fruit." Helen admired the salads—thick rounds of sliced pineapple with blueberry eyes, raisin noses, strawberry mouths and kiwi ears.

After lunch, Kathy sent Allison upstairs to her bedroom to watch *Goodnight Moon* on her mini DVD player.

"I'm not sleepy," Allison protested. Her lower lip quivered.

"You don't have to take a nap," Kathy said. "Just watch one movie while I talk to Aunt Helen; then you can come downstairs."

After Allison was settled in her room, Kathy said, "If I tell her she doesn't have to take a nap, she'll be out cold in ten minutes." She poured Helen a second glass of wine, then brought out a bag of Pepperidge Farm Milano cookies. "Coffee?"

"No thanks. I'll stick with jungle juice," Helen said. "Tell me where you have to deliver the money tonight at nine o'clock."

"On top of the Dumpster in the abandoned strip mall on Manchester," Kathy said. "The one where we threw away the stuff after we buried Rob. I can't believe I just said that sentence. I'm a suburban mom."

"If you want to stay one," Helen said, "we have to find this creep. Do you think he followed us there?"

"I thought we were careful to make sure no one followed us," Kathy said. "After he called yesterday, I drove around the strip mall again. There's a little cafe across the street, Jackie's Fine Eats. Maybe he parked there and watched us. You can see the Dumpster from the cafe window."

"I'll go there tonight and watch for him," Helen said. "I'll settle in at seven o'clock and drink coffee."

"That will work," Kathy said. "Jackie's cafe closes at nine."

"Good," Helen said. "I'll follow him after he picks up the bag."

"How?" Kathy said. "I'll be driving the minivan."

"I'll rent a car," Helen said.

"That's more money," Kathy said.

"What's another hundred or so after ten thousand?" Helen said. Did she just say that?

"Let me call the rental car place on Manchester." Kathy got out the Yellow Pages and dialed her phone.

"The agency has a car, but it's a little small," she reported. "They'll deliver the car here, and they can pick it up tomorrow morning."

"I'll take it," Helen said.

After Kathy hung up, she said, "I wonder if that dirtbag knows you're in town."

"Do you even know if the blackmailer is a man?" Helen asked.

"I don't know what he is," Kathy said. "He uses one of those voice changers. The first time he called, he had a Darth Vader voice. Now he sounds like a little girl. That's even creepier than Darth Vader. But the speech patterns seem the same. He started out with 'Greetings and salutations' like he did the first time. He said he saw Tommy—"

"Did he use names?" Helen said.

"Yes, he knew my boy's name, your name, and Rob's name, and he knew that Rob was your ex-husband. He called on our landline."

"So he knows I was your divorced sister in town for a visit," Helen said, "but he doesn't know you well enough to have your cell phone number. That tells us something."

"Not much. Our number is in the phone book. The whole neighborhood knows you're divorced," Kathy said. "You know how upset Mom was when you dumped Rob. She used to buttonhole people at church and talk about the shame of having a divorced daughter. Most of those people wouldn't have my cell phone number, either."

"Someone saw what actually happened, though," Helen said. "He had to, if he knew Tommy hit Rob with his bat."

"His aluminum bat," Kathy said. "He even knew the kind of bat."

"Your neighbors can look right in your backyard," Helen said. "You're surrounded by houses."

"Old Mrs. Kiley lives next door," Kathy said. "She's about ninety, but she goes to bed right after dinner. The Kerchers were on vacation in August, and no one was home at their house. The Cooks live on the west side, but their view is blocked by our house and that big tree."

"Well, somebody saw us," Helen said. "Which one of your neighbors needs money?"

"They all do," Kathy said. "Do you know what it costs to heat these places? The only person we can eliminate is Horndog Hal."

"The guy who was supposed to be at choir practice, but he was tuning up his girlfriend in his SUV on the church lot," Helen said. "His SUV was parked there when we dug the grave in the church hall basement. He still having an affair with Mrs. Snyder?"

"Mrs. Snyder's husband found out and beat Hal silly. I doubt he'll be able to stray for some time if his bruises are any indication. He's been walking very slowly, so I don't think all the damage was to his face. Hal says he tripped over his kid's tricycle."

They heard the sound of cars in front of Kathy's house. She peeked out the window and said, "There's your car now and the rental company's van."

Helen watched the lanky driver extract himself from the

green Neon one limb at a time. She ran out with her license and credit card and signed the paperwork, and the van took him back to the office.

"They weren't kidding when they said your car was small," Kathy said. "Our fridge is bigger."

"It's the right size to get me where I'm going," Helen said. "I need to buy some pepper spray. That blackmailer is going to have some face time he'll never forget."

"There's a sports store about two blocks away," Kathy said. "It sells joggers' self-defense kits with pepper spray on a rope."

"Good," Helen said. "I'll wear it around my neck. Won't have to dig for it in my purse when I spray this guy."

"Helen, what happens if he gets mad and reports you?"

"If he lives in this neighborhood, that blackmailer has as much to lose as we do," Helen said confidently, though she knew that was bravado. "Don't worry. Once he gets that spray in his eyes, he won't be threatening anyone."

"I don't want to leave Allison alone while you shop," Kathy said. "Do you mind driving your car?"

"Two blocks isn't far," Helen said. "I need the walk."

"But you're tired," Kathy said.

"A walk will wake me up," Helen said, striding out the door. The first block seemed unnaturally long. Helen wished she'd taken her car. By the second block—her sister must measure blocks in country miles—Helen was drenched in sweat. The sports store had the pepper spray canister, and Helen wore it home. The walk back was even hotter. The sun punished her like a boxer going for the heavyweight title. Those shade trees must be for show, she thought. They sure aren't making these streets any cooler.

Kathy met her at the door and said, "Helen, what did you do?"

"I walked two blocks," Helen said. "How many miles are in a block here?"

"It isn't that far," Kathy said. "But you are my older sister." Accent on the "older." Kathy gave Helen an irritating smirk. "Maybe you need a nap."

Helen was ticked off. First, Derek at the gym said she

was out of shape; now her sister implied she was old. "I'm not sleepy," she said. "I'm only two years older than you. Is Tommy home? I'd like to see my nephew."

"Albert Pujols is having batting practice in the backyard," Kathy said. "Take a cold glass of water and go watch him."

Helen poured herself a generous glass of white wine instead. She couldn't face the sight of her nephew swinging a bat—or the awful memories of what happened when he hit his uncle Rob—without wine to fortify her.

Tommy would be a big man like his father. At ten, he had a pink sunburned face and straw-colored hair lightened by the sun. His eyes still had their boyish innocence.

"I get to use a real wooden bat and baseball when I play in the park," Tommy told her. "I still have to use an aluminum bat and those stupid foam baseballs in the yard. Mom is worried about the neighbors' windows."

Helen eyed the windows surrounding the yard and wondered which neighbor was blackmailing them.

Tommy loved having his own audience. Helen pitched, and Tommy did his own color commentary in the time-honored practice of baseball-loving boys.

"He hits! He scores! The crowd goes wild!" he yelled.

Kathy poked her head out of the back door. "It's six thirty, you two. Tom is home and dinner is ready. Helen, you need to leave soon. Come in and wash up, both of you."

Helen gave her brother-in-law, Tom, a warm hello and assured him that everything was fine. It was a pebble of a lie compared to the boulders she was already carrying. Then she kissed her sister good-bye.

"Good luck," Helen whispered. "I'll watch for you from Jackie's Fine Eats."

"I recommend the chicken and dumplings and gooey butter cake," Kathy said.

"How can you even think of food now?"

"I'm scared," Kathy said.

"Don't be," Helen said. "Just drop the bag and go home. Leave the rest to me. We'll get this creep."

CHAPTER 24

"**M**a'am, you have to wake up now," the server said, gently shaking Helen.

Helen sat up, confused. There was a plate with a few crumbs of gooey butter cake on it in front of her. They didn't serve that in Florida.

The confusion was clearing now. She wasn't in Fort Lauderdale. She was in St. Louis. She'd fallen asleep after dinner at Jackie's Fine Eats.

"Oh my God. What was I doing?" Helen moved her hand and slopped coffee on the table.

"You fell asleep." The server had kind eyes, a turquoise uniform and a name tag that read MAGGIE.

"What time is it?"

"Four minutes after nine, ma'am." Maggie blotted Helen's spilled coffee with a napkin. "We close at nine o'clock. You looked so tired I didn't have the heart to wake you, but now we have to lock up."

Maggie was as thin as her no-color hair. Helen saw the cafe's chairs were seat-down on the empty tables and a busboy was mopping the floor.

The fog of exhaustion, travel strain and wine was

clearing. Helen had eaten her chicken and dumplings, then ordered dessert and coffee. She'd watched the Dumpster in the deserted strip mall across the street. She must have fallen asleep before she finished the coffee.

She was awake now. In the dim light of the streetlamps, Helen could make out a pale mound on top of the Dumpster. The ten thousand dollars was in place. No sign of her sister's minivan. Helen had slept through Kathy's money drop.

Luck was with her. The blackmailer hadn't arrived yet to pick up the money. Helen had to leave now. She had to be in her car when the crook took the money.

"What do I owe you?" Helen asked.

"The chicken special comes to $12.32 with the cake and coffee," Maggie said. Her fat-free frame showed she didn't indulge in gooey butter cake. Helen thought the cake was worth a few calories. Okay, more than a few. She remembered her mother's recipe. A single coffee cake in an eight-inch square pan had a whole stick of butter and an entire box of confectioners' sugar.

She glanced at the big clock over the counter. It was six minutes after nine.

Helen saw a dark car pull next to the Dumpster in the deserted strip mall. The blackmailer! She dropped a twenty on the table and searched for her car keys.

"Your keys are on the windowsill," Maggie said. "I'll get your change."

"Keep it," Helen said, her eyes still on the blackmailer's car. She watched a hand snake out of the driver's window, and the reusable Schnucks bag was gone from the Dumpster top. He had the money.

Eight minutes after nine. The blackmailer's car turned onto traffic-clotted Manchester Road. Helen had to catch him. She ran for the cafe door, jumped in the rental Neon and hit her knee on the steering wheel.

Helen cursed, started the engine and pulled the Neon to the edge of the parking lot, ready to dive into the traffic. She couldn't. A fleet of cars rolled down Manchester, blocking any entrance on her side of the street. The blackmailer's car was getting away, blending in with the other cars. She could still see the taillights, but they'd soon disappear.

Then Helen caught a break. She spotted a small opening in the traffic, right in front of a speeding Peterbilt truck with a candy red cab. Helen swung out onto Manchester in front of the tractor-trailer, then floored the Neon. The rental car sat there like a rock. The trucker blasted his horn. The truck's massive grill filled her rearview mirror. Just when Helen thought her life was over, the Neon woke up and chugged down the road.

Helen breathed a sigh of relief. The trucker shot her the bird. She knew she deserved the single-finger salute.

She wasn't sleepy now. Adrenaline arced through her system. Luck was with her. She could see the taillights of the blackmailer's car just over the next rise. Helen put the pedal to the metal, and the little Neon lurched forward.

The blackmailer's car roared through the major intersection at Manchester and Lindbergh. The light turned yellow, but Helen's rental car sailed through, accompanied by a chorus of irate honks.

At the top of a hill, the blackmailer's car signaled and made a right turn into a side street. Helen followed, hoping she could get closer now that they were off the busy main road. She pushed the Neon up to sixty miles an hour on the residential street, but she couldn't catch up to the blackmailer's car.

It stayed tantalizingly within sight. Helen couldn't get close enough to see any details. The make, the model, even the color remained a mystery. Was it black? It should be—the blackmailer should have a car the color of his heart. But it could be dark green, or even midnight blue.

Helen had no idea if a man or a woman was driving, but the blackmailer drove at a steady pace and handled the car well. She could barely make out the top of the blackmailer's head over the headrest. If she went just a little faster, she might catch up to him on the curve.

Helen floored the Neon again, and the little car leaped

forward with a shudder. There was a burst of shrieking sound, and flashing lights strobed through the quiet street. A police car was behind Helen.

She pulled over, and the Neon creaked to a stop, engine pinging. She presented her license and rental car papers to the cop.

"You were going sixty-five in a forty-mile-an-hour zone, ma'am," the officer said.

"I'm sorry, Officer," Helen said. She tried to look contrite. It wasn't difficult. She was truly sorry—that she'd gotten caught.

"I'm here visiting my sister in Webster Groves," Helen said. "I know that's not an excuse, but I was hurrying home. I'm supposed to watch her kids."

"So you endangered the lives of other families with your reckless driving?"

"I'm sorry," Helen repeated.

"When do you go home to Florida?"

"Tomorrow," Helen said.

"Drive slowly to your sister's house," the officer said. "I'm going to let you go with a warning."

"Yes," Helen said. "I will."

Damn, the blackmailer got away, Helen thought. This traffic stop just cost me ten thousand dollars.

"Ma'am?" the officer said.

"Yes, sir?"

"Most people say thank you when they don't get a ticket. I did you a favor."

CHAPTER 25

. . . .

"He got away," Helen said, limping through her sister's back door at ten o'clock.

"How?" She could see the worry in Kathy's eyes. Her sister would be a little grayer after this visit, thanks to Helen's mistakes.

"I fell asleep at the diner."

Helen had tried on various lies as she drove slowly home after her encounter with the traffic cop. They all sounded like fabrications. She decided to follow the timeworn advice: Always tell the truth—there's less to remember. Helen couldn't stomach one more lie right now, though she expected she'd go back to her regular diet of deceit when she returned home.

Kathy did not take the truth well. She shouted. It was a whispered shout—Kathy never forgot she had two children asleep upstairs—but it was forceful.

"You fell asleep! I told—" Kathy put the brakes on her anger, stopped abruptly, backed up, then said in a milder tone, "I told myself you were too tired to be watching for anyone. I should have made you take a nap. I should—"

"This is my fault," Helen said. "Thank you for not saying 'I told you so.'"

"I wouldn't say that."

"No, but you thought it," Helen said. "This is my mistake. It's been one long mistake since the day I said yes to Rob. You warned me not to marry him, but I was hell-bent to walk down that aisle. Hell-bent is the only way to describe that marriage." She sat down wearily in the kitchen chair and put her head in her hands.

Kathy hugged her sister and asked, "What can I get you? Coffee? Water? Wine? More food?"

"Nothing," Helen said. "I wanted to tell you about my failure before I went to bed."

Kathy sat down next to Helen and asked, "Was the night a total loss? Did you learn anything?"

"The driver is definitely not your ninety-year-old neighbor, Mrs. Kiley," Helen said.

"Then you saw him," Kathy said.

Helen heard the newborn hope in her sister's voice and killed it. "No. I couldn't tell you if the driver was a man or a woman, or if their hair was white or coal black. But I live in South Florida, and that makes me an expert on elderly drivers. No one as old as Mrs. Kiley could have driven so fast or so smoothly. The blackmailer had night vision and good reflexes."

"Well, that's something," Kathy said.

"I paid dearly for that knowledge," Helen said. "It's not worth ten thousand dollars."

"What are we going to do?" Kathy asked. "Do you think he'll want more money? What will happen to my poor Tommy if this gets out?"

Kathy wept soundlessly, tears running down her face and dripping on the tabletop. She didn't bother wiping them away. Those silent, hopeless tears tore Helen's heart. She wanted to reassure her sister that the blackmailer would go away. But Helen knew better, and so did Kathy. A comfortable lie wouldn't help them. If they were going to save Tommy, they had to face facts.

"Yes," Helen said. "That SOB will definitely call again."

She reached for a paper napkin from the holder on the kitchen table and wiped away her little sister's tears.

"He's doubled the amount with each demand," Kathy said.

"It's only been two payments so far," Helen said.

"First five thousand, then ten thousand. You've paid fifteen thousand dollars in less than two months." Kathy's voice was rising again. "At that rate, he'll go through your savings and my kids' college fund in a year or so. How are we going to stop him?"

"We'll catch him next time," Helen said. "We have no choice. I'm supposed to be a detective. I should have known better. That kind of surveillance takes two cars."

"So you're going to tell Phil after all," Kathy said. Anger and betrayal flattened her voice.

"No, I'll keep my promise to you," Helen said. "I don't like lying to Phil. It may cost me my marriage. But I'll make that sacrifice for Tommy Junior. The new generation comes first. My Phil is like your Tom. He'll go trustingly to the police and destroy both our families. I don't believe the police or the courts will do the right thing, and I have the personal experience to prove it.

"We still need two drivers, but next time, you're going to drive a second tail car. You'll make the drop, park your van in a side street, then get into the second car. I'll rent another car and park it nearby. Then we'll both tail him. We're going to show this dirtbag that sisterhood is powerful."

"I wish you'd said he wouldn't call again," Kathy said. "You're telling me what I need to hear, not what I want to hear. I'll jump every time my phone rings from now on."

"You'll have to live with that," Helen said, "the way I live with my lies to Phil."

"And my lies to Tom," Kathy said. "I used to worry that we didn't have enough money and wish we both didn't have to work so hard to make ends meet. Now I'd do anything to return to those days."

"At least the blackmailer lost the power to surprise you anymore," Helen said. "We've gained that much. Next time he calls, see if you can stall him another day."

"Helen, what were you going to do if you caught the blackmailer?" Kathy asked. "Did you have any kind of plan?"

Helen didn't, but she wasn't going to say so. She had to protect her older-sister status as the sophisticated, worldly one. "If you'd seen someone burying a body in a church basement, what would you do? I mean, before we got involved in this mess?"

"I'd call the police, of course," Kathy said.

"So why didn't our blackmailer call them?"

Kathy shrugged.

"Because he—or she—has something to hide," Helen said. "If Horndog Hal was the blackmailer, he couldn't call the cops because he was running around on his wife. He'd have to tell them why he was in that parking lot instead of at choir practice."

"Maybe it's someone who needs money," Kathy said. "Their kid needs braces, or they're starting a college fund."

"They wouldn't risk blackmail charges for legitimate expenses," Helen said. "Every parent in your neighborhood needs that kind of money. They can borrow it or get it from their families. Look out your kitchen window."

Kathy dutifully went to the window and pulled back the print curtains. The moon shone on the quiet old houses. Helen heard the faint sound of a distant television. The leaves rustled.

"You're surrounded by solid citizens," she said, "but one of them has something to hide."

"Then the blackmailers are the Cooks on the west side," Kathy said. "The Kerchers were on vacation then, and it couldn't be Mrs. Kiley."

"Did the Kerchers have a house sitter while they were gone?" Helen asked.

"No. But they hired someone to come by and take care of the dog," Kathy said.

"Mrs. Kiley lives alone, right?" Helen said. "Does Mrs. Kiley ever have anyone over?"

"Her son comes once a week to do her yard work, and her daughter checks on her every day. She cooks dinner for her college-age grandson. I think she went to bed early that night. But I don't know for sure."

"We weren't exactly able to check who was coming in and out of her house," Helen said. "We've broadened our suspect list. Our blackmailer is someone who doesn't want police attention. He—"

"Or she," Kathy added.

"Right. The blackmailer is sneaking around on a spouse, embezzling money, maybe running up gambling debts. Could be they're sick of their life and getting money together to leave here and live in Tahiti. For whatever reason, they want to stay under the official radar."

"It's a good theory," Kathy said. "But I don't know how it can help us."

"Keep an eye on your neighbors," Helen said. "Keep an ear out for gossip. If you find out anything useful, let me know."

Helen thought she'd done a good job of cobbling together a blackmail plan on the spur of the moment. She glanced at the cheerful rooster clock on the kitchen wall, crowing over this gruesome discussion of murder, blackmail and secret burial. "It's after midnight. I need some sleep. I have to see the lawyer tomorrow."

She tried to reassure her little sister. "We'll get him," she said in a forced, bright voice. "We'll make him stop. We have no choice." Her smile slipped, and she went wearily to bed.

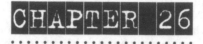

CHAPTER 26

. . . .

"How did the interview with your lawyer go?" Kathy asked as Helen jumped into the waiting minivan outside Drake Upton's office in downtown Clayton.

"I need to get to a bank, quick!" Helen said.

"Is there an emergency?" Kathy didn't wait for Helen to answer. The minivan charged into the suburb's concrete canyons, threading the maze of streets.

"Not yet," Helen said. "I'm trying to prevent a problem. I have one bit of good news: Drake said that ten-thousand-dollar withdrawal I made probably won't be reported to the IRS if I don't do it again. Banks are required to report ten-thousand-dollar withdrawals, but if it only happens once, they tend to forget to report it."

"You told him about the money!" Kathy said. She slammed on the brakes at a red light.

Helen braced herself, and her seatbelt snapped. "He's a lawyer. He's sworn to confidentiality."

"Did you tell him why you needed that ten thousand dollars?" Kathy couldn't keep a quaver of fear from her voice.

"I said an old Florida boyfriend has some embarrassing photos of me in bed with him. Drake knows I'm newly married. I said I didn't want Phil to find out, so I was going to pay the blackmailer to go away."

"Helen! How could you do that to yourself?" Kathy asked.

"Better me than Tommy Junior," Helen said. "Drake turned so red, even his patrician dome was scarlet. He's a Harvard man, so maybe I should say his head was crimson."

"Be serious!" Kathy said. "What did the lawyer say?"

"Drake said I should go to the police with my problem and they would be sympathetic. I explained why that wouldn't work. I said my new husband was a private eye and knew the local police. Phil would find out about the photographs.

"Drake fluffed himself up like a hen and said he would never suggest ignoring the laws of the land, but if he had a similar problem, he'd open a second bank account. Then he'd take the money out of the two accounts in five-thousand-dollar increments."

"Do you think any risqué photos of Drake Upton ever made the rounds?" Kathy asked.

Helen laughed. "Not a chance. Drake is too stuffy. That man wore a club tie with his bib."

"You'd be surprised what the quiet ones do," Kathy said. "I had a supervisor like that when I worked in an office, before I married Tom. Mr. Graham was the dullest, quietest man I ever met—a stuffed shirt. His wife found out he had a mistress in San Francisco. He took a business trip there. His wife was supposed to join him on the weekend, but she showed up early and surprised him in bed with his honey. He lost everything in the divorce, including that shirt."

"I wonder if Drake Upton wears his black executive-length socks when he's in the sack," Helen said.

"Stop it," Kathy begged. "St. Louis is a big small town. I've met that man. What if I run into him again? I won't be able to look him in the face."

"So stare at his shoes," Helen said.

"I'm going to have to wash my mind out with soap,"

Kathy said. "My brain is seared by thoughts of Drake Upton cavorting between the sheets."

Kathy giggled. Helen snorted. The two sisters burst into hysterical laughter, then guffawed until they had tears in their eyes. "Enough," Kathy said. "We're at Highway 40. Which bank do you want to go to?"

"Your bank," Helen said. "I want to open a savings account there with half of my three hundred thousand."

"That much?" Kathy said.

"I hope we don't have to make another blackmail payment," Helen said, "but I want the money ready when he strikes again. You'll be co-owner of the account, with your name on the signature card."

"You said you'd come to St. Louis the next time he calls," Kathy said. Helen saw her little sister's lip tremble.

"You look like Allison being sent upstairs for a nap," Helen said. "I will, Sis. I'll come home like I promised. But Phil and I have our private-eye business now. I may not be able to get back to St. Louis immediately if we're working a case together. This is just a precaution if I can't drop everything and fly to St. Louis. That way you can take the money out yourself."

"I don't want to," Kathy said.

"Of course you don't," Helen soothed. "But we have to plan ahead."

Kathy wasn't soothed at all. Helen tried to distract her. "Where is my favorite niece?"

"It's nap time," Kathy said. "I asked Mrs. Kiley to watch her. We're lucky we live next to an older woman who loves kids. We have a better television, so Mrs. Kiley watches her soaps at our place and gets paid a little. Here's my bank."

The cube was just as beige as it had been yesterday, and the rectangle of grass in front was still bright green. Helen opened a savings account with Kathy as co-owner.

"Will this account show up on my taxes?" Kathy asked the bank clerk.

"The taxes are paid by the first Social Security number on the account," the clerk said. Helen thought Kathy looked relieved.

Helen transferred $150,000 from her old St. Louis bank to the new account.

When the sisters left the bank, Helen checked her watch and said, "It's about time for me to get to the airport."

"I thought it would be," Kathy said. "Your suitcase is stowed in the back of the van."

The highway to the airport was lined with signs advertising the local casinos.

"You and Tom ever go to the casinos?" Helen asked.

"That's one vice we've managed to avoid," Kathy said. "Locals get sucked into the casino life way too easy. Ruth at our church has a daughter who gambled away her home. Lost the mortgage payments at the casino. The daughter handled the family finances. Her husband didn't know what was happening until he saw the foreclosure notice. By then it was too late."

"I read where St. Louis is the sixth-biggest casino-gambling destination," Helen said. "This city is ahead of Tunica, Mississippi, and Reno, Nevada. Nobody thinks of it that way."

"We pretend the casinos don't exist," Kathy said, "until a family member develops a gambling problem."

"That strengthens my theory that our blackmailer ran up a big debt," Helen said. "Start listening for clues that one of your neighbors likes to hit the casinos."

"Why would they talk about gambling if they're in trouble?" Kathy said.

"They might say they went to the casino for brunch or to see a show," Helen said.

The long shadow of a jet slid over the roadway. "We're almost at the airport," Kathy said. "Did your lawyer have any word about your IRS case?"

"No progress yet," Helen said. "Drake wants to set up a meeting with them. He says the IRS wants me to pay taxes, not overwhelm me with penalties. I hope he's right."

Kathy pulled the minivan in front of the airport terminal.

"I can't believe we're at the airport already. It seems like I just got here," Helen said.

"You did," Kathy said, handing Helen her suitcase. She kissed her sister good-bye and said, "Beautiful, clear sky. Not a cloud anywhere. It should be an easy flight home."

It was. Helen's plane touched down at the Fort Lauderdale airport fifteen minutes early. Phil was waiting at the gate. Helen ran to him, suitcase bumping over the colorful carpet.

"I missed you," she said, throwing her arms around him.

They exchanged light kisses and conversation on the way to the parking garage. While travelers rushed past them, Helen told her husband about Kathy and Tom and her niece and nephew. She waited until the parking garage door was in sight, then mentioned that her lawyer was planning to set up a meeting with the IRS. They pushed through the air lock into the evening heat. Phil didn't ask any more questions about Helen's tax problems. "Your manager called this morning," he said. "Derek wants you to report to the gym tomorrow."

Helen sighed. "I knew it was coming. I have to work on Shelby's case."

The soft, salt-tinged Florida humidity felt like a welcome caress to Helen. "I think it's cooler here than in St. Louis," she said.

"I drove the Igloo," Phil said. "Thought you'd appreciate the cool air."

Inside the PT Cruiser, Phil gave her a deeper kiss, then stopped.

"What's wrong?" Helen said.

"We have to work tonight," he said. "Mark Behr's old friend Danny Boy Cerventi will be tending bar at Granddaddy's. I've been there enough that I'm becoming a regular. Danny starts drinking most afternoons, and he's pretty bombed by evening. I thought we could sit at the bar, have a burger and a beer, maybe talk about old times."

"I'm always willing to eat a burger in the line of duty," Helen said solemnly.

"This time order your own fries," Phil said.

"Let's go there now," Helen said.

"Can't. You need to go home and change. Granddaddy's

is a bit of a dive," Phil said. "You're too well dressed. Ditch the pantsuit for jeans."

"With pleasure," Helen said.

It was Helen's favorite time of day, when the setting sun stained the subtropical sky a delicious pink. The icy white Coronado apartments turned a soft peach and the palm trees cast long blue shadows. Margery was waiting in one of those shadows, wrapped in cigarette smoke.

"Hey, gumshoes," she hissed.

"Huh?" Phil said.

"Got the drop on you," Margery said. "There's a dame out by the pool waiting to see two shamuses."

"Shelby?" Helen asked.

"That's her," Margery said. "She's here for the dope, if you get my drift." She blew a cloud of smoke at Phil and Helen.

Margery dropped the forties talk and led them to the pool. Shelby was dressed for work Florida style—a yellow summer dress and heeled sandals—and chatting with Peggy. Pete watched their client. Helen thought the parrot had a skeptical look.

Shelby smiled and waved when she saw Helen and Phil. "Thought I'd better stop by," she said. "You haven't been returning my calls. You two been busy with my case? I want to know how the investigation is going."

"Pete and I better turn in for the night," Peggy said, getting up from her chair.

"Bye!" Pete said. Margery had melted into the shadows.

"I've seen Bryan every day the gym has been open," Helen said. "He usually works out four to six hours a day. He was at the gym at six o'clock the morning Debbi was murdered, but the police wouldn't let anyone inside. Bryan spends a lot of time with his trainer, Jan Kurtz, but their relationship is professional. There's no one else he's interested in."

"There is," Shelby said. Helen thought she saw tears sparkling in their client's eyes. "He's been restless as a caged cat since the gym closed. He wanted to show houses this afternoon but said he didn't have time to clean his car because he had to go running. I said I'd take his car in to be washed.

"I found an open condom wrapper under the front seat. I'm on the pill. Why would a married man need a condom?"

"Maybe it fell out of a client's pocket," Helen said.

"I don't think so," Shelby said. "He's up to no good. I know it. I hate being a fool. You wouldn't understand."

"You'd be surprised," Helen said.

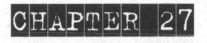

CHAPTER 27

Helen walked into Granddaddy's Bar and stopped dead. Phil ran into her back.

"What's wrong?" he whispered. There was no need for him to lower his voice. The customers were screaming at the Marlins game on the three big TV screens. Cries of "Yeah!," "Go, go, go!" and "Boo-yah!" drowned out everything, including the game's announcer.

"This is like walking into that video of Mark's birthday party," Helen said, "except the bar is a quarter century grimier. I think these are the same people, too, just older."

The men definitely had useful jobs in an area better known for beach bums. Sitting at the long, dark-wood bar (also jumping up and down, cheering and twirling) were mechanics, cable-company workers and hurricane-shutter installers, all holding beers. Helen knew their occupations by the trucks parked in the lot and the uniforms on their backs.

The rest of the customers wore T-shirts, mostly Marlins shirts.

The neon palm tree was still on the wall, but one side flickered. Helen thought the booze brands had gone down a notch since the 1986 video. There were no fancy blender drinks on the menu board. Helen was one of the few women in the bar. Even in jeans and a shirt, she was the best-dressed woman. Granddaddy's was no longer a place to bring a date.

Danny Boy Cerventi was behind the bar. With his drinker's potbelly and scrawny arms and legs, he looked like a spider with a bad haircut.

"Danny Boy looks about the same," Phil said. "His hair is just as black."

"It's dyed," Helen said. "I can see that across the room."

She and Phil gently pushed their way through the beery, cheering crowd. Helen found an empty barstool by the register, Phil stood behind it. Helen could see Danny Boy's bloodshot eyes and the road map of red veins on his nose. He wiped his hands on his dirty apron and said, "You brought the old ball and chain tonight, Phil."

Helen ground her teeth at that remark but remembered they were here on a case. Once they found Mark's murderer, she'd never have to go to this dump again.

"I've been telling Helen your burgers and fries are the best in Lauderdale," Phil said. "She wanted to see for herself."

Danny Boy grinned, revealing stained, ratlike teeth. "Is that what you're both having—burgers and fries?"

"Medium rare for Helen and walk it through a warm kitchen for me," Phil said. "Two orders of the fries and two beers." Helen nodded. Beer wasn't her first choice, but she knew better than to order white wine in a dive.

She was surprised by the photo of Mark Behr on the wall next to the cash register. That was him, wasn't it? She leaned in for a closer look. Time hadn't faded that glorious fiery hair. It was definitely Mark, raising a frosty mug of beer in a smiling toast.

Another picture in a heavy oval frame hung above the register, a brownish photo of an old man with a black handlebar mustache.

When Danny Boy returned with their food, Helen said, "Is that your grandfather up there on the wall?"

"Sure is," Danny Boy said. "Bought this bar with the money Granddaddy left me in his will. That's how the bar got its name. I keep his picture here to honor him." Helen heard him slur "picture" as "pick-shure."

"He has a terrific face," Helen said. "Makes you want to order a beer."

"Good idea," Phil said. "I'll have another beer. What about you, Helen?"

"I'd better switch to club soda," she said. "I have to work in the morning."

"Work," Danny Boy said, "the curse of the drinking class." He laughed uproariously at his own joke, as if he'd just heard it for the first time.

"I hate to drink alone," Phil said. "Can I buy you a Heineken, Danny Boy?"

"Don't mind if you do," Danny said. "I like a little Heinie." He leered at Helen and spritzed soda water into a glass for her, then filled two frosted mugs with draft beer. He moved with the slow, precise movements of a longtime drunk. He slid one beer toward Phil.

"Perfect draw," Phil said, holding up his mug and admiring the golden brew. "Not too much foam on that beer."

"I've had some practice," Danny said, and winked at Helen. He gulped down the beer, then drew himself another. His hand slipped on the tap handle. The beer was getting to him. Helen hoped he'd be drunk enough to answer their questions.

"Who is that handsome man in the photo next to the cash register?" she asked.

The smile slid off Danny Boy's face. "An old friend," he said. "Mark Behr. That photo was taken at his thirtieth birthday party. He had one hell of a party here that night. I still have the video to prove it. He's dead now, poor bastard."

"Was he an actor?" Helen asked.

"No. Mark was good-looking enough to be one. He was a mechanic, believe it or not."

"He could definitely drive my car," Helen said, and grinned at Danny Boy.

Phil frowned. He didn't like Helen flirting with the drunken bartender. Too bad, she thought. We're on a case.

"Mark drove a lot of ladies wild," Danny Boy said. "He used to hang out here at Granddaddy's. It's sort of our clubhouse, except they pay me for the beer."

Danny Boy laughed hard again—too hard—then turned serious. "I got outta high school, but I never left high school. I don't need a reunion. My friends are here 'most every night. That bald guy there in the gray shirt? That's Bobby. He used to be a plumber. Damn good one, too, until the economy tanked and he lost his job. Now he's my day bartender. Hey, Bobby!" he yelled over the boozy crowd.

Bobby was sitting two seats down at the bar. He raised his beer in Danny Boy's direction, then went back to watching the game, his arm draped around a bottle blonde on the stool next to him.

"Jack there with the marines tattoo works for the phone company," Danny Boy said. "I like him anyway. Hate the phone company, though. Hell, Jack hates it, too, but he won't admit it.

"See the guy in the khaki uniform at the end of the bar? That's Tom, another old friend. Tom still has all his hair; it's just grayer. He installs hurricane shutters. I got lots more friends, but those are the only ones here now. South Florida's not known for what you'd call a work ethic, but these guys break their butts all day. They come here to unwind."

Except for Bobby, Helen thought, who stays here after work.

"Did you always want to own a bar?" Helen asked.

"Me?" His hard, harsh laugh had a sorrowful sound. "Old Danny Boy here was gonna be a filmmaker. Not a moviemaker, nothing common like that. I was going to be an artiste." He crooked a pinkie in a mincing gesture. "Danny Boy was going to win awards at Sundance. I had that kind of talent. I'd make films with messages. You know what they say in Hollywood: If you wanna send a message, get Western Union. Wonder if they still say that. Do people even know what Western Union is, except for old farts like me?"

Danny looked lost for a moment. Sweat rolled off his

forehead, and his badly dyed hair stuck to his scalp. He poured another beer with shaking hands and took two deep drinks. Danny put down the nearly empty mug and asked Helen, "Know what happened to my film career? I work three afternoons a week before the bar opens for a video-duplication service, dubbing wedding and anniversary tapes onto DVDs. If I hear 'Proud Mary' one more time, I swear I'll machine-gun the whole wedding party.

"That's my big film job. I don't get any Sundance awards for my work. Mostly I hang out here, drinking beer with my friends, killing time until it kills me. Turns out my career as an artiste peaked the night of Mark's birthday party. That's the last movie I ever made. The last picture show for me and Mark both." Danny gave a high-pitched giggle.

"What happened to Mark?" Helen asked.

Danny looked like he'd been punched. "Sad case, Mark." He shook his head. "He was the best and brightest of us, and he put a bullet in his brain. Shot himself in the head. Just as well, I guess. If he lived, he'd be as old, fat and fucked as the rest of us. We're all fifty-five now, and none of us are what you'd call beauties."

"Hey," Bobby yelled. "Speak for yourself. I look pretty damn fine, and Tiffany here thinks so, too."

Tiffany had bright yellow hair, short shorts that exposed veiny legs, and a tube top that showed a flabby cleavage. She giggled girlishly, and Bobby patted her double-wide rear end.

Helen saw a flash of movement in a back doorway and whispered to Phil, "I need the restroom. I'll be right back."

Danny didn't even notice that she'd left.

Helen recognized the doorway. Mark's last birthday cake had been carried through it by the sequined, shoulder-padded woman in the old video. The doorway opened onto a short, dark hall ending in a back room. The restrooms were in the hall. Helen thought she saw someone she knew in that room. She used the restroom, then peeked in the back room. The small room seemed even more crowded because of the hulking customers crammed in it. They looked like bodybuilders.

Helen recognized Tansi from Fantastic Fitness. Her bright green sweats made her look like the Geico gecko. The lizardlike bodybuilder was talking to an iron pumper the size of a furnace. Helen didn't see anyone drinking anything.

Bobby the day bartender blocked her way into the room.

"May I help you?" he asked. His tone was not friendly.

"I thought I recognized someone back there," she said. Tansi didn't look up.

"I'm sure you didn't," Bobby said. He escorted Helen back to the bar, then took a seat next to his date, Tiffany.

"Where's Danny Boy?" Helen asked Phil.

"He went for another keg."

"I saw Tansi in the back room," Helen said. "A bunch of bodybuilders are in the back. Bobby steered me away from there."

"Think Bobby's up to something?" Phil asked.

"Definitely," Helen said. "None of those bodybuilders are buying drinks."

"I'm guessing they're buying something else," Phil said.

"I'm back, Phil," Danny announced, lugging an aluminum beer keg. He put it behind the bar and hooked it up to the beer lines. "Damn kegs are getting heavier. Either that, or I'm getting old."

"Not a chance, buddy," Phil said.

"Aw, don't lie," Danny Boy said. "I got a mirror. You know the one good thing about being this old? My sister Linda finally got off my back. She's a bigwig in Sunset Palms government. My sister the big shot. Got her photo taken with Jeb Bush when he was governor. Keeps it in her office. Sis is always after me to be somebody like she is. Too late now."

His face collapsed suddenly. Danny Boy put his head on the bar top. His drunken laughter turned into tears—the harsh, hard sobs that men make. "It's too late for me, and it's too late for Mark.

"Too late," he cried.

"Hey, there," Phil said. "You okay?"

Bobby stood up and lurched behind the bar, his yellow-haired girlfriend following. "He gets like that sometimes," Bobby said. "He'll snap out of it, won't you, Danny?"

Bobby put his arm around Danny Boy and said, "You're tired, Danny. Go home and take a nap. Tiffany and I will watch the bar for you while you rest. You can close out the register in the morning when you feel better."

"Go home," Danny Boy mumbled. "Good idea. I'll go home." He untied his apron and reached under the bar for his keys.

"Give me your car keys. I'll drive you," Phil said.

Danny Boy refused to surrender them. "No way," he said. "I'm in charge here. I'm giving myself the night off. Bobby said it was okay."

Phil tried to wrestle the keys away from Danny Boy, but Bobby stopped him. "He drives home like that every night," Bobby said. "He only lives two blocks away. He can't get into any trouble in that little distance."

Helen and Phil watched Danny Boy crunch his way across the gravel parking lot toward a beat-up pickup, crying drunkenly, "Too late. Too late. It's all too late."

CHAPTER 28

H elen counted sixteen people lined up outside Fantastic Fitness at five thirty the morning it reopened after Helen found Debbi Dhosset's body. Sixteen surly people, judging by their body language.

Helen shivered at that chilling memory, though the thick air felt like lukewarm soup. She'd parked the Igloo near a white Crown Victoria that screamed "unmarked police car."

Was Homicide Detective Evarts Redding on the scene? She might need him if the crowd turned unruly.

Bullet Head, the club member who'd slammed his fist against the door five days ago, planted himself in her path. His beefy sidekick blocked the rest of the sidewalk. The pair made Helen walk around them. She noted with satisfaction that the knuckles on Bullet Head's right hand were scabbed.

The gym blazed with light. Odd. Usually the lights weren't on inside until Fantastic Fitness opened. Bullet Head and his friend crowded behind her as she unlocked the front door and punched in the access code.

They started to push inside, but Detective Ever Ready confronted them at the door. "Back up," he said. "Gym doesn't open for another half hour."

Bullet Head and his pal stopped shoving but didn't move.

"I said back up," Ever Ready said, "or I'll slap the cuffs on you. Give the cleaners room to leave."

Five brown-skinned men and women in navy uniforms, clutching buckets and mops, hurried to a pale van. Helen slipped in after the cleaners, and the detective locked the door.

"You're here early," Helen said.

"I've been waiting to talk to you," Ever Ready said. "Sit down in that cubicle." It was not a friendly invitation.

Helen sat. The desk was polished and the room smelled of lemon wax. Helen didn't see any of the fingerprint powder the crime scene workers had been using the day she discovered Debbi. The suffocatingly clean room could barely contain Helen, plus Ever Ready's pillowy gut and towering outrage.

"I asked you for Evie Roddick's address," he said. "I'm still trying to get hold of her. I can't find her. Her husband says he hasn't heard from her, either."

"I thought he said she moved out," Helen said.

"He did, but one little lady doesn't disappear off the face of the earth."

"Maybe she's in danger," Helen offered.

"Maybe *she's* the danger," Ever Ready said. "Maybe Evie Roddick wanted to kill Miss Dhosset."

"Evie couldn't hurt anyone," Helen said. "She's too small."

"Exactly why she'd want the victim dead. She's small and sneaky. Evie Roddick didn't need muscles to kill Miss Dhosset. The medical examiner says the victim died of a fatal overdose of steroids, oxycodone and fat burners."

"So Debbi's death was an accident. Or suicide," Helen said hopefully. "Suicide would make the most sense. She was upset when she couldn't compete in the bodybuilding contest."

"Bull," Ever Ready said. "Miss Dhosset was in her twenties. Plenty of time to compete again."

Debbi had said the same thing, Helen thought. Am I actually agreeing with him? Not for long.

"Evie Roddick murdered her," the detective continued. "The fact that she ran away after Miss Dhosset died tells me your Evie killed her."

My Evie? Helen wondered. How did Evie get to be mine? "I haven't seen Evie since I left the gym."

"Exactly," Ever Ready said, as if she'd proved his point.

"We don't live near each other," Helen said. "I've never seen Evie anywhere but at Fantastic Fitness."

"Then you call me, missy, the minute Evie Roddick shows her face here again. She's guilty. I know it. And I know you and that manager, Deter—"

"Derek," Helen corrected.

"Whatever his name is. You're covering up for her. Find her, or I'll lock you both up."

He marched out of the cubicle, massive gut vibrating with each step. It wasn't six in the morning yet, but Helen was shaken by the homicide detective's threats. He seemed determined to railroad Evie, and if he couldn't get Evie, he'd go after Helen and Derek.

The righteously ripped Derek was waiting for Helen at the reception desk. The early-morning light gilded his muscles.

"Is Detective Redding gone?" Helen asked.

"At last," Derek said and sighed. "He said he wanted to give you what he called 'a piece of his mind.' That man doesn't have any pieces to spare. He's after your hide."

"Yours, too," Helen said.

"I know it," Derek said. "He made that clear. Be glad you weren't here these last few days. He terrorized the staff and the customers."

"I thought the gym was closed," Helen said.

"He tracked the customers down at their homes and offices," Derek said. "He made the staff come in for questioning. I'll be lucky if we don't lose all our staff and our members by the time his investigation is over."

His coffee skin had a gray tinge. Derek looked weary. "He let me bring the cleaning crew in at midnight last night. They just finished."

"Place looks good," Helen said. "You got the broken glass repaired in the weight room, too."

Derek looked uncomfortable. "Helen, before we open, I want to talk to you. You need to work out more if you want to keep this job. Everyone at Fantastic Fitness has to be fit. You look good, don't get me wrong, but you have to take off a pound or two around the middle."

Helen glanced down guiltily at her gut. One piece of gooey butter cake and a couple of fries shouldn't have made that much difference. She conveniently forgot last night's beer, burger and fries.

"I had to make a quick trip home to St. Louis," Helen said. "It's hard to lose weight when you travel."

"I understand, but I need to see results soon. I'll help you work out, okay? End of lecture." Derek flipped on the pounding music. "Turn on the TVs, please."

"Which channel?" Helen asked, then realized it wouldn't make any difference. Debbi, the only person who cared, was dead. Helen turned on CNN. Might as well please the living Heather.

"Battle stations," Derek said. Helen took her place behind the reception desk and pasted on a smile.

The fitness fanatics pushed through the doors, eager to mortify their flesh in fat church. Soon the weights were clanking, the bikes were whirring and the treadmills were turning. Basketballs bounced off the floors and racquetballs off the walls. Watching that rampant energy made Helen feel tired, and her night at Granddaddy's Bar didn't help.

At six ten, Bryan, Shelby's sizzling-hot husband, walked in with "What a Waste" Will. The two men were so deep in conversation that they handed over their cards without a nod to Helen. She checked them in, and they continued their intense conversation all the way to the men's locker room. Their faces were chiseled and their bodies were breathing sculptures.

Those men were too beautiful in a city known for hunks. Was Bryan having an affair with Will? That could be why he left an open condom packet in his car. But everyone knew Will was faithful to his partner. He was just friendly.

How friendly? whispered an ugly little voice. Everyone

finds Will irresistible. Maybe Bryan strayed to the other side of the fence.

"Helen! How have you been?" Carla asked. The brown-eyed receptionist hopped behind the desk and checked the computer. "I'm ready to work. Looks like a full house. How pissed are the members?"

"They'll get over it," Helen said. "Wow. Look at you. Did you spend the last five days at a spa?"

"Hah! That fat, stupid detective put me through the wringer for hours. When I started to cry, he finally sent me home. I spent the rest of the time by the pool, recovering."

The sun gave Carla's tanned skin rosy overtones. Her curly hair snapped with energy. Tight black shorts and a red top showed off her toned figure. I should hate her, Helen thought. She makes me look bad. But Helen couldn't help liking the bubbly Carla.

"Wish I looked that good when old Ever Ready finished with me," she said.

"Are you coming to the East Coast Physique Championships to see Paula compete?" Carla asked. "She's going out for the Women's Bikini competition. The whole gym is going to cheer her. Derek will be there, and Jan, Bryan, Will, me and all Paula's little pets on the treadmills."

"You mean the suckers," Helen said. "I like to watch them try to hold in their guts when she passes."

Carla laughed. "If they worked that hard the rest of the time here, those dudes might actually impress her. We want to show our support for Paula. I have an extra ticket. It's at the Lauderdale City Auditorium. Please come. You'll have a blast."

I can watch Bryan and Will together, Helen thought. Maybe I'll catch them off guard and in each other's arms.

The gym doors parted, and Paula paraded through, a blinding vision in white spandex and shimmering pale hair. She presented her card at the desk.

"Are you wearing that suit for the competition Saturday night?" Helen asked.

"This isn't a competition suit," Paula said. "It's a plain old workout suit. I'm wearing white with crystals. Sparkly suits look better for evening competitions. One more coat of tan and I'm ready to go."

"We'll be there Saturday night to cheer for you," Carla said. "You're going to win."

Out of the corner of her eye, Helen watched the overweight men on the treadmills. Already they were struggling to hold in their guts and making subtle shifts in their gym clothes to look better. Paula strolled by on her way to the women's locker room, blissfully unaware of the havoc she caused to their hearts and abdominal muscles.

The treadmill men had just let their fat flop back when Paula came hurrying out of the locker room. The guys nearly herniated themselves trying to suck their guts back in. Once again, Paula didn't notice.

"Excuse me," she said to Helen and Carla. "We're out of towels in the women's locker room."

"I'll get them," Helen said.

She opened the towel closet, flipped on the light and saw a pale leg hanging out of the overhead vent.

CHAPTER 29

"**N**o!" Helen screamed. "No!"

The body fell out of the overhead duct and landed on a pile of towels. The small, rumpled form of Evie Roddick sat up. She blinked in the bright overhead lights and shook her gray hair.

Helen's high-pitched screams carried over the televisions, the gym equipment, the ball games and the music. Evie didn't seem to hear. She pulled the legs of her gray sweatpants down to her ankles, then dug her socks and gym shoes out from under a pile of towels and put them on.

Helen didn't stop screaming until Evie stood up and brushed off her dust-streaked sweats. "Helen, there's no reason to be upset," Evie said, as if gym members fell out of air ducts all the time. "I'm sorry I scared you, but I'm fine."

"Well, I'm not," Helen said. She flopped down on a stack of white towels as if a puppeteer had cut her strings.

By that time, Derek and Carla were in the doorway of the towel closet.

"Where have you been, Evie?" Derek asked, sounding like an angry parent. "The police have been looking for you."

"Home," Evie said in a small voice.

"Oh, no," Derek said. "Don't lie to me. For the last five days, the police have stopped by your house almost hourly. When the cops weren't at your house, they called and harassed your husband."

"Good!" Evie said. "Peter deserves it."

"Well, I sure as hell don't," Derek said. "We've been trying to find you."

"You have my address," Evie said.

"Not the right one," Derek said. "Quit evading my question."

"I was staying with a friend," Evie said.

"You're lying, Evie. What were you doing in that air duct?"

"I left something in there the other day, before Debbi died. I went back to get it."

"That's why we have lockers," Derek said. "When did you get here?"

"This morning," Evie said. Her eyes shifted. She looked ready to bolt, but Derek blocked the door with his massive bulk.

"I don't think so," Helen said. "I've been on the desk all morning, and I didn't check you in."

"You were busy," Evie said. "I swiped my card myself."

"You're not in the computer," Carla said. "I checked a few minutes ago when I came on duty. I didn't see your name. And this isn't the first time you didn't check in."

"The computer malfunctioned," Evie said.

"It's working fine," Helen said. "The police have made our lives hell because they want to talk to you."

Tears ran down Evie's face, but she said nothing. She sniffled and wiped her face on the sleeve of her baggy sweatshirt.

Derek knelt down in front of her and said softly, "Evie, you can tell us. We need your help or we're going to jail. Where were you, please?"

"I was right here," Evie said. "At the gym. I've been living here since I walked out on my husband three weeks ago. We had a fight and Peter hit me. I can't live with a man who abuses me. He said he was sorry, but he refused to get counseling. Peter said it was my fault that I made him angry.

"I took seven hundred dollars out of our account, but that's not enough money for an apartment. Now I sleep in the women's lounge at night and use your facilities."

"I never see you when I lock up, and I check both dressing rooms," Derek said.

"I hide in a toilet stall while you close up. Those long doors don't show my feet. If I don't leave the lounge area until the staff comes in at six a.m., I don't trip the security system. I sleep on the couch. It's surprisingly comfortable, and the towels make good blankets. I drop them in the dirty laundry basket when I get up, and nobody knows I spent the night here.

"When the gym gets busy, I dress up nice, go out for food and look for a job. I haven't found one yet."

"How can you look for a job?" Helen said. "You don't have a car."

"I've walked to every store for three miles up and down Federal Highway. I take the bus, too. I've been looking and looking, but nobody will hire me. I haven't had much work experience. Now you're going to kick me out and I'll be homeless, too."

"Have you seen a lawyer?" Helen asked.

"They charge too much," Evie said. "If I see a lawyer, I can't afford to eat."

"How do you eat?" Derek asked.

"When I go out, I have a meal at the pancake house. Then I come back here to the gym and check in officially. If I get hungry the rest of the day, I drink the ice water from the pitchers in the lounge or buy protein bars."

"No wonder you're so thin," Helen said.

"The police have been crawling all over this place," Carla said. "Why didn't they find you?"

"I heard the screaming when Helen discovered Debbi's body. I ran up here to the towel closet. It's my alternate hideout. I'm small, and I can fit into the air ducts. I removed the screws on the cover with a quarter and hid them in the back of the top shelf. They're still up there."

"How do you get up into a seven-foot ceiling?" Derek asked. "You're only five feet tall."

"I'm five-one," Evie said, indignant that he'd underestimated her. "I take off my shoes and hide them under the towels, then climb the shelves like a ladder, stand on top, take off the duct cover and crawl in. I'm small enough that I fit inside.

"That's what I did when the police were here. I pulled the duct cover in after me and held it in place while they looked around. They didn't stay long. The CSI woman dusted for prints, but she'd expect to find them on the towel shelves."

"How long were you in that duct?" Helen asked.

"The police left at eleven the first night, so I guess maybe sixteen or seventeen hours. I climbed down and opened the door a crack. The lights were off, but the security system was on and I didn't want to set it off. I slept on a pile of towels in the corner there, then stayed in here the whole next day."

"What about when you needed a bathroom?" Helen asked.

"There's a liter bottle in the corner," Evie said, and hung her head. "I covered it with a towel, too. I'm sorry. I'm scared and I haven't had anything to eat but my emergency stash of PowerBars I kept under the towels."

"Good grief," Derek said. "Let me get you some food. Then I'll call Detective Redding."

"No!" Evie said. "I heard what he said. He'll arrest me. I didn't kill her."

"We have to call the detective," Derek said. "He wants to talk to you."

"He wants to throw me in jail. He thinks I'm guilty." Evie wept so hard, Helen thought her small body would come apart.

"I have to call him," Derek said. "Otherwise, he'll close this gym down and then you'll be homeless and we'll be out of jobs. I promise we'll do our best to protect you, Evie, but we have no choice."

"At least let me shower and eat before you turn me in,"

Evie said. She looked pitiful with her dirt-smeared face and oily hair.

"I can do that," Derek said. "You clean up, and I'll go out for food. What would you like: a pizza, hamburgers, a roast beef sandwich?"

"A chicken," Evie said. "A whole roast chicken. From the supermarket. And chocolate cake. I have the money. I can pay for it."

"I'll buy it," Derek said. "My treat. Take your shower, and by the time you're finished I'll be back with your food. Don't cry. We'll find the real killer. When this is over and we know who killed Debbi, I'll give you a job here. You'll make enough money so you can rent your own place."

"You promise?" Evie said. Helen couldn't bear to see the hope shining in her eyes.

"Have you ever known me to lie?" Derek said.

Right now, Helen thought. To save your job.

Carla watched the reception desk, and Helen stayed with Evie while Derek went for food. Evie came out of the shower wrapped in towels and hot steam, then blow-dried her gray hair until it shone. When she was dressed in clean gym clothes, she joined Helen in the lounge with the tropical furniture. They were alone. The bright-colored upholstery seemed to mock their somber mood.

Evie was so slender and pale, she looked like a child. Her worries were real and grown-up.

"I didn't do it," Evie insisted.

"I believe you," Helen said. She did. More than she believed Derek.

"What am I going to do, Helen?" Evie asked. "You know that detective will arrest me. I don't have any money for a lawyer. My husband won't help. Peter would be thrilled if I was locked up for murder. He hates me. He wants me out of his life."

Helen wasn't going to give Evie false assurances. They both knew that roast chicken Derek was so eager to fetch would be her last meal as a free woman.

"When Detective Redding takes you into custody, he'll read you your rights," Helen said. "Tell him you want a lawyer. He has to get you a public defender. Don't say a word unless your lawyer says it's okay."

"I've heard public defenders aren't very good," Evie said. "But I guess you get what you pay for."

"Not necessarily," Helen said. "There are good ones. I'll do my best to help you. My husband and I have a detective agency."

"Really? And you'd help me?" Evie held on to this frail hope as if it were the last lifeboat off the *Titanic*.

Helen felt like a fraud. She couldn't help her own sister, but she was volunteering to help this woman.

"I can't make any promises," Helen said. "I'm only a trainee. I wouldn't want Derek to find out what I really do."

"No, no, I won't say a word," Evie said. "But thanks for caring."

There was a knock on the lounge door. "Evie," Derek said, "I have your dinner ready in the sales cubicle."

The desk was spread with a whole roast chicken, mayonnaise potato salad, white rolls, a bottle of wine, a cup of coffee and an entire chocolate cake.

"It's lovely. Would you like some?" Evie asked.

"It's your feast," Derek said. "Eat up." The delicious scents of warm chicken and hot coffee were calling to Helen, but she was too ashamed to ask for any.

Evie ate it all, down to the last chicken wing. "Are you sure you don't want any cake?" she asked, cutting herself a giant wedge.

Helen started to say yes, but Derek's frown and head shake stopped her.

After Evie finished her coffee and the last crumb of cake, Derek said softly, "Evie, I have to make that call now. But there will be a job for you when this is over."

"I understand," Evie said. Helen heard acceptance and sadness in her voice.

"I'll stay with Evie while you make the call," Helen said, hoping to spare her the humiliation of Derek asking Helen to stand guard.

"I haven't much time left as a free woman," Evie said. "At least I had a good meal."

Helen felt pity for the small woman, who struggled to find a bright spot. "If the worst happens, remain silent," she told her. "You don't have to talk to the detective without a lawyer."

"I promise," Evie said. "You've promised to help me."

So I have, Helen thought. Why? She already knew the answer: I've failed so much already. I have to succeed at something.

"Detective Redding is going to arrest me," Evie said. "It's probably for the best. I'll be safer in jail."

CHAPTER 30

The Coronado Tropic Apartments had started its sunset salute early. Phil, Margery, Peggy and Pete the parrot were lounging by the pool when Helen came home from the gym.

"Well, look what the cat dragged in," their landlady said. Margery grinned like a Cheshire cat herself, nearly disappearing in a wreath of smoke.

"Awk!" Pete shuffled restlessly along Peggy's shoulder. Mentioning cats made the little bird nervous. Pete looked like a green-feathered fashion accessory on Peggy's cool blue caftan.

"Helen, did you have a bad day?" Peggy said. "You look wiped out."

"I am," Helen said. She sat down at the umbrella table. "We found the missing Evie. That horrible detective Ever Ready came racing over and clapped her in jail."

Helen told them how Evie had fallen out of the air duct where she'd been hiding and Derek had turned her in. "I guess he had no choice, but Ever Ready's mind is made up. When Evie refused to speak without a lawyer present, the detective said, 'That's further proof you're guilty.'"

"Awk!" Pete said.

"You said it, Pete. It's not proof of anything," Phil said. "She's entitled to a lawyer."

"I know," Helen said. "It's more proof the detective has jumped to another wrong conclusion."

"How about a glass of wine?" Margery asked. "It's a new box."

"I'd better stick to club soda," Helen said. "My boss is after me to lose weight."

"You look fine to me," Phil said. "I like your curves."

"Did I tell you I love you?" Helen kissed Phil. "I have to choose between my curves and my job. Derek insisted I work out for an hour before I left the gym today, even after that awful scene with Evie." She couldn't keep the resentment out of her voice.

"I'll get you a club soda, since you provided the sweat equity for our business," Phil said.

"How is Shelby's case going?" Peggy asked.

"Not well," Helen said. "Shelby insists her husband is cheating on her, but I can't really go into the details. We have to protect our client's privacy."

"What privacy?" Peggy said. "Shelby told everyone at work that she found an open condom packet in Bryan's car and she'd hired detectives."

"I've been watching her husband at the gym," Helen said. "I've never seen Bryan even flirt with another woman."

"Doesn't he have a hot-looking woman as a trainer?" Peggy asked. "Jan somebody?"

"Jan Kurtz. Their relationship is professional, so far as I can see."

"What about a man?" Margery said. "Could be that he's having an affair with one of those hunks at the gym. Bryan is surrounded by sweaty temptation. This is Fort Lauderdale, where the boys are—and I'm not talking about that old movie."

"It's possible Bryan may be having an affair with a gay guy at the gym," Helen said. "I've seen him with one who's good-looking and a real sweetheart. They've had some intense conversations, but no touching or kissing that I could see."

"You can't follow them into the men's room," Margery said.

"No, but the straight guys don't tolerate sex in the dressing room. They complain at the reception desk if they see two men making out, so I'd know if they were carrying on in the lockers.

"I don't have any proof that Shelby's husband is straying," Helen said. "I hope I don't find any. What if I discover Bryan is having an affair with another man? If that turns out to be true, I don't want to break that news to his wife. That could be a real blow to her image of herself. Should I tell Shelby the truth or return her money and drop the case?"

"You know the answer." Margery sounded stern. "Rob cheated on you for years. You didn't like being the last person to know."

"At least he went after other women," Helen said.

"You didn't find that much comfort in that fact at the time," Margery said.

"From personal experience," Peggy said, "it's more humiliating to be kept in the dark. I'd rather know if my man was straying. I felt like a fool when I found out, but I survived. Now I'm glad that jerk took off. I'm dating a much better man. Danny is my dream lover."

"Good boy!" Pete said.

"Yes, he is," Peggy said, petting her parrot softly on his back. "And a good lawyer. Shelby is paying you to tell her the truth, Helen. You'll be doing her a favor if you find out Bryan is playing around. My boss is getting divorced, and he spends all day hanging around Shelby's desk. He practically drools on her. She keeps telling him she's married, but the whole office can see the sparks between them. Shelby's not the type to play around. I'm sure she'd fall in love with him if she was free."

"Don't play God," Margery said. "If Shelby's husband is playing around with anyone, male or female, she needs to know. She wants to know. She'll survive. You certainly did."

Phil returned with a frosty club soda topped with a lime wedge for Helen and a second beer for himself.

"Well, I'm making progress," Phil said. "I thought there was something missing to Mark's accident report."

"Why?" Helen asked.

"Because those cops weren't the best investigators, but they were thorough about their paperwork. I spent the day searching the old records at Sunset Palms and found two more pages to Mark's accident report. It's some kind of addendum to the original report. It was filed in the wrong folder and forgotten. Took me four hours to find it. Going through those paper files was dusty work. I needed this." He raised the beer in a toast.

"What did the new pages say?" Helen asked.

"Didn't get a chance to study them," he said. "The office was closing at three. The records clerk will fax them to me first thing tomorrow. Did you see what happened to Danny Boy after he left the bar last night? I saved the paper for you."

Phil handed Helen the local news section. "Check out the first story. Danny Boy Cerventi was arrested for a DUI last night. Must have been while he was driving home from his bar. He's been released on bail."

"You offered to drive him, too," Helen said. "His friend Bobby said he couldn't get in trouble on the short trip home."

"Looks like he managed after all," Phil said. "I was curious about Danny. He talks too much and drinks too much. Strikes me as a man with a guilty conscience. I did a background check on him. No arrests, wants or warrants. Then I checked the county records.

"Danny Boy's grandfather had left nothing but a small policy to cover his burial. He didn't leave his grandson enough to buy a beer, much less a bar. I'll say this: The old man was respected. He had a nice write-up in the paper when he died.

"I learned something else, too," Phil said. "Remember the mustachioed gent hanging over the bar?"

"I assume you're talking about a photograph?" Margery said.

"He is," Helen said. "Danny Boy told us that was a picture of his granddaddy. He said he inherited a lot of money from the old man and named the bar in his honor."

"I saw Mr. Cerventi's obituary picture," Phil said. "Danny Boy's grandfather is not the man in that photo."

CHAPTER 31

"Hey, Danny Boy, you shouldn't be drinking soda water," Bobby said, taking a seat at the bar at Granddaddy's. "Let me buy you a beer."

Last night, Bobby and his yellow-haired girlfriend had tried to help Danny. His old high school buddy had tended bar for the rest of the night when Danny left. He'd also insisted that the drunken Danny could drive himself home without Phil's help. That had led to Danny's DUI.

Now Bobby was tempting the bar owner with a beer. Some friend, Helen thought.

Danny was sober tonight, but Helen wondered how long he'd stay that way. Temptation beckoned from every corner. Liquor bottles glowed. Beer was poured into frosty mugs. Friends offered him drinks and pushed cold beer bottles his way.

Danny fended them off and clung to his club soda, seething with red-eyed anger.

Helen watched the spectacle from her seat next to Phil at the bar. She was sipping her own club soda and listlessly picking through a salad with no dressing—and no flavor.

She speared a rubbery slice of boiled egg and chewed it mournfully.

"I can't drink, Bobby," Danny Boy said. "I told you. My sister Linda will ream my ass." The skinny bartender rubbed the seat of his jeans and said, "It's still sore from the chewing out she gave me when she bailed me out last night."

"She didn't have much to chew on with your bony ass," Bobby said.

"I promised Sis I'd lay off the sauce," Danny Boy said. "This isn't the first time I got stopped for a DUI. Linda says this is absolutely the last time she can pull strings and make the charges disappear."

Danny took a sip of club soda, winced in distaste and turned to Phil. "Did I tell you my sister Linda is a big deal in Sunset Palms?"

Alcohol didn't change Danny, Helen thought. He was just as repetitious sober as he was drunk.

"Is that right?" Phil said.

Danny leaned in closer to his new friend. The bartender needed a shave and a clean shirt. And a bath, Helen thought. Danny didn't seem to remember Helen from last night. She kept silent, hoping he wouldn't notice her. She decided now would be a good time to check out that back room. She slid quietly off her barstool and headed toward the restrooms. Danny was droning on. Bobby was watching his friend.

The noise level was even louder in the back room tonight. Helen stuck her head in and saw four bodybuilders and a red-haired woman. Heather from the gym. She said something, and the big lugs around her laughed. She was holding the only drink in the room, a glass of something clear and fizzy. Helen heard a heavy footstep in the hall behind her and darted into the restroom.

What was Heather doing here? she wondered. Flirting with the bodybuilders? Did she buy something for Debbi's fatal fruit smoothie?

Helen slid back into her seat. Danny didn't notice. Phil patted her leg.

"Linda had her picture taken with Governor Jeb Bush," Danny confided. "Keeps it on the wall. Sis knows everything going on in town."

"Like what?" Phil asked. Helen watched her husband artfully draw Danny into more conversation. How could he stand the boredom?

Danny lowered his voice. "Like she says there's some kinda detective going through the city files, looking for information about how Mark Behr died."

"Mark Behr." Phil pretended to search his memory for the name. "Is he the good-looking guy in that picture?"

"That's him," Danny said. "My sister says Mark's brother, Gus, is the one who is stirring trouble. I know he's got the money to do it. Gus charges an arm and leg at that carrepair shop of his. Now Linda says Gus has hired a detective to look into Mark's death."

"Who's the detective?" Phil asked.

"Don't know," Danny Boy said.

"I thought your sister knew everything in Sunset Palms," Phil said.

"She does. She'll find out," Danny said. "We gotta make Gus stop."

"Why?" Phil said.

"'Cause he'll ruin everything, dude. Can't have an outsider poking around in our business. It's private-like."

"Privacy is important," Phil said.

"Damn right. What that detective wants to know is none of his business. What time is it?"

Phil checked his watch. "Two minutes after eleven."

"I've had enough of this pee-water." Danny slammed down the club soda on the bar, and the liquid slopped on the wooden top. "I made it to eleven tonight without a drink. I can't stand being here anymore. I'm going home."

He yelled, *"Any cops in here?"*

The other customers looked up at his shouted question. The music stopped. Even the televisions were suddenly quiet. Danny heaved himself up onto the bar and screamed, *"I said, any cops in my frigging bar? I'm warning you now.*

*Go ahead and follow me home. I'm sober. You won't get me
tonight, assholes."*

Bobby reached up and helped his friend climb down
from the bar. "Dude, have a drink and chill," he said. "You'll
feel better after a beer. You need to relax."

"Can't," Danny Boy said. "I'm too angry. People are
meddling in my life, detectives are sticking their noses
where they don't belong and now my sister is telling me
how to live. It's gonna stop now." He tore off his stained
apron and threw it on the bar. "Watch the bar for me, okay,
Bobby?"

"It's late, dude. I got work in the morning."

"You don't have to come in until ten o'clock. I'll pay."
Danny opened the cash register and took some bills out of
the till. "Here's fifty bucks. Take the keys. You know how to
lock up. I need to get out of here now."

"Thanks," Bobby said.

Danny didn't wait to hear Bobby's thanks before he
walked out. The customers watched Danny Boy's exit in
silence. Then the music blared again and the TV volume
went back up. Once again men were watching the ball game,
drinking, cheering and slapping one another on the back.

Helen gave up on her limp salad. "Can we leave now,
Phil? I have to go into the gym at ten tomorrow morning."

"I'll drive," Phil told her, and Helen happily handed over
the keys to the Igloo. She was tired. "How do you think
Danny's sister found out about you?"

"Records clerk probably told her," Phil said. "She was
protecting her job."

"Think you'll still get the rest of Mark's report faxed to
you tomorrow?" Helen asked.

"I hope so. I made the request in writing. Danny's sister
knows there's a paper trail, so she'll be careful that I get
some response. I just hope the clerk doesn't fax me two
pages of gibberish instead of the actual report."

"I learned something, too," Helen said. "I saw more
bodybuilders in that back room, and Heather from my gym.
She was the only one with a drink."

"Did she see you?" Phil asked.

"No, and neither did Bobby."

"Good," Phil said.

Helen was half asleep by the time they were home. The Coronado Tropic Apartments shimmered in the moonlight. A soft breeze stirred the pool and made the palm trees whisper in the dark. Helen sighed and leaned against Phil. "We're lucky to live here. It's so beautiful."

"Are you happy?" Phil asked her.

"Oh, yes."

"Sorry we started our agency?"

"Never," Helen said. "I like having our own business. I just wish I didn't have to work out at Fantastic Fitness."

"You can stop that as soon as you solve the case," he said, patting her bottom. "I like you the way you are."

She gave him a lingering kiss on the doorstep to his apartment. "I like this living arrangement, too," she said. "Sleeping at your place makes us seem like lovers."

"We are," he said, and kissed her.

As Phil unlocked the door, they heard his phone ringing.

Helen's heart was pounding. "Midnight phone calls are always bad news. I hope it's not my sister."

Phil put the phone on speaker so Helen could hear the conversation.

"Phil, it's Gus." Helen hardly recognized the burly mechanic's voice. He sounded frightened. "You and Helen got to get over here. There's blood everywhere."

"Are you hurt?" Phil asked. "What about your wife? Should I call an ambulance?"

"I'm fine. Jeannie is spending the week with her sister in Vero Beach. I was working late at the shop and just walked in. Somebody broke in. My living room is a mess."

"Is the burglar in the house?"

"I checked," he said. "It's empty."

"Get out of there now, Gus," Phil said. "Call 911."

"I'm not calling the police until you see what he did first," Gus said.

"Helen and I can be there in fifteen minutes. Give me your address and go sit in your car until we get there."

"I'll wait outside for you," Gus said. "I can't look at it anymore. It's awful."

Helen thought she heard tears in his voice.

"I don't understand what happened," Gus said. "I don't know why they brought Mark back and splashed blood all over. Get here fast, okay?"

CHAPTER 32

"**M**ay you live forever, and may I never die."
The cheerful voice gave Helen chills. She watched the beautiful Mark Behr lift his beer in his last toast. He was smiling, golden—and dead for a quarter of a century. Helen viewed the dead man through a veil of blood spattered across the television in Gus's living room.

She watched Mark blow out the candles on his cake. The screen went dark, and the blood looked even grislier. Then the scene started again. Mark raised his beer in that deadly toast and smiled through the blood-splashed TV screen. He blew out the candles, and the blood-drenched screen went dark again.

Helen watched spellbound as Mark gave his fateful toast three times.

"That's enough," Gus said. "I can't stand to watch it anymore." He started to turn off the television.

"Don't touch it," Phil said. "The police need to dust your television for prints. Tell me again what happened."

It was after midnight. Gus was bleary-eyed and grease stained. Helen, Phil and Gus made a weary cluster in Gus's living room. The blood-splashed television sat on a dark wood stand across from a beige brocade couch flanked by cut-crystal lamps. The dark coffee table was crowned with a silk flower centerpiece. The blood-drenched television looked like a Halloween prop in this traditional living room.

"Can we go in the kitchen?" Gus said. "I haven't showered, and I'm walking on this beige carpet in my work shoes. Jeannie tries to keep this room nice."

He seemed more comfortable in the cheerful kitchen, splashed with bright tropical oranges, blues and yellows instead of blood. They sat down at the oak kitchen table.

"Coffee?" he asked.

"No," Phil said. "We need you to tell us what happened. Then we'll leave and you'll call the police."

"I got home about midnight," Gus said, "and came in the front door. I was in the hall there, and I heard a voice. I knew Jeannie wasn't home. I stood in the doorway and listened. It took me a minute to realize it was Mark talking. I hadn't heard him for so long. I was tired and confused, but I knew something was wrong. I tiptoed out to my car again, got a tire iron out of the trunk, then went back inside.

"The lights were off, but the TV was on in the living room. That old tape of Mark's birthday party was playing. Except it's not a tape. That's a DVD. I don't have a tape player anymore. I watched it twice before I noticed I was looking at it through a red haze. There was blood everywhere—on the TV set and the stand. My wife's going to kill me when she gets home."

Phil went back into the living room, scratched a speck of blood off the TV with his fingernail and tasted it.

"Phil!" Helen said. "What are you doing?"

"It's not real blood," Phil said. "It's fake blood, like you get at a party shop. Real blood would start to darken by now. This should wash off, Gus. How did the burglar get inside?"

"Broke the slider in the rec room at the back of the house."

"Anything taken?" Phil asked.

"Not that I can see. I checked our bedroom. I keep about

a hundred bucks in cash in the top dresser drawer. It's still there. So is our checkbook. Jeannie's good jewelry, her mother's silver, our laptop and camera are fine. I noticed my desk was messier than usual. The copies of your contract are gone."

"Someone heard you'd hired detectives," Phil said. "Whoever it was wanted to know who we were."

"That's bad," Gus said.

"It's inconvenient," Phil said. "But it tells me we're on the right track. Someone doesn't want it known that your brother was murdered."

"So are you guys in danger? Do you need to hire body-guards?"

"We're fine," Phil said. "We'll have to be on guard, but we're paid to do that. You have to report this to the police. You've put it off long enough."

"Don't worry," Gus said. "I'll tell them about the break-in so my insurance will pay for the broken slider. That contract is none of their business. The cops screwed up Mark's murder investigation the first time. They're not getting a second chance for a cover-up."

"You have to tell them," Phil said. "Somebody already told Danny Boy's sister that you hired a detective, but Danny didn't know the name. Now that your contract is gone, whoever did this found out it's Helen and me."

Gus shrugged. "So? Danny's a drunk and a blowhard."

"His sister isn't," Phil said. "She's quite a power in Sunset Palms. She got Danny released on bail. She can make trouble for us. I'm wondering if your sister, Bernie, is behind this break-in."

Gus glared. "You're joking, right? Bernie? She wants nothing to do with this investigation. She's pissed I hired you. She called and gave me holy hell after Helen talked to her."

"She wants to stop the investigation, Gus," Phil said.

"She's mad at me, too," Helen said. "I went to her house. Bernie doesn't want you stirring up the past."

"You know she lives way out in Weston," Gus said. "You

think she drove forty minutes to throw fake blood on my television?"

"She wants to scare you, Gus. She succeeded," Phil said.

"No, she didn't. I'm not scared," Gus said, but Helen saw the worry in his eyes. "I'll tell you why my sister didn't do this. Bernie couldn't transfer a tape to a DVD. She has to call me to reset her VCR clock. Besides, she has a key to our house. She wouldn't have to break the slider."

"She could have hired someone, Gus," Phil said. "She's got the money. She wanted this to look like a break-in."

"My sister would never do that."

"Look, Gus, you've reopened Mark's death investigation. Your sister wants to forget her past. It's possible she contacted Ahmet Yavuz and he got someone to do the dirty work."

"You're full of shit!" Gus said, pounding the table. "My sister has had nothing to do with that drug dealer. You're ruining her name. First you tell me Mark had to rescue her from Ahmet's house. Now you're telling me she vandalized my home. This is my little sister. My brother died to save her."

"So he did," Phil said. "And your sister became a model citizen, just like Ahmet."

"She wouldn't betray her own brother," Gus said.

"Your brother is dead," Phil said. "In her eyes, he can't be hurt anymore. She can. What if her husband finds out about her past—drug dealers and mental hospitals? Ahmet doesn't want his past unearthed either. They have that in common, and they'll unite to save themselves. You're in danger."

"I can handle it," Gus said. He sat up straighter and tried to suck in his gut, but that only made him look older and more out of shape. The circles under his eyes were as dark as his gray work shirt.

"I don't like you accusing my sister," Gus said, his eyes narrowing. "She was a little wild when she was young, but Bernie's a respectable executive's wife."

"Who wants to stay that way. She knows all about

blood," Phil said. "Real and fake. Your brother's death has been forgotten for twenty-five years."

"Not by me," Gus said, stubbornly.

"Exactly. That's the problem," Phil said. "Your sister wants Mark to stay buried as a suicide. You think Mark's death was murder. You got us to investigate, and now we agree with you. We're looking for proof.

"If you're right, that means there's a murderer out there who wants us to stop. Someone with a lot to lose. It could be your sister, Bernie. It could be Ahmet Yavuz. It could even be Mark's old buddy Danny Boy."

CHAPTER 33

The baby wouldn't stop crying. His angry, urgent howls sliced through Fantastic Fitness. The child's screaming drowned out the clanking exercise machines, the thumping basketballs and the pounding music. It disrupted workout rituals and assaulted eardrums like a hot spike.

Finally, Heather, the lushly curved gym member with the red hair, had enough. She climbed off her stationary bike and marched to the reception desk. "Helen, what's wrong with that poor baby?" she asked. "The kid's been crying for twenty minutes. I can't concentrate."

"Me, either," Helen said. "I'll see if Jen needs help in Kiddy Kare."

"Kid's giving me a headache," Carla said. "I'll watch the desk while you check with the sitter."

The gym's playroom was painted in bright colors—yellow, blue and green. The baby in Jen's arms was a raging red. The frazzled babysitter was white with worry. Her hair had escaped its ponytail, and her shirt had slid out of her jeans. She walked the little boy up and down, rocking him and trying to soothe him. It didn't work. The baby continued yelling.

Helen was no expert on babies, but this one looked

about eight months old. She could see hot tears running down the little guy's face. He stopped, took a deep breath and shrieked again.

"Shhh," Jen said, patting the sturdy little back. "It will be okay, Adam. Mommy will be back soon."

Adam's sobs went up another ten decibels.

"I'm getting worried," Jen said. "Adam has a fever. His mom dropped him off and promised to be right back after she toured the gym. Logan just signed her up as a member. You know him?"

"He's the super salesman with two Testarossas," Helen said.

"And too much testosterone," Jen said. "Logan and Mommy—her name is Megan—went off to see the gym. She's a tall blonde with tanned legs and a ponytail. They've been gone twenty minutes. Adam won't stop crying. Megan needs to get this baby to a doctor. He's burning up."

"I'll go look for them," Helen said.

Logan wasn't at his desk in the sales area, and there was no leggy blonde, either. Helen ran upstairs. She saw two guys playing a brisk game of racquetball and a lone man lifting weights, but no couple touring the gym. No sign of Logan and Megan downstairs. Bryan and "What a Waste" Will were running side by side on the treadmills, sweating manfully. Helen ducked into the women's locker room to see if Megan was checking out the facilities and ran into Beth.

"Hi, Helen," Beth said. "Remember me?"

Beth was undressing after a grueling workout. Her sweaty hair was plastered to her neck. She peeled off her wet top. Her outfit wasn't as revealing as the one she'd worn last time. Helen would never forget Beth's eighty-dollar bribe for information about her married boyfriend.

"Of course," Helen said.

"Could you get more towels, please? I want to shower, and I'm half-dressed. I can't go out to the towel closet like this."

Helen ran down the hall, opened the closet and saw a flurry of movement—a swish of blond hair, a flash of tanned legs and a man's bare back.

"Eeeek!" the woman screamed.

"What the—," the man shouted.

"Megan? Logan?" Helen asked.

Megan grabbed a towel and draped it over her bare top. "It's not what you think," she said.

"Spare me," Helen said. "Megan, your baby is sick and needs you right away."

Logan zipped his pants, straightened his polo shirt and slid out the door while Helen gathered an armful of fresh towels.

Megan wasted no time pulling on her clothes. Her black bra and skintight tap pants were more suitable for a Victoria's Secret catalogue than a gym. "Look," she said. "I'm not proud of what I did, but I don't have much money. Logan promised me the first week free if I'd hook up with him."

"Everyone gets the first week free when they sign up," Helen said. "You got a scumbag as a signing bonus." She shut the closet door and dropped off the towels for Beth.

Back at the reception desk, Helen told Carla what she'd seen in the towel closet.

"I warned you that Logan was a sleaze," Carla said.

"Too bad I got to see it for myself," Helen said. "Should I say anything to Derek?"

"Won't do any good," Carla said. "Other women have complained. Management doesn't care what Logan does, as long as he exceeds his monthly sales quota."

"Excuse me." A man at the counter waved to get her attention. "My name is Nick. I'm new here, and I need help."

Nick was twentysomething with brown hair and a boyish face. Helen couldn't help staring at him. Nick seemed so—well—normal, after the ripped, stripped and chiseled Fantastic Fitness freaks.

"Where do I sign up for aerobics classes?" Nick asked.

"Right here," Helen said. "There's step aerobics at two this afternoon and freestyle aerobics at five o'clock."

"Do I pay extra?" he asked.

"No, they're part of your membership," Helen said. "You realize you'll be the only man in the class."

"I certainly hope so." He gave Helen a heartbreaker smile and went upstairs.

"Nick seems sweet," Helen said.

"If I have a son, I'm naming him Nick," Carla said dreamily. "All Nicks are hot. We've got another one at the gym who would make you forget Phil. Then there's Nick Jonas."

"The Jonas Brother? Cute, but a bit young," Helen said.

"Nick Nolte, Nick Cannon—he's with Mariah Carey. Nick Lachey is another one."

"Who's that?" Helen asked.

"He's engaged to Vanessa Minello. She used to be an MTV host," Carla said. "Naming a boy Nick almost guarantees he'll be smoking hot."

"Saint Nick may have a high body mass index, but he never forgets Christmas," Helen said.

"I was talking about real people," Carla said.

"Excuse me." The small voice belonged to a small woman. The brunette in the red Nike suit was so short, her head barely reached the top of the reception desk. She looked around uneasily, then put two tens on the counter top and said, "Has Nick arrived yet?"

"Which one?" Carla asked, stepping up to the computer. "Nick B. or Nick S.?"

"Nick S.," the brunette said.

"Sorry," Carla said. "He was in at six this morning. He's gone."

"Oh." The brunette's shoulders slumped and she slunk off to a treadmill. Helen noticed the two tens were gone.

The small brunette reminded Helen of another tiny gym member, Evie, who'd been branded as Debbi's killer. "Any word about Evie?" Helen asked. "I watched that brute Ever Ready arrest her for first-degree murder. He hauled her off in handcuffs, poor little thing."

"Nobody here has talked to her," Carla said, "but Derek is half-crazed that Debbi's death will hurt the gym. He overheard Ever Ready on the phone talking about the autopsy report with the medical examiner's office. Debbi overdosed on steroids, fat burners and oxycodone. The report didn't say if her death was an accident, suicide or murder. Ever

Ready jumped to the conclusion that Debbi had been murdered. He insists Evie killed her."

"He's wrong about Evie," Helen said.

"Maybe not," Carla said. "Ever Ready bragged that he'd found out Evie's estranged husband, Peter, had had knee replacement surgery three months ago and the doctor had given him a prescription for oxycodone for the pain. Ever Ready found twenty-one tablets left in the huge bottle. Evie's prints were on it, as well as her husband's. Peter couldn't remember how many tablets he'd taken or if Evie had helped herself to any. Ever Ready is saying Evie took her husband's tablets to kill Debbi."

"She's been living at the gym for three weeks," Helen said. "Did she go back home and get the pills?"

"I didn't say it made sense," Carla said. "But that's what Ever Ready says she did."

"The only part I agree with that detective about is that Debbi didn't kill herself. She told me she was going to compete in another bodybuilding contest."

"She could have won," Carla said. "Poor Debbi. She was difficult, but she had talent. Her wake is tonight. Are you going?"

"I guess I should," Helen said. "I did find her body."

"The funeral is tomorrow," Carla said. "Derek will represent the gym. I'll go with you to the wake after work."

Helen looked doubtfully at her clothes.

"Your outfit is fine," Carla said. "You're wearing a white shirt and black pants. Oh, lord, look who's coming in. Debbi's two would-be trainers, Kristi and Tansi."

Kristi wore an orange suit over her grotesque physique. The hyperdeveloped Tansi's gray-green suit made her look so reptilian, Helen expected her to flick out her tongue.

"Helen and I were just talking about Debbi's wake," Carla said as she checked them in. "Are you going today?"

"Can't break training," Tansi said. "The East Coast Physique Championships are almost here."

"Debbi would have wanted it that way," Kristi said solemnly.

Helen wanted to heave a computer at the muscled monsters. "But you trained her."

"She overdid it and ruined everything," Tansi said. "She couldn't have competed this time anyway."

"We know she's upstairs cheering us on," Kristi said, looking piously at the ceiling, as if heaven were just west of the basketball court. "We have to win this one in her name."

"Debbi believed God wants us to make something of ourselves," Tansi said. "We are fresh canvas, waiting to become works of art."

"You two are definitely pieces of work," Helen said. Both bodybuilders smiled as Helen's insult sailed over their heads.

Carla reached under the counter and pulled out a frosty liter bottle of water. "Mm," she said, smacking her lips. "This is so good and cold. May I offer you a bottle?"

The two women looked at Carla like she'd staggered into a temperance meeting with a fifth of bourbon.

"No!" Kristi said. "Drinking water so close to the competition will bloat us. We can't even suck ice cubes."

"Too bad," Carla said, taking a long drink. "You don't know what you're missing."

The two ran off for the dressing room as if the devil were chasing them.

"That was mean." Helen giggled.

"They deserved it," Carla said. "Heartless creeps."

Helen tried to hide a yawn.

"You look tired," Carla said. "Job getting to you?"

"Up late last night," Helen said.

"You newlyweds," Carla said.

I wish, Helen thought. She and Phil hadn't gotten home from Gus and his bloody television until nearly two that morning.

"I saw Tansi the other night at Granddaddy's Bar with a bunch of bodybuilders," Helen said.

"What was she doing in a bar if she can't even have an ice cube?" Carla asked.

"That may be where she gets her steroids," Helen said. "I saw Heather there, too."

"I don't see any signs that Heather uses," Carla said.

"What about selling steroids?"

Carla shook her head. "I don't think Heather and Tansi run in the same crowd."

The rest of Helen and Carla's shift was a blur of routine tasks—checking members in and out, fetching towels, refilling the water pitchers. In the mirrors, she saw Jan Kurtz put Bryan through his paces on the weight machines.

At seven thirty the evening receptionist arrived, and Helen and Carla left for Debbi's wake. Carla drove them in her red Mustang.

The funeral home was mournfully bland. The other two viewings were for elderly people. Helen saw men and women with walkers and white hair going into those rooms. Debbi's viewing was a bizarre oasis of color. Her mother, Susan, greeted them near the coffin. She was a generously built woman slipcovered in sorrowful black.

"We worked with your daughter," Carla told her.

"Would you like to see her?" Susan said.

"Yes," Carla said.

No, Helen thought, but she knew they couldn't leave without viewing Debbi's body. Might as well get it over with. Susan escorted them to the black coffin, as shiny as a snowmobile. Helen tried to hide her shock when she looked inside. Debbi was buried in her posing suit, the tiny black bikini with the yellow sparkles. Her strawlike hair had been smoothed into a golden cap.

"Doesn't she look amazing?" Susan asked.

"Yes," Helen said, truthfully. She'd never seen anyone laid out in a four-hundred-dollar bit of sparkling spandex.

Carla's eyes bulged. She and Helen carefully avoided looking at each other.

The corpse was as bronze as a sun god. "Debbi was going to get another coat of spray tan before her competition," Susan said. "I think the undertaker did a beautiful job."

Debbi's steroid acne was skillfully hidden. The cratered skin that would have kept her out of the competition was covered by the lower half of her coffin. Her jaundiced eyes were closed forever.

"She looks competition ready," Carla said.

"I'm sure she would have won," Helen said.

"She's beyond all that now," Susan said. "I'm not into bodybuilding. I guess you can tell by looking at me. But my Debbi was a champion. There's real prejudice against pumped-up women, but my girl fought it."

"Please accept our sympathy," Carla said. Helen patted the grieving mother's hand. A shadow crossed her path as a hulking bodybuilder approached.

"Aunt Susan," he said. "I'm so sorry."

"Oh, Mike! Let me take you to see her," Debbi's mother said. "She wanted to be just like you."

As the couple reached the coffin, Helen heard him say, "Great abs! You don't see many women that ripped."

Susan started sniffling. Helen and Carla had to steel themselves not to run for the door. They were quiet on the ride back to Helen's car. They didn't want to laugh at Debbi, but they didn't know how to handle that bizarre wake. Silence seemed the only option.

When they were in sight of Helen's car on the Fantastic Fitness lot, Carla said, "Do you think Evie killed Debbi?"

"Not a chance," Helen said. "Evie was scared of her own shadow."

Helen flashed back to that scene in the women's lounge while she and Evie had waited for the homicide detective. Evie had been frightened then, but not about her impending arrest. She'd gone meekly to jail.

What did Evie mean when she'd said, "I'll be safer in jail"?

CHAPTER 34

Helen felt like a zombie in a low-budget horror movie: half-alive with staring eyes and smeared makeup. She'd spent her evening in a funeral parlor with a corpse in a spangled posing suit. Now she dragged herself through the door of Phil's apartment at the Coronado and flopped bonelessly on his black leather couch.

"I'm so glad to be home," she said, and sighed.

"Quick!" Phil said, grabbing her hand. "Don't get comfortable. We have to go to Granddaddy's Bar."

"Now? It's after ten o'clock," Helen said.

"Exactly," Phil said. "My Spidey sense says that Danny Boy won't be sober tonight. Not when he's at a bar with friends buying him drinks."

"Let me sleep," Helen said. "It won't do any good to see him. Danny must know we're the detectives investigating Mark's death. His sister would have told him."

"We'll surprise him," Phil said. "He's drunk. We'll get the drop on him."

"Did you say 'get the drop on him'? Have you been watching old movies again?" Helen asked. "Forget going to that bar. This dame hasn't had dinner yet."

"You can get a burger there. I've fed Thumbs." Phil pulled her off the couch and pushed her toward the parking lot. "Hurry."

"I'm never going to lose weight eating bar food," Helen grumbled.

"You don't need to," Phil said, opening the Igloo's passenger door. He patted her bottom as she sat down.

"Easy for you to say," Helen said. "Your boss doesn't think you're fat. Did you get Mark's accident report from Sunset Palms yet?"

"I waited by the fax machine all day. Nothing." The PT Cruiser roared into life and the air-conditioning blasted out cold air. Helen was reviving.

"I'm going into that office tomorrow and pick up the report personally," Phil said.

"What if the clerk won't give it to you?"

"Then I'll remind her about the paper trail and threaten to call the Florida attorney general. That should shake it loose."

Two of Phil's predictions were correct. Danny Boy was at the bar, and he was drinking—alone. His friends were engrossed in the Marlins game. Danny huddled over a nearly empty mug at the bar, surrounded by a wall of seething silence. His bloodshot eyes looked like they were bleeding. His T-shirt was dirty, but Helen could read it: 24 HOURS IN A DAY. 24 BEERS IN A CASE. COINCIDENCE? YOU BE THE JUDGE.

Helen judged that Danny had downed at least half a case.

"Phil!" he cried when they sat down. Danny Boy didn't seem to notice Helen. "What can I get you?" Sour sweat poured off him. He was drunk. Tonight he didn't slur his words so much as speak them with an odd, heavy emphasis.

"Helen and I will have burgers, and I'll have a cold beer. What are you drinking, Helen?"

"I want a beer, too," Helen said. Damn the diet. She needed a drink after Debbi's wake.

Danny slid two beers in thick frosted mugs their way.

"Get ready to run," Phil whispered to Helen. "I'm going to try something with Danny. It may set him off."

Phil lifted his mug to Danny Boy and said, "May you live forever, and may I never die." That was Mark's toast on the ancient tape.

Danny paled, even in the bar's dim light.

"You burned a DVD of Mark's last birthday party and put it in Gus's VCR, didn't you, Danny? It has your fingerprints all over it."

"Does not," Danny said. "I wiped them." He realized what he'd said and sobered up fast.

"You've got the know-how," Phil said. "Why did you do it, Danny Boy?"

"For Gus's own good. I had to warn him," Danny Boy said. "If the wrong people found out someone is looking into Mark's death again, Gus could get hurt. My sister Linda called and told me there was a detective nosing around in the files." Danny Boy didn't seem to know he was looking at that detective.

"You killed him," Phil said.

Danny Boy moved in closer. He smelled rank, a combination of sweat, dirty clothes and stale beer. Helen saw an enormous blackhead on his left cheek. She stared at it, fascinated. There was a stray whisker growing beside it. "No, dude, you got it wrong," he whined. "Mark was out of control. He talked too much when he got his crazy spells."

"You were afraid Mark would tell everyone you were selling drugs," Phil said. "You and Mark were dealing together, weren't you? That's how you got this bar. You bought it with drug money."

"I inherited the money from my grandfather," Danny said. "That's his picture over the bar."

"Bull," Phil said. "I saw your grandfather's obituary. He was clean-shaven. That guy has a mustache. You didn't inherit anything from your grandfather. All he left was enough money to bury him. You made the money for this place selling drugs. Mark used his drug money for his brother Gus's car business. You had to shut up Mark when he started babbling."

"No, you got it all wrong," Danny Boy said. "Mark had these crazy spells when he'd say Ahmet was the devil. He didn't make any sense when he talked like that. Gus put him in the loony bin after he found Mark walking naked down Dixie Highway."

"Mark was crazy, but he wasn't violent," Phil said.

"He was around us," Danny said. "Mark was crazy *and* violent, especially when he did coke. We were all afraid of him—me, Bernie, his own mother. Gus was the only one who could deal with him. You never saw the Mark we did. He wanted to die. Whoever killed him did Mark a favor. He was off his head and didn't want to live like that. The doctors couldn't regulate his medicine."

"Of course they couldn't," Phil said. "Not with all the coke he took."

"Coke was the only thing that made him feel better," Danny said. "Mark knew he was getting crazier. He couldn't work. He couldn't get it up anymore. He couldn't sleep. He was afraid he'd spend the rest of his life in the psycho ward."

Danny was desperate to make Phil believe him. Helen thought the bartender was telling the truth.

"Two weeks before he died, Mark begged us to kill him. He asked his friends, one by one. He couldn't do it himself. He was too Catholic to commit suicide, but he didn't want to be a burden to his family. You weren't there when he was walking around with a butcher knife, begging us to help him die." Danny made it sound like an accusation.

"Killing Mark was a kindness," he said. "It was putting him out of his misery like a sick dog."

"So you shot him like a dog," Phil said.

"No!" Danny Boy was sobbing now. "No, I didn't kill him. I swear. Mark was going apeshit, freaking out all the time. He cut his wrists once at my house. Got blood all over the john. I had to repaint the walls. That pissed me off. He wouldn't get better. He wouldn't. I didn't do anything to help him. I wished he was dead."

Danny Boy's rubbery drunk face was sloppy with tears. "When I first heard he was dead, I was relieved. That's what I felt: relief. My best friend, and I wanted him dead. I can't stand myself. I've pissed my life away. Mark killed himself. He succeeded at that, too. I wish I had the courage to do what he did. I wish someone would put me out of my misery."

He reached under the register and pulled out a .44 Magnum. Helen froze at the sight of the huge, heavy gun.

"Put that gun down, Danny Boy," Phil said, his voice low and careful.

Danny waved the gun at his head, then his chest. "I don't deserve to live," he said. "I'm lower than whale shit."

Helen reached slowly for her beer mug.

Danny's eyes stayed locked on Phil's. Tears ran down the drunken bartender's face, but he was defiant. Only the emotional wobble in his voice betrayed him. "I can do this," Danny said. "I can get out of this. All I have to do is pull the trigger and it will be over."

"Do you think your death will bring back Mark?" Phil asked. "Don't waste your life, too."

"Too late," he said. "I've screwed it up royally."

No one in the noisy bar noticed the drama at the register.

"You don't want to die, Danny," Phil said softly.

"I don't want to live," Danny said. "I'm a failure. My sister has to save me. I threw away my talent. It's too late. Mark and I, we were dealing drugs; you got that right. We made a fortune. The money was rolling in. We couldn't spend it fast enough. I was going to start my own film company in Hollywood as soon as I had enough. But I didn't kill Mark. I swear it. Mark shot himself, and then I was too scared to go on dealing. I kept the bar and never touched coke again. I've been drinking beer ever since."

"Who was your supplier? It was Ahmet, wasn't it?" Phil asked.

"Yes."

"Did Ahmet kill Mark?" Phil asked.

"I don't know," Danny Boy wailed. "No! Mark killed himself. He hated Ahmet. Mark kept saying if he killed Ahmet he would save the world. Mark didn't make sense when he said shit like that. Ahmet doesn't deal anymore. It's over for him. I want it to be over for me, dude."

Fat tears of self-pity ran down his stubbled cheeks.

Helen was disgusted with Danny's dramatics. She

thought the bar owner wasn't serious about shooting himself. But he was holding a loaded weapon. He might kill an innocent beer drinker.

Danny tightened his grip on the trigger. Phil was too far away to grab the gun from him. Time for shock treatment, Helen decided. She moved closer to Danny and yelled, "But what will I tell Mark?"

"Huh?" Danny Boy looked her way in drunken surprise. He finally saw her.

Helen swung her heavy mug with both hands and hit him in the face. Beer spattered everywhere. Danny Boy crashed into the back bar. The gun went off with a sound like a cannon.

Then there was a great silence.

CHAPTER 35

"I am such a coward," Danny Boy said. "I can't even kill myself."

The scrawny bartender sat blubbering on the floor behind the bar, wallowing in self-pity. His forehead was covered with a red curtain of blood. The sharp stink of spilled liquor, gun smoke and cordite was overpowering.

Phil moved carefully behind the bar and took the weapon from Danny Boy's hand. Danny didn't seem to notice. Phil unloaded the gun. The cylinder did not open smoothly, the way guns did on television. Phil removed the remaining bullets and dropped them into his pocket.

Helen watched, dazed and unmoving. Her eyes couldn't quite focus, and the gunshot blast had left her ears ringing. She finally managed four words. "Did Danny shoot himself?"

"No," Phil said. "His head is bleeding because you conked him with a beer mug. He fell backward into the liquor bottles and smashed them. He cut his hands on the broken glass."

"He fired the gun," Helen said. "I heard it."

"He shot the neon palm tree," Phil said.

Helen noticed that the flickering glow on the wall was gone. "It was dying anyway," she said, her laugh too high-pitched.

Phil moved quickly out from behind the bar, gently placed the empty gun on a stool, and put his arms around his wife. "You saved him," he said into her ear. "He'd be dead now if it wasn't for you."

Helen burst into tears. "I'm sorry, I'm sorry. I'm such a girl," she said.

Phil held her and said, "Sh, it's all over now. He's safe. You're no girl. You're an amazing woman. You moved in and saved a life. You risked your own. I'm so proud of you." He kissed her tears away.

Danny, alone in his private misery, wept and rocked himself back and forth.

The gun blast and broken glass drew the other drinkers. They gathered in a knot near the bar. Bobby pushed his way forward. "He keeps that gun under the register for protection," he said. "Put it back."

"Right now he needs protection from himself," Phil said.

Bobby tried to reach for the gun, but Phil blocked him. He was taller than the flabby bartender and fitter. He glared at Bobby, and Bobby backed away. Phil pulled out his cell phone, called 911 and reported Danny's accident.

Bobby protested from five feet away. "Hey, dude, that's not cool. Call his sister Linda. You don't have to bring in the cops."

"Covering up for Danny hasn't done him any good," Phil said. "He needs stitches for those cuts."

"I can take him to the ER myself," Bobby said. "Nobody has to know. We can say he had an accident."

"Don't you get it?" Phil asked. "He's drunk and he tried to kill himself. I want to talk to his sister. How do I reach her?"

"I'll call Linda," Bobby said. "But she's going to be pissed."

"Too bad," Phil said.

Distant sirens settled the debate. Customers slipped out

the back door at the sound. Danny's good-time friends were deserting him.

Helen could hear the gravel crunching in the parking lot as they hastily drove away. By the time the police arrived, only Helen, Phil and Bobby were left standing. Danny Boy wept incoherently on the floor behind the bar, covered in blood and broken glass.

"What have we here?" the lead uniform cop asked. He had sergeant's stripes, grizzled hair and a weary attitude. Danny continued rocking and mumbling that he was a failure. He didn't respond to the officer's questions.

Phil presented his PI credentials, then told the sergeant about Danny Boy's suicide attempt. He pointed to the gun on the bar stool and handed the cop the rest of the bullets. Then Phil bragged that Helen had stopped Danny from killing himself by hitting him with the beer mug.

"Nice move, ma'am," the officer said. "Maybe you knocked some sense into him."

Helen nodded. She followed Phil's lead. She'd noticed he never mentioned their investigation into Mark's death. She gave her story, talking quickly and trying to make sure her facts dovetailed with Phil's account.

Bobby knew the officer. When it was his turn to talk, the bartender downplayed Danny's distress. "He gets these moods, Sergeant Rick. You know what he's like. But it's nothing serious. This outsider"—he pointed at Phil—"made a big deal out of it."

"He should," the officer said. "Danny Boy's been causing the night shift a lot of trouble lately. It's illegal to discharge a firearm in city limits, especially a weapon that may be unregistered. Attempted suicide should always be taken seriously."

"But Linda—," Bobby began.

"I don't care how important his sister is," Sgt. Rick said. "I'm not having a homicide. Not on my watch."

He looked Bobby in the eye. "And if I see any more Incredible Hulks hanging around that back room, I'll haul your ass to jail. Got it?"

The paramedics had stanched the worst of the bleeding and strapped Danny Boy into a stretcher. They were wheeling him to the ambulance when a short, thick woman marched through the barroom door.

Linda Cerventi, Helen thought. Danny's sister. Linda's features were indistinct, as if a mediocre sculptor had made her face by pressing clumsy fingers into clay. Her eyes were angry. She barely gave her bleeding brother a glance before she turned on the officer. "What's going on here, Rick?" she asked.

"Your brother appears to be drunk," he said. "We'll have him tested at the hospital to make sure. Witnesses say he was threatening to kill himself and discharged a weapon indoors. That woman there"—he nodded at Helen—"saved his life. You owe her thanks."

Linda glared at Helen, and she figured she'd get those thanks when she won the lottery.

"Lucky for both of you, he shot the wall," Rick said. "He's on his way to the hospital."

"Why didn't you call me?" Linda asked. "I thought we had—"

Sergeant Rick stopped her. "I've been patient enough, Linda. I've respected Danny and you and your precious career. But for the second time this week, Danny's been a danger to himself and others. I have to think about the safety of the other citizens of Sunset Palms. And I don't like that side business Bobby is running in the back room. It stopped tonight. Here's my card with the case number and my phone, if you want to call me. I've had enough. Oh, and my name is Sergeant Markban."

They watched the weary officer depart in silence. Helen wondered if the sergeant had had enough trouble for tonight, enough of Danny or enough of taking orders from Linda. Maybe all three.

"Linda, I tried to—," Bobby said.

"Shut up," Linda said, her voice like a slap. "You were supposed to watch Danny Boy. You failed. Were you too busy drinking with the boys to keep an eye on him?"

Bobby's silence was his only answer. Helen wondered if Linda paid Bobby to be her brother's keeper. "And that back room stays closed. Understand?" The bartender slunk away, and Helen heard a car start up.

Linda turned on Phil. "As for you, what gives you the right to stick your nose in my brother's business?"

"When he started waving a .44 around a crowded bar, he stepped outside your family circle," Phil said. "Let me introduce myself. I'm the detective asking for the last two pages of the report on Mark Behr. The Sunset Palms records office was supposed to fax them to me today, but the clerk didn't."

"I told Rachel not to," Linda said. "Mark Behr's death is none of your business."

"Oh, but it is," Phil said. "Unless you want TV reporters here talking about the dramatic rescue of a drunken, gun-toting Danny Boy by an unarmed woman. That would be my agency partner and wife, Helen." He squeezed her shoulder.

"I'm good friends with Valerie Cannata, the reporter for Channel Seventy-seven," Phil said. "She would love to feature you and your cozy relationship with the powers that be in Sunset Palms on her investigative show, *Double or Nothing—A Seventy-seven Exclusive Exposé*. Two sevens could be unlucky for you, Linda. Sweeps are coming up, and television stations want hard-hitting news. Valerie would like nothing better than to expose the corruption in your town. I could point her toward a good source, a sergeant who's tired of doing you favors."

Linda didn't bother to stall or deny. "What do you want?" she asked.

"Those two pages, Linda. I want them faxed to this number." Phil handed her a Coronado Investigations card.

"I sent that paperwork to our storage facility," she said. "It will take three days to get it."

"You have two," Phil said.

"I'd have to do a special requisition and get approval from the head of the records department."

"You can do it," Phil said. "You're a big shot. You have two days. After that, I go to Channel Seventy-seven, and Valerie Cannata gets a lucky break on a Double Seven exclusive."

CHAPTER 36

"I t's two in the morning, Helen," Phil said. "Do you have to go to the gym tomorrow?" The couple had crept into Phil's Coronado apartment like burglars, trying not to awaken the sleeping complex.

Helen yawned and tossed her white blouse into the laundry basket. Even her shirt looked exhausted.

"No," she said. "I'm going to jail."

Phil raised one eyebrow.

"I want to see Evie, the gym member who was arrested for Debbi Dhosset's murder."

"I didn't realize you were friends," Phil said.

"We aren't," Helen said. "She's innocent, Phil. She didn't murder Debbi. I want to find the real killer."

"Very noble," Phil said. "But Evie's not a paying customer. We're a two-person agency with two cases we haven't solved yet. Can we afford to help her get out of jail?"

"Evie is our free advertising," Helen said. "We have no budget. You've been too busy to hang around the courthouse and latch on to an up-and-coming law firm. How are we going to find new cases?

"We won't be getting any word-of-mouth business from our current ones. If I prove that Shelby's husband is cheating on her, she won't want to tell the world. Gus won't want publicity about his brother's murder, not with his family's past—and that's if we find Mark's killer."

"And prove it after twenty-five years," Phil said.

"Exactly." Helen kicked off her shoes, then peeled off her black pants, sparkling with bits of broken glass. The pants followed the shirt into the basket.

"If I save an innocent woman railroaded on a murder charge," Helen said, "that television reporter you mentioned—Valerie what's-her-name—"

"Cannata," Phil said.

"Valerie Cannata will beg for that story," Helen said. "Florida is a death-penalty state, so I'll have saved an innocent woman's life. Valerie could splash our name all over the television. We can't buy that kind of advertising. TV viewers will see that Coronado Investigations is smarter than the police. We'll be the agency to consult when someone has a hopeless case."

"Good thinking, partner," Phil said. He kissed her.

"How do you know Valerie Cannata, anyway?" Helen asked.

Phil's face was expressionless. "She's an old friend."

"Not that old," Helen said. "I've seen Valerie on television. If I remember right, she's dark-haired, tall and thin. Did you meet her when you were a PI?"

"A gentleman never tells," Phil said. "Are you going to compare notes with my old flame?"

"So that's how it was," Helen said.

"We were both single." Phil stripped off his shirt while Helen admired his chest. "Val moved on to someone better. So did I." He kissed Helen again, a deeper kiss.

"I'm not jealous of your past," Helen said. "I want your future. You wouldn't happen to have Valerie's cell phone number, would you?"

"I might," Phil said.

"I'm going to ask her for help," Helen said. "I'll tell you about it when I get out of the shower."

She felt better after a steaming shower. Wrapped in a towel, Helen slid into bed beside Phil.

"I found Valerie's number and keyed it into your cell phone," he said. "I added her office number. Now tell me why you want to reach her."

"I think Debbi was murdered, just like that detective said. But I don't think Evie killed her. Heather gave her a fruit smoothie right before she died. She and Debbi had a big fight over a TV channel at the gym. It was a stupid fight. Heather said that fight poisoned the atmosphere and she wanted to make up and gave Debbi a drink she made herself. What if she'd mixed in some oxycodone and it killed Debbi?"

"Over a TV channel?" Phil said.

"Ever Ready said people have killed for less," Helen said.

"Possible," Phil said.

"How about this scenario? Debbi's two trainers were shooting steroids. The whole gym knew that's why they went out to the parking lot at three o'clock. They got their protégé hooked on 'roids. They had her use fat burners and bodybuilding powders. Longtime bodybuilders get injured and gulp pain pills. They'd be more likely to give Debbi oxy. The drugs probably came from the back room at Granddaddy's Bar. I saw one of Debbi's trainers there."

"But why kill her?" Phil asked. "I thought they wanted Debbi to jump-start their new careers as serious trainers."

"Debbi couldn't compete in her first match—because of their bad advice. She was crazy with rage. Maybe Debbi threatened to expose her inept, drug-using trainers. If that happened, she could end their bodybuilding *and* their training careers. Poor Evie was living at Fantastic Fitness. She was good at hiding. Maybe she saw the trainers kill Debbi and now she's afraid of them."

"Lotta maybes there," Phil said. "Do you really think Evie was frightened enough to risk prison? A women's jail is not a ladies' sodality."

"Evie was broke, hungry and homeless," Helen said. "She slept at the gym in the women's lounge, in the towel closet, even in an air duct. Prison promised a bed and three squares. In her situation, that could look good."

"Better than the death penalty?" Phil said.

"That would be many years in the future," Helen said. "Evie needs help now. I want to persuade her to talk. If my theory is right, I'll set a trap for the killers. Valerie will get an amazing story, and we'll get publicity."

"How will you persuade that homicide detective he's wrong?" Phil asked.

"I won't have to," Helen said. "There's an ambitious uniform, Officer McNamara Dorsey. Officer Mac would love to help Ever Ready retire."

"Then what will you do for the rest of the day, hero? Rest on your laurels?" He was teasing her.

"I'll go to the bodybuilding championship and cheer on our gym members."

"Impressive," Phil said.

"I can't fight for truth and justice single-handedly," Helen said. "I have to be a good team player." She kissed Phil good night and sank into the pillow.

Helen felt like she'd slept seven seconds instead of seven hours when the alarm blasted her out of bed at nine o'clock.

The Harriet Brackensieck Women's Correction Facility of Broward County—better known as Brackie—was on a barren stretch of Highway 27 near the Everglades. As Helen drove past sun-strafed scrubland, shabby houses and dying businesses, she was grateful for the Igloo's cool air. She hoped Evie would see her. Prisoners had the right to refuse any visitor, one of the few privileges they retained.

Evie not only agreed to talk to Helen; she was grateful for the visit. Helen was surprised to see a smiling Evie sit down in the booth behind a Plexiglas shield. The tiny grayhaired woman looked better after her short stint in prison. She'd put on a little weight and seemed rested. The old jail was not air-conditioned. Huge fans on stands barely stirred the hot, heavy air. Evie didn't seem to notice the heat.

I'm right, Helen thought. A prison bunk was more comfortable than the Fantastic Fitness couch. Evie no longer has to worry about money—just her freedom.

Evie lifted the phone receiver to talk to Helen. "I didn't think you'd remember me," she said. "The only person I talk to now is my lawyer, and she's young enough to be my daughter. Nancie Hays gives nice pep talks, but I don't think she has much hope. It's not bad here, really. I do have to work, and there's no air-conditioning in our dorms, but heat never bothered me. I can take education courses, too."

Helen had never heard Evie say so much the entire time she'd known her.

"I'm here for a favor," Helen said.

"Do you really think I can do anything for you?"

"You can tell me why you said you'd feel safer in jail," Helen said.

Evie's eyes shifted to the floor. She wouldn't look at Helen. "I'm getting a divorce. My husband, Peter, is mean."

"Has he threatened you?" Helen said. "We can get a restraining order. I can have someone talk to him for you."

"No! Don't do that!"

"Why not, Evie?"

"Because . . ." Evie stopped.

"Because that's not why you're afraid, is it?"

Evie nodded, like a little girl caught with her hand in the cookie jar. Helen held her breath, waiting for Evie to stand up and say the interview was over. Evie stayed in her chair.

She wants to tell me, Helen thought. Might as well try out my theory. I have nothing to lose.

"Let me say it, if you won't," Helen said. "You know who killed Debbi. You saw a lot of things when you lived at the gym. You saw Debbi's killers."

Evie's face crumpled, but she said nothing.

"Tansi and Kristi murdered her, didn't they?"

Silence.

"Please," Helen said. "Please tell me what you heard. Her trainers could hurt me, too. Ambition and steroid abuse are dangerous combinations."

"Even if I told you, that homicide detective wouldn't listen," Evie said.

Progress! Helen thought. "No, but your lawyer would. And so would an investigative reporter. You've been jailed unfairly, Evie. You could sue the city of West Hills and Detective Evarts Redding for wrongful arrest. You'd have enough money to live on when you got out."

"They could still kill me," Evie said.

"Not if you're free and they're locked up. Please, Evie, tell me. What did you see?"

"I'm sort of shy," Evie said. "I don't like undressing in the locker room where everyone can see me. I change in the toilet stalls. They have long shutter-type doors, so you can't tell if anyone is in one. Debbi came into the locker room, crying. I was afraid to come out after she threw that weight at me. I peeked through the slats and watched, waiting for her to leave. Instead, Tansi and Kristi came in soon after her. They're a weird pair."

"Kristi looks like a space alien," Helen said. "Tansi looks like a lizard."

Evie managed a weak smile. "Both of them screamed at Debbi," Evie said. "They told her she overdid it and didn't eat enough and that's why her skin cratered.

"Debbi was sobbing. I felt sorry for her, even if she did try to hit me. She was so young, and she'd invested so much effort in her bodybuilding. Debbi said it was her first competition and she'd followed their advice. She said she was going to tell everyone that Tansi and Kristi were terrible trainers and used steroids. She'd get them kicked out of the competition and barred from the gym."

Evie took a deep breath, as if she was glad to have that off her chest.

"The trainers tried to calm her down, but Debbi got angrier. She said she was starving and her back hurt and now she'd suffered for nothing. Tansi, the creepy lizard, gave her an energy bar from her gym bag. Debbi gobbled it like a wild animal.

"Kristi said that she had some pills for the pain.

"'Are they illegal?' Debbi asked.

"'No,' Kristi said. 'I got them from my doctor. Lots of important people take this stuff, even a big-time radio guy. You'll feel better, I promise.'

"I heard a funny metallic noise. Tansi was removing the

bar for the shower curtain in the back corner. Those metal bars sort of sit in shallow cups. She lifted up the bar, slanted it down, and these pills poured out.

"Kristi told Debbi she could take six pills because they were about the same size. Tansi poured her a plastic cup of water. Debbi took the pills.

"The two trainers said she'd feel better after a shower. They said they'd made a slight miscalculation in her food and water intake, but now they knew better. She'd win the spring competition for sure.

"Debbi took a shower. Tansi put the cup in her gym bag, and they left. I waited until those two were gone. I heard Debbi turn off the water. She was dressing in the shower stall in the back. She couldn't see me. That's when I ran out. I left the gym to find a job and then came back later."

"You never saw the body?" Helen asked.

"I never went in the locker room that night. I slept in the women's lounge. I heard you come in and turn off the alarm system, and I hid in the towel closet. You discovered the body, and that's all I know."

"Evie, why didn't you tell that to the detective?"

"I tried. He wouldn't believe me," Evie said. "He was sure I killed her. I was afraid of Kristi and Tansi. They were cold. I watched them kill Debbi, though I didn't know it. They never said a word to each other. They just did it. I'm safer here in jail. Some of these girls are tough, but they're no crazier than Debbi in a 'roid rage. They get punished if they start fights."

"Debbi's killers can't hurt you if they're in jail," Helen said.

"But how do we catch them?" Evie asked. "Tansi and Kristi are there almost every day. They always go out at three for their parking lot shoot-up."

"I know," Helen said. "Let me arrange everything. How do I reach your lawyer?"

"You'd really do this for me?" Evie asked.

"No," Helen said. "For me."

CHAPTER 37

By two fifteen that afternoon, Helen's team was in place. Lawyer Nancie Hays, investigative TV reporter Valerie Cannata and Officer Mac Dorsey were at Fantastic Fitness.

Helen introduced them as three potential new members and made sure they got guest passes. She'd already warned them they would have to listen to a sales spiel first.

Nancie said she'd endure it for her client. Officer Dorsey said she'd listen to anything if it would force that homicide detective into early retirement. Valerie Cannata said she'd do it, but "I have to cancel an interview with the mayor."

"It's worth an Emmy," Helen promised.

"It better be," Valerie said.

It has to be, Helen thought. Things have to start going my way. It's a good sign that I got all three people I needed here on short notice, isn't it?

Helen was desperate, hoping for magic where none existed.

"What color is the locker room floor?" Valerie asked.

"Gray tile," Helen said.

"Dark or light?"

"Slate gray," Helen said.

"Good," Valerie said. "I'll bring our new 'spy cam' in a dark gym bag. We can tape what happens with a hidden camera."

After directing the trio to the Fantastic Fitness sales department, Helen checked in at the reception desk with Carla. Even her colleague's brown hair looked perky this afternoon.

"I didn't expect to see you," Carla said. "Why are you here on your day off?"

"Derek wants me to lose weight," Helen said.

"You don't need to," Carla said.

Helen shrugged. "I need this job. I thought I could exercise better when I wasn't so tired after working all day."

"Such a diligent employee," Carla said, and grinned.

Helen waved at Derek as he headed upstairs. "Afternoon, Helen," the day manager called. His Caribbean accent had lost its charm for her. She hated his insistence that she was overweight.

Helen commandeered the treadmill by the door as her lookout. Officer Mac Dorsey took the empty treadmill next to Helen and watched for their prearranged signal.

When Helen stopped her treadmill, Officer Dorsey would wander back to the women's locker room. As soon as Evie's lawyer, Nancie Hays, saw the police officer in the doorway, she would hide in a shower stall.

Valerie, the TV reporter, was already in place on the other locker room bench, painting her lips. Her gray gym bag with the spy cam was planted under a bench, the tiny lens aimed at the back shower. It melted into the dark tile and the shadows.

Valerie had dressed for success. Her red-hot satin jersey workout suit would look dynamite on camera. She was too famous to hang around the gym unnoticed, so she covered her dark hair with a blond wig. If any gym member started toward the back shower, Valerie would enter first and keep it off-limits.

When the trainers came into the dressing room, Valerie planned to hide in another shower.

Meanwhile, in the front of the gym, Helen was sweating, running and watching the clock. It refused to move.

Two eighteen p.m. Nothing.

Two twenty-three p.m. No sign of the Alien or the Lizard.

Two twenty-seven p.m. The two trainers usually didn't arrive for another three minutes at the earliest, but Helen was tiring. I'm not out of shape, she told herself. I was up late again last night.

She dialed the running speed down to a leisurely pace and hoped the pair would arrive before she collapsed.

Officer Dorsey was running at the fastest speed and not even breaking a sweat. Helen hoped the police officer would have the energy to chase Kristi and Tansi if the trainers made a break for the door.

Helen tried to convince herself that her plan would work. Officer Dorsey had already checked the murder book and confirmed that the crime scene techs had pulled prints off the shower bar where Evie said the drugs were hidden.

Officer Dorsey did warn Helen that Detective Ever Ready had built his case on one cold, hard fact: Evie's estranged husband had a prescription for oxycodone for pain. Evie's prints were on the bottle along with her husband's.

Two thirty-one p.m. Helen's heart was pounding, but not from the exercise. Come on, you two, she prayed, as if that could make them appear.

Tansi and Kristi walked through the gym doors at two thirty-three p.m., hair styled, spray tans glowing. Helen shut off her treadmill, nearly collapsing with relief.

Officer Dorsey switched her machine to the cool-down mode, ran for another thirty seconds, then ambled toward the locker room.

Tansi and Kristi were schmoozing at the reception desk with Carla, pumping up support for the bodybuilding competition.

"I'll definitely be there," Carla said. "The whole gym is going." She didn't mention that they'd be cheering for Paula.

"It starts at five," Kristi said. "We have our suits packed

and ready. All we have to do is show up in front of the judges and then pose with our trophies."

"You sound confident," Helen said, strolling over to the desk.

"Winners are always confident," Tansi said. "A cheering section helps, though. The judges are more likely to vote for a popular choice."

Helen wondered if that was true.

"Don't worry," Carla said. "We'll all be cheering."

"Do you need a ticket, Helen?" Kristi said. "We have extras."

"Already have mine," she said. "There are some new members here today. I saw one head for the women's locker room. Maybe she'd like to go."

Helen followed the two trainers to the locker room. She poured herself a cup of water in the women's lounge while she checked the locker room. The curtains were half-pulled on the showers where Valerie and Nancie were hiding. Officer Mac Dorsey was stretched on the lounge couch, drinking water.

Tansi the lizard approached Officer Dorsey tentatively. "Excuse me," she said. "I'm a trainer and a competition bodybuilder. So is my friend Kristi."

The Alien gave a spooky smile.

"We have some extra tickets to tonight's East Coast Physique Championships. Would you like one?" Tansi asked.

Officer Dorsey pretended to consider the offer. "I might," she said slowly. "What's it cost?"

"It's free," Tansi said.

"The price is right," she said. "I am curious about bodybuilding. I'm thinking of getting into it myself."

"You're fit enough," Kristi said. "We train novices. We could give you a special deal if you're interested. Come to the event and see if you like it. We need more serious women contenders."

"It's a high-energy crowd," Tansi said. "People cheer for their favorites. You don't have to, but we'd like you to cheer for us. We're in the Women's Bodybuilding Over Thirty class, right after the Women's Bikini class. We're on at eight o'clock."

"I could do that," Officer Dorsey said, "but I'd only cheer if I thought you were better than your competition."

"No doubt about that," Tansi said. "Want two tickets? Maybe your boyfriend would like to go."

"No thanks," Officer Dorsey said. "I'm not inviting him to drool at babes in bikinis. He can do that at the beach. I'll be seeing you." She took a ticket, tossed her water cup and went out the door. Officer Dorsey plastered herself out of sight against the wall, next to Helen.

In a nearby mirror, Helen could watch the two trainers search the locker room. "Anyone in here?" Kristi called, raising her voice. "Hello?"

No answer. Valerie and Nancie kept quiet. The camera stayed hidden.

"Good," Tansi said. "It's empty. Keep an eye out, Kristi, while I get the oxy."

Tansi pulled the shower rod off. A rain of tablets was pouring out when Officer Dorsey strolled back into the locker room. This time, she showed her credentials and identified herself as Officer McNamara Dorsey of the West Hills Police Department.

"Interesting medicine bottle you've got there," she said.

Tansi jumped, and a dozen or so tablets hit the tile floor with tiny *tics*. She paled under her fake tan and said, "I have a prescription."

"Really," Officer Dorsey said. "Does that give you the right to dispense medication? You gave six tablets to Debbi Dhosset. Add that to the steroids and the fat burners, and you gave her a steroid speedball. Ms. Dhosset died of an overdose."

"You can't prove that," Tansi said.

"Oh, but I can," Officer Dorsey said. "Our crime scene techs took prints off that rod. We also have a witness who saw you give those tablets to the victim."

Two shower curtains slid back simultaneously, revealing Valerie and Nancie.

"And there are two more witnesses here today," Officer Dorsey said.

"Three," Helen said, stepping into the room.

"We also caught it on camera," Valerie said, pulling the gym bag with the spy cam out from under the bench.

Officer Dorsey turned to the two stunned bodybuilders. "That should be enough evidence to get a search warrant for your cars. I bet we find some controlled substances. But we can talk about that back at the station. Let me advise you of your rights," she said, and gave the familiar police chant beginning with "You have the right to remain silent. . . .

"Now, about those lawyers," Officer Dorsey said. "You may want to call them, or you may want to talk to me first and then call your attorneys. I can't make any promises, but I could make recommendations if a person was helpful.

"So, ladies, which one of you is going to sell out your partner, hmm? Let's make a deal."

CHAPTER 38

. . . .

"And now, ladies and gentlemen, it's time for Women's Open Bikini, Over Fifty class," cried the tuxedoed announcer at the Lauderdale City Auditorium.

Six women, spray-tanned and leggy, paraded onstage in five-inch heels and sparkly bikinis. Helen figured they were wearing more shoes than swimsuit. Each had a white competition number button clipped to her suit.

Helen couldn't believe these women were more than fifty years old. They had the bodies of twenty-year-olds. No, they were thinner than twentysomethings. The layer of fat under their skin had been stripped off, leaving lean, graceful bodies. They moved like gazelles in stilettos.

The crowd roared. It was only forty minutes into the program, and the spectators at the East Coast Physique Championships were wildly enthusiastic. The grim auditorium was some seventy years old, with stained concrete risers and hard wooden seats. Clouds of grease from the concession stands hung in the air.

This audience was definitely made up of spectators in the bodybuilding world. Most were overweight and getting more so. They stuffed themselves with food forbidden to bodybuilders—greasy pizza, cheeseburgers and fries. The thickset man on Helen's left was crunching through a tub of buttered popcorn while he watched the underfed women. The hefty teenage boy next to him sucked on a chocolate shake.

On Helen's right were Carla and the Fantastic Fitness gang. Carla sipped bottled water. Next to her, Beth and Jon lived on love. The cheating couple stared into each other's eyes and held hands under their programs. Logan, the super salesman, was telling red-haired Heather about his Testarossas. She looked bored.

In front of them, Bryan sat between his trainer, Jan Kurtz, and "What a Waste" Will. Where was Will's trainer? Helen wondered. Was Bryan here to meet his trainer tonight? Or get closer to his gay friend, Will? Or neither one? The situation definitely needed watching. Maybe now that Bryan was away from the gym, she could catch him with his honey. She needed a report soon.

Tansi and Kristi, the overconfident bodybuilders, were not going to collect their trophies tonight. They were detained at the West Hills police station by Officer Mac Dorsey. Poor Evie was still in jail. Who else was missing from the Fantastic Fitness group?

The day manager.

"Where's Derek?" Helen asked Carla.

"He's manning our membership table in the lobby," Carla said. "He volunteered to take the first shift."

"But he won't be able to cheer for Paula."

"Sure he will," Carla said. "He'll stand at the entrance and see the show. Nobody's going to sign up now, and no one will steal our membership forms. I'll sit there after Paula's bikini competition."

Good, Helen thought. After Paula struts her stuff, I can go home. That's enough teamwork.

"Look what I brought for Paula." Carla showed Helen six red roses stashed under her seat.

"Nice. What happens if she doesn't win?" Helen asked.

"She will," Carla said. "If not, then I have a bouquet."

"Forty-two! Forty-two! Forty-two!" the crowd chanted as a long-haired blonde posed in front of the judges in a sparkly hot pink suit and clear high heels.

"Quarter turn to your right," the head judge commanded, and Number Forty-two turned to the side. She was so thin, her midsection looked concave.

"That's my wife, Jasmine," said the popcorn cruncher on Helen's left.

"I can't believe she's over fifty years old," Helen said. "She looks fantastic."

"Seven percent body fat," her husband said proudly. "She really knows how to flare her lats."

"Face the back," the judge said in a flat voice.

Number Forty-two gave the judges her back view. She pulled up her long blond hair to show her shoulders and thrust out her haunches as if she wanted the judges to mount her. Those weren't her lats, were they? Helen wondered. No, those were glutes. Sweet Gloria Steinem, why was this woman letting herself be judged like horseflesh?

"Great ass!" shouted the chocolate-shake guzzler.

"My son is proud of his mother," Mr. Popcorn said.

He was cheering for his mother's rear end? Helen didn't want to think about that. "Amazing," she said. It seemed the only word to describe the scene.

"You should have seen Jasmine last week," Mr. Popcorn said. "She was perfect. Then she started drinking water. She knows better: no carbs and no water before the competition. Too fattening and bloating. But she wouldn't listen. I caught her sneaking downstairs to the kitchen at two in the morning to suck ice cubes. I should have put a padlock on the refrigerator. Now she looks like she walked to Lauderdale." He stuffed his mouth with more popcorn.

"I think she looks terrific," Helen said.

"Not when you see her through my binoculars," he said. "The judges don't look at her the way you do."

Helen peered through the glasses, focusing on the emaciated beauty bending her body into absurd poses in her skimpy, sparkling suit. She wanted to kidnap Jasmine, take her out for a good meal and then give her a body-image lecture.

"She's not smiling," her husband said.

"She looks good," Helen said. The audience seemed to agree. They yelled "Forty-two! Forty-two! We want Forty-two."

"Now turn and face the judges," the lead judge ordered. Jasmine smiled, bowed and walked off the stage to thundering cheers.

Jasmine was definitely the crowd favorite. They were indifferent to Numbers Twenty-eight and Thirty and actively hostile to Thirty-three, another gazelle in a gold sequin suit with a pearl pendant between her globular breasts.

The crowd heckled the poor creature with cruel taunts: "Eat a potato chip!" "Two words: Olive Garden!"

"Get a Twinkie!" yelled a woman whose massive breasts nearly wobbled out of her tube top. She'd obviously followed that advice many times.

"Bring back Forty-two," the crowd screamed. The judges brought back all six contestants for one more turn around the stage, then retired to choose the winner.

"Carla," Helen whispered, "is this for real?"

"Very," Carla said. "These women are serious about this competition. Don't mistake it for real fitness. These are freakazoids. For some, it's the only recognition they'll get. They see themselves as athletes. They may look good onstage, but they starve and dehydrate themselves to get that look. Paula's competition is up next. She's the only Fantastic Fitness person left in the show. After that, I go work the membership table. I hope Paula wins. Here's the announcer. The judges have made their decisions for the Over Fifty class."

The man looked bizarrely overdressed in a black tux after the nearly naked contenders.

Number Thirty took third place. The chief judge put the bronze medal around her neck with Olympic Games solemnity. She received modest cheers. Number Twenty-eight looked disappointed with her second-place medal but graciously bent her neck to receive it.

Two bodybuilders carried out the massive first-place trophy, brimming with finials, urns, and winged figures, and layered like a brass wedding cake.

"And the winner is . . ." The announcer paused dramatically. The audience moved like a restless beast, waiting to roar approval or disappointment. Would the winner be the dislikable Number Thirty-three or the popular Forty-two?

"Forty-two! Forty-two! Forty-two!" the crowd chanted. So did Carla and the rest of the Fantastic Fitness party. Helen raised a questioning eyebrow.

"It's okay to cheer for her," Carla said. "We don't have anyone from our gym in this class. Maybe they'll cheer for Paula when she's up."

"Forty-two!" the announcer cried, drawing the two words out.

"Yay, Mom!" the milk-shake guzzler hollered.

"Smile, damn it," screamed her husband. "You won!"

Helen didn't know if Jasmine heard him or not, but she put on a wide smile. She posed for pictures next to the gigantic trophy, then carried it off as if it were made of seafoam.

"Congratulations," Helen said to Mr. Popcorn.

"She'll be up here shortly," he said. "You can tell her yourself."

The nearly naked Jasmine ran lightly up the steps to her family's seats and hugged her husband and son. Even in the dim light, Helen could see the contest had taken its toll. Up close her hair was like straw, and her skin sagged from malnutrition. But her smile was dazzling.

"I just wanted to say hello," she said. "Then I want some food. Does the concession stand carry my kind of food?"

" 'Fraid not," her husband said. "But we'll take you to dinner to celebrate."

The announcer was back. "Ladies and gentlemen, we have the Women's Open Bikini, Over Thirty class." Four women pranced out and lined up against the back curtain. Number Twenty-two wore a green suit covered with what looked like sparkly algae. Number Thirty-eight wore red with silver spangles. Number Eleven strutted out in yellow with gold sequins. Paula was Number Nine. She seemed to roll out on castors.

Paula had the same hypnotic effect on the rowdy audience that she did on the gym members. She looked like a snow queen in a sparkling white bikini and sandals with icicle heels. The audience was awed into silence while the judges called her poses and she made her elegant quarter turns.

Only when Paula was back in her original place did the audience erupt into applause. Carla led the cheer: "Nine! Nine! We want Nine!" The rest of the audience picked it up. The other three contestants didn't seem to exist. No one cared that Thirty-eight carried off the third-place medal or Eleven won second place. They were chanting "Number Nine! Number Nine!" A few parodied the line from the Beatles' song, that slow, monotonous repetition of "Number Nine, Number Nine."

Paula's win was a foregone conclusion. She glided up to accept the monster trophy, posed prettily for pictures, then carried it off as if it were made of feathers.

"Can you get that huge trophy in the Fantastic Fitness Hall of Fame?" Helen asked Carla.

"We'll make room if we have to," Carla said. "There's extra space since you-know-who won't be getting their trophies tonight. They must be so disappointed."

Helen hoped they were charged and arrested by now, but kept quiet. Officer Mac Dorsey had handled their takedown discreetly. The gym was nearly empty at that hour. Dorsey had allowed the gym to put an OUT OF ORDER sign on the hallway to the women's locker room while the crime scene techs worked. The few gym members who came in that afternoon used Derek's private restroom upstairs. Derek didn't quite comprehend what was happening, but he was cooperative.

The facilities were open again before the evening rush. Kristi and Tansi went quietly to the police car, possibly hoping to avoid unwanted attention.

When Helen left the gym, Valerie was doing a stand-up in front of the cameras in the parking lot. She'd thanked

Helen for the story and asked for an interview. Helen had begged off until after the East Coast Physique Championships. They'd set an appointment for eight o'clock that night outside the auditorium.

It was seven thirty now. Helen made her way down the concrete stairs to congratulate Paula, who was surrounded by well-wishers and haloed with white-hot success.

Carla rushed up to her first, presented the roses and kissed her. "You were awesome!" she said. "You look incredible. You made us look fantastic. Sorry. I have to dash."

The platinum blond Paula held her roses while cameras flashed. Helen saw tiny tears glitter on her cheeks. They went well with the sparkles on her white bikini.

Helen reached out and squeezed Paula's hand. She was rewarded with a queenly nod. Helen slipped away while Bryan, Will and Jan pushed forward with their congratulations.

Helen wanted to check her hair and makeup in a mirror before her television interview with Valerie. She'd never been to this auditorium and couldn't find the restrooms. She thought she'd followed the signs that said RESTROOMS THIS WAY, but after several minutes she wound up in a narrow, nearly deserted passageway with six doors painted dull green. None of the doors had signs.

The first door was a storage closet crammed with signs and easels. Helen shut it.

The second was another closet stacked to the ceiling with cases of soda and bottled water. Time was passing quickly. It was seven forty-two.

Helen opened the third door and stared into two surprised eyes. Carla's eyes. They were peering over a muscular back. Carla gave a little shriek and untangled herself from Bryan Minars.

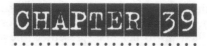

CHAPTER 39

● ● ● ● ● ● ● ● ● ● ● ● ● ● ● ● ● ●

Helen and Phil were awakened by loud pounding on the door to Helen's apartment. A woman shouted, "Wake up! Open up! Hurry up! You're on TV!"

Helen sat up and blinked at Phil. She was still stupid from sleep. Phil was more alert. He hopped out of bed, pulled on his jeans and ran to the front door.

"It's Margery," he called as their landlady swept past him in a purple chenille robe trimmed with whiffs of cigarette smoke.

Margery commandeered the clicker and flipped on Helen's television. "I don't have time to explain," she said. "Watch this. Helen, get in here before you miss your fifteen minutes of fame. Why is this on Channel Ten? Your television should be permanently tuned to Channel Seventy-seven after what that reporter has done for you."

Helen stumbled out of the bedroom in jeans and a white shirt, hair uncombed.

"Coffee!" she said.

"Your shirt's buttoned crooked," Margery said. "You can have coffee later. Right now, you need to see this special report. It's on after this commercial."

Margery took Helen by the shoulders and steered her to the turquoise couch next to Phil, then sat in the chair alongside them. Thumbs jumped in her lap, and Margery dumped the cat on the floor.

"Go shed on someone else," she said. The offended cat settled himself in Phil's lap.

They watched the last seconds of a fabric softener ad while Helen struggled to gather her scattered thoughts.

Carrie, the early-morning show anchor, said, "Lucky Double Seven brings you twice the hard-hitting local news of any other South Florida station. We've learned that a fifty-year-old Fort Lauderdale woman was jailed for a murder she didn't commit. Reporter Valerie Cannata tells you about an innocent victim of misguided justice—and the private eye who saved her from death row."

Valerie, wearing that eye-catching red workout suit, stood in front of Fantastic Fitness. She described the murder of Debbi Dhosset. "The twenty-two-year-old victim OD'd on a kind of bodybuilder's speedball of oxycodone, fat burners and steroids."

A photo of Debbi in her posing suit flashed on the screen, followed by the mug shot of Evie. The accused killer looked as harmless as a kitten.

"This woman, Evie Roddick, was arrested by West Hills homicide detective Evarts Redding for the murder of Debbi Dhosset. The homicide detective said her motive was revenge after Debbi threw a hand weight at her in a steroid rage while working out at the gym.

"This woman, a Fantastic Fitness employee, was convinced that Evie Roddick was innocent and proved it." Helen was standing outside the Lauderdale City Auditorium.

Helen winced at herself on-screen. "My hair looks awful."

"Shut up!" Margery and Phil said together.

Valerie was talking again. "Helen Hawthorne is a private eye with Coronado Investigations, a Fort Lauderdale agency owned by Hawthorne and her husband. Helen did the investigative work that helped free Evie Roddick, even visiting the woman at the Harriet Brackensieck Women's Correction Facility of Broward County."

The camera showed file footage of the grim jail, surrounded by razor wire.

"Coronado Investigations uncovered the true killers," Helen said on camera. "But we couldn't free Evie on our own. We needed you, Valerie."

"Kiss up!" Margery said, and grinned.

"Clever move," Phil said. "You mentioned our agency name, too."

Now Valerie was standing in front of the gym again. "Yesterday, this reporter was at Fantastic Fitness when the actual alleged killers of Debbi Dhosset were in the women's locker room. The victim's two trainers came to retrieve their stash of illegal drugs, hidden in a shower rod. West Hills police officer McNamara Dorsey took them into custody at the gym. We caught the scene with the Channel Seventy-seven spy cam. Watch."

Helen couldn't take her eyes away as the slightly blurry footage unfolded.

Valerie continued to explain: "Officer Dorsey said steroids, a controlled substance used illegally by some bodybuilders, were discovered in a vehicle belonging to one trainer and parked on the Fantastic Fitness lot. Both women were arrested and charged with first-degree murder."

Helen watched Tansi and Kristi being led to Officer Dorsey's car on the gym lot amid a carnival of police lights. The scene made an unforgettable ending to Valerie's story.

"I like that 'actual alleged killers' phrase," Helen said.

"It's awkward, but it makes the station lawyers happy," Margery said.

"And I'm a trainee, not a full-fledged private eye," Helen said.

"So you want a correction?" Phil asked.

Carrie, the news anchor, was back on-screen. "As of six o'clock this morning, Evie Roddick is still in jail," she said, "but authorities promise she will be released as soon as the paperwork is completed. Ms. Roddick's attorney, Nancie Hays, would not comment on whether her client will sue the

city of West Hills for false arrest. We'll have exclusive updates on the story as it unfolds."

Her co-anchor, Jason, said, "That's an amazing story."

"There's more," Carrie said. "Tomorrow, reporter Valerie
Cannata will tell us about the high-pressure tactics a Fantastic Fitness salesman uses to sign up new members. Here's
a preview from that special investigative piece, 'Promises,
Promises.'"

Helen watched a blurry spy-cam shot of the sales area
and heard a man say, 'You be nice to me and I'll be nice to
you. Extra nice. For a whole week.'"

"Logan!" Helen shouted. "That's Logan, working his
'one week free' scam to score with Valerie. I'd recognize
that scumbag's voice anywhere."

"That's good, I guess," Phil said.

"Good! It's terrific. Logan should have been fired ages
ago."

Thumbs patted Phil's face lightly with his big six-toed
paw and meowed.

"Breakfast time, buddy?" Phil asked the cat. "Good. I
need coffee."

Thumbs crunched his dry food and his owners drank coffee in Helen's kitchen. Phil spent a half pot of coffee prais-
ing Helen.

By her third cup, Helen said, "Today I have to tell Shelby
I caught her husband with another woman. I had no idea
that Bryan was having a fling with Carla. I was stunned
when I opened that closet at the auditorium. So were they.
I'd asked Carla if she ever got any bribe money from
women asking about Bryan. She said, 'No woman's dropped
twenties on me to find out if he's at the gym. His wife works
out here, too.' She was the one who wanted to know when
he was at the gym and she could check the computer herself. That liar."

"Technically, she didn't lie," Phil said.

"She sure didn't tell the truth," Helen said. "Now I have
to break the news to Shelby. I dread that."

"It won't be much of a surprise," Phil said. "She already
suspects. Shelby wants to know. That's why she hired you."

"I know she did," Helen said. "I also know how much it hurts to hear that news. At least she won't find out her husband was unfaithful the way I did. I surprised Rob in the act with our neighbor Sandy. I felt like a fool."

"I know you did," Phil said, folding Helen into his arms. "But you divorced him and then left St. Louis and drove until you found me here in Fort Lauderdale."

"It wasn't quite that simple, but I did find you and I'm glad," Helen said. Her man smelled of cinnamon and morning coffee. She didn't want to leave his embrace, but she pulled herself away.

"Might as well get it over with. How early can I call Shelby?"

"It's almost seven o'clock," Phil said, checking his watch. "That's when she came to see us the first time."

"Bryan's usually at the gym around six," Helen said. "I'll call her now and set up an appointment for eight this morning."

Shelby Minars refused to wait until eight o'clock for the final report. She stormed over to the Coronado Investigations office at seven thirty-five. Helen and Phil heard their client running upstairs to Apartment 2C.

This morning, Shelby was dressed for the office in a pink suit. The Red Hots toes were stashed inside black heels. Her hazel eyes burned with anger.

Shelby could barely sit still in the yellow client chair long enough to hear the news.

"He's at the gym right now," Shelby said. "What is that lying bastard doing? Or maybe I should say *who* is he doing?"

"Your husband appears to be having an affair with a woman who works at the gym as a receptionist," Helen said. "Her name is Carla. I caught them together in a storage room at the Lauderdale City Auditorium at seven fifty-two last night. I didn't take photographs, but they were embracing. Carla's blouse was unbuttoned and her pants were unzipped. So were your husband's."

"I don't need photos of that cheating scum," Shelby said. "I got the picture a long time ago. I wanted my suspicions confirmed." She burst into tears. "I'll kill him. I'll kill him."

"No, you won't," Phil said. He handed her a tissue. "We talked about this before. You can't make threats like that. If anything happened to Bryan, we'd have to tell the police, and you could go to jail. He's not worth it."

"You're right," Shelby said, sniffling. "He's not. I won't kill him. I'll strip him of every last nickel. Do you mind if I make a call?"

"Go right ahead," Helen said.

Phil was right, Helen thought. Shelby had been expecting this news. She pulled out her cell phone and called a number in her directory. "I'm on hold," she said. "I'm calling the toughest divorce lawyer in Lauderdale for an appointment."

There was a pause, and then Shelby said, "Nine o'clock this morning will work for me." She snapped her phone shut.

"Here's our bill," Helen said. "Might as well pay it now and save yourself a stamp."

"Good idea," Shelby said. She wrote the check without a complaint.

"Bryan will probably spend his usual five or six hours at the gym today. That will give me time to see the lawyer, change the locks and throw his stuff out on the lawn. He can go live with that Carla. We'll see how much she likes him when he has no money."

CHAPTER 40

"**D**erek wants to see you in his office right now," Carla said when Helen arrived at the gym that morning.

The Fantastic Fitness phone was ringing wildly. Carla grabbed the receiver and said, "Yes, ma'am. The manager is busy now. I'll have Derek get back to you. What's your phone number?" She wrote it down and hung up.

The phone rang again. Carla repeated her promise to have the manager return the call, then wrote down another number, and the phone rang for a third time.

"I'm sorry, ma'am," Carla said. "May I put you on hold?"

Carla stopped juggling the phone long enough to tell Helen, "You'd better get upstairs fast."

She didn't mention their surprise meeting in the storage closet last night. Maybe she didn't have time. The phone rang yet again, and Carla put that caller on hold, too. The phone's red HOLD lights were blinking like demon eyes.

Carla's own eyes were red, and she had an ugly zit on her not-so-perky nose. She also had an annoying smirk on her face.

Helen ran upstairs to Derek's office. She'd had enough

of Fantastic Fitness. She couldn't wait to say she was quitting.

Helen never got the chance.

"You're fired!" Derek said before she even knocked on his door.

"Fired? Why?" Helen said.

Derek stood up, outrage etched in every muscle of his body. There was no music in his Caribbean lilt now, only anger. Each word was clipped and precise. "You brought an undercover police officer into this establishment. You sneaked in that TV bitch. She brought a hidden camera inside the women's locker room without my permission. You got two gym members arrested on this property for drug dealing and murder."

Derek paused for a breath. He was so angry, Helen feared he'd stroke out in his office.

"And if that wasn't bad enough, that same TV reporter also investigated my best salesman. Tomorrow, she's going to say Logan tried to coerce her into having sex with him for a week's free membership. What do you have to say about that?"

"It's true," Helen said. "It's all true and you know it. You knew those two trainers used steroids and gave them to poor Debbi. The whole building knew why they went outside at three o'clock every afternoon. You should have barred them from the gym. But you kept silent because you wanted their trophies in the Hall of Fame case downstairs.

"You knew Logan did sleazy things when he sold memberships, but you ignored the complaints. You didn't care and you didn't stop him. You wanted those sales.

"Poor little Evie was railroaded into jail with your help while those two steroid-using monsters roamed free in this gym. You didn't care about that, either.

"So, yes, I did it. It was the right thing to do. I don't understand why you're firing me."

Derek's voice dropped to a deep rumble. "Because of you, I've lost my best salesman. Because of you, members are quitting this gym by the dozen. Because of you, Fantastic Fitness is associated with murder and drug use. Because of you, my gym gets more bad publicity with every news update on Channel Seventy-seven. That's why I'm firing you. Besides, you're fat. You were supposed to lose weight and you didn't. Those are the reasons why you're being fired. Got it? Get out. *You're fired! Fired! Fired!*"

Helen opened her cell phone and said, "See that? You're looking at TV reporter Valerie Cannata's personal cell phone number. When I call her, she'll listen. She got two good stories from me this week. Let's go for three. If I tell her I was fired because of her investigative stories, she'll plaster this gym's name all over the television for a week. You'll have seven solid days of local coverage."

Helen pressed the CALL button.

"Wait!" Derek said. "Stop! Don't call that reporter. What do you want? Your old job back? I can give it to you. I'll even give you a fifty-cent-an-hour raise."

"I want the raise," Helen said, "but you can keep the job. Give them both to Evie Roddick when she gets out of jail. You promised to find her work here if she went quietly with Detective Evarts Redding. She kept her end of the deal. Now you keep yours."

"I don't know if she's qualified for a job at this gym," Derek said.

"You definitely need someone to answer the phone and take messages," Helen said, looking at the blinking lights. "Evie's skinny, so she'll fit your important employment criteria."

"There may not even be a gym for her to work at, thanks to you." Derek sounded bitter.

"She'll have a fresh job for her résumé," Helen said. "You aren't going to close next week, or even next month. Maybe if you hire Evie, you'll get some positive press from Valerie. Evie could save this gym."

"But—," Derek said.

"You don't have to thank me," Helen said. "But there is one more thing I want to make clear: I'm not fat. Got that? You've been spending too much time around gym rats. This is what a normal woman looks like."

Derek managed a nod.

"Good-bye," Helen said. "I'll check back in a week and make sure Evie has her job. If you're lucky, you'll never see me again."

Helen ran lightly down the stairs. The front door *whooshed* open. Helen hoped she was walking through it for the last time.

CHAPTER 41

H elen was so happy to be out of the gym, she skipped
to her car. Unfortunately, the Igloo skipped, too.
The Cruiser hesitated when she hit the gas pedal.

Helen checked the gauges, but they looked normal. The
car didn't make any strange noises, and it got her home.
Helen hoped that meant the problem wasn't serious. She
patted the faithful Cruiser on the fender and ran upstairs to
the office of Coronado Investigations.

Phil looked up from his computer and smiled. "That was
fast."

"It didn't take me long to quit—or get fired," Helen said.
"I'm not sure which it was. Either way, I'm free of that
place. One case down, one to go. You were supposed to get
the fax from Sunset Palms this morning. Did Danny Boy's
sister have the clerk send those two pages?"

"I got one page. The great Linda Cerventi faxed it with
her own two hands," Phil said. "Looks like the real thing,
too. It's from Mark's police report."

"Where's the second page?" Helen asked.

"She says she'll have it this afternoon."

"Hah!" Helen said.

"I suggested that Linda might want to watch Channel Seventy-seven, especially the exposé by Valerie Cannata. Linda promised I'd have the other page by one o'clock."

"And you believe her?" Helen asked.

"Valerie is doing hourly updates of your story. She had live coverage of Evie leaving jail. Evie personally thanked you for saving her from death row. We'll have that paper from Linda in time. Meanwhile, there's plenty here. I've made you a copy. Read it and see if you reach the same conclusions."

Helen sat at her desk. The page was a Sunset Palms police form, the "Supplementary Investigative and/or Disposition Report on the auto accident/suicide of Mark Behr." It was dated July 15, 1986. The short report was written in that stilted police style, as if the officer was testifying. It said:

"Reference to the above incident, Bernadette Behr, sister to Mark Behr, contacted this officer, at which time the following information was obtained from her. Bernie Behr stated that Mark had been depressed and had often talked of suicide. Bernadette Behr stated that about one or two weeks before this incident, Mark had stated something about Ahmet Yavuz being the devil and he could kill Ahmet and then himself and this would stop Yavuz and save the world.

"Bernadette Behr was asked if Mark would have killed Ahmet Yavuz if he had seen him, with Bernadette stating that Mark probably would have. No additional information was obtained from Bernadette Behr."

The report had four boxes the police could check: "active," "cleared by arrest," and "inactive." Mark's case was checked "exceptionally cleared."

Helen read the report twice, trying to grasp it. "I keep reading this, but I'm not sure I understand it. Go over it with me: Bernie told the police Mark was suicidal."

"That's what the report says," Phil said.

"So Bernie stopped the investigation into her brother's death," Helen said.

"That's right," Phil said.

"That can't be," Helen said. "Gus told us his sister had stopped seeing Ahmet a week before Mark's death."

"Yes, he did," Phil said.

"Mark rescued Bernie from the drug dealer's house. Ahmet took her clothes so she couldn't leave. Mark wrapped his sister in a bedspread and carried her out of there. The rescued Bernie didn't want to go home to Mother, so she lived with her brothers in their bachelor apartment. She was too afraid to leave."

"That's what Joel told us," Phil said.

"Is Gus lying?" Helen asked. "Did Joel lie about Bernie's rescue?"

"I don't think so," Phil said.

"Then what's going on with this report?"

"If Gus and Joel aren't lying," Phil said, "then Bernie is."

"Bernie was afraid of Ahmet," Helen said. "She cut all ties with him. Why would she tell the police that Mark wanted to commit suicide?"

"I don't know," Phil said.

"Maybe the cops came to the apartment and interviewed her," Helen said.

"No, she made an appointment and went to the station," Phil said. "She gave the police a statement that her brother had mental problems and had threatened suicide. That's when the police stopped investigating his death."

"But what about the red flags we noticed—the gun, the shell casing and the blanket with the bullet hole?"

"The police ignored them once Mark's sister gave her statement," Phil said.

"Why would Bernie stop the investigation?" Helen said. "Why would she brand her brother a suicide? She was Catholic. Suicide is a serious sin in her religion."

"Bernie was trying to save herself," Phil said. "Her brother was dead. She was mixed up with a drug crowd. She didn't care if her brother was labeled a suicide. Bernie wasn't religious anymore."

"Where was Mark's mother?" Helen asked.

"Gus told us his mother was a ghost. She'd lost her husband and her son. She was dying of cancer."

Helen struggled with this information and still failed to grasp it. The conclusions were too distressing. "What Bernie told the police made Mark's case go away," she said. "It was closed. Not just closed—exceptionally closed. Gus was right. Someone in law enforcement was paid off."

"Not necessarily," Phil said. "Every case has loose ends. The police know that. This was a small force. Bernie gave them a way out, and they took it."

"Gus told us Bernie went to a psychiatric hospital after Mark died. I want to ask him about that incident."

"Why?" Phil asked.

"The hospital visit is a key to this case," Helen said. "I know it. I want Gus to tell me more about it."

"There's the phone. Call him," Phil said.

"No, I'll see him in person," Helen said. "The Igloo hesitates when I hit the gas. I'll take the car to Gus and have him look at it. Then I can ask him what happened when his sister was in the hospital."

"Your instincts have been good so far," Phil said. "I'll stay here and dig around in the computer for more information about Ahmet. He's the real mystery in this case."

Gus was in his office eating a turkey sandwich when Helen drove the PT Cruiser into the Boy Toys Restoration garage. The office was cool, but Gus's shirt was soaked with sweat.

"Heat getting you?" Helen asked.

"Yeah," Gus said. "It's brutal. I've got to lose weight. Jeannie has me on a diet. This time I'm sticking to it."

Helen wondered how often he'd made that resolution. His sandwich, a thin slice of colorless meat on whole wheat, had three bites out of it. Gus abandoned his low-fat lunch and said, "Do you have news?"

"Phil will have a report for you shortly. I have a small problem with my car and a question about Bernie."

"Car first." Gus listened to Helen describe the car's behavior, then said, "Sounds like it needs a new fuel filter, but I'll look at it. Now, what's the question?"

Gus seemed more comfortable working on the car while he talked, so Helen followed him into the repair area. Gus draped the Cruiser's fenders with the same care as if he were working on a vintage Rolls.

"After Mark rescued your sister from Ahmet, she came to live with you and Mark," Helen said.

"That's right."

"After Mark saved her, did Bernie ever call Ahmet?" Helen asked. "Did the dealer come see her? Ask after her?"

"Never," Gus said. "She was frightened. She cut all ties with Ahmet."

"Tell me about when your sister had a breakdown and went to the psychiatric hospital."

"Mark had been dead a month," Gus said. "Bernie was still living with me. Bernie quit eating. She lost, like, thirty-some pounds. She stayed in my apartment all day, holding Mark's old shirt and crying. She wouldn't get dressed. I got worried and called Mom. Mom wasn't doing too well herself. We took Bernie to the doctor. I had to carry her to the car in her robe.

"The doctor said she was depressed and anorexic. He wanted her committed to a psychiatric hospital. Mom hated shrinks, but she didn't argue with him. She didn't want to lose another child. Bernie didn't have the strength to fight anyone.

"After two weeks, the doc finally let her have visitors. She was lying in her bed like one of those stone figures on a tomb in an old English church; you know the kind I mean?"

"Yes," Helen said.

"She looked half-dead. She was pale and rigid and so thin she hardly made a mound in the covers. Her face was like a skull covered with skin. She was taking heavy drugs—legal, psychiatrist-type drugs—and her eyes were dull. She still had that incredible red hair. It was almost down to her waist, but it was crackly and dry. I couldn't tell if Bernie was awake or not. I stood there for a long time staring at her. Then I whispered her name.

"She sat up like she was eighty years old. 'You came to see me,' she said in this whiny voice. 'You didn't have to do that. I don't deserve it.' She started crying. I was afraid I'd upset her again.

"I said, 'Hey, it's okay.' I gave her a hug. She was so

skinny I could feel her spine through her hospital gown. It was like knobs of bone.

" 'I'm so ugly,' she cried.

" 'No, you're beautiful. You just need to gain a little weight. You've got great hair.'

"She wouldn't stop crying. She kept saying, 'It's all my fault. It's all my fault.'

"I tried to say it wasn't, but she wouldn't listen. I left her there, crying.

"The doctor said she would get better, and she did. Bernie was released about six months later, and she really straightened herself out. She went to school to become a phlebotomist; then she married a decent guy. Her husband's an executive. They have a good kid. My nephew's in college now. Whatever the doctor did to her at that hospital, it was the right thing."

Gus was poking around under the Cruiser's hood. Helen thought it was easier for him to examine the inner workings of a car than his own family. "Ah! Just what I thought," Gus said. "It was the filter. That's easy. I'll fix it in a minute."

Gus returned with the new filter, tinkered with the car again, then shut the hood. "That's it," he said, smiling. "Ready to go. Did I answer your question?"

"I still don't understand," Helen said. "Why would Bernie say Mark's death was all her fault?"

"Guilt," Gus said. "She felt guilty that she got Mark mixed up with that wild crowd. My sister made some bad decisions when she was young, but Bernie grew up. She's a good person now. You're good to go."

Gus wanted Helen to leave.

"What do I owe you?"

"No charge," he said.

It was almost one o'clock. Phil was supposed to get the second page of Mark's report. Helen hurried home.

The car was fine, but something was wrong with Gus's story. Something he couldn't see no matter how often he looked at it.

CHAPTER 42

The fax machine was humming when Helen walked into the Coronado Investigations office shortly after one o'clock.

"Is that the second sheet from Sunset Palms?" Helen asked.

"You must be psychic," Phil said. "Linda sent it right after she saw the latest Channel Seventy-seven breaking-news report. Detective Evarts Redding announced his retirement from the West Hills force. He wants to spend more time with his wife."

"We got him!" Helen said. She hugged Phil, then danced around the room.

"The city of West Hills spokesman said there was no connection between the detective's retirement and the stories on Channel Seventy-seven."

"Of course not," Helen said. "Enough gloating. Let's look at the rest of that Sunset Palms police report."

"It's a property sheet," Phil said. "The police kept Mark's wallet, ID, thirty dollars and a .32 automatic Mauser. The property sheet said a family representative should bring 'this with you at the time of claim. Property held in excess of six months will be disposed of in the manner prescribed under Section 1-16 of the Municipal Code.'

"The lower part of this report was a signed receipt. It says Mark's property was picked up by—" Phil stopped.

"Don't be a tease," Helen said. "Who picked up Mark's property?"

"Bernie," Phil said.

Helen sat down. "Bernie picked up Mark's gun and wallet?"

"That's what the report says. It was signed by a police captain."

"Bernie has the gun that killed Mark," Helen said. "If we get it, we can prove Mark was murdered. It can be checked for Ahmet's fingerprints. The police could do ballistics tests and see if it fired the bullets. Does she still have it?"

"I don't know. We can ask Gus," Phil said. "First, tell me how your visit went. What did Gus say about Bernie? Why does she blame herself?"

"Gus says she feels guilty about dragging Mark into her wild life," Helen said. "I think Gus is wrong about her reason. I'll call him about the gun. We just talked. It will seem more natural."

A young mechanic answered at Boy Toys Restoration. He said he'd look for Gus. Helen drummed her desktop impatiently while she waited.

After several minutes, Gus picked up the phone. "Helen, what's wrong with your car now?"

"It's fine," Helen said. "I have one more question. After Mark died, your sister went to the police station and picked up his property, including his wallet and his gun."

"I told you, that wasn't Mark's gun. He owned a .22, not a Mauser."

"Okay, she picked up the gun the police said belonged to Mark."

"Mom asked her to do that," Gus said. "The case was closed. Bernie offered to get Mark's wallet and gun."

"Does she still have the gun?"

"No," Gus said. "My sister threw it away as soon as she got it. Dumped it in the ocean off Dania Beach. Is my report ready?"

"Soon," Helen promised and hung up before he could ask more.

"The gun's long gone," Helen said. "What is the date on that report? When did Bernie claim Mark's property?"

"Two weeks after Mark's shooting," Phil said. "Gus says two weeks later Bernie was admitted to the psychiatric hospital crying, 'It's all my fault.'"

"It was all her fault." Helen stood up and paced the terrazzo floor. "She did something worse than introduce her brother to her wild life — if that's even what happened. Bernie was telling the truth. I'm going to Weston to have another run at her."

"She threw you out of her house," Phil said.

"She won't this time."

"What if she's at work?" Phil asked.

"She doesn't work all day every day. If she had the early shift at the hospital, she'll be home by the time I get there. If not, I'll camp out in her driveway until she does get home."

Helen drove to Bernie's house in the distant beige burb. The garage doors were closed on her tastefully bland mansion. Helen hoped Bernie's car was inside.

She parked the Igloo on the brownish pavers. Last time, Helen had driven Phil's black Jeep. If Bernie was peeking out the windows, Helen hoped she wouldn't connect this white car with the PI pest she'd thrown off her property.

Helen rang the doorbell. No answer. She thought she saw a curtain flutter upstairs. She definitely saw miniblinds and Roman shades discreetly moving in the nearby houses. The stay-at-home moms were watching, bless them. They'd help Helen get inside.

"Bernie," she shouted and rang the doorbell again. "Hey, Bernie, open up! I saw a friend of yours from the good old days. I'm dying to talk to you about him."

Up and down the quiet cul-de-sac, Helen detected minuscule movements at the windows. Helen pretended to be drunk, knowing that would attract more attention.

"Bernie!" Helen pounded on the door and slurred her words. "Wassa matter? Le's talk. C'mon."

Helen heard the clatter of footsteps on the marble entry. Bernie unlocked the door but kept on the security chain. Once again, Helen was shocked by the transformation from femme fatale to frump. Her beige hair matched her beige scrubs. Bernie was wearing brown Crocs.

Her voice was a witchy hiss. "What do you want? I told you to go away. I'm calling the police if you don't leave now."

Helen lowered her voice to a near whisper. "You can let me in for a talk or we can discuss this on your doorstep where all the neighbors will learn about your interesting past. As you heard, I can shout pretty loud."

Bernie held up her cell phone. "I'm calling 911 now."

"Go ahead," Helen said. "I can shout out your history before the cops get here. Bet your neighbors would love to hear about when you were a drug dealer's girlfriend. How about the time your brother dragged you naked out of Ahmet's place, wrapped in a bedspread? Go ahead, Bernie. Make that call."

Bernie glared at Helen as if she could make her head explode into a red haze. Helen stood her ground. Bernie took off the security chain, and Helen slid into the beige, mirrored hallway. Bernie blocked her from moving past the doormat.

"Stop right there," Bernie said. "You're not going any farther. Say what you have to say and leave."

Helen said, "Ahmet killed Mark, didn't he?"

Bernie looked shocked but didn't deny it.

Helen pulled some papers from her purse. "I have the police report right here. It has your statement that your brother threatened Ahmet's life. You called the drug dealer and warned him that Mark wanted to kill him. That's why you said Mark's death was your fault when you were in the hospital. You tipped off your boyfriend and got your brother killed." Helen held out the papers.

"Ex-boyfriend," Bernie said. She backed away from the papers as if they were poisonous. Bernie recited the dramatic facts in a flat, toneless voice. "I was trying to save

Ahmet's life. He didn't mean to kill Mark. It was self-defense."

"Is that why Ahmet used a silencer? The police found a blanket with a bullet hole in Mark's car. Blankets, pillows and couch cushions are used as silencers."

"It wasn't a silencer. That's not how it happened," Bernie said in that cold, flat voice. "Ahmet told me he had the blanket in his hand because he was moving an old mirror in the stockroom at his business. The blanket protected it. He looked out the window and saw Mark driving erratically into his parking lot. Ahmet grabbed the gun for protection and put the blanket over it. It was broad daylight. He couldn't go outside waving a gun."

"Why didn't he call the police?"

"People like Ahmet don't call the police.

"You know what he did for a living," Bernie said, her voice full of scorn. "Mark had a .22. He said he was going to shoot Ahmet. There was no reasoning with Mark. He was crazy. Bipolar is the name they use now. He said Ahmet was the devil and he would send him to hell."

She went back to that flat tone. "Ahmet said he couldn't get Mark to put down the gun. It was pointed right at Ahmet. Mark had his finger on the trigger. Ahmet fired first. Mark's foot must have hit the gas pedal then, and he rammed the building and hit a parked car.

"Ahmet ran over and threw his Mauser on the floorboards of Mark's car. The casing was already inside. Ahmet got the .22 out of the car, but he must have left the blanket behind. It was too late to pick it up. People were running out of the building."

"You believe that story?" Helen asked.

"Yes, but I knew the police wouldn't," Bernie said.

"You went to the police and closed out the investigation," Helen said. "You told the cops Mark had been making threats and talking about killing himself and Ahmet. You said your brother was suicidal."

"He was. I told the truth!" Bernie said. At last, a surge of feeling—for herself.

"Nobody tells that much truth about their brother,"

Helen said. "They might say their brother had some problems or he was troubled. You branded Mark a crazy man who was going to murder Ahmet."

"You're branding my brother as crazy," Bernie said. Her voice went flat again. "Saying someone is suicidal isn't the same. I suggested that Mark was depressed. My brother was ill and needed help."

"What was your mother's part in the cover-up?" Helen said. "She was in on it with you."

"Why do you think Mom was involved?" Bernie asked.

"Because you both told Gus the accident was in the wrong city," Helen said.

"My mother's dead. Leave her out of this." Another brief flash of anger.

"If she's dead, nothing you say can hurt her," Helen said.

Bernie took a deep breath, then said, "My mother and I didn't get along. While we were at the hospital together when Mark was"—she stopped, then said the word as if it hurt to speak it—"dying, Mom told me she had cancer. She said she was going to die. I cried and begged her forgiveness and promised to reform. We were afraid I wouldn't get a chance at a new life. The police kept coming to the hospital and asking me about Ahmet. They knew he was a dealer, but they hadn't caught him yet."

Bernie returned to reciting the powerful facts in that inhumanly calm voice. "Mom decided I should tell the police that Mark was suicidal. My brother was dead. It wouldn't make any difference to him. Mom wanted to save my future. I couldn't work at a hospital if I was mixed up with drugs. I did this with my mother's blessing. She traded her dead son's reputation to save her living daughter. We didn't lie about Mark. We told the truth."

"The truth sure set you free," Helen said. "When Mark's case was closed as a suicide, you didn't have to worry about the police looking into your life, either. I understand why your mother tried to save you. But there was more to it. You were still in touch with Ahmet. He wanted Mark's case closed, too, didn't he?"

"Yes," Bernie said. "But so did Mom. Closing Mark's

case helped both of them. So what?" She shrugged and tried to sound unconcerned. But Helen thought she saw fear in Bernie's eyes.

"So you picked up the gun from the police and threw it in the ocean. How much did Ahmet give you to get rid of his gun?"

Bernie jerked back as if she'd been slapped.

"Hit a nerve, didn't I?" Helen said. "You got Mark's wallet, his gun and his thirty dollars. Thirty pieces of silver, Sister Judas. How much did Ahmet pay you to get rid of the gun? Tell me or I'll tell your neighbors."

Bernie's voice trembled. "I got ten thousand dollars," she said. "But Ahmet subtracted Mark's cocaine debt first. I needed the money to go to medical tech school. I've lived a good life. I've atoned for what I did. I never touched drugs again."

"You sold out your brother," Helen said.

"So did my mother." The emotion flooded back into Bernie's voice. She was talking faster now, desperate to defend those decisions. "Mark wasn't supposed to die. I couldn't bring my brother back. He wanted to save me. I started my training with the money I got from Ahmet. I succeeded. I had to; don't you see? If I didn't, Mark would have died for nothing. Mom and I both agreed it was the right thing. I promised her I'd never see Ahmet again.

"After I came out of the hospital, Ahmet didn't want to let me go. He followed me. He showed up at school and begged me to live with him. He said he'd make me rich and I'd never have to work again. I wouldn't have to deal with blood and needles. But I didn't go with him. I made the hard choice. I've tried to be a good person."

"Is that why you cut your hair?" Helen asked.

"It made men crazy. I chopped it off and dyed it brown." Now Helen heard contempt. Was it for the men who loved Bernie for her beauty—or for herself? "I made sure no man like Ahmet would look at me again. I wouldn't have to worry anymore. It's what I wanted. I told you all I know. Will you go now?"

Helen left Bernie weeping alone in her beige mansion.

CHAPTER 43

"Bernie and her mother were both in on the cover-up for Mark's murder," Helen told Phil.

She was back in the Coronado Investigations office reporting on her encounter with Gus's sister.

"For the love of God, will you please quit pacing and sit down," Phil said. "I can't concentrate."

Helen tried to sit still, but it wasn't easy. Her interview with Bernie had left her restless and keyed up.

"I guess Roseanna Behr figured she made the right decision," Phil said. "She traded her daughter's future for her dead son's reputation."

"I wonder how Gus will feel about that deal," Helen said. "Is it time to tell him?"

"Not yet," Phil said. "There's one more mother mixed up in Mark's murder—Lorraine Yavuz, Ahmet's mother. The police report says he was inside his import-company building when Mark was shot. One of the witnesses was his mother. I checked the records. Mrs. Yavuz still lives in Lauderdale. Maybe she'll remember something about that day."

"You really think she'll say anything against her son?"

"It's worth a try," Phil said.

"Should I go see her in person?" Helen asked.

"No," Phil said. "Stay away from that man and anyone connected to him. I don't want his mother giving Ahmet your description. He's a killer."

"And a civic leader," Helen said.

"That makes him more dangerous," Phil said. "He has too much to lose."

"You don't think he'd hurt me and flee to Turkey, do you?"

"No way," Phil said. "Ahmet Yavuz is the Turkish version of John Smith. Despite their foreign-sounding last name, the Yavuz family is as American as Big Macs. They've been in the United States for four generations. Ahmet grew up in Fort Lauderdale."

"I'll call Mrs. Yavuz," Helen said. "I can pretend to be an old friend of Ahmet's who is in town on a trip."

"Use an airport pay phone so the call can't be traced back to you," Phil said.

Helen and Phil drove to the Fort Lauderdale airport together. Helen found a pay phone near the baggage carousels and punched in Mrs. Yavuz's number. Phil stood next to her holding a notebook in case she needed to write something down.

Mrs. Yavuz answered on the first ring. She was either drunk or lonely, or both. Helen struggled to hear the difficult old woman through the flight announcements and rattle of luggage carts.

"My son is rich and important," Mrs. Yavuz said, her words slurred. "He never comes to see me anymore. He's got this new business."

"Yavuz Elegant Homes," Helen said.

"Not that one. That's an old business. He's started a bunch of new ones. One's a propert—proppity—a real estate holding company. It's called Silverhall. Isn't that a pretty name?"

"Yes, it is, Mrs. Yavuz. Silverhall is a very pretty name." She signaled Phil and he wrote it down in the notebook.

"I like it, too," Mrs. Yavuz said. "I'm the CEO. My son made me a CEO and he still doesn't come to see me."

Helen took the pen from Phil's hand and wrote "she's CEO."

He nodded.

"Your son has come a long way," Helen said.

"Too far," Mrs. Yavuz said. "Too far to go back and see anyone from the old days. Like his mother. I won't be here forever, you know. I blame those Behrs for changing him. Ahmet went to high school with the sister. There were three of them."

The old woman recited in a singsong voice, "Once upon a time there were three Behrs: Mark, Gus and ... I can't think of the other."

"Bernie," Helen said. "The sister."

"You know her?" Mrs. Yavuz asked, sounding suddenly suspicious.

"I am an old friend of your son's, remember? I told you that. I talked with Bernie this morning."

"Yeah, right. You did say that. What's your name again?"

"Helen. Helen Hawthorne."

Phil was shaking his head no and signaling for her to stop. Helen scribbled: "She's drunk. Won't remember" on the notepad.

Phil wrote: "Don't tell her more."

"You there?" Mrs. Yavuz asked.

An announcement for flight 1506 to Tampa blasted through the airport.

"Yes, I'm not going anywhere," Helen said. She frowned at Phil.

"You said you just talked with Bernie today," Mrs. Yavuz said. "Sounds like you're at an airport or something."

"That's right," Helen said, hoping to coax the old woman back into a conversation.

"Look, no offense, but that slut ruined my son," Mrs. Yavuz said. "He's a success. Once Ahmet threw Bernie out on her trampy ass, he started going places. My son paid a buncha millions for his new house. He's got a wife, too, a good woman, not like that Bernie, and they have a son, Junior. My grandson is ten, but they never let Junior come see me.

"My boy Ahmet's completely changed. That wild Bernie Behr and her crazy brother did it. Ahmet was never the same after he hooked up with them. That Gus wasn't so bad, but those other two were hell on wheels."

A drug dealer's mother thought Bernie was trash? Helen didn't know what to say. It didn't make any difference. Mrs. Yavuz was happy to have an audience, even an unseen one. She kept talking.

"Ahmet won't come see me, even on Mother's Day. He's changed so much, and it's all the fault of that Bernie Behr and her brother. The wild Behrs."

She gave a cackling laugh, then lowered her voice. "Mark was nuts, you know. Shot himself."

That was the opening Helen needed.

"Where was your son the day Mark crashed his car into Ahmet's building?"

"At work," his mother said, sounding surprised Helen would ask. "Ahmet was at work like he should have been, even if Bernie's nutcase brother was threatening to kill him. My boy was no coward; I'll say that for him. He went to work even though he knew that lunatic was looking for him. I saved his life, you know. My boy would be dead if it wasn't for me. He gave me a job at his import company. I worked there. Made good money, too. Did you know that?"

"Yes," Helen said. "How did you save your son's life when Mark threatened him?"

"I said, 'Ahmet, you got a gun for protection?'

"He said, 'No, Mom.'

"I said, 'Well you better start carrying one. You better protect yourself.' I was so worried I gave him his father's old gun for protection. My boy would be dead without me, and he doesn't 'preciate what I did for him."

"What kind of gun was it, Mrs. Yavuz?" Helen asked.

"It was old. An old .32 Mauser. I was right, too. That crazy Mark Behr turned up at my son's business. My son shot him."

Helen felt her stomach clench. "Did Mark have a gun?" she asked carefully.

"Don't remember. He could have. Mark was threatening to kill my boy. He deserved to be shot. I miss my boy."

Mrs. Yavuz started crying and dropped the phone. The line went dead.

Helen hung up the pay phone and felt a wild surge of joy. She threw her arms around Phil and said, "We got him! We got him! Ahmet's mother admits she gave her son his father's .32 for protection, just before Mark's murder. That's the weapon that killed Mark. The one the police had. She said Ahmet shot Mark. We've tied the killer to the murder weapon."

Phil started steering Helen toward the parking garage.

"There's no statute of limitations on murder," Helen said. "We can reopen the case. Mark's killer will be arrested."

Phil looked at her sadly. "No, Helen. There is no case."

They were at the parking-garage elevator. Phil pressed the button for the second floor.

Helen was still celebrating. "I realize Mrs. Yavuz drinks a little, so she won't make the best witness."

"No, Helen," Phil repeated, but his words didn't register. The elevator doors opened. "The Igloo is parked in section J5," he said.

Phil tried to make Helen understand. "All her son has to do is visit Mrs. Yavuz and she won't testify against him. He'll make up some excuse and she'll forgive him. Even if she doesn't, we have the word of a drunken, confused woman. She didn't actually see Ahmet shoot Mark, and there is no gun. The police gave the Mauser to Bernie. They thought it was Mark's property. She threw it in the ocean."

"Oh," Helen said. She got in the Igloo and started it.

"The police never fingerprinted the gun," Phil said. "There is no evidence."

"So that's it," Helen said. Her elation was gone. "I guess we're ready to give our client his report."

"Not quite," Phil said. "I want to spend some time on the computer looking into Silverhall before we talk to Gus. Why don't you take a nap? Let me do some work."

Helen paid the garage fee. She had no intention of

taking a nap like a child. She wasn't sleepy. She was buzzing with energy. She would make Ahmet admit his part in Mark's murder. She could do that. Phil was right. She had the personal touch when it came to interviewing people. Thanks to her, Bernie had spilled her story. She'd gotten Ahmet's mother to admit she gave her son the murder weapon. Mrs. Yavuz said Ahmet shot Mark. Thanks to her clever questions, they had the whole story.

If Helen told Phil what she planned to do this afternoon, he'd have a fit. Helen knew it was okay to visit Ahmet's real estate office. Ahmet wouldn't shoot her in broad daylight in the middle of Fort Lauderdale.

CHAPTER 44

A hmet Yavuz was still a dealer. Now he sold something that had ruined almost as many lives as cocaine—Florida real estate. Buying and selling it was an addiction for many and destruction for some.

Helen parked the Igloo on the lot at Yavuz Elegant Homes in downtown Fort Lauderdale. The two-story office had a green awning and a sign with fancy gold lettering: WE HANDLE FINE WATERFRONT PROPERTY.

Helen's jaunty PT Cruiser looked out of place among the lot's shining, serious BMWs, Rolls-Royces and Mercedes.

Helen wanted to meet Ahmet, the man who had destroyed so many lives.

His waiting room belonged in a palace. Helen had never seen gilded French furniture like his outside a museum. Bewigged and beribboned aristocrats conducted frivolous flirtations on the tapestry mounted on the wall.

The gorgeous redheaded receptionist reminded Helen of a young Bernie, her flamboyant beauty toned down by a tailored navy suit.

"Do you have an appointment to view a property, Miss

Hawthorne?" The receptionist's voice was colder than the room's well-regulated temperature. She correctly assessed Helen as low-rent—literally.

"I have a quick question for Mr. Yavuz," Helen said.

"He prefers to meet by appointment," the receptionist said.

"It won't take but a moment," Helen insisted.

The receptionist was too well trained to sigh. "I'll see if he's available," she said and glided through the massive double doors opposite the tapestry. Helen tiptoed across the thick carpet and peered inside.

Mark had been right. Ahmet was the devil—at least, Helen thought that's how the devil would look. The dealer was an elegant older man with shining silver hair. His walnut skin looked hand polished and his suit was hand tailored. The receptionist approached him respectfully and relayed Helen's request.

"Come in, Ms. Hawthorne," Ahmet said. "That is you eavesdropping at the door, isn't it? A fitting pastime for a private investigator."

Ahmet's office was even more opulent than the waiting area. His extravagantly carved and gilded desk was an antique. So were the chairs. He did not invite Helen to sit down.

Ahmet had the glow only the very rich have. Helen studied his face for signs of evil. She saw only a businessman, gone a little fleshy from good living.

"Ms. Hawthorne, I do not know why you are harassing me and my mother."

His voice was smooth and educated, his face impassive. Helen fought to keep her face immobile. She was still stunned that he knew she was a private eye.

"Don't look so surprised, Ms. Hawthorne. Mother told me about your chat. She was so excited that my old friend Helen Hawthorne called to see how she was. Correct me if I'm wrong, Ms. Hawthorne, but we never went to high school together. You're from St. Louis. You and your husband Phil own Coronado Investigations. Your new agency has been getting a lot of favorable attention lately on television.

"Mother said you didn't really talk about old times, except for Mark and Bernie Behr. So very sad. That whole family is unhinged. First, their brother Mark tried to kill me. And we won't speak of his unstable sister. Now the third brother, Gus, who still refuses to accept Mark's unfortunate death, hired you to investigate matters that don't concern you. You've been questioning my poor mother.

"This has to stop, Ms. Hawthorne. I am an upstanding citizen. I do not have so much as a parking ticket."

"All that means is you haven't been caught yet," Helen said. She hoped her words would force Ahmet to react.

Ahmet merely looked bored. Helen wanted to wipe that look off his face. "Your mother told me about the gun," she said. "The .32 Mauser that killed Mark. She gave it to you."

Ahmet sighed. "When my dear mother called me today, I took her out to lunch. Mother and I agreed that I don't spend enough time with her, but that's going to change. She's moving into the Evesham Home today, and I've promised to bring her grandson to visit once a week."

Helen froze. The Evesham was where rich South Floridians stashed their inconvenient relatives. It cost a fortune and looked like a plush resort, but it was the modern equivalent of locking the crazy relative in the attic. The Evesham was where the rich could hide the drunks, the drug impaired and the deranged.

"Poor Mother drinks too much sometimes. When she does, she says the most outrageous things." Ahmet's voice was as soft as velvet. "Mother tripped in the parking lot of the restaurant after lunch and fell. She broke her arm. Bones are so brittle at her age.

"She needs extra care," he said. "Especially now. It's difficult to get into the Evesham Home, but I pulled a few strings. By now she should be in a lovely room overlooking the ocean. She has a big-screen TV to watch her favorite shows. But she's in a lot of pain. The doctor says she'll have to take drugs for a while. He said not to worry. Mother will be fine, but she will sleep most of the time. She needs to sleep to recover her health.

"Ms. Hawthorne, I had the resources to find out who you

are and where you live in ten minutes. I had the money to get my mother into the Evesham today, and they have a six-month waiting list. I have the power to pull your private-eye license. Oh, wait, you don't have one, do you? You're merely a trainee. I have the power to pull your husband's license and close your annoying little business.

"I'm not threatening you, Ms. Hawthorne. I'm telling you, so you know where you stand. I always like to know that. I'm sure you do, too."

Helen's last hope was gone. She couldn't bluff Ahmet into saying anything. But she would not run away. She looked him in the eye and said, "You killed Mark Behr. And you will get yours."

Ahmet didn't bother answering. He started laughing. It was loud and searing. Helen felt like he'd thrown acid on her. She'd been stripped naked by his contempt. She knew Ahmet would not harm her. She was not worth it.

Helen left Ahmet's office a complete failure. She could get nothing out of him because there was nothing in him. He was not some romantic figure of evil. He was a businessman. He'd killed Mark because it was expedient. He'd locked up his mother because she was inconvenient. He felt no guilt. He felt no remorse. It was just business.

As she drove back to the Coronado, Helen felt a great heaviness overtake her. She fought to stay awake and prayed she'd make it home before she fell asleep at the wheel.

Helen slept until seven o'clock, when Thumbs woke her up demanding his dinner. She fed the cat and saw the lights burning across the courtyard in the Coronado Investigations office. She remembered her encounter with Ahmet and felt hot with shame. She would never tell Phil what she'd done.

She had to see if Phil had learned anything about Ahmet. She wanted that man behind bars.

Helen ran upstairs to their office. A red-eyed Phil was squinting at his computer. The half-empty coffee mugs next to his computer testified to the intensity of his search.

"Mrs. Yavuz gave us a good lead with that Silverhall

name," he said. "Her baby boy hasn't abandoned his shady ways. He's set up some shell companies to flip high-priced real estate. His mother, his wife and his ten-year-old son are on the boards. Ahmet did a — well, a land-office business — "

Helen groaned at the pun. "I assume he made this money before the real estate slump."

"You bet," Phil said. "So far, I've found three properties he flipped for a profit of twenty million dollars total. I can't find any tax records."

"I thought those weren't public," Helen said.

"Not for ordinary people," he said, and grinned. "A supersleuth like me can find them. Seriously, Helen, I've only been at this a few hours. That information is out there, and I know how to look for it. When Ahmet applied for a loan to buy his new multimillion-dollar home, the bank wanted to see three years of tax returns, business and personal. Ahmet paid a lot of taxes, but nothing on those three properties."

"His son isn't in high school yet and the kid is already a tax cheat," Helen said.

"If I had more time to investigate, I know I'd find more dicey deals."

"You're not going to take more time, are you?" Helen asked.

"No, I want to end this case. I have enough to interest the IRS," Phil said.

"So we'll get Ahmet on tax evasion?" Helen asked.

"It's possible. Gus will want him in jail for murder, and that's not going to happen. We'll give our client our final report tomorrow morning."

"Can you do me one favor?" Helen asked. "Can you take me to see Ahmet's house?"

"Now? Tonight?"

"Yes."

"It's not where he lived with Bernie," Phil said.

"I know. I just want to see it."

"Then you shall," he said.

Ahmet Yavuz had his own elegant waterfront home in a pricey subdivision on Hendin Isle. His mansion was dark and lifeless, surrounded by a high white fence bristling with security cameras. A tough-looking crew-cut guard made the property look like an expensive prison. Helen could catch only a glimpse of the house. Its thrusting planes of cantilevered glass glittered like ice shards in the moonlight.

"Brr," Helen said. "I wouldn't live there if you paid me."

"I hope we'll help move him to less exclusive accommodations," Phil said.

Gus was polishing the bright red paint on a small, sleek sports car with graceful fins in front of Boy Toys Restoration and Car Repair. A long line of cars paused to pay homage to the gleaming antique stunner. Phil parked the Igloo in the shop lot, and Helen and Phil got out to admire the red car.

"That is awesome," Phil said.

"Is it an old Thunderbird?" Helen asked.

"Better," Gus said. "This baby is a 'fifty-nine Studebaker Silver Hawk. No rust, no dents, dual exhaust with glass packs." He patted one fin and smiled.

It was the last time Gus would smile that day. He was about to hear the Coronado Investigations report. They retired to Gus's office. Phil delivered the report, Helen at his side.

Gus was speechless for several seconds. Then he erupted into anger.

"So that's it! The killer gets off scot-free? My mother and my sister were in on the cover-up and Bernie gets away with it, too?" Gus asked.

"Your sister didn't get away with anything," Phil said. "Bernie did six months in a psychiatric hospital. She punished herself. That woman is carrying a load of guilt. She's suffering, Gus."

"What about Ahmet? Is he suffering in his mansion?"

"He'll get his eventually. Even Al Capone got his."

"I don't believe in that karma crap," Gus said. "I want my brother's killer in jail."

"He may still go to jail," Phil said. "But not for Mark's murder."

"Think what a murder trial would do to your sister," Helen said. "She's worked hard to become a useful citizen. Your brother loved Bernie. Mark wanted to save her. He succeeded. Don't undo all his good work. He gave his life to help her."

Gus's seething silence was ominous.

"I know this is hard to hear," Helen said. "Wait a while. See how you feel when you've had time to think it over."

"What do I owe you?" Gus asked, his face expressionless.

Helen handed him the bill.

Gus glanced at it, yanked open a drawer in his black desk and wrote a check. He tossed it at Phil.

"Don't bother coming back here if there's anything else wrong with your car, Helen," he said.

They left without a word. Helen and Phil had expected that Gus would be unhappy with them. Coronado Investigations could not use Gus Behr as a recommendation, but it didn't matter. Valerie Cannata's television exposé generated enough business to keep the fledgling agency busy.

Shelby Minars, their first client, stopped by Coronado Investigations in late September. She made a pretty picture in her blue dress, sitting primly in their yellow client chair. Her manners were softer and she seemed contented.

"I wanted to say that you can use my name as a reference," Shelby said. "I was unhappy when you first told me that Bryan was cheating on me. The truth hurt, even when I expected it. But now I'm in therapy and dating the sweetest man. I don't care if it is an office romance; I enjoy being with him. I wouldn't go out with him until I was free. He's divorced and soon I will be, too."

"Peggy mentioned that your boss had a crush on you," Helen told her.

"I like him a lot," Shelby said. Helen caught the hint of a blush. "I don't think he's the one, but he makes me feel like a woman. Thanks to Bryan, I'm an independent woman. Financially, that is. My lawyer made sure that Bryan gave me the house and a good income. My pride was hurt, but I'm better off with Bryan out of my life. He moved in with that woman, Carla." Shelby looked like she'd bitten into a lemon. "They're living in her cracker-box condo.

"He lost his real estate job; did you know that? He'd been using clients' houses to meet her. He'd tell the manager that he had a showing. You can guess what he was showing Carla. A homeowner came back early and surprised those two in the master bedroom. Can you imagine?"

"I'd rather not," Helen said, hoping to shut out the memories of the afternoon she'd stumbled upon her ex-husband with his paramour. "I'm glad you're happy."

Helen was surprised when Gus called their office at Christmastime. He sounded uneasy. "Helen, can I stop by and see you and Phil sometime? I got something I want to say to both of you."

"Sure," Helen said. "How about in an hour?"

Gus labored up the stairs to 2C with slow, heavy steps, carrying a small brown cardboard box with a red bow taped on it. "Nice office," he said. "Vintage, like my cars. Cool poster. Is that real?"

Phil beamed at the praise for his Sam Spade poster.

"Is it okay if I sit in that yellow chair?" Gus asked. "I'm still wearing my work clothes. I don't want to get grease on it or something."

"Don't worry," Helen said. "The vinyl upholstery is washable."

"Cruiser behaving itself?" Gus asked, as if he were checking on an adopted pet.

"It's perfect," Helen said. "I couldn't be happier."

Gus handed Helen the package and said, "This is for you."

Inside, Helen found two stainless steel oval rings, about five inches wide, and a steel crown-shaped object. They were arranged in a felt-lined box like jewelry.

"It's a stainless-steel gearshift frame set," Gus explained. "It's designed for the newer Cruisers. Fits over the gear shift and gives it a custom look. I can install it for you."

"Why, thank you, Gus," Helen said. "It's beautiful."

Phil admired the gift. "Should make an already good car look even better," he said.

"I've been meaning to come here for a while," Gus said. "I owe you an apology."

"No, you don't," Phil said.

"Hear me out," Gus said. He shifted in the yellow chair and jiggled his leg. He was not accustomed to making speeches. "I admit I was disappointed when you told me that Ahmet killed my brother and he couldn't be arrested because there wasn't any evidence. I wanted him to rot in jail for what he did. He not only murdered my brother; he helped kill my mother. She gave up after Mark died.

"I was shocked by your report, too. I never knew Mark rescued my sister from Ahmet's house. No one told me. Hearing it years later made it worse somehow.

"I also didn't expect my own sister to be mixed up in Mark's murder. I never dreamed that she'd called Ahmet to warn him that Mark had a gun after Mark rescued her. Bernie got our brother killed.

"I don't believe Ahmet shot him by accident or in self-defense, either. Mark owed Ahmet three thousand dollars for cocaine. My brother had thumbed his nose at Ahmet by hauling Bernie out of his house.

"I think Ahmet killed Mark to make an example of him. Drug dealers can't have customers or employees disrespecting them.

"Anyways, your report caught me by surprise. I said

some stuff I'm sorry for now. It takes me a while to get used to new information, you know? But I want to thank you for telling me."

Helen and Phil nodded.

"I saw the story on Channel Seventy-seven that the TV reporter Valerie Cannata did," Gus said. "She said Ahmet Yavuz has been indicted by a federal grand jury and will go on trial for tax fraud. They say he'll probably go to jail. You did that."

Helen and Phil neither confirmed nor denied Gus's speculation.

"The television reporter said Ahmet couldn't explain where he got three million dollars to start his real estate business. He set up some shell companies to fool the IRS, but they saw through that. We know he used drug money, right?"

Double silence.

"You and Phil sicced the IRS on him. You told me Ahmet would wind up in jail, but not for murder."

"I said he *might* wind up in jail," Phil said. "It's just luck that he got indicted."

"Right. I believe that like I believe Santa Claus is gonna come down my chimney. You pointed the feds in the right direction, and nothing you say — or don't say — can convince me otherwise. He's going to jail and he's gonna serve time. Hard time.

"Ahmet is used to fancy cars and a big mansion and elegant furniture. Living in an eight-by-ten cell with a toilet for the centerpiece will cause him real pain. That's fine by me. He deserves it. He's caused more hurt than he's ever going to feel."

"An indictment isn't the same as a conviction," Helen said. "Ahmet might win his tax-fraud case. But his lawyers will get most of his millions. If a man has no conscience, the best way to get him is through his wallet."

Gus laughed. "I like that. You got him good. Both of you.

"I hired you because I wanted to know what to say to my grandson, Gus the Third. I was worried he'd inherited some kind of suicide gene. I didn't know how to explain my brother.

"Now I know what I'll tell my grandson: the truth. His great-uncle Mark was a great man. Great men have great struggles, and they don't always succeed.

"Mark saved his sister, and that's what matters."

"Greetings, TV star," Margery said.

Helen's landlady was alone by the pool, bathed in purple dusk and soft clouds of cigarette smoke. Margery lifted up her glass of box wine in greeting. "I saw Coronado Investigations got another plug on Channel Seventy-seven."

"Was that cool or what?" Helen said. "Evie Roddick won her lawsuit against the city of West Hills and Homicide Detective Evarts Redding."

"Retired detective," Margery said.

"Gone for good," Helen said.

"He should be," Margery said. "The jury awarded Evie a cool seven hundred thousand dollars."

"I'm glad Valerie mentioned our part in freeing Evie," Helen said. "She didn't have to do that."

"Gave Valerie another chance to show that clip of her in the flame red workout suit in front of the gym," Margery said. "That has to be good for ratings."

"It's definitely good for our business," Helen said. "The phone's been ringing nonstop since the show aired tonight. Phil is answering the calls."

"You two got time to join me for a drink?" Margery asked.

"I will, as soon as I feed the beast," Helen said. "I'll try to pry Phil off the phone. Is Peggy home yet?"

"She and Pete will be out here in a minute."

"Phil and I will join you in five," Helen said.

Helen ran to her apartment, poured Thumbs some food, checked his water, then called Phil. Their office line was busy.

She opened her fridge and brought out a massive tray of cheeses, from sharp cheddar to creamy Brie. The deli had artistically arranged the cheese with grapes and apples. Helen peeled off the plastic wrap and poured crackers into a basket. Then she dialed their office number again. This time she got through to Phil.

"Ready with the wine and the presents?" she asked.

"Yes, but the phone keeps ringing," Phil said.

"Let the answering service take the calls," Helen said. "Otherwise, you'll be on the phone all night."

She held her front door open with her hip, carefully balanced the cheese tray and cracker basket, then set them on the umbrella table by the pool. She could see Phil on the stairs across the courtyard, carrying champagne in a bucket, glasses, flowers and a silver package.

Peggy and Pete were on a chaise next to Margery, bright spots of red hair and green feathers in the gathering dusk.

"What's this?" Margery asked when Helen and Phil arrived with the food and wine.

"Awk!" Pete said.

"We want you to help us celebrate our success," Helen said.

"We wouldn't have it without you," Phil said. He handed Margery a long, narrow package in silver paper. "Open it."

Margery ripped the paper like a hungry lioness disemboweling an antelope. "A check. What's this for?"

"Our office rent," Phil said.

"I didn't ask for that," Margery said.

"We owe you lots more than that," Phil said. "You and Peggy gave us our first clients. You got our business started."

"Helen gave you a jump start when she roped in that TV reporter, Valerie Cannata," Margery said. "And solving Debbi's murder was her idea."

"That helped," Phil said, "but we wouldn't have had our first cases without your help. Please take the money. You can charge us more if you want."

"No way," Margery said. "Your success has wiped away the memory of the tragedy in Apartment 2C. I won't forget that poor girl, but when you move your business to larger quarters, I can tell renters that a famous detective agency used to be in that apartment."

"We have no plans to move," Helen said. "We like it here."

Margery held up the check. "Think I'll keep it. Box wine doesn't grow on trees."

"That wine didn't grow on anything," Helen said. "It was created in a test tube."

Phil presented Peggy with a fragrant pink bouquet. "We also have something for you."

"Stargazer lilies," Peggy said. "They smell wonderful."

"Woo-hoo!" Pete said.

"And this is for Pete," Helen said. She handed the parrot a single green bean.

Pete took it in his foot, examined it, then dropped it on the pool deck. "Nite," he said.

"Pete!" Peggy said. "Bad boy!"

"Green beans are on his approved food list," she told Helen. "He can eat them."

"I feel the same way, Pete," Helen said. "Can he have one cashew?"

"Sorry, he's still overweight. The vet says he has to diet if he wants to stay healthy."

Pete eyed the fern in Peggy's bouquet. "I'd better put these in water inside," she said. "Ferns aren't on his approved list, either. We'll be right back."

"Open the champagne, Phil," Helen said.

After the champagne was poured and Peggy and Pete were back, Phil said, "A toast to the women who got us started."

They clinked glasses.

"And to the long life and success of Coronado Investigations," Margery said.

"Hear, hear." More clinking, then drinking. The four friends began spreading cheese on crackers and nibbling on apples and grapes.

"We need to catch up on what's going on," Margery said. "Tell us what you know about Evie's lawsuit. The part that wasn't on television."

"Her lawyer, Nancie Hays, is smart," Helen said. "Nancie worked out a good strategy for her client. First, she made sure Evie divorced her husband, Peter Willingham Roddick. Nancie handled the divorce pro bono. She got her client a settlement of one hundred thousand dollars. Once Evie was free, Nancie filed suit against West Hills and Detective Ever Ready."

"Was that pro bono, too?" Peggy asked.

"No, Nancie left the public defender's office when she filed that suit. She'll get forty percent of Evie's judgment."

"Awk!" Pete said.

"She deserves it," Margery said. "Nancie took quite a gamble quitting her job in this market."

"Nancie called us after she left the courthouse," Phil said. "Nancie wants to start her own law firm and hire Coronado Investigations to do her in-house investigations."

"No need to hang around the courthouse trolling for an up-and-coming law firm," Helen said. "Now we have one."

"More champagne!" Phil cried.

Helen savored the champagne and the good time with her husband and friends. She knew it wouldn't last forever, but neither would the bad times.

Thanks to wise investments, Evie was comfortably fixed when Fantastic Fitness of Fort Lauderdale closed a year later. She left her job at the gym with a glowing recommendation, which she plans to use on her résumé when she's ready to look for another job.

Tansi told Police Officer McNamara Dorsey the details

of the murder of bodybuilder Debbi Dhosset, as well as drug dealing with Kristi, her former friend. Tansi admitted that she bought illegal anabolic steroids and other controlled substances at Granddaddy's Bar from a man she knew only as Bobby, the day bartender.

Tansi pled guilty. Officer Dorsey told the judge that Tansi had cooperated in the investigation. The judge sentenced her to six years in prison. After her release, Tansi is barred from competitive bodybuilding.

Kristi, her former friend and training partner, was convicted of first-degree murder and more than twenty counts of selling illegal steroids, human growth hormone, oxycodone and other controlled substances. Kristi will have more than twenty-five years to develop her physique by natural means in prison.

Officer McNamara Dorsey received a commendation for her investigation of the murder of bodybuilder Debbi Dhosset. She became the first woman homicide detective on the West Hills police force.

Heather opened an organic fruit smoothie bar that caters to bodybuilders and health-food lovers.

Sunset Palms police, under the direction of Sgt. Rick Markban, raided Granddaddy's Bar and found a quantity of anabolic steroids, Ecstasy, human growth hormone, and other illegal substances with a street value of two million dollars. Bobby, the day bartender, was charged and convicted of multiple counts of drug dealing.

Danny Cerventi was not charged, possibly due to his sister's influence. But Linda was not able to prevent Granddaddy's Bar from losing its license. Sergeant Markban told the liquor commission that the bar was a source of drug dealing, drunken drivers, noise and nuisance complaints. Granddaddy's closed and the building is up for sale.

Danny still works three days a week for the video-duplication service, dubbing anniversary and wedding tapes to DVDs. He has a marked dislike for "Proud Mary" and walks out of places when that Creedence Clearwater Revival song is playing.

Sunset Palms recently laid off twenty-five city employees due to budget cuts. One was Linda Cerventi, Danny's sister. She is currently unemployed.

So is real estate agent Bryan Minars. Bryan broke up with his fiancée, Carla. He is using his professional skills to search for a new apartment.

Channel Seventy-seven investigative reporter Valerie Cannata's show, *Double or Nothing—A Seventy-seven Exclusive Exposé*, was number one during prime-time sweeps. So was her station. Phil and Helen keep their television tuned to that channel. Seventy-seven has been a lucky number for them.

Read on for a sneak peek at the next
Dead-End Job Mystery
by Agatha and Anthony Award–winning
author Elaine Viets,

FINAL SAIL

Available in hardcover from Obsidian

"**T**hat woman is murdering my father," Violet Zerling said. "We're sitting here while he's dying. And you—you're letting her get away with it."

Violet Zerling jabbed an accusing finger at attorney Nancie Hays. Violet was no delicate flower. She was twice the size of the slender lawyer and obviously upset.

Nancie wasn't intimidated by the large woman. The lawyer was barely five feet tall, a hundred pounds and thirty years old, but tough and adept at handling difficult people. She had faced down—and successfully sued—a slipshod homicide detective and the small South Florida city that employed him. She'd fought to keep an innocent woman out of jail. Now she didn't back away from Violet.

Nancie was all business, and so was her office. The carpet was a practical dark blue. Her plain white desk was piled with papers and folders. A workstation with a black computer, printer and fax machine was within rolling distance of her desk. Seated next to the workstation were the two partners of Coronado Investigations, Helen Hawthorne and Phil Sagemont. Nancie had called in the husband-and-wife PI team to help her new client.

Helen felt sorry for Violet, sitting rigidly in the lime green client chair. Her beige pantsuit was the same color as her short hair. The unflattering cut and drab color turned her face into a lump of dough.

Violet's clothes and shoes said she had money and spent it badly. Despite her sturdy build, she seemed helpless. Helen thought Violet could be pretty. Why did she work to make herself unattractive?

I'm not here to solve that mystery, Helen told herself. We have to save a man's life.

Nancie did not humor her client. "Violet, we've discussed this before," she said, her voice sharp. "Your father did not leave any medical directives or sign a living will. In fact, he doesn't have any will at all. Your stepmother—"

"That witch is not my mother," Violet said. "She is Daddy's second wife. She married my father for his money and now she's killing him. She wants his ten million dollars. He'll be dead soon, unless you do something. I need to save Daddy. Please. Before it's too late."

Violet burst into noisy tears. Helen had seen women turn weeping into an art form, shedding dainty droplets as if they were Swarovski crystal. Violet's tears seemed torn from her heart. Helen would bet her PI license those tears were genuine.

Nancie, Helen and Phil waited out the tear storm until Violet sat sniffling in the client chair. Then Phil handed her his pocket handkerchief. Helen loved her husband for that old-fashioned courtesy.

Violet liked it, too. She dabbed at her reddened eyes, then thanked Phil. "You don't meet many gentlemen these days," she said. "I'll have this laundered and return it to you."

"Keep it," Phil said. "That's why I carry one."

Violet stuffed Phil's handkerchief into a leather purse as beige and shapeless as its owner. The ugly bag was well made. It would probably last forever. Unfortunately.

"May I ask a question?" Phil asked.

Violet nodded.

"How does the rest of your family feel about your fight to keep your father alive?"

"There is no one else," Violet said. "I'm an only child. Daddy is the last of the Zerling family. He doesn't even have distant cousins."

"And you're not married, I take it?" Phil asked.

"I'm divorced," Violet said. "My husband married me for my money and the marriage was not happy." She looked down at her smooth, well-shaped hands. They belonged to a woman who did not work for a living.

"I might as well tell you," Violet said. "You and Helen are detectives. You'll find the whole sordid story of my divorce on the Internet. My marriage was miserable. My ex-husband drank and beat me. I had no idea he was like that when I fell in love with him. I was only twenty-one. Daddy opposed the marriage, but I had a trust fund from my grandmother, and I was determined to marry. My ex slapped me around on our honeymoon, and the marriage went downhill from there.

"I tried to hide the bruises, but I couldn't fool Daddy. He knew why I wore heavy makeup and long sleeves in August. He never said, 'I told you so.' But he was there for me. It took me more than a year to walk away from my marriage. After my ex put me in the hospital, I got the courage to leave him.

"He wouldn't let go of his meal ticket without a fight. He accused me of living a wild life. We were tabloid material for months. I couldn't have made it without Daddy. I changed my name back to Zerling after the divorce.

"My family's money never brought me happiness. I can't trust my judgment about men. I've set aside that phase of my life."

"Oh!" Helen said. She was a new bride and couldn't imagine life without love, though her first husband had been a disaster.

"It's better that way," Violet said. "I can't make any more mistakes."

Now Helen understood Violet's dowdy appearance. It hid a badly wounded woman.

"We aren't here to talk about me," Violet said. "I have to save my father."

"Violet, I wish I could do more," Nancie said. "Legally, Blossom is Arthur's next of kin. He's being given the best possible care, but he had a heart attack and he's in a coma."

"No! He was poisoned," Violet said. "She did it. That's why he's in a coma."

"There's no proof," Nancie said. "Your father's housekeeper, Frances, accused Blossom of poisoning Mr. Zerling. Fran took two samples to the police. They were analyzed. The so-called poison turned out to be harmless spices, turmeric and cumin."

"Fran was right to be suspicious," Violet said. "That woman never even scrambled an egg. Suddenly, she decided to fix Daddy a spicy curry dinner. A meat-and-potatoes man like Daddy, eating curry. Guess what? He got deathly ill after he ate it. Fran said she made a big pot of curry, but there wasn't a crumb left. That woman dumped it down the disposal."

"After her husband took sick?" Nancie asked. "You couldn't expect her to eat it."

"It disappeared before Daddy was sick."

"Blossom ate the same meal as your father," Nancie said.

"She poisoned Daddy's dinner," Violet said. "That's what I told the police. They didn't listen."

"They can't," Nancie said. "Not after Fran. The doctors said he had a heart attack. They didn't see any symptoms of poison."

"They didn't look. That woman's got a boyfriend," Violet said. "She left Daddy's house to meet a man. Fran saw her."

"Fran never actually saw Blossom with a man," Nancie said.

"That woman left at midnight," Violet said.

"She could have been going for a drive," Nancie said.

"Dressed in a short skirt and a low-cut blouse?" Violet asked. "Fran reported that woman's suspicious behavior to the police. Blossom fired my father's housekeeper. Threw poor Fran out of her home."

"Can you blame her?" Nancie asked. "Let's look at the

facts: Mr. Zerling has a heart condition. He uses nitroglycerin pills. He also took Viagra. That's not recommended for a man with his health issues. I'm surprised his doctor prescribed it."

"He didn't," Violet said. "His Fort Lauderdale doctor refused. Daddy got the blue pills from India. That woman told him he was a stud and he believed her."

"It's not illegal to encourage your husband to take Viagra," Nancie said.

"You didn't see the way she flaunted herself at him," Violet said. "I did. Daddy was taking twice the recommended dose. I know he'll pull through if I take care of him. Daddy is a fighter."

"What else could you do for him?" Nancie asked. "The doctors are doing everything they can. They say there's almost no chance of recovery. According to Blossom, your father said, 'If anything happens to me, pull the plug. I don't want to be a vegetable.' She wants him to die with dignity. Your father is an old man who's had a massive heart attack."

"He's only eighty-four," Violet said. "That's not old, not in our family. His father, my grandpapa, lived to be ninety-seven. His mother passed away at a hundred and two. Daddy could go on for another ten, twenty years, if he hadn't married that woman. She murdered him."

"Mr. Zerling is still alive," Nancie said gently.

"Not for long," Violet said. "He's on a ventilator. My father is unconscious, wrapped like a mummy in tubes and wires. That machine makes the most horrible sound. I tried to see Daddy in the ICU, but that woman won't let me in his room. She says I give off bad vibes."

Helen saw tears welling up in Violet's eyes again.

"That's her right," Nancie said. "Unfortunately, the law is on Blossom's side. The judge denied your petition for guardianship."

"If I may interrupt," Phil said, "I find it hard to believe that a businessman like your father didn't have a will or a medical directive."

"Daddy hated lawyers," Violet said. "After my divorce,

he set up a trust to run his companies if anything happened to him, and settled half his personal wealth on me. Then he made even more money. Daddy said he'd make a will when he was old."

"But he was eighty-four," Phil said.

"That's not as strange as it sounds, Phil," the lawyer said. "Even smart people aren't rational about wills. They're afraid if they sign one, they're signing their death warrant. They put it off until it's too late. Mr. Zerling is an amazing man, but he is old."

"Daddy is strong," Violet said. "He will get better."

He will recover—he won't. Helen rode that same seesaw during her mother's last illness. Her heart couldn't accept what her mind knew.

Nancie turned toward Violet and her voice softened. "Violet, dear, I know this is hard for you to hear, but you must prepare yourself for the worst. Your father may not recover."

From the depths of her beige purse, Violet pulled out a photo of a white-haired man on a glossy black stallion and handed it to Helen. She saw a square-jawed older man with a straight back and strong hands gripping the reins. He looked fit and muscular. Helen handed the photo to Phil.

"Look at him! Is this the photo of a man who would give up?" Violet's eyes burned with fanatic fire and her pale skin was tinged with pink. For a moment, Helen got a glimpse of the vital woman she could be.

"That's my father on his eighty-fourth birthday, three months before he met her," Violet said. "He barely looks sixty. Blossom has reduced him to a thing on a machine. Soon Daddy will be nothing at all. He'll be dead and she'll have his millions and spend them on her boyfriend."

"Violet," Nancie soothed, "you must be careful what you say. That statement is actionable."

"I'm saying it to you in your office," Violet said. "These detectives work for you, right?"

"Yes," Nancie said. "When Helen and Phil work for my firm, their investigation is protected by attorney-client privilege. Also, under Florida law, client communications with

private investigators are protected. They can lose their licenses if they breach confidentiality."

"Good," Violet said. "That means I'm doubly protected. I want to prove she's killing Daddy. Then I can be in charge of his care."

"Violet," Nancie said, "your father may not live long enough for that to happen."

"If you can't save my father, I want her in jail for murder. I have the money to get what I want.

"His millions may kill my father," she said. "I want my money to save him."